ISBN-13: 978-1494385743
ISDN-10: 1494385740

The Day Jesus Rode Into Croydon

For Josephine

Chapter 1

A Welcome In The Underworld

17th March, 1998.

The good thing about bushes is that they don't pretend to be something they're not. They appear as unwelcoming on the outside as they are to hide in. The genteel surroundings of this exclusive area of suburbia fail to make my mission any less dangerous.

I dreamed, once, of joining the fashionable elite. I wanted it all; the big house, the gravel driveway with the electronic gate. The same dream as the reality I see before me. How far away are those dreams now? Further than ever, no way back.
I was always different, never quite fitting in, waiting for that unknown something that would give my life purpose. Now, after everything, it's finally here. No longer will I be deceived by the lie that has fooled the world, instead I will wash away my sins in a glorious act of self-sacrifice. All I have to do is wait and be strong, knowing that the world finally needs me. Today Joseph, you will forego the dream for the greater good.

In the silent twilight the electronic gate opens and a black BMW rolls up the driveway. The voices within die to a whisper as my grip tightens on the crowbar, cold deliberate steel within the hands of the righteous.

I see you Anthony Chambers, Mr television celebrity.

I see everything.

Two Months Ago

My God, how did I end up here again? What happened to my dreams of escaping this town? Whilst everybody else my age is on the established path to social acceptance in this glorious age of the nineties, I find myself continuing to live the student life with seemingly less money and disturbingly, less hope. The dream is the nice house and the two weeks a year in the sun. What I've got is a crappy job, a residential history bordering on hobo serial killer classification, and I haven't had a holiday in years. Instead I seem to be stuck in the eternal British winter, briefly interrupted for a brief moment in July by a mischievous glimpse of an unfamiliar climate.

All of this brings me here, standing outside another shared house, awaiting another adventure with life's underachievers. Maybe this time things will be that bit more progressive, I won't be just filling in time as I move sideways into the shadows of a society that forgets.

Despite taking every necessary precaution to shield myself from the biting January wind, its path through a combination of coat, gloves and beanie hat (all black of course) meets with little resistance. Stamping my feet as I wait does little to relieve the numbness spreading across my face. If this little display of suffering is meant to attract sympathy, then it is magnificent in its failure to do so from the steady stream of schoolgirls passing on the other side of the street.

What brings me to this unfamiliar road? Can it really be Act 5, Scene 7 of the shared house experience, contained within the great suburban experiment? To put it precisely, I'm about to undertake a viewing of yet another house where the horror of my initial observations lead to the conclusion that I very much doubt change is on the cards this time either.

The loose fitting drain cover shifts underfoot as I push the gate. Before me lies a cracked garden path leading towards a Victorian terraced house. I check the upstairs window for

Norman Bates' mother before casting a sideways glance towards the faded traffic cone reclining happily in the hedge. Conveniently, it provides a distraction from a garden that only an estate agent could glorify. The shadow of the dilapidated porch looms over me as I reach for the doorbell.

It's soon apparent that there is, in fact, no doorbell. Instead, a wire pokes through a badly drilled hole in the doorframe. Next to this is the house sign, Malebolge. Sounds French. Thankfully it suppresses the immediate urge to touch the wire. I find a great first impression is not best given by someone in the throes of electrocution.

I give a friendly knock and wait. The last time I did this was for the house with Steve, or to give him his full title, Weird Bloke Steve. It soon became apparent that he was so called for his hysterical fear of fish, for sleeping in the wardrobe, and for having a bag of potatoes in his room for company. If he had told me this when I first moved in, maybe things might have worked out better. Of course it didn't really help matters when I maliciously brought goldfish home after one particularly intense afternoon drinking session. Yesterday morning I awoke to find a potato on the pillow next to me, and with that I knew it was probably time to move on.

The front door is eventually opened by a guy who is smaller than me and around the same age, possibly a little older. The unkempt bowl haircut and the Inspiral Carpets T-Shirt make it easy to determine that he stopped updating his image sometime in the early nineties. My first urge is to break the horrific news that The Stone Roses have split up, but I restrain myself out of politeness. More disturbing than any of this is the dishevelled blue dressing gown he is wearing. I say wearing, more accurately it is hanging from his slumped shoulders and open to reveal aged boxer shorts beneath. In his hand is a recently lit joint. I've seen my fair share of joints, but at nine in the morning it's still somewhat surprising.

'Yeah?' Manchester mutters lethargically in an unexpected Welsh accent.

'I'm Joe. I've come about the room in the house.'

'Oh yeah? ' says Manchester, pausing to allow his memory to catch up. In this moment of recollection he manages to find time to scratch his balls, with the joint still in hand.

'Yeah, no worries mate, I remember, sound, come in like,' Manchester confirms as he stands to one side and motions me in.

'Cheers mate,' I say as I enter. I'm in, but I want out.

'Joe right, I'm Danny,' he replies.

Behind me I hear him struggling to close the door before resorting to the tried and tested technique of kicking it at its base. In response the door flies into its ill-fitting frame, sending a shudder reverberating around the house. Danny squeezes between me and the wall as we make our way to the living room. The house instantly brings back memories of the countless places I've left behind. From the musty smell to the faded pattern of the carpet, I've been here before. The light shines through the glass panels in the door and catches the dust that glides effortlessly through the stale air of the hallway.

As I enter the front room, a joyous sight provides a welcome distraction. Aside from the two criminally unwashed sofas, one wall is completely devoted to the storage of music. CDs make way for vinyl, vinyl makes way for CDs. In the corner of the room sits a wide screen television with the latest games console next to it. Alongside is the best hi-fi system I have ever seen. A scan of the room reveals the speakers in prime acoustic positions.

'Nice,' I comment.

'You mean the records? What are you into?'

10

'Everything really; sixties, seventies funk, sci-trance, indie, jazz, blues...you know,' I recount, trying to appear knowledgeable by listing any credible type of music that comes to mind. I neglect to mention my Lionel Ritchie CD.

'Sweet,' Danny replies, and we exchange congratulatory nods for having found one another.

'Do you mind if I have a look?' I ask, gesturing towards the countless shelves and the contents within.

'Fill your boots son.'

As I scan the numerous rows of CDs, I'm disappointed to see that he has them arranged into genres. I'm an alphabetical man myself. Genre classification comes with far too many problems. Where do The Ozric Tentacles go? Psychedelic or hippies with guitars section? Where do Jamiroquai go? The acid jazz section or the bin? Periodically I pull an album out and provide comment. Danny, who has retired to the kitchen to make tea, provides his own thoughts, his voice travelling through the serving hatch and losing none of its accent along the way. He eventually returns to the room and plonks a heavily sugared tea in my vicinity. As I begin to study the post Syd Barrett Pink Floyd section, Danny flops onto the sofa opposite and begins to roll another joint. With impressive speed the flawless joint is constructed, lit, toked and then offered to me.

'You want a smoke?' Danny asks, leaning forward on the sofa in an enemy-of-the-establishment manner.

I'm about to decline his kind offer on the basis that I've been out of bed less than an hour, but then I take a swig of tea. A rancid *I do all my shopping at the local corner shop* taste hits the back of my throat. Luckily, I can tell from the smell that it's some serious skunk - it had better be if I'm going to get rid of the taste.

'Yeah, why not?' I reply, taking it delicately at the roach end.
'How's the tea?'

11

'Yeah it's good, nice one,' I lie in reply.

'You a Bond man?'

'Not with you.'

'Bond, you know... Bond,' Danny repeats, less than impressed with my lack of recognition.

'Oh Bond. Absolutely! I get annoyed that everyone says Connery was the best. There is absolutely no doubt that Moore was the peak of the golden age.'

'Good man. Let's gets it fired up on that matey,' Danny adds, nodding towards the games console.

'You're on,' I reply, happily obeying his instruction.

What ensues is over two hours of running around a virtual world, trying desperately to kill Danny, with little success.

'Man, just wait till my mates Squirrel and Pikey Chris come round, this is all we bleeding play,' Danny states, his concentration not wavering as he kills me once again with a flourish of button pressing. I wouldn't mind, but I was OddJob and you can hardly even see that little fella.

'Would love to keep playing but I've got a bit of business to attend to, know what I mean?' Danny adds with a knowing wink. Obviously the game is over and it doesn't take a genius to work out what particular line of business Danny is referring to. There is, of course, the strong possibility that he's tired of the countless victories, but I like to think that he knew my luck was about to turn.

'Do you want to see the rest of the gaff before I shoot off?' Danny asks.

'Yeah, if it's no hassle.'

'Right, front room.' Danny gestures at the room I've just sat in for the last couple of hours.

'Yep, got that,' I reply sarcastically as we both stand up.

'Kitchen,' he declares, climbing onto the other sofa and leaning through the serving hatch. Once he removes himself, I mimic the action. It's got walls, it's got windows, but your more traditional kitchen appliances are disturbingly concealed beneath dirty plates and pizza boxes.

'Hallway…stairs…' he announces, identifying each location as we pass through the respective zone.

'This will be your room,' Danny confirms, opening the door to a bedroom at the back of the house. Its most striking feature, apart from the wallpaper, is the absence of furniture. There's a bed, a wardrobe and a chest of drawers, but that's pretty much it.

'If you wanna move in, that's cool, you know, if you want it, like,' Danny adds as I stroll around the room, trying to find something to look at.

'How much is it?'

Danny answers by blowing air out of his cheeks, making his third joint of the morning waggle up and down.

'I dunno, say three hundred a month?'

'Three hundred, bills on top?'

'Yeah, why not?'

I could spend all day considering my options, but as with many things in life I act on impulse. Does it really matter that the house is a hole? Does it even matter that technically, it's worse than the last one? I know the answer to these questions should be yes but I can't help thinking that perhaps it's not that important anymore. It's not going to be forever; I've got plans.

'Okay, I'll take it,' I announce as if it's the most natural decision in the world. 'When can I move in?'

After a few deep breaths through pursed lips to illustrate the fullness of his schedule, Danny digs around in one of the pockets of his dressing gown, eventually retrieving a key that he tosses across the room. Naturally, I fumble the catch.

'Move in when you want pal.'

'Ah, nice one matey,' I reply with a smile.

How was I to know that come the next Saturday, and for many Saturdays thereafter, my life would change forever?

Chapter 2

Living For The City

The Manor and Toad is technically a local pub, and like any self-respecting local it comes with its own set of mysteries. Which year exactly did the crisps go out of date? Didn't they stop selling that beer from the faded pump in 1986? These are questions whose answers remain hidden in the mists of time.

The two policemen sitting in their car outside presented mysteries of their own. On the driver's side sat a small, fat man with a grey moustache, which lent no credibility whatsoever to the obvious wig that sat askew his head. The wig's striking auburn colour had deterred saner consumers long enough for its price to fall dramatically, at which point Inspector Polston had pounced on what he considered to be the bargain of a lifetime. That day marked his final transformation to sad divorcee - a process that had been gathering pace over the last couple of years.

Lying on the back seat asleep was the Inspector's dog, Callahan. A branch had diverged from the Yorkshire terrier breed at a singularly annoying point in canine evolution, forming a dog crammed with the abject frustration of a hundred snarling pit-bulls. The dog was asleep for the time being, and it was sensible to keep him that way. The last man in the world who'd disagree with this was Callahan's arch nemesis, Sergeant Walker, the final occupant of the car. He was a tall, thin man with his shirt sleeves rolled up and his tie loosened. His narrow face was dominated by a large hook nose, the curse of the Walker lineage. Despite this, his face and demeanour were instantly forgettable, something to which every woman he had ever tried to chat up would happily testify, if only they could remember.

Two doors down from the Manor and Toad was a Post Office that specialised in stamps, sweets in plastic jars, and being the subject of any number of CrimeWatch reconstructions. A string of local Post Office robberies had terrified the public, and it was simply a matter of time before the suburban crime wave hit this, the most robbed Post Office since seventy two year old Ernest Wilkins learnt how to photocopy his own pension book.

Polston's eyes never strayed far from its front door. A combination of experience and prejudice branded every customer a potential criminal. An old lady walked slowly past the Post Office, pushing a tartan shopping trolley, stopping outside to check the length of the queue. Polston decided to be lenient and allow her to go on her way; after all, he wasn't completely heartless. Callahan, now awake, disagreed strongly and made his opinion known with a constant barking. This was largely because he had caught sight in the rear view mirror of the sawn-off shotgun concealed under her coat as she made her way from the Post Office and around the corner.

Walker, like Polston, had also failed to notice. He was waiting for the one moment of glory that would propel him on an unstoppable trajectory towards promotion. It wasn't diligence (or in Walker's case, competence) that got rewards, it was results - and results were crucial to his master-plan. The plan came in three parts.

First, the ground breaking arrest from which fame and recognition would instantly follow. The second part was Polston, or rather his obstruction to the sergeant's career. Walker had been waiting years for the inspector to retire or die; he wasn't concerned which came first. The final part was to quash the scurrilous rumours that he was incompetent. He had long suspected Polston to be the source of this accusation. In reality, the inspector was merely the 352nd person to observe this well-known fact.

'You know boss, when I was at Goodison...' Walker remarked, referring to his oft-cited short-term assignment in the City.

'Shut up, Walker,' interrupted Inspector Polston, sighing with the realisation that he would have to talk to his sergeant again.

'All I'm saying boss is that when I was at Goodison CID, we did things differently. There are better surveillance techniques nowadays than sitting in a car waiting.'

'We've been through this Walker.'

'I think you would find the results would speak for themselves.'

'I don't care about what you did up at Goodison,' Polston replied forcefully, his frustration finally boiling over. 'Every bloody day I have to hear about how things were better at Goodison, it's driving me up the bloody wall. I wouldn't mind, but they sent you here because you were so bad at your job. Christ, we didn't even want you!'

The Inspector's anger was all too apparent, even to Walker's limited detective skills. He reluctantly remained quiet but silently fumed, making a mental note to move the Inspector's forced retirement forward on the master-plan.

Walker eventually broke the ensuing silence, roused from his thoughts by a fresh episode of barking by Callahan.

'Boss?'

'What is it Walker?' Polston sighed resignedly. The inspector had reset his Walker-tolerance scale and had returned to his normal background level of contempt.

'Why's Callahan barking so much today?'

'Because you're sitting in his seat Walker,' Polston replied.

Walker's rage prevented him comprehending that the dog had precedence in the seating arrangements. In truth, Callahan's barking was directed towards the three people emerging from The Manor and Toad opposite. Polston was only seconds behind his dog in recognising their significance. Walker wasn't even near.

'Well, well, well, look what we have here,' Polston remarked. Callahan's barking increased, congratulating his master and berating Walker for another failure.

'What's that boss?' Walker asked, his voice modulated to feign disinterest.

'There, coming out of the pub.'

'Isn't that Danny what's his name?' Walker asked, finally paying attention.

'The same. I've been after that little sod for years,' Polston replied.

'Who's that other bloke with the black beanie hat on?'

Walker failed to elicit an answer as Polston was already levering his frame out of the car with some effort.

'But boss, what about the surveillance?' Walker asked, leaning across the seats.

'Christ Walker, haven't you learnt anything? There are better surveillance techniques nowadays than sitting in a car waiting!'

Sergeant Walker watched Inspector Polston move across the street for a few moments and then when he was sure the inspector was no longer within earshot he arched around in the seat. Callahan stood on the back seat, seven inches of miniature menace growling at Walker and revealing two small fangs. Enacting master-plan Emergency Measure 14 he took a swipe at the dog, knocking him to one side. With his victim temporarily stunned, the sergeant exited the car to follow his superior. Callahan's barking, a declaration of his intent for revenge, was barely audible as Walker closed the car door behind him.

Chapter 3

Everyone's Friend, Uncle Ken

It's 2:30pm and I'm late. Not just a little late, I'm stupidly late. And Katie, in all her beauty, is not a girl to keep waiting. We've arranged to meet at our local, The Manor and Toad. To be fair, it's not the nicest pub in the world. From the lack of cleanliness to the decoration on a par with my new house, it's as if two decades went the same way as most of the customers. The beer tastes crap and the landlord Ken is the most miserable bastard you could ever hope to meet. In short, everything a local should be.

Regulars that have drunk there for years have been known to never set foot in the pub again after incurring the wrath of Ken. He is a man to be grudgingly admired for his opinions, despite the much-needed revenue his enemy, society, brings. Despite this, Katie and I always meet there. There is something to be said for the familiarity, even if it does come at a price.

On the way in I walk past an old lady pushing a tartan shopping trolley before I bear off towards the entrance. As I enter I'm struck how empty it actually is, even by the Toad's standards. Apart from Ken, who leans over the bar reading the local paper whilst noisily sucking on a pickled onion, Crazy Yvette is also in. I've heard she was a bit of a looker in her day, but she's doing well to conceal it now. Upon seeing me she starts to laugh hysterically, a toothless cackle from the very depths of insanity. It proves a momentary distraction. From behind I hear the voice that fills my dreams.

'I said two o'clock.'

Turning round to our usual seats I see her sitting there, Katie Rose, my one true love. Every time I gaze upon her I fall in love all over again. Her long red hair flows over her shoulders, her green eyes burning into a desire I've tried so hard to bury. Katie is my oldest and dearest friend, but I've always wanted her to be so much more.

'Hi honey, how's it going?' I say, snapping out of my daze and making my way across the stained carpet, a model of platonic greeting.

'Get us a drink and I'll let you know,' Katie replies, indicating the empty glass in front of her.

At the bar, Ken has never been a man to be rushed. During the necessary waiting period that he deems applicable, Crazy Yvette keeps us entertained with an old wartime classic. Ken finally decides I've waited long enough when she breaks into a fourth verse. With exaggerated effort he pulls himself away from the paper and lumbers across to where I'm standing. Some regulars say he fought in the war, but on whose side we're not sure.

'What do you want?' Ken asks coldly, the disdain all too apparent in his voice.

'Can I get a glass of red wine and a pint of lager for the lady?'

Ken mutters something incoherent as he makes his way over to the pump. After what seems an eternity he eventually returns, half dropping the drinks onto the bar so that the liquid slops over the side.

'Three pounds eighty,' Ken demands, looking at the five pound note that I subsequently provide in disgust. The very notion of having to get change seems to fill him with horror. For a brief moment I toy with the idea that he's descended from the same gene pool as bus drivers, especially when the thieving git returns with only ninety pence change. I could stay and argue, but returning to Katie alive is definitely worth more.

'So Miss Katie Rose, how are you on this beautiful day?' I ask, placing the drinks on the table.

'I'm fine thanks, more importantly how's you? How's the new house?'

'Yeah it's good. Danny's a top bloke. He should be popping in for a pint if you have no objection?'

'No worries. So how's it working out with the new surroundings and you know what?' Katie enquires with a lack of subtlety that only a friendship such as ours allows.

'I have no idea what you are talking about,' I reply, fully aware of what she is talking about. How could I not?

'The Thing,' she states as if it were the most natural thing in the world to talk about. Yet, I have no wish to discuss *the thing* and change the subject quickly.

'You still seeing Pete the Gerbil?' I ask at a tangent so far removed from the previous conversation you could drive a bus through it.

'Pete the Gerbil? Still insulting my boyfriends I see!'

'Only because I love you,' I reply. She obviously takes this as a joke but I must try harder to conceal my feelings, if only for my own sanity.

'Only because you haven't fallen in love with anyone else in a while,' she replies before continuing. 'Talking about love, have you thought anymore about that invite to Beth's wedding?'

Beth? I hear you ask. There are plenty of other things I need to tell you about but let me explain to you about Beth, before somebody else does.

It was a long time ago, long enough for me to know that I shouldn't still be thinking about it. I was living in one of my first shared houses when I fell desperately in love with one of my housemates, the aforementioned Beth. If she was The Premiership, then I was the *Sunday morning down the park with a hangover* league. More importantly, she was a world away from the past I was trying to forget, but more of that later.

21

Beth was my salvation from a person I didn't want to be anymore. She even had nice friends, particularly one Katie Rose. We were together five months before things started to go wrong. Specifically, it went wrong because of some guy who I like to call Knobface. It's all quite confusing, but to cut a long story short, I was a participant in a rebound of quite staggering proportions. It took a hell of a long time to recover from that. I'm not sure I have completely. But it was not without its positives, and this is where the beautiful Katie Rose comes into the story. During my time with Beth I knew I was growing closer to Katie, a lot closer than was probably healthy given that I was in love with her friend. So when Beth went walkabout with Knobface, Katie was happy to transfer her friendship to me. Since then of course I have fallen in love a thousand other times for a thousand different reasons, but none of them were Katie. It's not too late, I'm waiting for the right moment to tell her. A week ago Beth (or rather the soon to be Mrs Knobface) came careering into my life again via an invitation to their wedding. Why? Was it some sudden pang of guilt? I had tried so hard to block her out. What a way to be reminded, a knife to the back, somewhere between the heart and the brain.

'Oi! Are you listening to me?' Katie bluntly interrupts.

'Sorry, what?' I ask, my thoughts banished to the dark corners of my mind.

'Beth's wedding?'

'Ah, no I don't think so.'

'Are you sure?'

'Yeah, I'm sure about that.'

'I just thought…' Katie persists.

'So how's Harriet?' I ask, trying desperately to change the conversation. For this purpose even using Harriet, Katie's housemate, will do. Christ, I'd settle for anything.

Two more rounds follow, two more spins of Ken roulette, each time resulting in a house win. Then the doors swing open, not unlike a wild west saloon except in more dangerous surroundings. In walks Danny, everything a cowboy should be but without the hat.

'Waaahaaayy!' Danny exclaims as he spots us.

'Good day to you old boy,' I reply in greeting.

Danny would respond, but he is already on his way to the bar: alcohol first, pleasantries later. This is the first time he's been in The Toad, so Ken makes him wait that bit longer than the norm.

'I think that bloke likes me,' Danny states as he finally joins us at the table with a pint of the cheapest yet strongest lager.

'Only if he thought you were never going to come back again,' Katie comments.

'Well hello,' Danny says, flicking from strong welsh accent to Leslie Phillips the minute he first lays eyes on Katie, the dirty pervert.

'Hi, I'm Katie.'

'Hi, I'm Danny.'

'Hi, I'm Joe,' I add, despite the fact that I live with one of them and am secretly in love with the other.

'So how are you getting on with this annoying git then?' Katie asks Danny, a sly grin on her face.

'What can I say; the man thinks The Stone Roses were better than The Happy Mondays. He's got problems.' He winks at Katie, the dirty pervert.

'Oh, please, not another one. I've had to spend years listening to Joe going on about music.'

'Ah, come on I'm not that bad,' I retort.

'Yes you bleeding are! If it's not music you're talking about then it's your useless football team. If it's not football then you're probably talking about Beth,' Katie replies harshly. She oversteps the line sometimes.

23

'She's got you there matey,' Danny chuckles, the dirty pervert, before continuing. 'Hang on, Beth? Isn't that that bird you keep banging on about?'

'You've heard about that then?' Katie asks sarcastically.

'Bloody hell, once or twice.'

'Sorry, is this anti-Joe day?' I interrupt. These are supposed to be my friends.

'Oh honey, you know I'm only kidding,' Katie replies and leans across to kiss me on the cheek, concealed by a hug. Perhaps she knows she went too far? Perhaps she just simply wanted to kiss me? Interesting. Regardless, I watch Danny's gaze drop to his pint. Not today my friend.

Faced with these shocking accusations of repetitiveness by my friends, one an angel, the other a wannabe gangster, I decide to move the conversation on.

'Anyone want a game of pool?'

'Yeah, I feel like a win,' Katie replies and Danny nods his head in agreement.

Three frames later and it's all over for me. I don't mind the initial beating by Danny; after all he has nothing else to do with his days except practice, probably. Then Katie has her turn to do the same. At the end I give a few subtle hints to indicate that I threw the match like a gentleman, although that's not specifically true as such. The third frame is reserved for the winners, but I have lost all interest in this stupid game by now.

'So what do you do for a living Danny?' Katie asks as she leans over the table, lining up the black ball. Stop looking at her arse Danny, you dirty pervert.

'Ah, you know, bit of this, bit of that. You could say I'm in the supply and demand business.'

'You're a drug dealer then?' Katie correctly surmises. She may cultivate an air of delightful innocence, but she's not stupid. Besides, his weak cover story wouldn't fool a goldfish with ADHD.

'Yeah, pretty much,' Danny replies as he sees the ball sail into the pocket.

Three pints later I conclude that I might as well turn my lunch break into an afternoon off.

'So what now? Anyone fancy hitting a club?' Danny asks.

'It's four o'clock on a Tuesday afternoon you plum,' I reply, suppressing the urge to frequent the kebab shop.

'Another pint then?'

'Afraid not Daniel, four's my limit on a school night.'

'Me neither, I should go back to work for a couple more hours.' Katie adds. Bless her; she's the model of professionalism.

'Well I'm not drinking with that miserable bastard', Danny states, nodding his head in the direction of Ken. 'Give us a minute to finish my pint and I'll come with you as far as Loop Road, got a bit of business down that way.'

As we file out of The Manor and Toad, the bright winter sunshine delivers a welcome sobriety to my mind. It's still on catch up though, as I inadvertently step into the path of the old lady from earlier. As she wheels her shopping trolley over my foot she seems to mutter an obscenity at me in a deep masculine voice. What the hell are they putting in Ovaltine these days?

'Oh nuts!' Danny exclaims, drawing my gaze away from the old dear and towards the two men crossing the road with intent, towards us.

'Hello there, Daniel,' the fat one declares as he steps onto the pavement. His thinner compatriot with one hell of a nose halts abruptly beside him. It doesn't take a genius to work out who they are, after all I should know. If it looks like a copper,

25

speaks like a copper and smells like, well I don't know what that smell is, it's probably a copper.

'Well, hello Inspector Polston,' Danny replies confidently. I guess I wasn't wrong, an inspector no less.

'Just passing, Daniel. Thought we would come and say hello,' he states. I've no idea who the other geezer is, but that doesn't stop him entering the conversation.

'Keeping your nose clean are you Danny boy?' he asks as we look at each other and ponder if this constitutes irony.

'I'll do the questions thank you Sergeant Walker,' the inspector interrupts forcefully. This exchange takes everyone by surprise and a brief silence ensues. I cast a sideways glance to Katie to check she's okay, after all that's my job. Behind her, I notice the old dear is now negotiating her trolley into the Post Office, no doubt to menace them with her driving skills.

'Keeping your nose clean are you Danny?' Inspector Polston continues followed by a noticeable shudder as he realises his repetition of the sergeant's question.

'Always Mr Polston, upstanding member of the community me.'

'It's Inspector Polston, you little shit,' Polston blurts, little droplets of his saliva flying in an arc through the air.

'I'm sorry, inspector,' Danny replies, any sense of genuine apology a long way off.

'Go on, get lost,' Polston retorts, flicking his hand in a dismissive fashion, suggesting we make in the opposite direction. I know from experience that this is an instruction worth following.

'Pleasure meeting you again officer,' Danny replies, and being of a like mind we start to walk away as an alarm goes off nearby. I don't need to look to know that as Katie walks beside me there is a definite sense of events being frowned upon. Yet again she is witness to another unwelcome encounter. She knows what it means. She knows that out of the three of us, I have the most to lose.

'Always watching Danny boy, always watching,' Polston shouts from behind.

As we walk past the Post Office, the old lady from before almost takes my face off as she rushes out of the door and onto a waiting electric scooter.

'I never miss a thing,' the inspector continues shouting, but the rest is drowned out as the shopmobility demon wheel-spins away. Soon she is a blurred figure on the horizon as we put a welcome distance between ourselves and the police. As we turn into the next road, Danny leaves us to conduct his business down Loop Road. This I'm more than happy with, I have no desire to draw attention to myself any more than I have done so already in this life.

'So, Coffee?' Katie asks, my mind waging a titanic battle of suggestion verses reality. Did she mean coffee or *coffee*?

'I think we need to discuss "the thing",' she continues. No, she didn't mean coffee. She meant anything bloody but.

Chapter 4

Living On Planet Gong

There's the past, and then there's the distant past. I have to start at the beginning if I want to tell you about what comes later. Some people already know: a certain young lady unquestionably does, she tells me enough. However, she wasn't there. No one was.

Let me explain. Let me show you.

A light breeze catches a pile of leaves and whips them into a frenzy above the road. As the leaves settle back, a ball sails through the air and pierces their gentle movement. The ball is quickly followed by a hungry pack of ten year olds chasing it in the name of football.

Go back.
Remember.
There is laugher and shouting.
I remember. That was around the time it started.
Now old Mr Thomas is coming out of his house at the end. It sounds like he's confiscated their ball, ha-ha.
It's as if I'm still there. A movement in time.

Saturday morning, 8th September 1979

I can only guess at what my brother and his friends are playing now instead. I could go and look, I could even go outside. I won't. I'm quite happy here. I am a normal kid. At least I think I am. Besides, who is there to play with? Sean is four years older than me, a fact mentioned eight times already today what with it being his birthday. His friends are the same age and I have no place there, they've told me that. I don't want to play with them anyway, not when the music chart is on television. Cliff Richard is still top with 'We Don't Talk Anymore', which I can't stand, whilst my Boomtown Rats are in free fall. A small disappointment, but not one I'm going to cry about. Anyway, it doesn't matter, my fourth-favourite programme on the list is on next.

Rentaghost
Blake's 7
Grange Hill
Noel Edmund's Multi Coloured Swap Shop
Tiswas (for when Keith Chegwin is on Swap Shop or one of Noel's jumpers becomes too much)

As Noel opens the show, I hear the footsteps of my Mum on the stairs. It's so predictable. The minute one of the top five is on she'll be in here like a shot to do her cleaning. She doesn't realise the top five are set in a routine that can't be broken. The door opens and in she comes, smiling, as if that will make things better. At least it's only smiling. If she's not cleaning, or arguing with dad, or preferring Sean to me, she's talking, and that inevitably ends in questions. I don't like answering questions, no one understands the answers. Mum sits herself on the sofa beside me, no doubt to give me the predictable hug prior to the questions. I watch the red digits on my new digital watch change before she makes her move.

'Oh mum, please don't start hugging, Noel's about to do something funny!'

'Why don't you go outside and play?' she quietly whispers in my ear. I know what she's after. She wants me out. They all want me out.

'I'm quite happy here thanks mum.'

I have no desire to go outside, to be laughed at. I want to stay right here.

'It will do you good to get outside.'

'Mum, I'm watching this!' I reply.

'They don't bite you know,' she softly mutters as she releases me from her hug. Maybe they won't, but they will laugh and kick and they will make me cry again.

'Mum, please. I just want to watch Swap Shop!' I state firmly.

'You could take your Lego outside to play with. You're good at building things. I just want you to be happy.'

'I am happy. I like Swap Shop. It's my fourth favourite programme.'

'Are you sure?'

'I'm okay Mum, honest.'

For once, she takes me at my word and makes her way from the front room, smiling all the way. She doesn't understand, no one does.

Five minutes later, as I listen to my mum humming Cliff Richard in the kitchen I hear the front door open. This is followed by the sound of Sean's thumping footsteps as he runs up the stairs. Seconds later the footsteps return as he bounds his way back down. I know what's coming, I've been expecting it. A thud travels through the house as he jumps the last few steps and then he is in the front room within seconds.

'I'm going to play my present from Mum and Dad!' Sean declares, struggling to conceal a grin. Under his right arm is his silver tape player that he got for his birthday. My parents knew that this was what I wanted for my birthday, further enforcing the undeniable fact that he was their favourite. I knew it, Sean knew it and my parents knew it, not that they were ever going to admit it. Birthdays were the worst as he always got better presents.

'I'm watching television,' I reply, hoping he will just go away.

'No, you're not. You're just pretending because you're mental.'

'Shut up Sean. I don't want to hear your tape player. Leave me alone!'

'Yeah, well it's my birthday.'

'So?'

'So I can do what I want!'

'I'm watching television.'

'Of course you are nutter.'

'Mum!' I shout at the top of my voice. I can imagine her in the kitchen now, wearily getting up to sort out another problem between her favourite son and the mental one. The threat of her coming doesn't stop Sean however. He slides the silver tape recorder onto the floor, switching the television off as he does so.

'I was watching that!' I shout.

'Now what tape shall we listen to?' Sean speculates, a finger to his pursed lips. 'What about this one, nutter?'

The first song starts and the synthesisers fight their way from the speaker, loud enough to hammer home the fact that Sean has everything and I have nothing. Yet it's not quite loud enough to conceal the footsteps in the hallway. I hear the door open, but my eyes never stray from the tape recorder. Sean instinctively looks up and that's where he makes his mistake: he misses everything. The tape recorder emits a loud, sickening bang that echoes around the room. Sean turns round with a jump to see a gentle wisp of black smoke rise from the cassette player and slowly dance in small circles before disappearing into the room. The smell of melting plastic slices the air. It is now my turn to conceal a grin as I see the tears begin to form in the corners of his eyes.

You remember that well don't you? You remember every moment. For those few brief moments you were the king of the Morgan children, and all it took was some subtle modification to the cassette player with a screwdriver earlier in the day. Mum used to say that you were good at building things. She never suspected that you much better at destruction.

It may have seemed like a disaster to Sean at the time, but things were easily corrected when he was the favourite. A few fake tears, boo-hoo, my tape player's broke, next thing you knew it's three days later and you were on the way to BurgerWorld to make up for it.

Tuesday afternoon, 11th September 1979

I never got to go for a BurgerWorld meal when it was my birthday. Mum said it was only fair that Sean got another present after the accident with the tape player. An accident? Of course it was. As we park in the town multi-storey car park my Mum's asking me to stop complaining. Why should I?

'I never got a BurgerWorld when it was my birthday!' I complain for the fifth time.

'You're having one now aren't you?'

'I wanted one then. I don't want one now, with him!' I reply, nodding with anger towards Sean who unsurprisingly got to travel in the front seat.

'I want to go home and watch Rentaghost!' I demand.

'We're going for a nice meal and that's the end of it, okay?'

'I can walk home. I don't mind.'

My Mum turns around in her seat and gives me a serious look that she reserves for these sorts of occasions, and that's her final say. The thing is, I never lose.

As we walk through town, I stride ahead. It's all in the plan. If we are quick enough then we can get home in time. Walking on my own gives me time to think. Wouldn't it be good if you could actually rent a ghost, like in the programme? What would I do with my own ghost? Obviously I would want him to haunt Sean. I'd want a particularly nasty ghost for that. Then I would get him to haunt that doctor who says I have an attention problem. I'll show him who's mental.

I'm here. Thirty minutes to the start of Rentaghost. It can be done. Mum and Sean finally turn up two minutes later as if nothing matters. Of course it matters, everything matters. Three minutes after we have sat down to eat our meals, I've finished. Now I have to wait for them. Come on, come on, tick tock, tick tock. And then I see that smug grin on his face. Sean knows. He knows about the routine, he knows how important this is, and he knows what will happen if it's broken. He picks a piece of lettuce from his burger and nibbles on it slowly. He knows, and he's making me pay. A familiar feeling wells in the bottom of my stomach. I try and control it but it is already making its way up my chest and around to the back of my neck. Within seconds it has burst into my skull and I can feel it swirling around, looking for a way out. The thoughts reverberate around my head and I grit my teeth to stop them spilling out.

You fucking sly mother fucker! You fucking moron! I'm going to wipe that smile right off your face! You hear me? I'm going to kill you! One night, when you're asleep, I'm going to make you pay! You hear me? It's not going to be quick. I'll bash your head in with your beloved fucking tape recorder!

No. Not here. Not now. Keep it inside. Remember what the doctor said to do when this happened.

I close my eyes and sit on my hands. I'm counting, I'm counting.

Fucking doctors! They don't know me. They don't know a fucking thing about me!

8, 9, 10 …..

Fuck them! Fuck them all!

14, 15, 16 …..

They don't know what's wrong with me. No one does.

22, 23, 24 …..

Why can't anybody help me?

35

31, 32, 33, 34, 35, 36, 37, 38 …..

It's passing. I can feel it, draining from my skull, flushing itself through my body, fading into the background. But it's still there; it's always there.

When it feels okay to do so, I open my eyes and take my fists out from under my legs. As I work my fingers so that the feeling returns, I look around the table.

Nothing!

They haven't even noticed, and they don't know how close they came.

Five minutes later Sean has finished his burger and is now sucking his milkshake so that it lasts a lifetime. Rentaghost is nearly on. If we leave now then I can catch most of it.

'Mum, please can we go now?' I ask softly.

'Don't worry, we'll make it back for your programme,' she replies, not even considering the time. I need this. I need to see this programme. I deserve it. I fought the anger.

'Please mum, please; Sean can finish his milkshake in the car.'

Doesn't she hear the desperation in my voice?

'We're not going till we are all finished, understand?' she answers in a firm voice.

'But…'

She looks down at me and everything in the room goes out of focus, all except that grin on Sean's face.

'But Mummy…' I plead with every ounce of strength. I'm hardly even here.

'Sit down and be quiet,' she half shouts, before looking around the burger bar to see if anyone heard.

'I am sitting down you stupid bitch!' I scream at her, the voice fighting its way past clenched teeth.

A pause before my mum answers.

'What did you say?'

1, 2, 3, 4 …..

I say nothing. The numbers weren't quick enough, can't do anything about it now. Not grinning any more, are you Sean?
'What did you say?' my Mum repeats, this time in a louder voice.
I'm saying nothing. I can feel my rage, a whirlwind of intensity rolling behind my eyes, no escape. A grin spreads across my brother's face again.

55, 56, 57, 58 …..

Rentaghost came and went. You caught the episode a few years later but it wasn't the same. Then again a lot of things had changed by then. Sean certainly didn't know what was to come.

Chapter 5

Sitting On A Sofa With A Katie Or Two

'Do you really need three sugars in your tea?' Katie asks, delicately placing the mug on the Swedish coffee table.

'Absolutely,' I reply.

A good cup of tea guarantees that by the bottom of the mug both the lecture from Katie on the way home and the resulting tension between us now will be forgotten. In the meantime I almost wish for Katie's housemate Harriet to turn up to provide a distraction, even if I know the short term effect will be heavily outweighed by the long term unpleasantness. How else would I describe a once-upon-a-time girlfriend of two weeks' duration who dumped me because I got in the way of her acting career? A one-sentence role in The Bill five years ago doesn't constitute a valid profession in my opinion. Katie is the polar opposite of Harriet: a stable life, obligatory savings account, everything in fact I seem to missing. Katie could change me but despite my best efforts, she doesn't seem to be in the changing business, at least not on a personal level. So while I wait for the Universe to change in accordance with the amount of tea drunk, or for a failed actress to return from the dole queue, afternoon television provides a welcome distraction.

Katie and I watch in silence as we fume at each other. I gave up long ago trying to construct words from the anagram game currently on screen. The presenter launches another joke into the mists of mediocrity, which is greeted by a sympathetic chuckling from the studio audience. One of the contestants, an eighty year old woman, is desperately trying not to swear after spending the last twenty minutes being humiliated by a fourteen-year-old boy with life-threatening acne. The next game starts and I watch the strangely sexy assistant place the letters on the board, the first three coming out as W, A and N. My hope that the next letters miraculously deliver K, E and R are soon dashed. Instead she whacks out D, R, A, B, E and E, seemingly with no desire to rig the deck for mischief. The old woman makes a six letter word, acne boy triumphs again with eight, both scrape past my three letter effort. And then it's over to Dictionary Corner with Anthony Chambers, well known television celebrity whose smile could halt the collective menopause of a thousand housewives. I can't stand the bloke.

Suddenly the front door slams and Katie and I divert our attention to the raging storm approaching. With alarming and possibly paranormal speed, Harriet enters the living room.

'How did it go?' Katie asks, even though Harriet's forthcoming answer and the truth are most likely two differing things. If acting were the ability to mask pure rage with unbelievable politeness then we would be in the presence of De Niro.

'Ah, you know,' Harriet replies in her soft Scottish accent as she collapses onto the sofa opposite us. 'Said they would let me know, though they were impressed with my portfolio.'

Her four seconds of fame in The Bill flash through my mind with amazing clarity.

'Oh that's good then,' Katie replies comfortingly.

'Oh, hi Joe,' Harrier says, acknowledging my presence after every other item in the room.

'Hi, Harriet.' I reply with a sincerity surpassed by the same aforementioned items in the room.

'Oh, tea!' Harriet comments and without hesitation she is off to the kitchen.

'Yeah I might not take it though if that film role with Jack Connolly comes up in the next couple of weeks,' Harriet continues, her voice fading as she slips into the next room.

'You didn't tell me she had gone for an audition for a film with Jack Connolly?' I ask Katie. It may not be a sparkling conversation piece, but conversation it is nevertheless, and I can't stand the silence any longer.

'Who is this Jack Connolly anyway?' Katie asks, her eyes not once moving from the screen to indicate that I'm far from forgiven just yet.

'You're kidding me?'

'Nope,' Katie replies, her attention switching from the anagram game credits to me, somewhat reluctantly.

'Jack Connolly is a legend!' I reply with enthusiasm. I know I have mere moments while the adverts roll to provide a succinct description of one of light entertainment's most infamous characters.

'Jack Connolly, you know ... actor, starred in low budget, short running soap operas years ago,' I continue as Katie flicks channels to another quiz show.

'Nope, why's he so famous?'

'Well, he's not really, it's just his career has a certain Troy McClure-esque nature to it.'

'A Trot ma what?'

'A Troy Mc…, oh don't worry about it,' I reply, seeing that her interest has long since disappeared. The new quiz enters its final round presented by Anthony "God has given me omnipotent powers to be on every single television channel" Chambers. The questions start to roll. Years of practice have conditioned me to pretend not to hear when not knowing the answer. Hopefully it gives the impression that I know but can't be bothered to reply. I pass the time by pondering the history of Jack Connolly, and wonder if there is a book in it somewhere.

Ten years ago would place me firmly in the Beth era. For Jack Connolly, this was just the beginning. It all began quite innocently enough with a starring role in a popular soap

41

series. They even gave him awards for it. That soon stopped when a slight misdemeanour on his part became national news. The event in question was being observed subtly slipping out of a suburban brothel. 'I was shocked by his brazen attitude!' one onlooker commented. Unfortunately said onlooker just happened to be located in the bushes opposite, equipped with a telephoto lens on his camera. You have to give it to the man: if you're going to fall, you might as well do it straight onto the front page of the biggest selling Sunday newspaper. Did I mention the drug allegations as well? So it was farewell to soap operas for Jack, hello to the rocky climb back up. He never made it, of course. Still, a bit of infamy does get you an occasional low budget film or the odd Channel Five reality show. He's still out there, somewhere. Which brings us to Harriet. I grant you I would be more impressed with a Pacino or Ford but Jack Connolly is Jack Connolly and Harriet is, as always, Harriet.

'What's the capital of Norway?' Anthony Chambers asks from the safety of his television screen. I know this; it's time to stop thinking about defunct television celebrities, it's time to impress.

'Stockholm!' I exclaim hurriedly.

'Oslo!' Katie counters.

'It's Oslo,' Anthony Chambers confirms as Katie looks at me with pity. Thankfully the look is short lived as the phone rings, and like a shot Harriet picks it up in the kitchen. Her quiet tones attempt to mask the essence of the conversation and she almost pulls it off.

'Bastard Connolly!' Harriet shouts as the phone is slammed back onto the hook.

'Guess she didn't get it then?' Katie muses.

'I guess not,' I reply.

'Lord Palmerston!' Katie blurts out to answer another of Chambers' questions. I, of course, choose to answer neither that one nor the many others that follow.

Without a sound, Harriet suddenly appears in the doorway. Despite her best acting attempts, which are seldom up to the job, I see the hurt in her eyes.

'I'm going to learn some lines babes,' Harriet announces, and without waiting for a reply she makes her way up the stairs, stomping so heavily it could double for Judgement Day.

'Okay honey, see you later,' Katie replies sympathetically, her voice chasing Harriet up the stairs as a bedroom door is slammed in frustration.

With just the two of us remaining, the previous awkwardness returns to the fore. Katie and I are at an impasse. Richard and Judy, or conversation? It's a close one, but I decide to be brave.

'I just don't see the problem with me living with Danny,' I start, returning to the main point of her lecture on the way back from the pub.

'Look, Danny seems alright. But are you sure living with a dealer is a good idea?' Katie asks, finally turning to face me. We are straight back into it.

'Come on, you know that's all talk. He thinks he's the Welsh Pacino,' I reply.

'You keep saying that you want to live this ideal life like everyone else, mortgage, girlfriend and all that...'

'I'm working on it, but I don't see what any of this has to do with Danny?'

'Well, because he's a smoker and you are... shall we say, delicate?'

'Let's not go over this again. That was just a problem in the past!' I answer, protesting history, even if it is anything but. She knows that this is the last thing I want to remember.

'You may be trying to bury it, but if you don't accept it then you will never let go. Smoking and all the other stuff is just your way of blocking it out.'

'I don't smoke anymore!' I lie.

'Bollocks don't you.'

'Look…..' my hands are gesturing, trying to grasp an answer out of the air.

'All I'm saying is, we all need help sometimes, I'm your friend and I'm trying to help you now. '

'I….' I try to comment before she interrupts again. She isn't finished yet but I can feel myself getting angry with her. No answer I give will ever make her understand, but I'd at least like the opportunity.

'You are living in another shared house and your life rotates around smoking gear.'

'It's not about the bloody Swedish furniture and mortgage. It's about wanting to be happy!' I reply forcefully, my anger spilling over. 'You know I can't just get the suburban life with a click of my fingers. There are other things to consider.'

'Your past?' Katie asks.

'Yeah, that for a start.'

'But you have to if you want to move on.'

'Yeah, well these things take time. In the meantime I'm quite happy living with Danny,' I reply, wanting to draw this conversation to a close. I know it will never end, not until she has emerged victorious. She may be a friend but she is also a pain in the arse. I know I have to leave soon or it could get very ugly.

'Let's just agree to disagree,' I suggest.

'Just for a change,' Katie replies, her eyes glancing towards the ceiling in resignation. I let her have her moment as it's obvious she will never see my point of view. Yet it's a point worth making, and I illustrate it by rising from the sofa into the heavy atmosphere between us and make my way to the front door.

'Joe!' Katie shouts after me as I further my point by closing the door behind me. That will teach her. I don't know how I can even think that I want us to be together sometimes. I love her but I want to kill her.

44

As I turn onto the main road I look at my watch. Ten minutes to walk home. Once there I can forget all about Katie and whether she is right or wrong. Instead I intend to concentrate on more important things, namely an evening drinking tea, smoking dope and playing Danny's games console. Last night it took me four bloody hours to get up to level three on a game called Inferno! Even then I couldn't defeat the whacking big dog at the end with three heads. Katie says I lack motivation to change my life, but motivation, albeit misdirected, will get me to level four tonight.

My thoughts are suddenly diverted as a pamphlet-waving Christian jumps out from the shadows directly in front of me. These new guerrilla-warfare tactics they use nowadays don't even give me the chance to cross the street.

'Can I interest you in the word of the Lord?' the fresh faced girl asks.

'Not really my thing,' I reply, hoping this will send her on her way.

'You're making a mistake,' the girl replies.

'Sorry?'

'It says in Ephesians 2:8 that….'

'I'm sorry I'm in a bit of a rush,' I interrupt. Neighbours will be starting soon.

'Can't you spare a minute for your own salvation?' comes a grave voice from behind. Looking around, I see I have fallen for the classic pincer manoeuvre: the young girl stopping me, the older guy trapping me from behind. I give a few moments thought to whether I can indeed spare a minute to gain some credit with the man upstairs.

'I wanted to get home for Neighbours,' I declare. Joseph, the points from the heavenly jury are in: nil point.

'There are cross roads in life Joseph. The devil doesn't want you to stop at them anymore, he wants you to keep going on the road to damnation,' the older one philosophises.

45

'I understand that but, hang on, how did you know my name?'

'It's our business to know,' the young girl replies. It's the first time I've ever seen that, Christians waiting for you with name in hand. They're good, I'll give them that.

'I have to go, I'm sorry,' I reply and take a sideways step out of the human sandwich with the evil filling. I barely make ten metres before the older man speaks again.

'You forgot the important bit.'

'The pamphlet?' I speculate, turning and facing them but continuing to walk backwards.

'Ephesians 2:8. For it is by grace that you have been saved, through faith – and this is not from yourself, it is the gift of God.'

'That's very nice but....'

'For we are God's workmanship, created in Christ Jesus to do good works, which God prepared in advance for us to do.'

'Well thanks for your time,' I reply and turn forwards again, just in time to notice the lamp post, currently two inches from my face, and closing. With a dull thud, flesh and bone meet cold cylindrical steel, the physical pain minuscule compared to the embarrassment. I glance around to see if anyone noticed but there is no one, just an empty street. Not even the Christians, although I concede that they may have been scared off by my blasphemous mutterings and 16th Century swearwords. I start to walk again, giving the lamp-post a wide berth and an evil stare, leaving it to wait for its next victim. Only ten minutes to my house, ten minutes to warmth, ten minutes to television, ten minutes to a nice cup of tea.

Chapter 6

Cook For A Lifetime, Leave To Burn

Polston's three-bedroom house wasn't shabby by design, but it was in a state of equilibrium between natural decay and minimal care. The inspector had neither the time nor the inclination to notice. The house and Polston were fading together, a fate sealed the minute his wife and daughter had left in search of a life that Polston could neither offer nor comprehend. Returning from work, the inspector took a rewarding seat in his worn armchair, his supine body collapsing against the floral pattern, his hand gripping a can of real ale. A little of the ale jumped from the can and onto the sponge that was softly erupting from a gash in the arm. Callahan nestled at his feet and they both fell into an uneasy sleep. Within seconds the inspector was snoring loudly and his grip on the can began to slip, tipping it sufficiently for a dribble to escape and fall onto Callahan's head. Callahan woke from a delightful dream where he was eight foot tall and savaging Sergeant Walker, and in a half doze he made his way the short distance to his master's tie and began chewing on it, before laying down and drifting back to sleep. The dream soon resumed, with the tie cast in the role of Sergeant Walker's leg.

Twenty minutes later, Polston awoke with a start, his own vivid dream coming to an abrupt halt and bringing the inspector back to the world of the living. As he tried to recollect his dream further, his attention was diverted to the wet phlegmy sounds emanating from the floor. Arching over with some difficulty he noticed Callahan chewing on his tie, and made a mental note to get one of Walker's ties for the future. Relaxing back in the chair, Polston flicked on the telly

47

but quickly lost interest, his mind drifting back to the dream. Something to do with the Post Office... No, not the Post Office, something about the conversation with Danny? There was something important about it. Yet it wasn't Danny that seemed to be rousing his suspicions, it was the slightly less dishevelled character with him. Although Polston didn't know his name, there was something about him. Was it a memory of the boy from the past or simply natural suspicion? Recently the distinction between the two was becoming blurred. A look in his eyes, perhaps? Polston knew when someone was hiding something; it was all in the eyes. Surely it was no coincidence that the Post Office was robbed as he was talking to Danny and the dishevelled one? That's it, it must have been a clever distraction, these guys were professional, the scruffy one probably the brains behind the operation, Polston thought. The inspector made a mental note to get Walker to conduct immediate surveillance. It was a lead at least, enough to convince Chief Inspector Goss that the afternoon hadn't been a complete cock up. Polston suddenly became aware of the empty can in his hand and the wet patch on the carpet. The inspector raised himself from the chair and made his way to the kitchen, passing a half full sink, complete with floating grey scum happily navigating around the bowl. He forced the can into the bin, which was fast approaching maximum slope instability, and retrieved another can from the fridge. Returning to the front room he slumped back into the armchair and watched a few seconds of television flicker by. He was tempted to put on one of the special videos that he kept hidden in the side cabinet, but decided to search a few more channels instead. Delightfully the next channel he fell upon was a show presented by one of his favourite women. She descended the lit stairway like a fake Liverpudlian second coming. No special video required, thought Polston.

'Come on Callahan, come on,' he spoke hurriedly, rising from the chair with purpose. Callahan awoke excitedly and followed his master into the hall. When they both got there, Polston quickly turned and returned to the front room, closing the door behind him. As he settled back into the chair he could hear the padding of Callahan's paws on the other side of the door. Burying the feelings of guilt, Polston ensured that the curtains were drawn. Operation Lightning Hand began.

50

Chapter 7

Solitude Can Do Strange Things To A Boy On Planet Gong

I had it all planned out and it could have been beautiful. I'm watching the film of my life, becoming one with the memories.

Friday Afternoon, 12th October 1979

Behind me is the door that leads to the Headmaster's office. Not the headmaster's office in my normal school, oh no. I'm not allowed back there since I rubbed Johnny McGregor's face in the gravel. Instead they keep talking about this place. A school for difficult children they say. How can I be above average intelligence one moment, and difficult the next? If you ask me, which no one seems to be doing, it makes no sense. I don't have a problem. I don't!

I can hear them talking behind the door; not the actual words, but I can hear them. Talking about me behind that door aren't you? I want to cry but I've already tried that and it didn't work. I promised myself they won't see me weak again.

The door opens and a middle aged man in a suit and tie emerges from the haze of cigarette smoke within.

'Come on in son, your mum and I would like to talk to you,' he requests. I'm sure you would, you dirty fucking pervert.

My mum turns round to see me as I enter. I know you're just trying to scare me Mum. You won't send me here. You love me, remember. I take a seat next to Mum as the headmaster takes his opposite.

'Hello there, you remember me don't you? Mr Brown. I've been speaking to your Mum again,' he begins. 'Now you know why you're here, don't you?'

'No,' I reply. Tactics.

'Well son, both your current school and your parents feel that you would be better suited if you came to school here. We think we can help you understand your problems, and with some hard work, help you to overcome them.'

'I promise I'll be good!' I cry, scrunching my eyes to make the tears appear. Mr Brown looks across the desk and gives a thin smile to my mum. Well he would wouldn't he, the dirty fucking pervert. Leave her alone, stop looking at her.

'Well son, you've said before that you would make a considerable effort to improve your behaviour,' Mr Brown pauses as he starts to flick through a pile of papers on his desk, 'and here we are again after a recent incident where…'

'I didn't mean to hurt him!' I interrupt.

'…where you rubbed a boy's face in gravel, do you remember that?'

'Yes, but he was nasty to me!'

'And what did he do to warrant such an attack?'

'Scarred for life,' my mum suddenly contributes. Thanks Mum, you shouldn't have.

'He called my mother a fucking whore!' I reply, my head bowed but with my eyes watching carefully to monitor their reactions. My version of events is not strictly true. Johnny McGregor tackled me when we were playing football. I'm Kevin Keegan and he's Kenny Dalgleish: he had to pay for making for making the European footballer of the year fall over and cut his knee. Truth or not, doesn't my mum realise that I did it for her?

'Now I don't think you need to repeat that do you?' Mr Brown replies abruptly.

I'm quiet.

'And then there is your behaviour at home... tell me about your brother Sean?'

I'm not saying anything. I can feel it again.

1, 2, 3 ...

It's like a black cloud forming behind my eyes, if I can only..

4, 5, 6 ...

Suddenly Mum interrupts the silence. As she speaks, I feel it ebbing away, draining to a small point.

'We just don't know what to do, Mr Brown. We treat them the same but he just never seems happy, always wanting what Sean has.'

That's 'cause he has everything, you stupid cow! Come on Mr Brown, time to earn your money or do I have to start counting again?

'Well sibling rivalry is quite common, but I must admit usually not to this degree. In this case I believe we could see significant results with attendance. Now normally we wouldn't accept an induction without meeting the boy's father as well...'

'He's very busy, works awful hours, he wanted to come today but something came up at work I'm afraid.'

What's an induction? Who cares? Obviously my Dad doesn't as he can't even be bothered to turn up. He's more interested in wearing a suit and going to work than looking after his son. He's never even told me what he does. Something that makes a lot of money because we've got a nice house, better than anyone else's at school. More than enough to buy me the Star Wars X-Wing Fighter that I want. A few seconds later Mr Pervert remembers that I'm actually in the room and turns to me.

'Now son, you know what happens at this school don't you?'

'But I want to go home,' I reply in a weak voice. I can feel tears welling up, real tears.

'You're going to come and live here with us. We are going to help you with a more structured approach to your schooling than perhaps you have had previously.'

What's he talking about? Surely they can't be serious about sending me here?

'Of course son, we'll have some fun along the way.'

No. No way. You're not serious. I know your idea of fun. You want to bum me. No way. No fucking way.

1, 2, 3…

Mum please. Why don't you understand? Why the fuck don't you understand you stupid bitch?

4, 5, 6…

What if I smash your face in, pervert? You wouldn't be so keen on having me at your stupid school then!

7, 8, 9…

Fight it. Come on, bury it.

10, 11, 12…

Don't let it get you. Use the numbers!

13, 14, 15, 16, 17, 18 …..

'I just want to go home Mum, please let me go home!' I plead, tears starting to roll down my cheeks.

'And how often will he come home?' my mum asks the pervert as if I'm not even here.

'Oh, every half term and holidays. It will be strange at first for the whole family but you'll find it gets easier.'

Hello, didn't you hear me? Look, I'm crying. I'll be good, I promise. Look at me, look at me.

'Well I shall speak to my husband tonight and hopefully we can have it arranged by the date you mentioned.'

'Excellent. I think that just about covers everything.'

43, 28, 11, 79, 81, 4...

The rest is a haze. Faces look out from the fog, scared faces. There are sounds, things hitting the floor as they are swept from the table. A grainy feel of the plastic of the chair on my fingers as it leaves my hands and crashes into the window. Pain now. Pain from the weight pushing me to the floor. Get off me you dirty pervert fuck! The smell of the dust on the wooden floor beneath my face. Get the fuck off me! I know what you're thinking, pervert. So fucking what! My mum loves me, she won't make me come here.

Later that night I'm lying in bed. I've been here since we got back. I can hear the house and the voices within, monotone voices droning through the floorboards, straight through the grain of the wood, straight through the skin and the bone of the fingers that block my ears. There's the distinctive drawl of my father's voice.

I wonder what I'll ask for Christmas this year?

Now the voice of my mother.

Maybe I should ask for something educational. They'd like that.

'Christ, I work all day and I have to come back to this!' Dad shouts. Yes, something educational, that's what I'll ask for.

'You can't even look after your own son!'

Stop it. Please.

'I don't care what it takes, he's going to that school.'

I can't hear you. I can't hear my mum crying. I can't hear anything.

Three weeks and everything in between. Like a runaway train. You remember a lot of things about your childhood. A lot of things you wish you couldn't remember. If you could forget then maybe now you wouldn't have those urges.

Tuesday, 6th November, 1979

I hate it. When are they coming to take me home? I hated it yesterday when I arrived, and I hate it still. When are they coming to take me home?

I share my dorm room with four other boys. They were apparently out of control before they were even brought here. What kind of idiot puts someone like me with kids like this? They are nothing like me. Three of them are hard and the other one is quiet. I'm troubled, apparently. They've already seen my weakness, no matter how deep I tried to bury my face in the pillow last night. Eight hours of crying was enough to place me squarely at the bottom of the food chain.

This is how it seems to work. Michael Richards is the boss. He's what they would describe on Police 5 as stocky, with hair that looks like it hasn't been washed for weeks. By all accounts, by his recollection anyway, the last hair wash took ten teachers to hold him down. Of course it's not true, but who's going to argue with him? Next in order are Bobby Johnson and Dean Robinson; smaller and younger, but still much larger than me. They know their place and they've already determined mine as well. Seconds in command, Avon to Michael's Blake. Where Dean is thin, Bobby has a boyish chubbiness and a habit for eating in as slobbish and uncouth a

56

manner as possible. Scum, both of them. Therein lies the balance of power, but the last position is up for grabs. Eric Porter is the last member of the dorm. He has a lanky and fragile frame which compliments his submissive nature. Greasy hair, stupid face. I know what you're thinking, Porter. You've been waiting a long time for someone else to turn up to share in the pain haven't you? Well I hate to disappoint you but that's not going to be me. I've got plans. In the meantime, just another night and then Mum will see sense and come to take me home. She has to. So while I wait I'm lying on my top bunk in my Transformer pyjamas for just one more night. Eric sleeps on the top bunk opposite, beneath me Bobby, and on bottom bunk opposite, Dean. A single bed sits adjacent to the bunks, Michael Richards's territory. Bobby and Dean aren't allowed to go near, so the same rule most definitely applies to Eric and me.

It's late now. Dean and Bobby are talking into the night. Then silence as the footsteps of Mr Carter pass by the door. Whispers now. What can be said in whispers?

'Morgan!' Bobby whispers from the bunk below. Maybe I can get away with not answering. I'm asleep. I can't hear you. I can't hear anything.

'Morgan!' it comes again. 'We're gonna get you tomorrow, you fucking poof!'

'You gonna fucking die, rich boy!' I hear whispered from across the room. Dean's contribution this time.

'And then I'm gonna fuck your mum,' Bobby whispers from beneath.

They try desperately to stifle their laughs. They try and fail. Too busy to notice me anymore.

1234567891011121314151617181920212223242526272829 303132...

No more numbers. A rage, instant and uncontrollable, uncontainable.

'Fuck you, you fucking motherfucker! Fuck you, fuck you, fuck you!' I shout, my face tightening as the words spill out of my mouth. My chest tightens as the rage takes hold. And then as instantly as it arrived, I feel it falling away.

'You little bastard!' Bobby speaks out from below. His voice is filled not with fury, more disbelief, pride forcing the reply. As he speaks I feel the bed shudder, accompanied by the sound of sheets moving against skin as he leaves his bunk. The fury has drained, a mere shadow of itself. Left behind is a void, quickly filled by fear, travelling through my body as if I were drowning in it.

I must defend myself. I must survive.

The fear is washed away as a new feeling of strength enters. I turn onto my side and raise my leg, arching it behind me. From my advantageous position I see Bobby's head emerge from the bunk beneath. Bad move, Fuckface. He starts to turn, his head following his shoulder in the movement. Mere moments before I swing my leg, connecting with that fucker's face, Michael's voice fills the room. Its deep tone carries authority.

'For fuck's sake, shut up! I'm trying to get me some kip here.'

Bobby is the first to speak. 'I'm gonna kill this little fucker!'

I can feel the tension in my leg, the eagerness of my subconscious mind to strike.

'Go to fucking sleep!' Michael shouts. It fails to stop Bobby and I can see his face turning towards me. With gritted teeth he starts to draw his arm back, his hand already in a clenched fist, preparing.

'You fucking......' Bobby spits. My leg is shaking. I don't know if it's fear or just the effort of restraint. Michael speaks again, this time louder.

'I said go to bed, for fuck's sake!'

'But this …'

'I'm not in the fucking mood Bobby, alright? Sort it out tomorrow.'

'But Mickey, you were asleep, you didn't hear what this little fuck said!'

Footsteps, outside on the landing suddenly interrupt the argument. The landing light is turned on, its brilliance puncturing the darkness in our room as it streams around the frame of the door. Bobby returns to his bunk with impressive speed and silence. The sounds of sheets being moved back in the pretence of saintly sleep form a backdrop to the footsteps now outside our door. I settle back into a more realistic sleeping position.

A pause.

The door is opened about a foot and Mr Carter's head enters first, followed by his bulky frame and furious temper.

'I heard you little bastards, I heard you. I'm going to be right outside this door waiting for you. The next time I catch you speaking you will all be in detention and that's just to start with.'

The door closes quietly and darkness returns to the room, all except the halo of light that surrounds the door. If the light remains on then Mr Carter is still around. I'm safe for now, even as I listen to the whispers that begin again.

'You're gonna pay, rich boy. I'm gonna kick your fucking teeth in. You're a dead man Morgan, you hear me.'

I hear you. Eric hears you too. The vacant expression on his face in the bunk opposite hints at painful memories. You should be happy Eric, I've just taken your place.

Over the next couple of hours I watch and listen. Eventually Eric's eyes close and he falls into the most comfortable sleep he's probably had in months. From across the room Michael

59

falls into a deep sleep, soon followed by Bobby and Dean, no doubt dreaming of revenge. It is only then that I allow the darkness to gather itself in the corner of the room. At the beginning it is just a dark form, consolidated from other shadows cast there. Only I can tell it is something different. Suddenly two pale grey eyes open in the gloom to observe their new surroundings.

Chapter 8

From Suburbia With Love

I'm half asleep aren't I? What was I was dreaming of? Something about the past?
Open your eyes Joseph, open your eyes.

My eyelids open, it's a tremendous sight. 12 o'clock on a Saturday, another week of work vanquished and one month today of having moved in and moved on. My arm extends towards the bedside cabinet and I grope hopelessly for the telly remote sitting amongst the empty coffee cups, flicking on the telly when it is finally located. It's the perfect start to the day as the theme tune to footy focus begins, God bless you BBC. Now I admit that my interest in football has waned somewhat in recent years, strangely coinciding with my team's relegation to the depths of mediocrity some years before. And so to offset those memories, amongst many others, I decide to roll a joint. Once the craft is complete, I pass the time with Gary Lineker and Mary Jane for company.

A few minutes into this beautiful moment a small hot rock falls unnoticed from the tip. First to arrive is the faint smell of burning, then comes the searing pain amongst my chest hair. Looking down I see a familiar wisp of smoke rise from my chest and like any person on fire I become an exaggerated maniac and flip onto my side, the scooby falling to the bed in a burning path of destruction. Do you never learn Joseph? Its molten evilness is making its way straight through the bed sheet, forming another singed hole amongst the multitude. Returning to manic status I go on the attack, brushing the bed vigorously so that the scooby pops out of its ever deepening indentation and with an enthusiastic leap, accepts its fate and drops to the carpet intent on one final mission of reducing my deposit. However it is no match for me as I hit an exaggerated area of the carpet with my sandal repeatedly. I am victorious, but at a price. All this excitement has thrown me from my comatose state and reluctantly I get up to face the day.

'Alright my boy,' I say to Danny as I enter the front room, the games console staring up at me from the heavily littered floor. The stereo thankfully provides a distraction as a new song breaks in. From his extensive collection, the boy Danny has chosen to welcome the weekend in with Twelve Steps by Spiritualized, a great song although I'm always disturbed by the police sirens in the middle.

'Alright Joe lad. What you up to today?' asks Danny from the kitchen, half yawning as he takes a bite from last night's pizza.

'Should be popping into town in a bit,' I reply as the games console and I share a look.

'Sweet.'

'Might crack on with level 4 for a while first though.'

'Bollocks to that, you'll be on there for hours you sad bastard. Want a cup of tea?' Danny asks.

Having experienced the dire tea making skills of Danny on numerous occasions, I am tempted to decline the offer. Still tea is tea, so I politely accept. A few moments elapse with the sound of drawers being opened before he finally emerges and places the cup in front of me. Of all the things missing in this house, for example any form of food, there is always a ready supply of tea, bless him. Danny grabs his mobile and keys with disturbing enthusiasm from the same table as my newly arrived tea.

'Got a bit of business to attend to,' Danny declares as he quickly disappears into the hallway.

'Put me down for an eighth!' I shout after him.

'London Town or town town?' he asks as I hear the sound of the door being wrenched open.

'Town town and don't forget the eighth!' I reply.

A few moments after Danny leaves my eyes inevitably focus on the games console. Okay you bastard, just don't let me play you all afternoon. Taking my cup of tea with me as I kneel on the floor to switch on the console I take a huge swig before I realise my mistake. Mr *I get my tea bags on special offer at the corner shop* strikes again.

The tea doesn't get any better by the fourth time I fall foul of yet another flying bowler hat, courtesy of my arch nemesis OddJob. There is nothing left to do but to take the brave step of actually making a cup myself. Entering the kitchen I consider my own meagre supplies before coming to the conclusion that I don't actually have any tea, crap or otherwise. So, in true house mate fashion, I begin to look through Danny's cupboard. There is no immediate tea like packaging so I search a bit harder. After all, although Danny's previous efforts are spectacularly poor, I am convinced that it is indeed tea that he is using. I eventually come to a battered tin box with chips of the green paint missing, revealing the golden hue of the brass underneath. Upon opening it, it looks and smells like tea so I congratulate myself on a spot of theft well done. After switching the kettle on and then waiting an eternity for it to boil, I consider the possibility that the electricity has been cut off - always a danger in my line of accommodation. Eventually returning to the front room with tea in hand, I give Bond a miss as M files my score as equivalent to the 00 geezer who gets killed in the first five minutes of every film. Instead it's on to Inferno and to where I left off on level four. Despite twenty minutes of effort and colourful language I can't just seem to get past the wolf at the end of the level. It's bloody impossible. Mind you, I am on my third joint by now. Then suddenly I remember the tea, how could I forget? I take a huge swig and the taste - or should I say the cold repugnant filth - loiters around the back of my throat before I refill my cup in a quite disgusting reflex action. Bloody Danny! Such a horrific experience brings Plan A to the forefront of my mind. A plan of devious proportions that I devised last night. I may not be able to make a decent cup of tea or be any good at computer games but I can at least do something about one of them. I'm going to buy my own games console. I could of course use the money I was saving for a holiday or a new car or a mortgage or whatever the establishment is spending it on nowadays. Or I could go into town and buy the games console and through a combined effort of stealth and sneakiness, hide it in my room and practice Bond like crazy. Come the day, Danny's face will be priceless as I crush him when he is least expecting it. No choice really, especially as controlling impulses has never been my strong point.

Today's drive into town is different from the normal commute I have to undertake for the purposes of work. Five days a week, five days of meaningless toil for the man. Still, beats the alternative. I pull up at the traffic lights, a red sports car pulling up alongside. I stare across jealously at the car and in return the beautiful young woman driving stares back. Crikey! I know what Bond would do in a situation such as this, a race off the lights through the suburban streets, a match between her foreign sports car and my symbol of British car manufacturing at its best. She looks at me with a smile and sends a deep powerful rev to the engine. Bizarrely, she actually seems to be on the same wavelength. I rev my twenty year old car in response, the dashboard shaking uncomfortably as I do so. The Austin Maestro may not look like much but she's got a few surprises left in her.

Amber. She's off, immediately taking the lead. My Maestro stutters under the sudden request for acceleration before stalling with a mechanical noise not previously encountered in the entire history of the automobile. Bugger! Looking up, I see the sports car disappear around the corner, coincident with my 00 status being revoked at MI6. Perhaps M will let me stay on and look after the stationary cupboard after my latest disgrace to the organisation. On the third attempt, the engine starts again and I begin to crawl up the road. It's hard not to notice the uncomplicated hand gestures from other drivers as they overtake. The only thing to do is ignore it, to turn up the radio and drive.

Half an hour later, my failure is forgotten as I stash the games console into the boot of my car, now parked in the multi-storey. Since I am on a roll towards financial ruin, why stop there? I leave the car park and head towards the record shop. When I get there, first stop is the soul section until I realise I have all of Stevie Wonder's stuff. I then move on cautiously into the new world section but not having a cardigan I move on swiftly. I skirt around the heavy metal section because my clothes aren't black enough and my hair is far too sensible. There is only one place left to go and it's the worst: rock and pop a.k.a Browsers' Paradise. I'm starting to think that maybe Ken has the right idea in his whole hating society thing. A through F is crammed with the enemy and so I go straight towards D to see if Jim Morrison has made an amazing recovery from death and reformed The Doors. It takes a good half hour before I eventually leave the shop after buying A Northern Soul by The Verve and Brushfire Fairytales by Jack Johnson.

Walking across the town square, my record shop bag swings with my stride and gives me a distinctly feminine look. I look across and see a gang of teenagers sitting on the steps drinking cider. A brass band plays somewhere nearby. And then emerging from the shopping centre is one of the greatest sights I have ever seen. She is beautiful, a vision in the crowded town square. As I pass some bloke in a Salisbury's supermarket uniform she is passing the Big Issue salesman twenty feet away and moving into the crowd, heading in my direction. I watch her all the way, unable to draw my eyes away from such stunning beauty. It is as if she is the personification of everything radiant, served up in the middle of suburbia, untouchable but utterly desirable. She has a kind face with a little make up, her stunning long brown hair falling over her shoulders in exquisite folds. As she gets nearer I can see that her small rectangular glasses compliment her stunning blue eyes while she is dressed perfectly, utterly devastating to the male species. In all of her beauty she retains a hint of the girl next door. I would love to live next door to her, and if she moved then I would too. A little obsessive? Maybe. Entirely legal? I doubt it. In all of this there is something familiar about her. Behind the vision which is sending my senses into submission there is something else, and as she gets within ten feet it occurs to me. Beth! There is only one thing to do in such a situation, run away. I search the crowd for a way out, but fate is not so kind. The crowd parts like fluid waves leaving a corridor of space with me at one end and her at the other. I must use my last resort, to lower my head and walk straight past. As my head begins to drop I can see that she is looking straight at me, a puzzled look on that beautiful face. There is a slight change in her posture and an alarming change in direction. She can smell the fear, she is heading straight for me. Help.

'Bruce!' she exclaims as she gets within a couple of metres of me. I look up and as I do so a number of realisations enter my mind. The first and most important is that I have seen Beth's face in my dreams for years but this is not how I remember her. There is Beth in there somewhere but it is hidden behind the face of someone different. It sounds harsh but Beth was never this beautiful. The second realisation is that if this isn't Beth then why is she heading towards me, thinking she knows me and calling me Bruce? Who the hell is Bruce? There must be some lucky bastard lurking behind me and I am just a minuscule obstacle in her attempt to reach him. How the fuck does someone called Bruce get a girl like this? At least it will be over soon once she passes. It's all a simple mistake on my part.

Any logical explanation is shattered as she throws herself at me, slightly jumping upwards so her arms wrap around my neck, her cheek softly connecting with my shoulder. The force of our meeting has caught me unaware and I stumble backwards. All this takes a matter of seconds but I am confronted by a wealth of sensory input, physically and mentally. Asides from the whole it's not Beth/this girl thinks I'm Bruce situation I feel her hair brush my face, her soft bosom pressing into my chest and the warmth of her upper arms against my neck. Before I can correct her mistake, logical reason is suspended and I am controlled by the most basic instinct, to move away so that she can't feel my erection that is rapidly building. After the slight stumble backwards I push forward gently, pressing into her bosom a little whilst trying to regain stability, ready for my escape. She continues to hug me and then begins to jump up and down excitedly against me like it was Christmas. This isn't really helping things with the little fella although I doubt that that term could be entirely accurately applied at this moment.

'Oh Bruce, it's so good to see you!'

Now I'm thinking to myself that there could be a number of scenarios. Perhaps a simple case of misidentification? Perhaps she is pissed? And through all this, I hope and pray that she hasn't noticed my erection because if this Bruce turns out to be her brother then it could get very complicated. I begin to pull my head away from her so that she can see my face and realise her mistake. I have to be gentlemanly in this situation, despite how nice it is to be hugged by a beautiful complete stranger. And I still haven't said anything yet. Our cheeks touch slightly as I move my head and it comes as a shock when she kisses me passionately. A sweet tender kiss which my eyes instinctively close to; soft, unrushed, a feeling of the unfamiliar flooding my mind with excitement and pleasure. I am too caught up in it to realise that this is not really acceptable practice with complete strangers, even ones that are drop dead stunning and so I do the unthinkable, driven by impulse, I kiss her back. It takes a few seconds to realise the inevitable, for my mind to refocus on the event, and I still haven't said anything yet. What the hell am I doing? I'm about five seconds away from having to sign a register at the police station for the rest of my life. I start to pull away reluctantly, slowly, our lips gradually parting as if we have been in love for years but have only just realised it. Illogically I think of Katie as I do so.

'Oh Bruce, I thought I would never see you again,' she mutters softly. The sound of her speaking the name Bruce strikes terror into me and a new feeling of guilt envelops me. How could I have allowed this to happen? I need to say something clever so that the whole confusion is immediately resolved, both of us departing with pride yet humour at such a simple mistake.

'Hi, how's it going?' I ask her as if I've known her for years. Why the fuck did I say that? My eyes close with resignation, a new low in the collective stupidity of the human race. When I open my eyes again I see a middle aged bloke glancing at us as he passes, carrying shopping bags as his wife talks to him. We make eye contact but he looks quickly away as if he has been caught out looking at someone else's girlfriend, although this is as far from the truth as it could be.

'Oh Bruce,' she replies, her hot breath against my neck as her head tilts upwards. The concern for my erection returns and I can feel it absolutely stonking against her. She must be aware of it too as she continues to hug me. Lucky that, because if she moved I could have someone's eye out. I know I should just walk away from all this, but I can't, not without a limp. Besides, once I tell her that I'm not Bruce and that it's all been a big mistake, I can't see her being as accommodating. There is only one option left, to carry on the pretence and think very boring, very un-stimulating thoughts. In my mind I am trying to put up some shelves at home. Why has she walked in the room naked? Why have I grown a handle bar moustache, ja? This is not helping.

'It's good to see you as well,' I say dryly, trying to keep conversation and imagination separate. It occurs to me that I don't know her name but at least that makes two of us.

'Oh Bruce,' she whispers again. I wonder what this Bruce is like and that he must be an amazing guy if someone who looks like me could ever get a girl like this. I can imagine a picture of myself as Bruce, sitting in a hut in the Antarctic with a blizzard hurling itself at the windows, whilst his evil impostor enjoys this moment in his absence. There is a look in her eyes of longing and history between them. She has probably been searching for him for years and she ends up with me. Perhaps she is mad, as well as pissed.

'Oh it's so good to see you,' she continues, her fingers gently running down my cheek. I can't detect the smell of alcohol on her breath.

'You too,' I reply in a deep coarse voice that I imagine Bruce would speak with. It may sound manly but it distinctly lacks sincerity.

Her head takes a short jolt backwards, her face a look of bewilderment.

'Bruce, you do remember me don't you?'

Oh shit. She's rumbled me.

69

'Yeah of course I do!' I reply in a less dramatic tone. Perhaps a smile and a small laugh will reassure her.

'Bruce, it's me, Mia. It hasn't been that long has it?' She asks.

'No of course it hasn't, I've missed you so much Mia,' I reply. I question why I am saying all of this. Beautiful girls often make me think illogically but never to the point of insanity. The mention of her name seems to reassure her and we kiss again.

'So how long have you been back? What was it like?' She asks as the kiss ends.

'Yeah, it was good,' I reply, whatever it was. 'Haven't been back that long,' I continue whilst I scratch the back of my head. I wonder why Bruce could let someone like this disappear from his life and into the arms of his evil impostor.

'Oh come on, stop being modest. Come on tell me all about it,' she asks again and I'm terrified that she is pressing the question. Can't she just leave it?

'It was good,' I say, nodding my head forward and back. 'Let me tell you about it over a drink.'

My first thought is one of congratulation at having evaded the question, quickly followed by despair at the dawning realisation of what I've said. My intention wasn't to ask her out, I'm just trying to bluff my way out of an ever deepening hole. Someone get this man a shovel.

'Let's go then!' she says, lightly taking my hand in hers. All I know is that I'm scared and am in way over my head. My erection is lessening however, presenting the perfect opportunity to escape.

'I'd love to but…' I mutter scratching the back of my head again.

'Oh come on,' she appeals. My God she is beautiful.

'Ummm, I've got…' I hesitate, struggling to think of something, anything. 'I've got this thing and then I've got to go and ….' I reply with ridiculously little conviction.

'A couple of drinks Bruce, that's all.'

The ground beneath my feet in my little hole has now given way and I can feel myself falling.

'Please?' she asks, her head falling to one side.

'Yeah sure,' I reply and as I speak the words, sensible Joe who for the majority of my life has never taken a bit of interest in my well-being suddenly makes his presence known.

What are you doing? I hear him ask.

I have no idea really.

She's gonna rumble you?

I know.

Then why are you doing it?

I don't know.

Why don't you just leave now?

I don't know.

You know you're taking advantage of her mistake don't you?

Yeah of course but she's fit.

Not very noble is it?

Not really but can you please lend a hand instead of constantly asking questions? I need all the help I can get right now.

Sorry not my line of business. See you on the other side you immoral bastard.

And so with my nemesis departed I am free to engage in dastardly acts of deception.

'Where shall we go?' I ask.

'Your choice,' Mia replies, her hand tightening in mine.

The first place that enters my mind is The Manor and Toad and I dismiss it as quickly as it emerged. I can't think of a quicker way to make a girl go right off you than to take her to the villain pub.

'What about the new Wine Bar?' I reply, congratulating myself again for the sensible answer.

71

Either I am getting better at this speaking to women thing or it may just be my bluffing skills are far in advance of my own expectations. We've sat in the wine bar for at least a couple of hours and during that time she hasn't given the slightest indication that she suspects a thing. No, I don't know how either. Eventually of course, every conversation has its end. We step out into the late winter afternoon of the best day of my life and kiss again. It is just as beautiful as before and it lingers before she slowly pulls away, our lips parting and leaving a feeling of mystery and sudden loss. As her hand leaves mine she rummages in her deep jacket pocket and emerges with a small rectangular piece of paper folded down the middle. Before I have any chance to study it further she kisses me quickly before turning, smiling and leaving. Please don't go. I continue to stand there and watch as she walks up the street. It is only after she gives me one final smile as she slips around the corner that I dare to look. With some trepidation, I unfold the piece of paper as a feeling of excitement and nervousness overwhelms my senses.

A phone number. Her phone number!

I look at the people in the street and want to hug them all as a broad grin erupts onto my face. Unconsciously I play the slip of paper around my fingers, feeling the dry texture on my fingertips before I slip it securely into my own pocket. This small piece of paper may now be the most valuable item that I possess, it wouldn't be hard. There is only one thing left to do, get back home and fit in as much boasting to Danny as Saturday evening will permit.

My thoughts are full of joy as I turn to head in the other direction. Before I have even taken a step, I nearly shit myself when a tramp appears out of nowhere. My eyes don't have time to focus on the mass of hair and crap a few inches from my face before the rancid smell of urine hits me.

'He took me there, ya bastard!' the tramp spits into my face with a foul breath of dog end tobacco and super strength cider.

My body doesn't jump, neither does it fall, it shudders as if I were an immovable object was hit by an unstoppable force.

'Fu...' I attempt imaginatively to reply but he doesn't give me time to finish.

'And I saw a man, ya bastard, whose app..., whose appear... whose app... app...'

'Fucking hell man!' I manage to contribute during a pause in stuttering.

'Whose app... app... appear...' he continues in a mad filthy rant. It seems that he doesn't even acknowledge my part in the discussion. It's as if I'm not even here.

'Look mate,' I counter in the beginnings of a plan to escape.

'Whose appearance was... was... was like bronze!' The tramp blurts out at considerable speed. His primary mission seems to be to deliver his speech despite the difficulties in speaking it. It doesn't appear that his intention is to scare the crap out of me, which is a shame because he's doing a remarkable job at it. He concludes this difficult sentence with his head twitching to the side and looking at the floor like a small ashamed child.

'Ya bastard, ya fooking bastard!' he shouts again with renewed confidence. I conclude that I've tried speaking to him, I even tried reasoning with him, sort of. There is nothing left to do but to walk away. As I give the nutter a wide berth I hear him mutter at a barely audible volume something about a gateway. My pace increases just as his stutter is seemingly cured.

'Son of man, look with your eyes and hear with your ears and pay attention to everything I am going to show you, for that is why you have been brought here.' The volume of his voice increasing as I thankfully put more distance between us.

'Tell the house of Israel everything you see!'

As I round the corner his voice suddenly stops and I am away, I am free from him. Christ and they said I had problems.

Chapter 9

Mr Smith Goes To Scumtown

Bounding up the pathway and up to my front door I feel like I have a secret. Still, as I turn the key in the lock and force the door I should at least try and maintain some essence of composure. I will never be the Fonz but I should at least try. I might just casually drop what happened with Mia into the conversation, I might not. I walk the short distance to the front room with an exaggerated stride, turning into the room to observe Danny rolling up a good six-inch joint.

'Mate, you wouldn't bloody believe it!' I say before I have even sat down.

'Eh?' Danny replies, raising the joint to his lips.

'I was in town right?'

'You wanna game of Bond?'

'Not at the moment dude,' I reply, slightly annoyed with the interruption.

'Noodle Pot?' Danny asks, offering me the remnants of his cold dinner on a fork.

'Ah, no thanks,' I reply politely. 'I was in town right, and I see this girl coming down the steps...'

'Hang on a minute mate,' Danny interrupts again, this time in response to the Rhubarb and Custard ring tone emanating from his mobile. Leaning forward with no great speed he grabs his phone which is vibrating its way across the small table, through the remnants of marijuana and roach material.

'Yeah, no worries,' I sigh.

'Just another punter I expect,' Danny speculates as he raises the phone to his ear and waves the joint in my direction which I willingly accept in consolation.

With my moment of glory in a state of suspension I watch the television and wince as the nation's favourite Liverpudlian light entertainment star strikes up an insane cackle disguised as a song. No choice really than to listen in on Danny's phone conversation instead. In truth I would probably be listening anyway, even if Audrey Hepburn were on telly naked with a number of phallic shaped objects made of cheese.

'Fucking punters,' Danny complains as he returns the phone to the table. 'So who was this girl then?'

'Oh yeah,' I reply, trying to give the impression that I had already forgotten about it.

Danny clears his throat unsubtly, gesturing for the return of his creation. I reluctantly comply.

'I was walking through town right...'

'Yeah, and you saw this girl coming down the steps.'

'Yep, spot on, and I thought it was Beth, I've told you about Beth haven't I?'

'Once or twice you repetitious git,' Danny replies. In the one month we have lived together we have established a friendship where trading insults is wholly acceptable if not expected. 'So, how long is it since you last saw Beth?'

'I dunno, five, six years or something,' I reply, fully aware that it's been nine years, four months and thirteen days.

'Did she recognise you?'

'No... well, yes, but it wasn't Beth you see.'

'How did she recognise you if it wasn't Beth?'

'Yeah well that's the thing,' I reply, glad that I can at last get the story out. Sod the Fonz approach, I need to tell someone.

All of a sudden the front door is forced open, the door swinging wildly into the other side of the living room wall with a bang. Oh Christ! It's either the filth, come to take away Danny or worse-case scenario...no it couldn't be.

'Oh fuck!' Danny exclaims quietly.

From the hallway and at a considerable volume comes an unfamiliar voice.

'Alright boys!' the visitor announces, the words drawn out with emphasis.

'It's Smith the landlord,' Danny warns in whispers as he leans forwards.

The door to the living room flies open and he enters the room. From the cowboy boots on his feet to the mass of black curly hair and razor sharp sideburns, Mr Smith doesn't seem like your average landlord. He holds a can of Guinness in his right hand, while in his left is a white carrier bag with more of the same.

'Alright boys,' Mr Smith repeats as he collapses onto the sofa next to me, taking a huge swig from the can. I shuffle myself away from him a little but this only encourages him to spread his legs further apart.

'Alright there Mr Smith,' Danny says, halfway between a question and a statement.

'Not too bad Danny boy, not too bad at all,' Mr Smith replies before draining the can.

'Excellent,' Danny responds coldly, obviously taking little joy from this sudden visitation.

'This your new house mate then?' Mr Smith asks, gesturing in my direction.

'Yeah, I moved in a while ago,' I reply nervously as he takes another can from the bag and opens it with some gusto, the spray firing onto the carpet.

'I don't care who you have in here as long as I get me money.'

'No problem there,' Danny replies.

'Better fucking not be, Daniel. You don't want to cross me, I know people,' Mr Smith declares, his tone changing quickly to menace.

'Of course.'

'I've got contacts, I'm a face, remember that!'

With some shock I see that he has finished another can in an unbelievable time, falling from his hand to the floor. A mixture of foam and liquid slowly spills onto the carpet. From the corner of my eye I see Smith follow my gaze before leaning over to inspect the damage.

'You'll have to get that cleaned up lads.'

'No problem,' I confirm. I'm starting to think that maybe my worst fears would have made a better visitor.

'So, got my money then?'

'Yep, no problem, would you like to step into my office?' Danny enquires.

Both Smith and Danny leave the room and enter the kitchen to sort out the rent. I can only conclude that Danny must have a stash of money hidden somewhere in there. I make a mental note to check when Danny is out. Not to steal, just to know. I get up and close the front door, previously left wide open and then return to the living room and make a futile attempt to tread the spill into the carpet with the sole of my shoe. The conversation from the kitchen is muffled until Mr Smith starts shouting.

'Don't fuck with me Danny boy, I'm a player!'

Any reply on Danny's part is interrupted by the hollow metallic sound of an empty can hitting the worktop. A few minutes later they both re-enter the room. Mr Smith looks a little disconcerted which I put down to a short period of abstinence from alcohol, a conclusion verified as he makes a beeline for the plastic bag and takes out the last can. 'Right boys, it's been a pleasure,' Smith exclaims. As much as I doubt his sincerity, this all seems like part of the monthly routine for him and Danny.

'Always Mr Smith,' Danny confirms with a lie.

'Got to get back to collecting rent from the usual muppets, these things don't run themselves you know.'

'Business good is it?' Danny asks as he settles back into his original position on the sofa.

'Not too shabby my boy, although a bit of extra money is always welcome. Might have to make the missus get another part time job,' Mr Smith declares, laughing hysterically before adding in my direction 'that's Mrs Smith to you son, or Renee if you've got the money.'

'Stay lucky boys,' he mutters, lighting a cigar as he leaves. As he walks from the front room to the hallway he flicks ash onto the floor and reaches inside his trousers to adjust himself. The front door is opened with force and slams into the other side of the living room wall, again.

'Is he always like that?' I ask as I get up to close the door.

'Yeah pretty much,' Danny replies. 'So what happened with this girl then?'

Finally I can tell my story, no more needless phone calls, no more visits from a homicidal madman.

'What girl?' I reply, acting uninterested.

'Some bird in town or something.'

'Oh yeah, where was I? I was walking across the town square...'

'Yeah yeah, met this girl and she looks a bit like Beth, bit rough was she?'

'No, this girl was stunning!' I exclaim vehemently. I have to defend her.

'Go on then, town square, beautiful girl,' Danny prompts, emphasising the word beautiful with a camp expression.

'So she comes up to me and thinks I'm someone else. Then all of a sudden she's kissing me.'

'Why was she kissing you?'

'Because she thought I was someone else remember. Anyway, we ended up going for a drink.'

'You sly old dog, you didn't take her to that shit hole did you?'

'No, to the new wine bar.'

'Good work fella,' he replies in congratulation.

79

'Anyway she was amazingly beautiful, did I mention that? Then she gave me her phone number so I should be seeing her again.'

'Nice!' Danny says in his best Leslie Phillips impression.

'Oh and then some tramp had a pop at me outside.'

'Wasn't her dad was it?'

I close my eyes for a few brief moments before I continue.

'Nope, just your usual run of the mill twat.'

'So when are you going to see her again?'

'Dunno, might give it a couple of days, play it nice and cool and all that.'

'Wanna borrow my mobile?'

'Daniel, I am not going to explain the finer points of relationships to you.'

'Bloody hell. One minute she mistakes you for someone else, and then you go for a drink whilst informing her of her mistake. Next thing I know you're in a relationship!'

Despite my best attempts to tell the story in a flattering light I have given too much away. I might as well tell the truth now as that's what mates are for, a bit of piss taking, a bit of advice.

'Ah, well that's the problem. She thinks I'm this bloke called Bruce. You remember the mistaken identity bit?'

Danny straightens in his chair and chuckles to himself.

'You immoral bastard!' he concludes.

'Eh?'

'You didn't tell her did you?'

'I meant to,' I say, trying to act innocent as if I never got the chance.

'So when you gonna tell her?'

'I was thinking that I could try and get away with it,' I reply, despite how ludicrous it sounds as I say the words.

'She'll rumble you within a week you sad bastard!' Danny chuckles as he rises from the sofa and moves to the kitchen. It's true, I accept the sad bastard classification but if this is the only way that I get to see her again then so it must be. We only spent a few hours together but I can't get her out of my head.

'Wanna a cup of tea?' Danny asks as he leans through the serving hatch.

'Nah, I'm alright mate,' I reply. I don't quite fancy taking the *is it tea or is it liquefied crap* challenge. 'Not if you're still using that corner shop crap.'

'Nah, got some new stuff earlier. Some bastard kept nicking the old stuff.'

'Oh go on then,' I reply, prepared to take the risk.

A few moments later Danny re-enters the room and places the cup in my hand. I take a small apprehensive sip but any disgusting taste is cleverly disguised with an overpowering sweetness.

'Bloody hell how many sugars did you put in this?'

'Dunno, your usual five probably.'

'It's three you moron!'

'Got a bit of business,' Danny states as he shovels his collective crap into his pockets and makes his way to the front door.

'Okay matey, have a good one.'

'Always,' Danny replies, wrenching open the front door and leaving at a speed dictated by a demanding clientele and the promise of a profit unknown to the taxman. That's all well and good but he's left the bloody front door open as well. Still, short term memory loss is a cross we all must bear.

After getting up and closing the front door, I return to the front room and suddenly remember that it's Saturday night and I have nothing on. Just me and, if I'm not mistaken, a large chunk of gear that Danny has just left lying around, silly boy. I skin my first joint before flicking between channels, passing a low budget movie and the sight of Jack Connolly as the hero. Two channels later I come across the lottery show.

81

Salvation awaits. The familiar face of my television nemesis, Anthony Chambers grins at me as the first ball begins to roll down the tube.

'4!' The voice over guy announces. Looking down at the crumpled ticket pulled from my pocket a few seconds earlier, I realise that my dream of buying a football team has disappeared yet again.

'1!' My yacht vanishes.

'14!' The plan to buy a few ounces of gear seems no more.

'12!' Oh come on.

'9!' You bastards!

'5!' Oh like I care anymore.

'Well I hope you were lucky,' Anthony Chambers announces from the safety of the screen. No I wasn't you cock.

'Screw you Chambers!' I shout back and flick the television off in disgust.

In the silence I look at the games console and it in turn looks back at me. No, consider the plan, play in secret on my new purchase, make Danny think I've lost the skills and then one day …. Bam, I thank you. The last thing I want to do is get drawn into some stupid game where I can't beat the end of level wolf demon and then in walks Danny to reset the plan to day one. I could ring Mia? Why not? Well to start with there's the whole playing it cool thing. Then of course there's the danger involved with that first phone call, especially after a few joints. What else is there to do in situations such as these? Well there's always tea. I make my way to the kitchen and spend a couple of minutes searching through Danny's cupboards in search of his money stash. When that fails I resort to my original plan. Although that untrusting bastard has hidden his money elsewhere I do find the battered green tin from earlier. It's his own fault really that I indulge in his unwitting generosity. The exercise is complete when I test out my new four sugars ideology.

82

When I return to the front room I decide to put Wish You Were Here by Pink Floyd on the stereo. This is by far The Floyd's finest work and I feel it is only appropriate to celebrate accordingly. Another joint Joe my boy? Why thank you, don't mind if I do. Once I finish my creation I start on another for no other reason than to fill the time. The Floyd have started to go all synthesiser on me as I search amongst the wreckage of our front room for a lighter. When I eventually find one nestled in a teacup, I lie back in the seat and gaze at the yellow stained ceiling, raising the flame to the tip. You can't beat relaxation like this, there's nothing better. On the third drag I notice something from the corner of my eye. For a second the television flicks itself on and then off again. I shake my head thinking that cheap bastard Danny has only gone and brought the cheapest telly on the market. Look there it goes again. Typical, I expect he'll want to go halves on a new one when I tell him. Maybe I won't, maybe I'll let him break it on his own.

Two seconds later, shock, horror, on it comes. This is getting stupid now.

Off.

On...

Shouldn't you be turning yourself off by now? I hope you realise you are interrupting a moment I was having over here. Right that's it, I'm unplugging you, I hope you're happy now.

As I raise myself from the seat the white noise disappears and the screen returns to darkness. Except it's not because I can see shadows in the darkness. I inch closer to the screen to make out more of the detail. In the centre of the darkness lies a dark grey form. The more I look, the more obvious it becomes. The form has edges, edges of a chair, with someone in it. Suddenly I am reeling back as the screen floods with colours. No sound, just images. Images of some bloke walking along the road. I recognise that road, it's the one

83

outside my work. No it can't be. Don't be so bloody stupid. It's ..... The bloke walking down the road, it's me, or at least it looks like me. Maybe a little older, maybe a little scruffier. Perhaps it's just someone who looks like me. What poor sod looks like me? No one! Well, no one except Bruce. For the second time today has he entered my life, unexpected, unwelcome and most of all in very unusual circumstances? If this is Bruce then why is he now walking up the path to my house carrying what seems like a games console in a bag? Why is he forcing the door open using my special technique? What the fuck is going on? Thoughts enter my mind with amazing speed but with a distinct lack of clarity. All except one, why isn't there any sound? I grab the remote with my left hand whilst my right frantically pushes buttons on the stereo until Dave Gilmour stops halfway through the first line of track four. The volume bar on the television screen slowly creeps upwards from its half way position. By the time it gets to the three quarters mark it's blindingly obvious there is no sound. That is until...

I AM, YOU ARE, WE ARE CRAZY booms from the stereo and scares me shitless. It would seem that for all of my uncoordinated button pushing the stereo has simply moved onto the next CD in the rack and increased the volume ten-fold to something roughly equivalent to bowel emptying. Worst still it's one of Danny's crazy sixties psychedelic jazz albums. Looking away from the screen for a second I locate the power button for the stereo and it dies instantly, thank God. My eyes instantly return to the screen to witness Bruce now kissing a girl outside the wine bar in town. Not just any girl, Mia. I can hardly contain my anger, doesn't he realise that I got there first? I was pretending to be him long before he arrived. Now some tramp is having a go at him. Good on the tramp! Go on, punch him in the face.

Wait. That's my girl and my bleeding house. What the fuck is going on here? Further scenes roll and I struggle to sort out the truth. It's all there, Saturday with Joe, filmed with precision. The screen goes black with the realisation.

'What the…?' I mutter softly through waves of fear.

The darkness on screen begins to relent, grey shadows creeping out to form three dimensions. A silver hue glides across the tangled branches of what seems like a bush. I can just make out the darkened form of someone crouching within, a metallic glint from an object beside him. The darkness returns and the scene is extinguished by the night.

'For God so loved the world that he gave his only begotten son, that whoever believes in him shall not perish but have eternal life,' comes a soft voice from the telly. I recognise the quote, not because I'm religious in a Dot Cotton kind of way but because we learnt that sort of thing at school. The darkness begins to lift from the screen to reveal the shadowy figure of the man in the chair again. I don't know what this is I'm watching but I'm pretty sure it's not Jackanory in a power cut.

'It is time to wake up from the dream of your life, Joseph. It is time to believe. We will meet soon, you and I, and I will show you a world that you thought only existed in your mind,' the figure whispers as he leans forward in his chair, his form catching a light somewhere off to the side. One side of his face is cast in a faint yellow glow and there is something I recognise but I don't have time to ponder this small detail as a more pressing question is at hand.

'How do you know my name?' I ask the shadows as they begin to fall away. 'How the fuck do you know my name?' I cry.

In response I am met by an unresponsive screen and blackness deeper than my worst nightmares.

Then it is no more. The television suddenly kicks back into life again with the fake Scouser murdering a Beatles track mere inches from my face. The show is reaching its conclusion and as she's making her way up the stairs and waving to the audience I can think but a single thought.

Christ, it's happening again.

Chapter 10

An Unwelcome Life On Planet Gong

I remember that Saturday, it should have been the day she took me home. I hadn't even contemplated any other outcome up to then. I was wrong.

Saturday, 10th November 1979

Most people get visits from their parents at this god awful place. Even Michael's mum and dad manage to draw themselves away from claiming the dole once in a while to visit their scumbag son. That's not quite how it works for my parents. They all came together at first, then perhaps my constant pleas to come home started to irritate my dad. So he tends to stay at home now, supposedly to look after Sean. Don't bother with the truth Dad. Sean won't come after I threw a chair at him. They blamed me of course. So it's just my mum now. I can always see the pain in her eyes and the fight within herself. It's only a matter of time before she admits her mistake, talks my dad round and I can go home. Perhaps as a bonus, they'll send Sean here? Today could be the day.

'Hello honey!' she cries as I walk towards her at a slow pace to emphasise my sadness. Of course she has to ruin it by rushing towards me, picking me up in her arms. I feel cold.

'Hi mum,' I reply unenthusiastically.

'Oh honey, are you okay?'

No I'm not okay! While you, Dad and fuck face sleep in your nice house, in your nice beds, with your nice things, I'm here, far from okay.

'What have you brought me?' I ask distantly, looking up to see a thin forced smile on her face.

'Oh honey, I'll show you in a bit. First things first.'

Take your time, why start caring now?

As we walk to the car, a new model I observe, she tells me that Dad couldn't make it again as Sean has been feeling poorly. Poor Sean, poor idiot Sean. Apparently he can't act in his fancy drama class at his posh school because of a sore throat. Why are you telling me? You keep talking all the way to BurgerWorld, why? I don't care about Sean just like no one cares about me.

Standard mega kid's meal. Ludicrously thick chocolate milkshake. It's placed efficiently on the tray and we walk down the stairs of BurgerWorld to the downstairs area. Within seconds of sitting she is reaching under the table for the bag she brought with her. Perhaps it's the silence, perhaps the feeling of awkwardness on her part that's making her go for the present already. The box comes across the table with a smile yet I receive it with a blank expression. And there it is. I have always wanted it, you might even say I have always needed it.

Star Wars X-Wing fighter with battle damage stickers.
Two 'AA' batteries required. Action Figures not included. Ages 4 and up.

This one thing should bring joy, yet all it does is remind me of the past. Besides she can't even get it right, already having put the battle damage stickers on before giving it to me. Can't she read? They are irremovable battle damage stickers. I don't want them on, it's ruined. Regardless, I accept the gift and utter a small soft thank you in return. Sadness is everywhere in my voice. To counter this, her happiness heightens. Small talk. Sean this, Sean that. New car, new life. Words drifting across the table, past my ears until the last one catches.

'How do you think you are getting on at school now?'

88

I've been waiting. Time for the plan.

'Well, I think I'm ready to come home.'

'Really dear?'

'Yes,' sounding grown up here. 'I think the teachers and psychologist have helped me to understand myself, to understand my problems.'

'That's excellent dear, good to know that you think you are making progress.'

'I've realised that my problems aren't solved by violence.'

'I spoke to that nice Mr Carter the other day and he said that he thought you were settling in better now,' she replies. That nice Mr Carter? How do you know? Don't misjudge the way he speaks to you Mother, he's a pervert, like all of them. Just one simple decision from you and we can end our association with that terrible place.

'I think I would like to come home now?' I ask.

'That's good honey but...'

But what, but fucking what?

'The teachers and your dad and I think that you should stay a bit longer. After all they are all there to help you.'

'But I'm okay now!' I state in a tone so full of disbelief that anything other than going home would be pure madness.

'I know you believe you are better dear but we aren't quite sure that you are ready yet. Mr Brown said you hurt another boy the other day. Did you really mean to set his jumper on fire with a Bunsen burner?'

'Of course not, it was an accident!' I answer and can feel tears starting to well up in my eyes. Fight it! Don't show her your weakness.

'You do remember what we agreed don't you? You can come home when Mr Brown and the psychologist agree that you are making progress. They don't feel that the episode with the Bunsen burner was an indication that you are doing as well as you could.'

Why should it be Mr Brown or some pervert doctor to decide when I am feeling better?

'You must stop getting angry all the time,' my mum adds.

'I didn't get angry Mum, it was an accident,' I reply weakly.

With a half-eaten burger in her hand she smiles her warmest smile at me. It's supposed to be a smile of understanding, she doesn't even come close.

'We just want you to get better then we can all go back to the way it was.'

'I am better!' my voice rising. This emptiness in my head is fading, she's not listening.

'Well…'

'Please mum, let me come home,' I plead.

'Look dear…'

'Please mum, please!' I plead again, a tear running down my cheek.

'We understand that….'

'Please, please, please!' my voice is getting quicker, higher pitched.

'When you are better I promise you can come home.'

No more numbers.

No more numbers.

No more numbers.

A rage enters my head, my eyes widen and my teeth clench as I begin to shout.

'I want to fucking come home!'

'Look young man…'

'I want to fucking come home! Why won't you take me home? What the fuck is wrong with you all?'

'Please my angel...'

Angel, you used to call me that once. I remember now. The memory brings a sadness washing over me. My face smoothly moulding itself to one of sorrow. The rage passes, just like it always does.

'Please let me come home,' I say, full of resignation and fear.

'Honey, please don't be angry, we are doing the best we can.'
From the corner of my eye I see a small fat man descend the stairs in a rush before he approaches our table.

'Excuse me madam.'

As if my mum already knows what he is going to say she apologises for my behaviour.

I'm the manager … *blah blah blah.*

My son I'm afraid has behavioural problems … *blah blah blah.*

I understand that Madam but I'm going to have to ask you both to leave … *blah blah fucking blah.*

'Do you have no consideration for people with medical problems?' She replies. Don't worry Mum, let me make it easy for you.

'Fuck off!' I shout at the fat man with the last remnant of rage splashing around at the bottom of my mind. Surprised by my own speed I snatch the X-Wing fighter from the table and run up the stairs, leaving my mum to finally catch up with me half way down the street. Say what you want Mum, it's all changed now. I may be staying but I'm no longer alone. He's beginning to form, he's beginning to live.

Before I know it, I'm back at the school. You can see why Mum wasn't so keen on exploiting the full time allowance. All I did was tell some fat man to fuck off.

There is only one place and one time when I am safe and that's when they sleep. In the meantime I have to wait.

The telly is already on when I get to the common room, casting shadows across the deserted beige sofas. The previous occupants obviously found something more entertaining to do, probably involving small animals and fire. I change the channel to BBC by reaching on my toes to the elevated set, just in time as the theme music for Blake's Seven begins. The last episode of the series starts and I slump into one of the

91

sofas, trying not to think of the germs contained within. The crew beam down to a planet that looks like Devon. I remember we went there on holiday once in happier days.

'Oi, Morgan fuck off!' exclaims a voice as it enters the room, Michael.

'But I was watching....'

'What did I say?' he replies with menace.

Without hesitation I leave, the common room as well as the dorm now out of bounds. There is only one place left to go. I have my X-Wing fighter stashed in the bushes by the lake. It is there that I head for the next couple of hours, comfortable in the surroundings of solitude, inventing the most fantastic of stories and ruling over my world. Soon everything has to come to an end though. The light has long since faded and the bell rings for bed. Whatever fate awaits, I must face it.

A feeling of nervousness fills my stomach as I make my way up the stairs. I want them to go on forever. But they don't and I soon find myself outside the door, my hand shaking as it grips the handle.

'Morgan, why the hell aren't you in bed yet?' Carter bellows as he makes his way round the corner. 'If you're not in that room in five seconds then you'll be in detention again.'

'Please, sir.'

'Morgan, I'm warning you.'

An involuntary reaction takes over and my hand obeys, revealing a room in near darkness. I can make out the forms of Bobby and Dean in the lower bunks, already asleep. My enemies are unaware, I arrive in secret. No way back, forward only. I cross the room in silence and begin to change quickly into my pyjamas, not bothering with the trousers and keeping my pants on for the purposes of speed. Get into bed, unseen, unheard. I quietly climb the steps to the top, the bunk groaning as I lower myself onto it gently, my legs sliding under the covers. Suddenly a snigger from beneath. Bobby and Dean are obviously still awake. Still, a snigger can't hurt me, it's just the inane mutterings of their stupid, childlike minds. They can't hurt me, I'm stronger than that. My legs move, the cold linen sheet swiftly moulding itself to my body as I slide further down. Then something else! The coldness of the bed sheets is replaced by a warm, slimy sensation on my left leg where it meets the mattress. A mere trick of the covers, nothing else. Yet as I continue to move my leg the feeling persists. The movement makes the folds of the sheet near my chest unfurl, releasing a dark, disgusting smell of shit.

No! No! No!

I move with speed, feeling my leg leave the smeared shit behind and jumping to the floor. Upon landing, my left leg buckles under me and shock waves shoot through the soles of my feet. And then comes the laughing. Bobby and Dean, hysterics. Michael, a deep raucous laugh. Eric, a distant high pitched giggle. Bad move Eric.

My mind is swirling with pain, humiliation, self-contempt, but no anger. When I need it most all that is left in this devastated shell is a terrible weakness. There is only one thing to do, an impulse action. I fling the door open and run down the corridor, into the shower room, turning on the tap to the shower and sticking my leg straight under. There is a slight knocking from the pipes behind the walls before a powerful spray of ice cold water is delivered straight onto my leg. The dark brown shit washes away reluctantly in horrid sticky flakes, holding on all the way. I must be clean, I must be pure, stepping under the spray completely in my pyjamas and pants. The water crashes onto my head and as it runs down my cheeks it conceals the tears. There I remain, shivering, humiliated, nothing to this world.

When I can bear the cold no longer, I step out and look for safety, finding the corner of the room and curling myself into a ball on the floor. Through blurred vision a shape begins to form in the opposite corner. The shadows join, the body becomes, eyes open. Then as thought follows sight, the eyes turn from a grey to a bright blue that pierce the night.

'I am here my friend,' it whispers.

I don't need to be afraid any longer. The game begins.

Chapter 11

The Ken Is Dead, Long Live The Ken

All in all, a month is a long time to have something on your mind. Especially things you don't want to remember. Let's replay events of that day shall we: town, Mia, home, smoking …. oh yes, the smoking. I suppose five (or was it seven?) Thai stick joints was enough to tip myself past breaking. So I ask myself, what's more likely? Visions of myself on television or a spot of good old fashioned paranoia? More importantly, how to stop it happening again? Well, I'm glad you asked. Abstinence, that's what. A change in lifestyle no less, despite the persistent temptation from Danny. Such a change of course has been markedly easier with Mia around. I haven't told her about it, of course. To her I'm still the same guy, albeit as Bruce still. No problems for me though, no hints of instability, no dependency on class C drugs. Joe is now Bruce and Bruce is the person that I've always wanted to be.

So how did Mia and I get from the drink in the wine bar to here? Two days later and over a moderately priced dinner we talked, we laughed, and Bruce and Mia fell in love all over again. And what I feared most never even came up. The danger of Bruce's past and Joe's present conflicting didn't even manifest. In fact she seemed almost reluctant to talk about our past, well hers and Bruce's anyway. Subsequently it has been remarkably easy to maintain the facade. And where's the harm in it, I ask? Mia gets Bruce and I get to be Bruce; everyone's happy. Plus, I'm actually enjoying the things she likes as well. Take for example that subtitled French film she wanted to watch. Once I got over the wanky direction and extended dialogue I discovered something: films actually have a plot to them. It's just much easier to recognise when cars aren't exploding or somebody's not getting whacked. There is only one thing left to do for our relationship to reach nirvana. It's coming, I can tell, but I haven't made the moves and she hasn't asked. Bruce is a gentleman and she is too wonderful. It has to be perfect, just like her. The perfect place, the perfect time, the perfect moment.

There is just one obstacle to overcome to complete my transformation. Today is the day she gets to meet my friends. They may not be the sort of friends that Bruce would choose, but for want of more ideal candidates I have to work with what I have. Katie and Danny are under strict instructions that I am now Bruce in Mia's presence, and you can imagine the sort of conversations that ensued. Danny was easy to convert to the cause once he moved on from sarcastic insults, even contributing with enthusiastic deception techniques. Katie as you would expect was somewhat harder to convince. It has taken a couple of weeks for the nagging to cease and for her to identify the multiple points where the whole plan will intrinsically fail. She's not exactly a keen participant but once I'd finished with logical reasoning, followed by moaning and self-pity, the only thing left was pleading. It took about a week for her to be ground down, surprisingly quicker than I was expecting. So tonight I am Bruce and I've made bloody sure that Katie and Danny know it. All I have to do is finish work and the evening will begin.

Mia is due to meet me outside work at half past five. The minute hand on the clock torments me from a dimension where time retaliates against its overlord, desperation. And just as it can't get any worse, the last two people that I want to enter the room, enter the room.

'Looking a bit smart today aren't you Joe?' asks Marshall the twat from human resources, accompanied by fellow fuckwit Magilton.

'Yeah, Joe, decided to move on from your gypsy look have you?' Magilton pipes up.

'No, I'm meeting my girlfriend after work,' I reply directly.

'Bloody hell, I didn't know the blind were allowed to date,' Magilton counters. 'I'll tell you what, Marshy boy here had a right couple of sorts last Saturday, didn't you Marshy?'

'Something to pass the time,' Marshall confirms. Who knows if it's the truth, who cares?

Perhaps if I don't reply they'll simply leave. Unfortunately Marshall and Magilton seem content to treat the silence as an opportunity to sit down and scan one of their sad boy racer magazines for stupid looking cars.

Ten minutes eventually grind their way across the off-white clock face until the magical time arrives, and I am free. Marshall and Magilton are still muttering about spoilers and stereo systems but their real reason for remaining is all too obvious. They want to see Mia, expecting her to be rough so that they can take the piss. I struggle to contain a broad smile spreading across my face as I wait for their assumptions to be shattered. And then there it is, my mobile ringing and it takes all the constraint I can muster not to jump up and laugh in the twats' faces. Answering, it is indeed Mia, as wonderful on the phone as she is in life, her voice smooth and seductive. As planned she is waiting outside and after hanging up I cross to the window to see her standing in the car park, two floors down. There she is, more beautiful than ever, wearing a long white dress with floral print, her hair tied back loosely.

'Hi honey,' I say, opening the window from above.

'Let's check out the minger,' I hear from behind, combined with the movement of shoes across cheap carpet as they approach.

'How's it going?' I ask, trying to ignore their oncoming presence.

'It will be better when you get yourself down here, Bruce,' she replies, cheekily and provocatively.

'I'll be down in a sec,' I conclude. She isn't just standing there, she is waiting for me, what am I still doing here? Just as I'm about to draw my head back in, the force of Magilton and Marshall pushes me forward once more as they attempt to look around me at Mia. I allow them this moment with pleasure and squeeze past them. There is a silence as they struggle to comprehend the unexpected sight which befalls them.

'Hi boys,' Mia says from below in the most seductive manner I have ever heard.

'Hello Miss umm....' I hear Marshall stutter.

'So are you friends with my Bruce?' she asks from below. Suddenly it occurs to me that they could blow my cover at any moment. Oh Christ!

'Bruce.....erm.....yeah' I hear Marshall reply. The name Bruce goes unnoticed as they stare in enchantment at her, drowning in her intoxicating beauty. I needn't have worried.

'Who's Bruce?' Magilton whispers.

'Shut up fool,' Marshall replies in equally hushed tones.

'Well boys it's been a pleasure but we have to go down the pub now,' Mia confirms from below, terminating the conversation to my obvious delight.

'Ummm...okay.' Marshall replies in a disappointed tone. He knows he has just witnessed perfection personified but has been turned away before he can fully appreciate it. He comes back inside, with the knowledge that, up this point, his life has been a complete waste. Magilton however elects to keep his head outside grinning inanely, before Marshall pulls him back.

'Joe, is she, like, you know?' Marshall asks as he closes the window. Before I can answer let alone understand the question, Magilton interrupts.

'Why does she call you Bruce?'

'Oh, she thinks I look like Bruce Willis,' I reply without a hint of hesitation. I must be getting better at this.

'Bruce Forsyth more like,' Magilton retorts. His subsequent laughing at his own joke is short lived as Marshall gives him a backwards slap to the arm.

'What pub you going down then?' Marshall asks.

'Manor and Toad, you know it?' I reply. Naturally we aren't going there but it seems appropriate to mess with the twats when the opportunity presents itself.

'Yeah, yeah,' Marshall replies and I can see his mind slowly working in the most obvious of ways.

'Oh well chaps, got to go and meet my girlfriend, catch you later,' I say, steering round the desks as I go in an exaggerated fashion. Perfection awaits and who am I to argue.

Mia and I arrive first. The bar is dark with subtly lit corners as house music pumps from the speakers. We settle in near the back on a sofa, separated from another sofa by a low table, room for Katie and Danny when they arrive. Our drinks remain untouched as we sit side by side, occasionally kissing, occasionally talking. During these moments without the soft touch of lips, I can't help but notice that she is looking around the room subtly but intently. She must be looking out for my friends. I can understand this, she's probably as nervous as I am. As if on cue, Katie walks through the doors, dressed in her office suit and looking traditionally Katie. I smile as she approaches and get up to hug her.

'Hi honey,' I say as we embrace. We keep the exchange brief given the circumstances.

'Hello there!' Katie replies, sitting on the sofa opposite 'You must be Mia?'

'Hi, Bruce has told me so much about you,' Mia replies with a smile.

'That's good to know,' Katie says, smiling in my direction.

'You look really nice,' Mia comments.

'Thank you.'

'Bruce didn't tell me how beautiful you were,' Mia comments kindly.

As she continues her warm series of compliments an image enters my head of the two in a lesbian embrace. I decide to contribute to the conversation rather than throw lager over my groin to calm things down.

'Danny should be here in a bit,' I say, directing the statement towards Mia.

'Yeah, I've just seen him down the road trying to buy a can of special brew off a tramp,' Katie adds. This is not wholly unsurprising but I don't want Mia to get the wrong impression (well, the right impression) before she has even met him. Thankfully she lets it pass and continues her conversation with Katie.

'So how do you know Bruce?' the beautiful Mia asks.

Katie replies with numerous muddled steps of misdirection, absent of any coherent detail. I'm proud of the brave new step she has taken. Then through the glass doors I see Danny eventually arrive, trying to push the door despite the fact that it opens outwards. Instead of pulling as he should, he instead opts for the method employed on our own front door. The glass door shudders on its hinges under excessive force before Captain Moron realises the obvious. This display of a general lack of cognitive ability is probably down to a few joints beforehand. Thanks a lot pal.

'Wahay!' Danny exclaims as he approaches, having finally negotiated the idiot trap.

'Alright matey,' I reply as he slumps into the chair opposite, next to Katie. Instead of responding he instead opts to talk to Katie first in his usual charming way.

'Alright treacle!'

'Danny,' Katie acknowledges distantly.

'Alright Danny,' I welcome again. It feels stupid to say this a second time but in a delicate operation such as this I have to direct the conversation.

'Alright there Bruce,' he replies, accompanied by a small thin smile aimed in my direction.

'Bruce…I mean Danny, this is Mia,' I say, panicking that the thoughts at the front of my mind have slipped out with ease.

'Hello there!' he says in his Leslie Phillips style. 'Fucking plum, doesn't even know my name.'

Although my face is calm, anger flies around my mind. If he ruins this for me then I'll bloody kill him.

'I mean after all the things we've been through, eh?' Danny continues. Why doesn't he stop bloody talking?

'Yeah sorry mate,' I interject. Come on Danny play the game.

'Used to get my name wrong all the time,' Danny declares, 'when we were in the Amazon.'

Shut up, shut the fuck up.

'Bruce, you didn't tell me you were in the Amazon?!' Mia asks excitedly. Thanks pal.

'Oh you know it was a while ago,' I say, trying desperately to think of a convincing lie.

'Was it after China?' she asks. I see Danny and Katie look at me with surprise. Hey, don't look at me, I don't have a bleeding clue either. Only now does it occur to me that in those precious moments together I should have subtly gleamed information from her about Bruce instead of constantly trying to avoid it.

'Yeah about that time,' I reply vaguely, which I hope gives off an air of coolness. I see Danny and Katie look at one another, my so called mate giving a nod of his head. I don't know if he is impressed or confounded by the lie, but I can guess Katie's thinking.

'Good times, good times,' Danny exclaims as he takes a sip of my beer.

'I'll go get a round in shall I?' Katie suggests, dragging Danny up to the bar by his sleeve. Thank you Katie, thank you so very much.

After they return the evening goes surprisingly well. I can't escape reality completely as Katie talks for a while about the latest gossip emanating from the Manor and Toad. Allegedly, Ken is housing illegal asylum seekers in his cellar, or so the rumours go. Three rounds later it's my turn to get the drinks. An action Katie seems intent on helping with. Cue a bollocking, I expect.

At the bar I lean across with my twenty pound note. If I can make this quick then I can avoid a lecture while limiting the damage being done by Danny in my absence. Killing two birds with one stone, so to speak. The barman takes my order and moves with speed to the pump nearby. I catch a glimpse of Danny leaning across the table, talking to Mia. He is either messing with the situation or is he is trying to chat her up. The dirty pervert!

'You know she's either incredibly stupid or completely unobservant,' Katie starts.

'Relax!' I say. 'Things are going well aren't they?'

'Bloody mystery to me how?'

With excellent timing the barman returns and places three lagers and a white wine in front of us. After parting with a sizeable portion of my disposable income, we make our way back to the table and Mia greets me in an excited fashion.

'You didn't tell me you played session guitar with the Rolling Stones!' she announces. I involuntarily close my eyes before opening them to see Danny smiling with his creation. You bastard!

'Oh, it was a while ago.'

'When did you learn to play the guitar?' she asks.

'It was probably when we were in the Amazon wasn't it Bruce?' Danny offers.

'Yeah about that time,' I reply. I can't believe that he gets enjoyment from watching me drown in his lies.

'Will you write a song for me?' Mia asks.

'Ummm…well you know these things take time,' I reply. This is a fricking disaster.

'Oh go on, this man's a genius. He could write one right here,' Danny adds, revelling in his role.

I'm in a hole, a very deep hole in a very dark corner. Mia wants a song and anything less may rouse her suspicions, besides the lie is happily snowballing away. Turning to Mia with a serious look I speak poetically in a monotone voice:

'Loving you...' a brief pause... 'is easy because you're beautiful!'

Despite the horror flashing around my mind I continue.

'Everything I do, I do it for you!'

Oh dear God. Not just plagiarism of the two worst songs ever recorded, but I've even managed to make them fit together.

'Genius man, absolute genius,' Danny cries as he struggles to contain his laughter.

'Excuse me I have to go for a waz,' Danny adds, quickly getting out of the sofa. The sight of Danny shaking with all the restraint he can muster as he disappears towards the toilets thankfully goes unnoticed by Mia.

All of a sudden a hand gently touches my face and I flinch, shocked by her touch.

'Thank you,' she whispers, leaning forward and kissing me on the lips softly. I'm embarrassed by Katie's presence but I'm more surprised that I've gotten away with it. During this brief yet sensual kiss I instinctively glance towards Katie who smiles and quickly looks away. She almost looked jealous.

When Danny returns the evening continues. Two more rounds occur, and with slightly unsteady legs we finally make

103

our way from the bar. Mia agrees we should walk Katie home, but this doesn't stop Danny offering a rather dubious alternative. Katie wisely resists half an hour of persistent requests to sleep with him. It's only what he deserves, the dirty pervert! Plus this way, once Katie is home, that will leave just Mia and me, and you know what comes next. Danny wanders off in the opposite direction in abject failure back to the house. With any luck I won't be joining him later.

Back at Mia's flat and with Katie safely deposited at her house we talk for a while, we drink coffee for a while, we kiss passionately. Unfortunately it doesn't go any further. I don't know if it's her holding back or me, or perhaps a combination of the two. The thought of spending the night with her is incredibly appealing but also very worrying. What if she is waiting for that special moment? What if I'm not good enough? What if I'm not Bruce enough? It's okay, I can wait because I respect her wishes. If Bruce's Bruce can be patient then so can Joe's.

I leave around eleven and walk back to my own house. After attempting to reprimand Danny (and failing to do so) I make my way to the secure surroundings of my bedroom to get in some Bond practice. I'll make Danny pay for his lack of co-operation. I change games after a while for Inferno, cracking on with level 5. I make my way across the gloomy river, strange bodies with sad faces coming at me from all angles, in ever greater numbers. With relish they tear me apart as Game Over appears on screen and I'm offered the chance of a replay. Um, no thanks. I am defeated, but there is always another day.

I drift into a contented doze on top of the covers and begin to dream of Mia. For once everything seems right. Maybe this is what being safe is all about?

Chapter 12

An Accessory To The Fact And His Faithful Nemesis

09:00am, Inspector Polston's Office.

Even given Walker's history of landing every rubbish job available, this was the worst so far. Conduct surveillance on somebody who may or may not be hiding something, Polston had ordered.

'So what's he done exactly?' Walker questioned.

'Nothing but that's not the point,' Polston replied, his eyes scanning the paperwork strewn across his desk.

'I don't understand boss.'

'You never do Walker. This is real police work. Call it a hunch, but this friend of that scumbag Danny is up to something.'

'But we have no evidence that he has anything to do with the post office robbery.'

'When have we ever needed evidence Walker?'

'Fair point,' Walker replied and with no other argument coming to mind he resigned himself to the job. It wasn't all bad, Polston seemed to be far too busy to join him. At last, he might get some peace.

'One last thing,' Polston muttered as Walker was making his exit.

'Yes boss, did you want to talk about my request for a pay rise?'

A prolonged period of laughing by the inspector suggested to Walker that this wasn't the case.

'No, I'm going to assign you a new partner for today.'

At last, Walker thought. His detective skills were finally getting the recognition they deserved. He could share his experience and skills with this new partner.

'You want me to teach him a thing or two about how to be good detective?' Walker asked before a fresh outburst of laughing by the inspector spoiled the moment.

'Not as such Walker, not as such. Think of him more as an equal,' Polston replied.

'Okay,' Walker sighed, frustrated that Polston had yet again failed to recognise his potential. 'So who is it?' he asked.

'He's behind you.'

Walker turned, he hadn't heard anyone come in behind him. Still, there was the hope that it would be a new female recruit at least. Walker looked behind and then to the sides in case he had missed something. There was no one behind him.

'There's no one there,' Walker commented.

'You're looking in the wrong place, look down,' the inspector ordered.

'Callahan?' Walker blurted, looking down and seeing the dog sitting behind him.

'Yes, Callahan,' Polston replied.

The inspector wasn't without his own plans. Knowing his sergeant didn't much care for his companion, Polston hoped that this would make the surveillance just that little bit more unpleasant for Walker. With any luck it might be the final straw in getting rid of him. Walker breathed in heavily. So this was what it had come to, a dog for a partner. His superior had obviously gone mad, but to object to such an order would not help with the master-plan. Let's help the poor old fool on his way, the sergeant thought.

'Okay boss,' he replied, attaching the lead to his arch enemy and making his way from the room.

10:00am to 14:00pm. No Activity.

Using his exemplary detective skills and making heavy use of the police database, Walker found himself outside of Joe's house. From there Walker tailed the suspect's crappy car to his work and waited. For most of the day Walker had sat opposite and not seen a thing. Any fool could see that this Joe had nothing to hide. He was just another of the many nobodies in this town. He needed to get off this job and move on. There was still the matter of the big arrest that the master-plan demanded.

Time for a break, Walker thought. Anything to get away from the constant barking of Callahan who was occupying the back seat. He had left the dog in the car as he made his way to the sandwich shop, secretly hoping that the criminal fraternity would steal his car and hold the dog to ransom. He had even left it invitingly unlocked. When he eventually returned, sandwich in hand, he found the car radio ripped out and Callahan soundly asleep on the back seat.

15:00pm. No Activity.

Six hours he had waited and not a thing. To entertain himself, Walker would intermittently shout 'Walkies!' Callahan would respond enthusiastically, standing up on the back seat and looking at Walker's reflection in the rear view mirror. The Sergeant's response was to not move a muscle, with a great deal of conviction. He gave up this torture after the eighteenth time when Callahan urinated over the back seat.

With the windows open in a futile attempt to flush out the smell, Walker started to think about Constable Rosario back at the station. He had previously regaled her in the canteen with stories of his success at Goodison and could tell that she was impressed. Of course there were always people trying to steal his thunder, that good looking Scottish bastard Fleck for one. With relish, Fleck had informed him that he had already taken her out, at least that's what Walker thought he'd said. He wasn't good with accents. Of course he was lying, or at least so Walker hoped. He had seen her a few days later but she hadn't recognised him, his forgettable face with the remarkable nose striking again. Walker decided to move Fleck forward on the master-plan, just behind Polston.

16:00pm. No Activity.
The sergeant had spent the last ten minutes arched around in his seat, staring directly at Callahan. The dog in return stared back and growled continuously.

16:30pm. No Activity.
Neither had broken the stare.

16:45pm. No Activity.
Callahan had by now been converted against his will into Walker's confidant. Walker told the dog an abridged version of his aspirations, his problems and his life in general. Callahan tired of the conversation after thirty seconds and went back to sleep.

17:00pm. Activity, and then some.
Walker was starting to drift into his own sleep when something unexpected happened. The first sight he caught of her was in the rear view mirror as she walked behind the car. From this brief glance alone he was able to determine that she was one of the most beautiful women he had ever seen. As she passed his window, it was as if everything he considered beautiful in a woman was present, heightened to an almost unbearable degree. A switch in his head, hidden for his whole adult life suddenly flicked on. In a serial killer it would have been quickly followed by murder. In a plumber it would have preceded an instant doubling of the bill. For a sexually repressed copper who was better placed to be selling kitchens,

it was the beginning of an obsession. What were the chances that his perfect woman would be walking past his car at that very moment? None, that's what. Walker didn't believe in fate but he did believe that things happened for a reason. She drifted past the front of the car in her flowing white dress with the floral print and with her long hair swaying seductively, Walker could hardly contain himself. He scanned her body as she moved, she was perfect from her slim hips and an ample bosom to the stunning blue eyes which shone through her rectangular glasses. There was no doubt about it, Walker was in love. All those years of waiting, all those rejections, they weren't the cruel hand of unattractiveness striking, it was destiny. He simply couldn't move his eyes from her as she came to a halt in the car park. He had never felt like this before but he knew that when one is confronted by unknown, unexpected feelings there is only one way to satisfy them. He had to have her, he would have her! For the next two minutes he watched, shortly before he screamed.

'No! Not him!'

Fresh from work, Walker's surveillance target came out and hugged her. And then he kissed her. Walker had never experienced jealousy like it and it astonished him. It took all of his will power not to go over and extend the full powers of the law and beyond in vengeance.

And then it became obvious. He finally knew what was going on. Polston had been right all along. This kid wasn't quite the innocent bloke that Walker had first thought. Here he was, kissing the girl of Walker's dreams. No one who looked like him got to go out with a girl like this. This Joe must have some power over her and Walker didn't like it one bit. It was his duty as an officer of the law and as a love struck fool to save her. The master-plan was complete. They would be begging for him back at Goodison once he had solved this crime. Just the sort of place where Walker and his perfect woman could spend the rest of their lives together.

From there the two of them moved off into town together. Walker jumped from the car to follow them, sure that she would be able to feel the beating of his heart as he trailed behind them. After a short walk they ended up at one of the new pubs. In they went and Walker watched from across the street. They kissed again and the sergeant nearly exploded.

'Leave her alone you bastard,' Walker spoke softly, his breath condensing in the air.

Walker watched another girl join them. His target got up and hugged her as well.

'The bastard must have some power over them both!' he whispered, casting a casual glance at his watch.

'Shit, the time,' Walker exclaimed, a little too loudly. 'That tosser will be wanting his dog back.'

Sergeant Walker rushed back to the car where Callahan greeted him with a snarl.

'Callahan,' the sergeant spoke, trying to catch his breath as he started the car. 'I'm about to solve the biggest crime this town has ever seen, I just don't know what it is yet.'

'What a plum,' Callahan replied but the language of dog meant nothing to Walker.

Chapter 13

Alan Hansen's World Of Decision

'Down the wing, down the fucking wing!' I shout.

Sometimes I don't know why I even come to watch my local football team. I mean look at him, a free player standing on the right and everyone in the ground can see him except that donkey in the middle.

'Come on town!' the crowd shout in a combined chant. Don't bother lads, we're 2-0 down and it's only the first half.

At least Danny is here with me to share in the pain. In truth, I don't think he really cares, if he did then he wouldn't be on his third joint before the interval. A deep pass from our own half flies in an excessive arc over the intended forward and lands somewhere beyond the corner flag. Amongst the cries of 'Fucking hell!' and 'Think about it, town!' from around me, I cast a quick sideways glance towards Danny and see him gently chuckling, soft rounded puffs of smoke emanating from his mouth that quickly dissipate into the air. To distract myself from my knob of a house mate I scan the faces in the crowd, I'm sure they never change. There's that old bloke in front who's been here since I was a kid. To the side is a woman who has been dragging her kids along for so long that I've seen them grow into an impressive criminal fraternity. Three rows back is a familiar face I can't quite place, a tall thin man with one hell of a nose.

'Oh for…..' I cry, tossing my head back in despair. 3-0 down and some of the crowd have just started cheering for the other side.

'Christ the opposition are awful,' Danny comments amongst the chanting.

'What do you mean…COME ON TOWN….they're playing really well.'

'You know the other side, the guys in red and white.'

'We're the guys in red and white you plum!' I exclaim. Only Danny could be so stoned that he has been supporting the wrong team all this time.

'Oh shit man, this stuff is good!' he says before following up with another raucous laugh. He offers the joint in my direction but I decline the offer as Henry Winkler pops up in my head and gives me the Fonz thumbs up.

Just before the referee blows his whistle for half time, Town manage, somehow, to scramble a goal in at the other end. It's a faint glimmer of hope for the second half but that's all it is. The players trudge off the pitch and the terraces begin to empty. A sizeable proportion of the crowd attempt to repress the memory of the last forty five minutes with unpalatable hot beverages and allegedly savoury snacks. Being an old hand at drinking crap tea, I fully intend to conform to their ideology, but only once the initial rush is over. With any luck I may miss some of the second half in the queue.

'What a pile of crap,' I comment to Danny as my eyes continue to scan the pitch despite nothing happening.

'Yeah,' he replies, struggling to hold back a fit of giggles.

'Man, do you have to smoke everywhere?'

'Do what? Did you say you wanted a smoke?'

'No, just forget it, alright.'

The half time mascot is out and running around behind the goal. I forget his name but he seems to be a chicken of sorts and over the years has affectionately become known as the Relegation Rooster. His antics are mildly amusing to the under tens until he trips on a clod of turf and lands face down, becoming instantly hilarious across generations. As he crashes down the entire end behind the goal respond with a jeering cry. To my left, Danny erupts into a high pitched fit of giggles and to my discredit I join in with the crowd. I know I shouldn't, it wasn't that long ago that people were doing the same to me. The cheering dies down as the mascot makes a rapid departure to the front of the family stand where he receives a lesser but still hurtful condemnation.

'What's that smell?' Danny asks, his mind now focused by an insatiable urge for munchies.

'That, my friend, will be the majesty of pies containing unidentified substances,' I reply, grateful for a common talking point. 'I'm going, you want something?'

'Yeah, get me two pies, a cup of tea and a Mars bar,' he asks. 'Hungry?'

'Like a fucking demon,' he replies. The munchies have him.

At the kiosk I join a huge queue of people, all talking about the match, or about other teams, or about their Saturday night. It takes an eternity to get anywhere near the front and by the time I do I can hear the second half beginning. Bonus! Eventually I get to order: three dog food pies, two cups of tea and one Mars bar for the cretin. I walk back along the queue with the hot tea already burning my fingers through the minimal thickness of the polystyrene cups. Trying to block out the searing pain, I pass the end of the queue and notice the guy with the hook nose, who seems to be looking in any other direction than mine. Bit strange that.

Emerging into the masses behind the goal I catch glimpses of Danny through gaps in the crowd. He seems to have taken the opposition launching another attack as a sign from Haile Selassie himself that he should light another pre-rolled joint. What a tit. Returning to stand next to him I deliver the pies, which he engulfs quicker than a hyena on benefits at an all-you-can-eat buffet. Each bite he takes seems to coincide with another goal conceded.

Five minutes from the end the other team launch an attack which finds our defence hopelessly stranded somewhere in the division below. The ball is passed along the wing and then crossed to just outside the penalty area where it finds their forward. He hits it first time, a sweet volley, everything it

113

should be except accurate. It sails a few feet over the top of the bar at terminal velocity. Danny's dulled senses fails to pick up the movement of the ball and as I duck rapidly to my right, the ball connects with his forehead and he performs an unintentional header a few rows forward. His eyes are full of bewilderment as he recoils backwards and is only stopped from falling by an old fella behind. The crowd jeer in response. This one event has livened up an entire half. Everyone is happy, except Danny. Does this stop me laughing? No, of course not. My enjoyment however is short lived as I look across to my house mate. Now that his thoughts have refocused and he has exited his stoned state in the most unpleasant fashion there is a look of deep humiliation in his face. The crowd continue to laugh, making snide comments with a wit I wish I possessed.

'Dude, are you alright?' I ask, clenching my teeth to fight off a second wave of laughter. He doesn't seem to hear me and my eyes flick back to the pitch where the opposing forward is raising his hand in apology.

'You fucking bastard!' Danny shouts at him.

The player bows his head and begins to jog away, shrugging off the remark.

I've seen Danny in a number of moods but this is the first time I have seen genuine anger. He is normally too stoned to manage anything asides from apathy. I suppose that his persona as a wannabe local gangster has led him to mistakenly believe that this is a personal insult upon him, a lack of respect as the mafia would say.

'Shit man,' I say as I hold his elbow gently, his stature still one of confusion and ungainly posture, swaying slightly.

'Fucking bastard!' Danny whispers into the noise of the crowd. It is just loud enough for me to catch and as I look at him, I'm sure that I catch a glimpse of a tear rolling down his cheek. Among the feelings of concern for my friend I can't help feeling that with shot-stopping abilities like that he could go in goal for us next week. The ref blows for full time and the 6-1 loss goes into the history books. A day in history when Town got spanked, I ate dog food and Danny got smacked in the face with a ball.

After returning home from the football I get a few hours of solitude whilst Danny retires to his bedroom. He claims he is going to get his head down but we both know that this isn't the entire truth. You never see Pacino cry, and Danny follows the example of the great man. I'm grateful for the time alone, it gives me the opportunity to complete level six of Inferno. Dreadful sad faces loom out from the darkness of a wretched wasteland, emitting woeful sighs as they approach. Only a lifetime wasted has delivered the skills to succeed, bobbing here, weaving there, whacking a few along the way. The hero approaches the main gates to the city, level seven and the screen fades to black. Happy with the work I have done I decide to call it a day. Fade to black.

Danny eventually manages to make it out of his bedroom and enters the living room. He seems remarkably happy, either because of the wonders of marijuana or because he's managed to fit in a wank, the dirty bastard.

'Cup of tea?' Danny asks as he crawls through the serving hatch. It would have been a lot easier to go around.

'Go on then,' I reply, sensing that everything is back to normal with him. I flick the games console off so that he doesn't suspect that I've been practising Bond - his time will come.

Returning to telly I get drawn into the national lottery as the kettle boils. I pull the crumpled ticket from my pocket and the numbers start to roll. They do seem oddly familiar, yet not familiar enough to match my selection.

'Well, I hope you were lucky,' Anthony Chambers declares.

'Fuck you Chambers!' I shout back. They say you have more chance of being hit by lightning than winning the lottery. I might go outside and fly a kite in a thunderstorm to get the electrocution bit out of the way. My failure for predicting random numbers slips from my mind as I flick channels and find re-runs of Monkey being shown. It's a joyous occasion to unexpectedly come across number 8 on my top ten list of favourite children's television shows.

'Alright kid?' Danny asks as he places my tea on the carpet in front of me.

'Check out Pigsy dude.'

'Joe, listen. I'm sorry about being a tit at the footy earlier.'

'That's alright mate, I'm used to it,' I reply.

'Look dude, I wanna make it up to you,' Danny announces as I light up a joint and give a dismissive wave to indicate it's all forgotten. Yes, I know, but it's only one joint and one joint isn't going to hurt anyone. Well two, if you count the one I had from Danny's gear whilst he was sulking.

'How about I make us something to eat?' Danny asks, and without hesitation I accept. It will save me getting a kebab later. You gotta love him.

Tiring of Monkey (my God, the sacrilege!) I flick the channels. On the first channel is the news. For what I can gather there is something about murder victims found in some pub cellar, David Beckham's new haircut, you know, the usual stuff. Shortly afterwards Danny re-emerges into the lounge with two noodle pots. When he offered me dinner this wasn't quite what I had in mind. Still, not even Danny can bugger up a noodle pot can he?

Turns out he can.

'What you up to tonight matey?' Danny asks, scooping an unstable portion of noodles onto his fork.

'I'm taking Mia out,' I reply with a feeling of pride.

'Nice one, where you taking her?'

'The fair that's just arrived in the park.'

116

'Cool, I'm heading down that way myself to see that dodgy fuck in Loop Road, I'll tag along.'

The last thing I need at this tricky point in our relationship is a typical Danny intrusion. I have to persuade him otherwise.

'Thing is mate, it was just going to be the two of us.'

'No worries, I'll just have a quick go on a couple of fruities and I'll shoot off.'

'No disrespect matey but I wanted it to just be us, you know.'

'I find your lack of faith disturbing,' he intones in his Darth Vader voice. 'You won't even notice I'm there.'

Somehow I seriously doubt this last statement but I don't have the heart to force the issue. He's tried to make up for acting like a tit earlier; the least I can do is meet him halfway. Besides, time is ticking. My noodle pot is no more and it's time for Joe to undertake the transformation to Bruce.

Ten minutes later I'm ready, going for a casual look of black cargo trousers and a white long sleeve t-shirt underneath a short sleeved grey surfing top. Just as I'm slipping on my new skateboarding trainers, Danny enters my bedroom without knocking.

'I could have been changing you bastard!' I exclaim as he lights up a joint in the doorway.

'You going surfing dude?'

'No, of course not.'

'Is Bruce a surfer?' he asks.

'Yeah, probably.'

'Lucky we don't live anywhere near the sea then,' Danny concludes, and on this occasion he's probably right.

I make my way from my bedroom and down the stairs. I hope that there's a distant chance that Danny has long since forgotten, but he too is coming down. Perhaps picking up on my concern, he makes an announcement at the bottom.

'Don't worry dude, you won't even notice I'm there.'

117

'You better not muck this up for me mate.'
'Hey, what could possibly go wrong?' Danny replies.

Chapter 14

Don't Have Nightmares, Sleep Tight

The smell of burger grease fills the air as the neon lights shine in the distance. The Fair, the last bastion of acceptable organised crime. Where else could they charge four pounds for the dodgem cars, while enforcing draconian laws of one way traffic and a collision free zone? We laugh at their rules, yet it doesn't stop the pikey hanging onto the back of the carts with the moral high ground that he alone can inhabit. When he's not spoiling the fun he's giving it all that to the teenage girls, trying to impress the impressionable. Let's not forget the ghost train, complete with the prior knowledge that it won't be the least bit scary. It does however allow a few brief moments with the lady of your choosing, laughing excessively at the effects to confirm your masculinity. The lady of my choosing this evening is of course Mia. But let's not forget Danny who insists on lingering on the grass bank while I wait for her, one side of our profiles in darkness, the other hewn in an orange glow cast from the nearby lights.

'You reckon she's blown you out?'

'Piss off you sad bastard!' I retort in our usual fashion. Of course I'm worried that she's blown me out. Bruce wouldn't worry because no one would blow Bruce out. But Joe's Bruce and Bruce's Bruce are two entirely different concepts.

A few minutes later all concerns are dismissed in a fiery blaze of glory as I see her walking along the bank. I've seen this scene before in a thousand films and it always ends well. Mia is the essential part of the script, perfect timing from the perfect leading lady. As she approaches she responds to my smile with her own *I'm gonna wake up any minute* version. I move forward and we embrace, followed by a kiss. I'm so caught up in the moment I almost forget Danny's presence. Almost.

'Go on, get in there son,' he encourages. In response we slowly break the embrace, her fingers lingering in mine for a few seconds.

'Hi Danny,' Mia comments.

'Alright treacle,' Twat Face replies. For a fleeting second I catch something. A look shared? A connection? They either fancy one another or absolutely hate one another. I think reason can work this one out. I'll put this one down to paranoia. Danny and Mia, no bloody chance.

'Right kiddies, I'm off to play the bandits, have fun,' Danny announces and true to his word, if not belatedly, he finally leaves.

'Catch you later,' I reply in an attempted friendly tone as he walks away. Truth is I want to run after him, to smash his face into the ground for even contemplating messing with Mia. I decide not to, Bruce wouldn't do that, but only because he wouldn't need to.

Mia and I kiss again. I tell her how much I've missed her and how nice she looks. A small voice at the back of my head tries to tell her that I love her but sensible Joe over-rules the impulse. Not now little voice, not now. The urge quickly disappears and the lure of the flashing lights nearby proves too tempting to resist. Mia begins to jog lightly towards the bewildering array of neon, taking me by the hand and dragging me towards it.

Two hours later we have gone on almost all of the rides, even the scary looking ones which Mia insisted upon. As she laughed in delight at the adrenaline rush, all I could think about was the level of maintenance undertaken on these potential death traps. We walk around the milling crowds containing a large proportion of small children clutching bags with lifeless fish floating inside. Rounding the corner of one of the arcades we are confronted by the Wurlitzer, its circular shape decorated with a multi-coloured display of light bulbs, half dead, half dying.

'Ooooh!' exclaims Mia as if a firework display was playing out a few feet in front of her eyes.

'Bruce...' she says slowly, her head turning to me and doing that look. It's the same look that she did when we first met in the town square. It's the same look which made me go to the wine bar. Importantly, it's the look that reaffirms my belief that she is in no way ready for my true self. When it comes down to it, I'm essentially blameless for not telling her the truth. The whole Bruce thing, it's kind of her fault.

'You wanna go on the wurly thingy?' I ask, already knowing the answer.

'Come on!' she shouts over the noise and starts to run again, dragging me with her.

I pay the extortionate price despite my looming financial ruin and we wait until the ride stops. The previous customers squeeze themselves out of the cars as new participants quickly squeeze in behind them. Mia and I choose a car just behind the barrier and we sit on the hard plastic seat, our legs gently touching. The ride starts slowly and then picks up speed, going faster than I was expecting. After two revolutions the speed, alarming as it is, seems to level out but worryingly seems to accompanied by a rattling somewhere beneath us.

'Scream if you want to go faster!' the pikey announces over the speakers. If anyone screams I'm gonna kill them, this is fast enough thank you.

The car spins like a drunk on a wedding dance floor and we enter the short tunnel for the third time. We are again bombarded with strobe lighting and then emerge just as suddenly into the cool fresh air and the darkness outside. As we spin past the entrance to the ride I contemplate making a leap for safety but sensibly decide against it. On the other side of the barriers a gang of kids are egging on two of their

121

friends to have a fight. The next time round I get to see how the fight is developing and I welcome the distraction. As the ride gets faster (thanks, pikey) my stomach starts to feels the force of the Coriolis Effect. Could two teenagers fighting be the last thing I see alive?

The sixth or seventh time around my attention is distracted by something else. A tall slender man dressed in a cheap dark blue suit and a moustache. He seems conspicuous in a CrimeWatch reconstruction kind of way. The next time around the ride begins to slow and the potential robber of female washing lines has already disappeared. He's obviously chosen not to come on this God-awful machine and I can't say that I blame him. The ride eventually comes to a halt and I have to pretend that I enjoyed it just as much as Mia, staggering from the ride with my balance well and truly screwed and onto the loving stability of wet grass beneath my feet. The ride begins again and I watch our car disappear into the tunnel with an acne-ridden teenage boy and his council estate girlfriend sitting within: good luck pal. The car behind follows them with only one person in it. I only catch a glimpse courtesy of the strobe lighting but it looks like a queasy version of that hook nosed bloke from the football earlier. I'm guessing by the rattling of the bar he is still stuck in the car from the last time around. What with him and Mr Weirdo, it must be sad lonely bloke night at the fair.

'You know what I want now? A nice fat greasy burger.' Mia reports as we pass the now full blown fight that's broken out between testosterone-fuelled twats.

'Then a burger it is,' I reply, the thought almost enough for me to bring up my stomach contents and put Mia off eating burgers forever. I'd rather have a cup of tea.

Halfway across the clearing to the burger van Mia turns to me and places a delicate kiss on my lips. Any chance of continuing the moment is lost as she declares that she has to go to the toilet and heads off in the direction of the bank of dark green portaloo toilets.

'Joseph?' a voice mutters hesitantly from behind.

As I turn I notice the strange bloke from the wurly thing standing behind me. His moustache and hair are as the police would describe: unkempt. My initial observation of him in a cheap blue suit is not entirely inaccurate. It is indeed blue and most definitely cheap because it's the uniform of the local supermarket Salisbury's. Down his left hand side are a number of smears, all varying in off white colours and seemingly encrusted on. Let's hope it's yoghurt.

'I'm sorry?' I reply, hoping that the weirdo will soon disappear.

'Are you Joseph?' strange man whispers urgently.

'Are you talking to me?' I ask and for the first time ever I say it without pretending to be Robert DeNiro in Taxi Driver.

'Are you Joseph?' he asks again, his whisper slightly louder and more confident.

'Yeah, my names Joseph, do I know you?'

'This is for you,' he replies, reaching inside his jacket and much to my relief failing to pull out a gun. Instead he thrusts a crumpled manila envelope towards me, which sensibly I decline to take.

'Sorry mate, I think you've got the wrong guy.'

'Or should I call you Bruce?'

To be confronted by a stranger is one thing, to be confronted by a stranger who knows the difference between my real self and my pretend version is very worrying indeed. I look into his eyes and can see the confidence of someone who either knows the truth or is a very lucky serial killer.

'Yeah that's me,' I sigh dramatically as the whole façade comes tumbling down around me. 'What do you want?'

'This,' the strange man replies, gesturing towards the envelope in his outstretched hand. 'It's a message from him, you must read it alone.'

'What's in the envelope?' I ask although I suspect it's a beating heart knowing my luck.

'It's a message from him.'

'Who's him?' I ask, totally confused by the conversation.

'I'm sorry,' he says, thrusting the envelope into my unwilling hands.

'I don't want this,' I reply, looking down. He takes the opportunity and begins to scurry off.

'Is this a wind up?' I shout, my neck craning upwards in an effort to talk over the crowds that drift between us.

'I'm just the messenger. It's your time now,' he shouts, disappearing into the shadows.

I take a few moments to duck and weave through the gaps in the crowd but there is no sight of him. All that is left is the envelope that I hold in my hands. Looking down, I see my name written in neat handwriting on the front.

'Man, this is weird,' I mutter to myself.

There is only one thing left to do. Maybe this was meant for me and maybe it wasn't, there is only one way to find out. I start to peel back the flap, carefully at first until a third of the way along I lose my patience and start ripping. Taking out the letter, I begin to read.

Dear Joseph,

Welcome to the new world, a world of truth and faith. It is a reality with the sword of Damocles hanging ever present overhead. The sword is the evil in the world; I am the thread that allows it to hang. It is on this thread that you will find life and freedom suspended. I assure you that of the many steps you take in life, reading on will be undoubtedly the most important.

124

What else could I do but read on.

I apologise for the methods employed in bringing you to us but as you will see, conventional means are easily dismissed in these times. I hold great faith that this letter will reach you without unnecessary involvement. By this time you will also have met the one known as The Messenger. You will also have discovered his vagueness in reply to your undoubted questions. This is the Messenger's instruction. He knows little, for his and our protection. Let me explain what has brought us to this point.

It is the uncertain factors in life, and indeed death which bind us. Yet it is fate that has brought us together. Providence has a plan for us all and this is especially true for you and me. I have witnessed your life, knowing what you were, what you are and what you will become. However fate isn't an unstoppable destiny nor is it resulting from the forces of chance. Fate is in the choices we make and the choices that are made for us. These troubled days hide your sins well, yet some of us are watching out of necessity, being watched ourselves by the guiding hand of fate. It is in our sins and their redemption that we find the faith and purpose in one another. Free choice is a gift to mankind but it does not excuse poor choices. These choices await you Joseph, fate has set a network of paths ahead of you. Each path has an end, which end you arrive at is decided by choice.

A new history is upon us, yet to be written and yet to be seen. We wish to ensure that the future is for all mankind. Others wish to seize its direction, to twist fate and make it their own. They wish to close the paths that have already opened.

That is why you have met the Messenger. This is why you read this letter.

You must be wary of the unexpected stranger.

You must be wary of the world around you.

Questions give rise to answers. Answers give rise to questions. I wish to show you what fate has in store.

Till next time,

The Prophet.

My mind is as dull as it is confused, my arm falling to my side, the fold of the paper resting between the light grip of my fingers. I look up to see if supermarket guy has reappeared to explain any of this. He hasn't, I wish someone would. It feels like this should all make sense, but the answer seems to slip away as I get near. Perhaps I should start at the beginning? Raising the letter once again I begin to read the first few lines, my mind focused.

'Sorry honey, the queue was terrible,' Mia announces, fast approaching from behind.

'Hi,' I reply, turning towards her and hiding the letter behind my back, 'I was just...'

'Just what?' she asks, smiling.

I want to confide in her, to tell her what just happened, what I think it means. Someone must be able to help. But Mia? No. She may be wonderful but she is still human. I know that look when you tell someone the past. The first look is the most telling. Everything after, the sympathy, the understanding, it means nothing, just blankets to hide their true feelings underneath. One day we may be able to move on from the Bruce situation and she will accept me as Joe. Can she accept me as Joe now? No. Can she accept me as Joe with a terrible, half repressed past? Definitely not. I slowly fold the letter behind my back and with the utmost stealth slip it into my back pocket.

'What's that?' she asks. Jesus, can't I get away with anything?

'Oh it's just…' and I struggle for a lie.

'Just…?' Mia asks, coming across all curious. Not now Mia, please not now. Think Bruce, think.

'My boss just gave me some urgent work that I need to do.'

'On a Saturday night? At the fair?' she asks, the curiosity in her voice now replaced with utter disbelief.

I fail to reply. I am far too consumed by the letter to be thinking of whether she believes me or not.

'Shall we go and get that burger?' Mia enquires.

'I'm sorry honey, this work thing. I really should get cracking on it. It's really urgent.'

I can't believe that I can't think of a better excuse, especially as I'm the last person in the world working on a Saturday night. I can see by the look in her eyes that the day Mia believes a story like this is the day the Devil goes to work in a snow plough. All I know is that I want to be on my own to face this.

'How long will it take?' she asks, sighing as she does so.

'Not too long I hope,' I reply. Maybe she believed me after all?

'Okay honey but you really should have a word with your boss about this. It's Saturday night after all!'

'I know. First thing Monday morning I'm going into his office to make sure this doesn't happen again.'

'You do that, now come on, drive me home or you'll be up all night,' Mia orders and begins to lead the way to the car park. Up all night working? Up until ten minutes ago I was hoping to be up all night doing other things. We walk the short distance back to the car park, yet it provides enough time for a heavy rain to start falling from a dark sky with no stars.

127

Ten minutes later we eventually find my car hiding under the shadow of the trees. I'm sure it was nearer than this. By the time we climb in both Mia and I are soaked through, my trousers useless against the rain. I just hope that the letter is okay.

It doesn't take long to drive back to hers. Outside we kiss quickly and I decline the offer of drying off inside. What's wrong with me? I can't believe I am passing up the opportunity of going inside and perhaps getting naked. Perhaps she would have got naked as well, you know, just so I didn't feel awkward. Instead an evening of lame excuses on my part shows no sign of abating any time soon. The second she closes her door I am driving away, making my way home through the torrential rain to read the letter again. I have to read it again. I have to know if it's happening again.

The minute I am behind the closed door of my bedroom I take the letter from my back pocket. It, like my stupid trousers, is completely sodden. Unfolding it, the top corner comes away as I lay it gently onto the bed. The rain has washed away most of the writing, the paper now a mass of blue streaks, however I can still make out a few words.

Blue mess blue mess redemption *something.*
Blue mess fate *blue mess* future.

Is that it? This can't be all that remains. I move it over to the side cabinet and hope that the letter will dry overnight, and that along the way the words will magically reappear from the chaotic scene within which they hide.

I lie back on the bed and stare at the ceiling, contemplating events. I must lie like this for hours and there is nothing worse than being awake in bed in the silence. I hear everything, from the sound of people outside coming home from nightclubs to the house settling down in the silence. Every creak sounds like an intruder and that bastard Danny hasn't even come home. He's probably passed out on some floor in Loop Road with a bunch of hippies. As I reach the early hours sheer exhaustion takes over and I fall into a disturbed, unpleasant sleep.

I awake at ten the next morning. The thoughts from the night before come instantly flooding back. The letter, here on the side…. The letter! Where is it?

Jumping out from under the covers, I check around the bed, around the bedside cabinet, all around everywhere. For the next hour I check the obvious, to the downright stupid. The letter is gone. No one has taken it and things have just become a lot more terrifying. But now at least everything finally makes sense.

Chapter 15

The Beginnings Of Servitude On Planet Gong

They called this the new decade, the 80s. It looked much the same to me on the outside. Inside it was so much different, not because of the change in decade but a change inside. The game had begun.

Sunday, 13th January 1980

My eyes hurt. It feels like they don't belong. And all because of Bobby having his Christmas money stolen, an act of revenge for the bed incident. He didn't take too kindly to that. Still it's not without its benefits; every so often I'll punch myself to keep the bruises fresh. The teachers may not care but my Mum will be outraged when she visits in a fortnight. It's all coming together.

In the meantime, Sunday morning in St Luke's, a small chapel on the grounds of the school. All detainees must attend the weekly church service. Walk, enter, sit, suffer.

The cold air has chilled the seat as I place myself on the hard wooden bench. I can see them looking.

'Have you seen his face?' they whisper.

'Who's face?'

'Morgan's.'

Next comes the inevitable arch around in the seat, spreading like fire throughout the congregation. Bobby is sitting like a champion in the row across from me, settled amongst the damned. Enjoy it, while you can.

'Love must be sincere,' the vicar drivels. What if love isn't sincere? I don't see love from those who claim to be my family.

'Hate what is evil...' the vicar continues. I know evil and it's all those who surround me.

'Cling to what is good.' Ha ha, where's the goodness? Where?

The rest of his speech passes me by. A vicar can't tell me what is right or wrong. There are others for that now. Looking to my right I see my enemies. There is Michael sitting at the end of the row, Dean and Bobby to his right. It's nearly over for me but it has only just begun for them. I feel my mind wandering as the spoken words drift by.

'Be devoted to one another in brotherly love.'

Boring.

'Honour one another above yourselves.'

Yawn.

Suddenly, the stained glass window behind the vicar shatters into a thousand pieces. Storm troopers swing through the remaining shards on wires, their guns drawn. It may only be a dream but it is no less painful for those involved. They throw the vicar to the floor followed by the sound of more of them bursting through the heavy oak doors at the back of the church, spreading out behind the last row of pews. No escape. Yet Michael still tries to run. I know I have the ability to defend him, to deflect the laser beams with my light sabre. I choose not to. I let him run a few yards before being gunned down, his last actions on this world that of a coward. I will of course put down this most villainous of incursions, but all in good time. Dean and Bobby are dragged from their pews next. They are executed then and there in the aisle for no other reason than I allow it. They don't even get a chance to plead for their dirty little souls as the lasers cut through flesh and bone. Within seconds they slump to the floor, burning bags of pathetic filth. They got what they deserved. Now I can get started. Just as I'm about to execute an acrobatic somersault over the four people to my right and into the battleground of the aisle, I am distracted. Amongst the scared faces ahead, one is looking around at me with a sense of understanding, his eyes somewhere between this world and reality.

The storm troopers fade as he continues to stare. What the hell is he staring at?

Michael, Bobby and Dean return to existence, unaware of how close they were to death.

The face with the knowing eyes continues to look … how… how dare you interrupt, my dreams, my plans for revenge.

The vicar's sermon returns.

'Do not take revenge, my friends, but leave room for God's wrath…'

The words bring me back to this world. The vicar must be aware that every Sunday his words sail through the empty minds of his flock. The last thing he would expect, asides from storm troopers, would be that someone would actually be listening. But I am, I've waited patiently for God's wrath. It's just that I can't wait forever. I will be the extension of God's hand, to punish those sinners who sin against me, to be God's wrath. It's coming, and when it does I know exactly where to start.

I'm shying away from the light, slipping into the recesses of the crowd as it makes its way up the aisle and towards freedom. We spill out of the doors and into a cold winter air that hits my face as I shove my hands deep into the pockets of my blazer. Breaking away, I descend the outside steps and into the gardens, my feet crunching the soft snow beneath my soles. Between crunches I hear a timid voice from behind.

'Excuse me?'

I turn to see the same kid again, the one who could see my dreams. He's probably my age but smaller, his hair a dusty brown with an unfortunate side parting.

'What do you want?' I reply. I don't have the time to speak to one of the lesser people when plans are afoot.

'Hi…. I'm Jimmy Christmas.'

'Nice surname, what do you want?'

'Bad isn't it, my surname? I might change it,' he babbles.

'What do you want?' I ask again, forcefully.

'I was wondering if you wanted to be friends.'

'Why would I want to be friends with you?' I answer, stifling a laugh.

'Well, I've heard you like Star Wars.'

'Yeah so?'

'And you've got the new X-Wing with battle damage, I've got the AT-AT walker …'

'How do you know that?' I interrupt angrily.

'I heard some of the older boys talking about it.'

'Who did you hear talking about it?'

'Those boys you share your dorm with, I didn't catch all of it but they mentioned the X-Wing and using it after the church service.'

'What?'

'Well I thought at first that they would be too old to play with it, but then I hoped that if you were all going to play then maybe I could join in.'

'The boys I share my dorm with?' I enquire, trying to fight the dread implications of Jimmy Christmas's revelation.

'I've got most of the figures as well.'

'What did they actually say?'

'I'm hoping my parents will buy me a snow speeder next.'

'What did they actually say?' I shout.

'Who?'

I don't have the time. I can still hear him talking nonsense as I start to run through the snow towards my secret hiding place. They can't know where it is, I've been so careful. The sound of my feet crushing the snow takes on a rhythmic beat as I get nearer the lake. Underneath the bush, my toys should still be there, they have to be. As I approach I extend my right arm, my hand hitting the tangled mesh of thin branches in an attempt to slow and turn. All this achieves is a searing pain as the branches cut into my outstretched palm. Stupid, stupid, stupid. And then I see what I already know to be true. My Star Wars figures are strewn and crumpled in the dirt. I drop to my knees and search frantically before turning my attention to the bush itself. Where is it? It has to be here. It's the only thing that connects me to the real world. My X-Wing fighter is no longer neatly secured in the dense undergrowth, nor is it lying amongst the wreckage of the battleground littered with sixty three Star Wars figures. Gone! They've taken it. They've fucking taken it. I leap to my feet and launch myself in the direction of the dorm. I veer onto the path, the sound of my feet changing as they pound the cold gravel pathway.

'Morgan! Stop running!' Carter shouts as I swerve round him. I can't stop. I have to get it back.

'Morgan! Stop running, you little shit!' he shouts again, his voice already fading as I round the final corner.

Every muscle is burning, my vision blurred, my heart racing. I'm not looking. I don't see Michael. Even though I hit him at speed, the only person affected is me. My legs fail me as I stumble backwards, my backside the first part of my body to hit the ground, quickly followed by the shock of the impact travelling up my frame. My arms splay out to grab anything to help but all this achieves is to run my hands across the rough ground, tiny bits of gravel imbedding themselves into my palms.

'Sorry didn't see you there Morgan,' Michael laughs from high above, a grin spreading across his stupid face.

There is a moment of silence as I look up at him. Then, gliding with menace behind him, Dean and Bobby enter my field of vision. All of them staring down at me now, laughing. Michael: the very sight of him makes me sick. Dean, he's no better. Bobby, the fat bastard just stands there trying to eat a pie in between laughs. Little flakes of pastry fly from his dirty mouth and fall onto me.

'See you later mong,' Michael spits and steps over me, 'Maybe we can play later eh?'

Dean begins to laugh raucously and is joined by Bobby once he has finished kicking gravel into my face. Seeing his shoe hit the ground at a sharp angle I turn my face to the right, judging the many points of impact by the searing pain that erupts on my cheek and hairline.

When they finally go, I bring my hands up from the pathway and turn them around. The gravel falls from my palms slowly, leaving indentations and blood to mark the encounter. I cast a cautious glance at the three of them as they make their way around the corner. Dean in one final insult raises his middle finger towards me. Gathering myself, I get up and gingerly make my way across to the steps. The pain stops the tears.

After climbing the two flights of stairs I arrive at the door. I don't know what lies inside but there is only one way to find out. I turn the handle and sweep into the room. The first things I look for are any obvious changes to my bed and unsurprisingly it has been disturbed. I don't believe that they would think I would fall for the turd in the bed routine again. As I climb the steps and peer over it would seem that they haven't bothered either. It is however as I was expecting. There, poorly hidden under the sheets is the missing X-Wing fighter. I may have accepted this present from my mum with little enthusiasm, but now that it has been taken from me its importance is so much greater. It is the link, and now it is broken. The cockpit has been smashed into a multitude of plastic fragments that lie scattered on the pilot's seat. The main damage however is to the lower left wing, having been completely snapped off. Along the break the plastic is stretched, its original beige colour now a vivid destructive white. I don't know where the rest of the wing is, who cares, it's fucking useless now. Those fucking bastards!

136

1, 2, 3 ….

Those fucking dirty bastards!

8, 9, 10 ….

Those fucking dirty ….

'What did I tell you about the numbers son? You don't need them anymore now that I'm here.'
The sound of the voice shocks me out of the anger. It belongs to salvation, to hope, a new life brought into this world to help me. The voice echoes from behind me and from inside of me, contained within the very fabric of the universe. I don't need to see him, I know he is there.
'What?' I mutter into the nothingness of the room.
'Don't lose the anger, don't get distracted.'
'But they broke my toy!' I stutter, tears starting to well in my eyes.
'Don't you dare cry! You're better than that.'
'I'm sorry but ….'
'Stop those goddam tears!'
As if on demand, the tears stop.
'What are you going to do now son?'
'I don't know.'
'You're going to make them pay aren't you?'
'Am I?' I question, not quite understanding.
'Yes you are, you're going to make them all pay.'
'Yes I am,' I whisper confidently. I can feel the anger rising in me once again. This time however it is different. It starts as a small drilling sound somewhere in my head before exploding through every living cell. No mercy, no morality, no fear.

'What are you going to do son?'

'I'm going to hurt them,' I reply, the anger now unstoppable, coursing through every element of my body and spilling into the air around me.

'Who are you going to hurt?'

'All of them. Every last fucking one!' I shout, spit flying from my mouth like venom.

'Then let's start shall we?'

I hear the door behind me open with a creek. One of them has come back, back to witness their victory. I can hear the rustling of clothes as he enters the room.

Have you come back to finish me off?

Closer now.

Just come a little closer.

Now!

I swing around, raising the X-Wing in my right hand above my head, increasing its speed as I complete the arc and bring it down on the temple of my attacker with a sickening crunch. As he stumbles from under the blow I start to fall over him, the force carrying me through. My right hand hits the floor along the bone and although this is only a dull pain, the shock propels the weapon out of my hand and skidding across the floor. No matter, I still have every advantage. I can hardly see, my eyes merely observing now. First a swift blow to the cheekbone rocks Michael's face back and forth, the next sends Dean's head to one side. I stagger to my feet and regaining my strength I deliver a kick to the ribs, Bobby's body shifting uncomfortably in response. Turning around I grab the cheap plastic chair next to me and hurl it onto Sean's chest. It bounces off him and into the corner. My dad lies beneath me now, his face bloodied and attempting to curl into a foetal position, shuddering from my justice. It is only then that I notice my breathing, short rapid breaths through my nose. My clenched teeth refuse to let any air through as my whole body shakes in its rage. And then there is the sound of the door creaking again. I am ready for whoever it is now; I want them to take in the scene of my opponent defeated. As I stand and revel in my power I want them to be scared.

Mr Carter enters the room and stands before me, first looking at my opponent on the floor and then straight at me. I can see fury entering his eyes, a more primitive, feebler anger.

'What the fuck have you done, Morgan?' he shouts.

Nothing. No fear, no anger, just a feeling of completeness.

'What the fuck! Get over there boy!' he screams, pointing me towards the corner. I do as I'm told, after all I've finished.

I wander casually over to the corner, leaning against the wall as he rushes over to the body on the floor. It is only now that my senses reawaken and I can hear the moaning.

'You have done well, Son.' says a whisper in my ear.

'I know,' I reply, sending the thought through my mind so that the only two people in the world that can communicate like this do so.

The congratulations come thick and fast in our private conversation as Carter turns the body over. My enemy is still breathing, more is the pity. Even with a face smeared in blood and eyes that are as vacant as my own the mop of messy hair on top of his slender face is instantly recognisable.

Poor old Eric Porter, in the wrong place at the wrong time; the wrong life. I warned you that you were about to enter the game but you didn't listen, did you?

Chapter 16

Tales From The Intercom

Four days off work. Four long, uneventful, non-threatening days. Under normal circumstances (and I will be the first to admit this) four days at home and getting paid for it is usually a good thing. This time however all I've felt is fear and disorder. Not even daytime television can block out the terrifying thoughts which run at the forefront of my mind, jostling for position. I do however possess extensive knowledge of how to make a Victoria sponge, restore an ageing house and the female menopause. That and my Bond is really coming on. You'd be surprised how easy it is to hide away from the world.

Danny turned up on the Sunday after the letter, explaining through blood shot eyes how he and Dodgy has come into possession of some rather fine mushrooms. I needed to speak to someone about it but how do you bring something like that up? I figured that if I gave off an air of mystery and sadness, he was sure to figure out something was wrong. As usual his observational powers were as acute as a mackerel. I'm kidding myself. There's only one person who can help. There's only one person who knows everything there is to know about me. I pick up the phone and dial Katie's work number.

'Hello, Katie Rose speaking,'

'Hiya Katie, its Joe.'

'Hi Joe, How's it going and why haven't I heard from you in ages?'

'It's a long story.'

'How long?'

'Well not so much long but complicated.'

'Complicated as in Mia dumped you complicated?'

'No, Mia is fine and we are still happy together, thanks for asking.'

'Then why haven't you been answering your phone?' Katie asks. I decline to mention the reason I haven't been answering is because I'm scared of who's on the other end.

'Look, I'm sorry for ringing you at work. Can you talk?'

'Not really. The police have just arrived.'

'What's wrong? Why are the police there?' I reply with an escalating sound of panic in my voice.

'Oh it's nothing. We've had this creepy looking guy with a hook nose hanging around outside all day.'

As Katie relates the story, the deductive part of my brain kicks in. A hook nose?

'But he left five minutes after we rang the police,' Katie continues.

Didn't that bloke at.........

'Did you want to meet up later?' Katie asks, unaware she keeps interrupting my logical reasoning. Oh sod it, I'll work it out later.

'Yeah, could do. Obviously the Manor and Toad is out.'

'Okay, come round to mine later and we'll take it from there. I'll be home at six.'

'Okay, see you then.'

'Take care,' Katie concludes.

I gently place the phone down and lie back on the bed. You take care as well Katie Rose; you don't know what's out there.

To pass the hours until then, I entertain myself by watching children's television. The problem with kids' television nowadays is that in the last ten to fifteen years a gold mine of quality has turned resolutely to crap. What happened to Rentaghost? What happened to the Mysterious Cities of Gold? What today's generation needs is another John Craven, complete with horrific jumper taste. Still I suppose it counts as good practice if I ever find myself unemployed. It doesn't escape my attention that if I don't go to work soon, the practice will soon become convention. When six o'clock approaches I'm out the front door and breathing in the fumes from the main street. Despite the smell, despite the dirt, I feel like a prisoner released. The outside has missed Joe and this town wouldn't be the same without me.

'Hi Harriet,' I announce as the Scottish one opens her front door.

'Oh hi Joe,' she answers and for a few brief moments she doesn't know whether to invite me in or tell me to piss off.

'Hi, I came round to see Katie.'

'She's still at work Joe,' Harriet confirms with a broad smile, probably fake, before continuing 'do you want to come in for a cup of tea and wait for her?'

As if knowing that I will accept she opens the door wider and begins to walk to the kitchen. Cheeky cow, she must think all I do is drink tea.

'Three sugars please,' I announce as I follow her in, closing the door behind me.

'Take a seat and I'll bring it through,' Harriet announces as she veers into the kitchen. I carry on my present course along the hall and into the lounge. As I place myself down on the sofa I sit up with my back straight, anticipating her return. I don't want her to think I'm too comfortable and familiar. Hurry up Katie.

Minutes later, Harriet brings in the tea, taking a seat on the same sofa. What follows is a few seconds of both of us trying to think of a topic of conversation. I really don't know what to say to her, apart from the obvious. What's preferable? A question with an answer that you don't want to hear or an awkward silence?

'So how's the acting business then?' I ask as my mind screams at me to go for retrospective awkward silence, awkward silence you fool.

'Oh you know, struggle as always,' Harriet replies.

'Did you ever get that part in that film with Jack Connolly?' I ask even though I know she didn't. Anything for conversation.

'No they gave it to some girl who was better looking,' she replies bluntly.

I know that I should say something reassuring at this point. It's a fine line. Does she really need a compliment from Joseph, the ex-boyfriend? What if she thinks it's insincere? What if she thinks I'm trying it on? She would bloody love that. I instead decline to rock the boat in shark infested waters and pass over the opportunity.

'So anything else in the pipeline?' I ask.

'What about you Joe? What have you been up to?'

'Usual stuff,' I answer, as far from the truth as possible.

'Oh, did you hear about that landlord at that pub that you and Katie drink at?' Harriet asks. Of course I've heard about it, the media have talked about nothing else. I must have seen the story a hundred times because I have seen the news a hundred times. *Neighbours* only fills a small proportion of the time for those under voluntary house arrest.

'Yeah crazy innit?' I reply.

'How many bodies is it now? Were they all locals?' Harriet asks.

'I think so. It sort of makes sense now.'

'It's absolute madness, right on your own doorstep and everything!'

'Yeah, seemed like such a nice bloke and all,' I lie.

With this, Harriet laughs dramatically, over-enthusiastically and unconvincingly. It is further confirmed to me why she gets so little work as an actress.

144

'Do you remember when you took me in there when we were going out?' she asks. How much more uncomfortable do you want me to feel Harriet? I realise how unromantic I was.

'Yeah sorry about that,' I reply, knowing that an apology means nothing to either of us.

'You know, I often wonder what would...........'

Before she can complete her sentence the front door opens and our attention is drawn towards Katie coming in.

'Hi sweetheart!' Harriet cries, almost in desperation. That makes two of us, love.

'Hi,' my saviour replies in a tired and resigned tone as she makes her way up the hall.

'Hi Katie,' I say, purposely louder and deeper than Harriet.

The door swings open and she enters the room, flinging her bag onto the armchair. I had forgotten how beautiful she is, had I been trying to ignore it?

'Good day?' Harriet asks.

'Nope, it was shit.'

Wanting to gain Katie's attention just for myself, I enter the conversation.

'Bummer,' I contribute, my left cheek rising into a sort of exaggerated Elvis sneer as I close my eyelid, giving a released-into-the-community wink. Quite what this facial expression is supposed to mean I have no idea. In reality it probably looks like a nervous twitch prior to declaring a love of pyromania whilst fiddling with matches.

'That bloody weird bloke with the nose turned up again.'

'Did you call the police again?' I ask.

'What's this? Was someone hassling you honey?' Harriet asks. Excuse me Harriet, do you mind? I was the one asking the question.

'It's nothing, just some weirdo,' Katie replies nonchalantly.

I can see Harriet's mind working. She's wondering whether to remind us all of her knowledge of law enforcement from her five seconds in The Bill.

'So did you ring the police?' I ask again. Don't you fucking dare Harriet!

'Yeah but he disappeared again, almost as if he knew they were coming.'

'Scary, so what did he look like?' Harriet asks.

'Dunno. Normal really, just had a really large nose. He looked a bit familiar but I can't place him.'

As she says this I can feel my brain kick into deductive mode again but before it can draw any conclusions it gives up on this tedious task willingly.

'Harriet I don't mean to be rude but do you mind if I speak to Joe in private? We need to have a chat about something.'

'Oh okay. Got to go and practice some lines anyway for an audition tomorrow,' she exclaims before heading up the stairs, reverting back to annoying actress mode. Yeah, thanks for that Harriet.

Katie listens to make sure she is out of ear shot before she starts.

'Okay first question Joseph. Where the hell have you been recently? I've hardly seen you.'

'Well I've had this thing you see...'

'You mean you've been seeing Mia?'

'A little bit but ...' I reply before stopping. Suddenly it all becomes clear. Katie didn't want to chat because she knew something was wrong. Katie wanted to chat so she could give me the Mia bollocking.

'That's not why I came round,' I state, hoping that this will be enough to end the offensive before it begins.

'If I can ask one thing,' Katie starts. 'How long can you hope to carry this on for? When she works it out and God knows how she hasn't already, she's going to dump you.'

And there it is. She couldn't bloody help herself.

'There's something different about her. She's not like the others,' I retort. Fight the truth Joseph, fight the truth.

'Why? Because she's mentally unstable?'

'There's something special between us,' I counter.

'Yep it's certainly special. But when she finally works it out, it will be me that gets to clean up the mess again.'

'What do you mean, again?'

'Mmmm,' Katie replies, pausing theatrically. 'How about everyone you ever went out with? You were even shattered when Harriet dumped you and she has about as much depth as a puddle.'

'Okay,' I sigh, 'can we move on?'

'Sure, but I thought this was what you wanted to talk about?'

'No, not at all, I'm quite happy with the situation actually, you're the person that launched into one,' I conclude. In fact I'm far from happy with the whole Mia situation. Every point Katie has made is completely valid but she is viewing it from an entirely different perspective. I need Mia, Katie doesn't. But this isn't about that, it's about the other thing. Except I don't know how to start. Even though I'm annoyed with Katie I want her to know. Maybe then she'll suddenly go *'Oh my god, my poor Joe, let me help you'*. Then we would hug and from the closeness of our bodies she would suddenly realise that she has always loved me. Then we would look at one another and kiss softly. Why exactly do I punish myself like this?

'It's a bit difficult really,' I pause. 'You see, well you know the thing? I think it's back except … except things aren't quite as they should be.'

'Okay' Katie muses 'Can I give you some advice?'

'Please do,' I reply. Please don't if it's where I think you are leading with this.

'Has all this started since you started to see Mia?' Katie asks, arriving at the inevitable with all the subtlety of a 747 landing in the crapper.

'Oh come on, not back to this again!'

'Has it?'

'Well yes but it's not because of her.'

'Of course it is, you're living a lie.'

'Please Katie, just listen. I'm trying to tell you something important here.'

'I am listening but the situation with Mia....'

'Will you just drop it?' I interrupt sharply, getting angry with her. No correction, I was already angry with her, I'm now furious. Why does it come down to this again? Small problem, Mia. Big problem, Mia. Wrong, wrong, wrong.

'Joe, it's everything about her. She might appear on the outside to be this beautiful, intelligent girl of your dreams but she also thinks you're someone else.'

'Yes she is all those things, but Katie it's not about her!' I reply. Why isn't she listening? Why does she have to undertake this character assassination all the time?

'The truth is, your relationship is doomed to failure,' Katie says. Why don't you listen? For fuck's sake why don't you listen just this once?

'Katie, I haven't told you everything.'

'Oh right, let me guess. You're going to tell me you love her right?' Katie continues. 'It's always the same. Every girl you go out with, you fall in love with,' she replies. That's bollocks, if only she knew that the only girl I've ever loved is her. And Beth of course. And maybe Mia.

'You haven't heard a bloody word I've said since you came in have you? I'm trying to tell you something here!' I shout.

'Please Joe don't get angry.'

'I'm not fucking angry!' I shout and of course I am.

'Look why don't you just calm down and we can talk about this.'

148

I know that would make sense. I know that if I simply calm down then we can work this out. I know all these things but I'm too far gone. It's a cascade effect in its purest form. Propelled by the anger inside, I stride across the room, past the sofa where she is sitting, feeling her presence now more than ever. A deep buried twinge of guilt tries to fight its way to the surface. No fucking chance. No fucking way. No apologies, no turning back.

'Please Joe,' Katie requests as I slam the door to the living room behind me and head towards the front door.

As I step outside and into the cold winter air, a blast of sunshine hits me, shaking me from my thoughts. I know I've gone too far as the anger subsides, a terrible purpose realised. Even if I wanted to go back and say sorry, events are now too far gone. As much as I want her to accept my apology and have her hold me and tell me everything will be alright, I know that everything will be far from just right. This is just the beginning. I pace up the road, my mind rolling with the after effects of the storm inside. I want to go back and apologise, but I won't, I don't want to have to say sorry.

Another street now. There's only one person who can really help, past the old oak trees, Mia's block of flats getting ever nearer. Within minutes I am climbing the steps towards the intercom, towards her. I should have come here first; after all she loves me doesn't she? She'll understand. That's more than bloody Katie can manage. First things first though. I hadn't planned it this way but if she's going to help then she has to know the real me. And that doesn't leave much room for Bruce. An inch from the buzzer my finger stops. Exactly what happens when I press this button? What sort of conversation will ensue? Something, I imagine, like this:

149

'Oh hi Bruce!'
'Hello.'
'Everything okay?'
'Not really.'
'What's wrong honey?'
'Well I think I'm seeing things.'
'Like what?'
'Where do I start? Firstly there was seeing myself on television and then when we were at the fair a bloke came up to me and gave me a letter from someone called The Prophet.'
'A letter?'
'Yes, talking about redemption for my sins or something. Problem is I don't know who the Prophet is and what he actually wants.'
'That's a bit strange.'
'Yes it is isn't it? Oh and now I think about it, I was attacked by a tramp when we first met and he may actually have nothing to do with this but he started shouting religious stuff at me, a bit like the letter.'
'Very odd.'
'Indeed but hang on, I'm not finished yet. The thing is, I have this past that you don't know about, well no one does except one person who I've just had an argument with and who may never speak to me again.'
'Are you seeing anyone at the moment?'
'Asides from myself on television, tramps knowledgeable in biblical matters and weird blokes that give out letters addressed from complete strangers, no.'
'Maybe you should?'
'Not quite finished yet my little fluffy bunny. I've also been lying to you by claiming to be someone from your past who just happens to look like me, but about whom you remember nothing, luckily. I've been trying to live his life with you and you know what, I really like it.'
'Are you insane?'

'Possibly, I don't know whether I am imagining all of this or if it's actually happening, can I come up?'
'Goodbye Bruce.'
'It's Joe actually.'
'Mia? Are you going to buzz me up?'
'Mia?'

My trembling finger remains an inch from the button. Oh Christ, what am I doing? I would be the first to admit that our relationship, having been built on complete deception, is not the most stable. Somehow (and I think you might agree with me here) revelations of such magnitude are not to be taken lightly. I do want to tell her, I want to run up there, tell her everything at a tremendous speed. Then maybe she'll forgive me and understand the sudden need for honesty. Is that day today? No. Drawing my finger away, Mia's intercom remains quiet, to be pressed again another day.

I descend the steps quietly, keeping low behind the tall hedge as I shuffle away. Once out of the way I break into a full blown sprint. I need to get home, the only safe place left. A ninety degree corner looms ahead and I take it at speed. My hand trails the rough texture of the brick whilst I take a poor racing line into it, coming out on the other side of the corner in an exaggerated arc. Before I can even realise what has happened the ground rushes up towards me. As I fall I get a sense, a memory perhaps of something similar having happening to me before. I've tripped over something, something soft, something angry. Even before I've finishing splaying myself all over the pavement I'm already looking back. I've only bloody tripped over a small Yorkshire terrier who has recovered from the blow and proceeds to snap and growl in my direction, fighting against the restraint of the lead. Following the lead up I see who is holding it. Bloody hell, it's that bloke from the football with the big nose.

151

'Shit, sorry mate!' I stutter.

'Ummm.......that's okay,' he replies hesitantly.

'Is your dog okay?'

'Don't worry about him, good evening,' he replies, ending the conversation nervously.

In an instant and as if the whole incident is forgotten, the bloke with the hook nose is making his way round the corner in the direction of Mia's flat. It is with great reluctance that the dog follows, fighting against the lead all the way. Gingerly I pick myself up and begin to stumble towards my own part of town. I can't believe I tripped over a dog. What a bloody idiot. Luckily that bloke with the hook nose... The hook nose! I saw him at the football! Then he was at the fair! Wasn't Katie saying that someone with a hook nose was following her? How many people can there be with a nose like that? Oh fuck. The letter was right all along.

You must be wary of the unexpected stranger.
You must be wary of the world around you.

From a stagger I break into a sprint, my mind full of panic. With a good fifty metres now between myself and the corner I take a risk and look back. My eyesight is good enough to see a nose, followed by a face, peeking around the corner, watching me.

Chapter 17

Unorthodox Policing Procedures No's 789 to 792

In an eternal labyrinth of walled corridors, Polston's office hid itself away in the depths of the station whilst everyone else had long since moved upwards towards the luxury of the sunlight. Polston however had remained, alongside an anarchic filing system and a disturbing scattering of evidence. Sergeant Walker was taking the familiar route to Polston's office, passing endless rooms with frosted windows and sinister shadows within. As he turned the corner, another corridor stretched out before him with Polston's door at the end. As he approached the door he could just make out the movements of the inspector behind, his well-rounded silhouette staggered into horizontal lines by the effects of the glass.

Walker entered the room and the actions of Polston were now clearer to see. With his back to the door the inspector was crouched next to his desk, flicking through piles of crumpled blue folders. Without turning the inspector spoke.

'What is it Walker?'

'Alright boss, you wanted to see me?'

'I wanted to know what was going on with....oh where is that file?' Polston exclaimed as he began to look through the pile for the third time, eventually admitting defeat before moving across to another pile in the corner. As he bent over, Polston's already low trousers provided scant protection to a dignity which had long since been lost.

'Yes, yes,' Polston muttered to himself softly as he paused at one of the files, half way down the stack.

'Anything I can help you with boss?' Walker asked in a hollow gesture.

'I'm up to my bloody neck in it with the Manor and Toad case, can't find a bloody thing!' Polston declared. In truth, the mess had been present long before Uncle Ken had even sealed up his first victim in the now infamous cellar.

For Walker, such a case could have been the big one, the essential cog in the master-plan. However with Polston distracted by the murder case, Walker knew he could continue his surveillance without undue interference. The more he watched Mia, the more he fell in love. The more he watched Joe, the more vengeful he became.

'How's the surveillance going?' Polston enquired casually, his mind elsewhere.

'He's our man, inspector, no doubt,' Walker blurted a little too quickly to seem natural. The sergeant suspected that Polston's question was a leading one. If the inspector was asking then he was thinking. And if he was thinking then this could only mean one thing. It was the beginning of the end, the end of surveillance, the end of watching Mia, legitimately at least.

'Walker,' Polston replied in a tired fashion 'I need proof. I need to know you aren't wasting your time on this.'

Walker tried to control himself. Wasting his time? Hardly, Walker thought.

'I don't think we should give up on him yet boss,' Walker replied, trying to add an air of professionalism. The sergeant knew that he had to think on his feet here. The thought of only ~~watching Mia~~ *ahem* monitoring the ongoing crime in his spare time filled him with utter dread. He had finally found something worth not going back to Goodison for and he wasn't prepared to give it up. It may not be in the detective handbook but what is the law if it isn't about saving young girls from corruption, he reasoned. Walker took a few moments to cycle through a number of options from his master-plan before continuing.

'Well, I followed the suspect and I've seen him conduct reconnaissance on a number of other post offices,' Walker lied.

'Of course,' Polston muttered to himself as nodded his head in agreement. 'I should have realised. Callahan was quiet all last night. He must have been thinking about the case.'

'What?' Walker replied in astonishment. The sergeant couldn't quite believe his boss actually considered the dog to have detective skills equal to his own. In truth, Walker suspected the dog was probably quiet because his main suspect had managed to trip over him the night before.

'I can always tell when Callahan is working on something,' Polston iterated.

'But he's just a dog!'

'Exactly Walker, exactly!'

Walker may have suspected dementia but he was now convinced that the inspector had just entered its final stages.

'I'm sure he will make his move soon and then we will have them,' Walker replied, urging his boss on.

'This could be your big moment Walker.'

'I won't stop until he's been arrested, I can assure you of that,' Walker offered with conviction in his most dynamic and professional voice.

'Well get going then,' Polston ordered.

'Yes sir!' the sergeant replied, turning towards the door.

'Oh, sergeant...' Polston called after him.

'Yes boss?'

'Aren't you forgetting something?'

'Am I?'

'Your partner.'

'My partner?'

'Your partner.' Polston repeated, crossing the room to one of the many filing cabinets, reaching into an open drawer and lifting out Callahan.

'But .... Do you really think …' Walker stammered.

Polston interrupted Walker with a look.

'Of course boss,' Walker surrendered. The sergeant couldn't believe the request but knew that sacrifices must be made to continue on the true mission.

After attaching the lead, Walker left the room, dragging the dog behind him. By the time he reached the end of the corridor he considered it safe enough to mutter his thoughts.

'A bloody dog for a partner!'

'Not just any dog, Walker!' Polston shouted along the length of the corridor. Quite how the inspector had heard him was a mystery. It couldn't have been superhuman powers because superheroes rarely came in the guise of overweight police officers nearing retirement and with poor personal hygiene.

As Walker was making his way up the stairs the inspector was relaxing back into his chair with a smile. Polston had begun to suspect that he may well have been wrong on the suspect that he had just sent Walker after. Yet he was more than happy to get rid of Walker for as long as possible. He couldn't risk having him stuff up the Manor and Toad case; it was too high profile for an idiot like him. It was also no secret that Walker couldn't stand working with Callahan. A combination of constant infuriation and the boredom of long hours of surveillance would be enough to send Walker over the edge. Polston sat back and congratulated himself on devising a plan that was sure to send the sergeant back to Goodison.

Chapter 18

Howard Marks Don't Come Round Here No More

My body rocks as I manoeuvre myself between the trees of level seven, Inferno style. From high above in the branches, birds swoop down with wicked faces, straight out of a Hitchcock nightmare. I duck, I weave, I run like the nutter I am. Eventually in the distance I see a light through the trees, a blinding white sand that stretches off into the distance, just as a glittering rain starts to fall from the heavens. Rushing onto the sand I come to a shuddering halt, brought to the edge of terror by a pain racing from my scorched feet to the tips of my fingers. The rain is not what it would seem, instead tiny flakes of fire falling all around me, forming the burning sand beneath my feet. Within ten seconds I am drained, no more energy, no more lives. I fall onto the sand and the flames have their victim. It's a stupid fucking game.

'Dude!' Danny shouts from outside my door.

In a flash I push the games console under the bed with my foot and flick the television off just as Danny with little regard for privacy crashes into my room.

'Man, you're still in bed.'

'I have been out,' I counter.

'What down the offy to get more cider?'

'I went round Katie's actually.'

'Nice, it's about time you got it on with her.'

'Piss off, she's my mate,' I reply, not sure I'm telling the complete truth.

'So you not interested in Katie then?' Danny asks with a sly grin.

'No of course not!' I assure him, unconvincingly.

'So you wouldn't mind if I had a pop then?'

Of course this bothers me, but I can hardly say no when I'm not even interested in her, which of course I'm not.

'Do what you want sunshine,' I reply, safe in the assumption that he doesn't stand a chance anyway. 'Did you actually want something?' I ask.

'What?' Danny replies blankly, starting to think about Katie in a number of provocative poses.

'The way you came in, looked like you wanted to say something.'

Danny's dope brain fails to hold onto whatever image he has of Katie when faced with an unrelated question. It takes a few seconds for the question to enter, the memory to recollect, the mouth to reply. A few moments for me to try and get a grip and not take everything out on Danny.

'Yeah mate, picked up some opiumated solid today. You want any? This stuff sells like a demon.' Danny offers, waving a small bag of the merchandise in the air to entice me.

'No it's alright mate, I'm not smoking at the moment.'

'I'll put you down for your usual quarter then shall I?'

'Honestly mate, I'm knocking it on the head for a while.'

'You serious?' Danny asks with a look of disbelief on his face. He'll try anything for a sale.

'Yep,' I reply. I don't tell him the reason is because I'm scared of what will happen if I do.

'Fair enough matey, I'm off to Loop Road to pick up another nine bar of this stuff.'

'Have fun!' I reply as he leaves the room.

I tried Katie and I tried Mia. That kinda leaves only Danny with which to discuss what's been happening: the letter, the nose, everything. To cut a long thought process short, that's no one that can help, then. So I let Danny leave without telling him anything. I'd get more sense out of a lobotomised unicorn, and they're not even real, unless you've been on the mushrooms. I sit in silence for a few moments before flicking the television back on and then watch the looped replay of my

158

death on the games console, the words Game Over plastered across the screen in mocking insult. Bloody Danny, why is he so useless? Well I'll get my revenge, you watch me. I'll start by tracking down his gear. I leave my own room and cross the landing, consumed by slight feelings of guilt that are easily suppressed, I'm just looking, not necessarily stealing. I approach the plain door with countless layers of white gloss and try the handle. Locked. Shocking that my own house mate doesn't trust me enough not to go snooping round his room. I give up on this futile quest when I hear the mobile ring from my own room, making my way back and retrieving it from the bed.

'Hello?'

'Good evening Joseph. It's good to speak at last,' the caller announces in a charismatic tone.

'I'm sorry, who is this?' I ask.

'I am the present where Abraham and Jeconiah came before me.'

'Eh? Is this double glazing?'

'No,' the caller sighs, 'I am the guided instrument, the extension of God's hand.'

An involuntary shiver runs through me as I realise who is on the end of the line. I was waiting but I wasn't expecting.

'Is this who I think it is?' I ask timidly, feeling my stomach turn. 'Is this the ….'

'Yes Joseph.'

'The…'

'Yes.'

'The Prophet?'

'Yes Joseph. The Prophet.' he replies. I feel like I'm catching up on a conversation that has been going on without me.

'Piss off you nutter!' I shout down the phone. In some ways I've been waiting, having formulated all number of logical arguments to make this go away. This is the first that springs to mind. I lower the phone from my ear and move my finger towards the disconnect button.

'I can give you answers to all your questions Joseph,' The Prophet's voice travels through the air. Against every impulse my finger moves away from the button and I raise the phone to my ear again.

'What do you want with me?' I whisper with a quiver in my voice.

'Perhaps we should meet to discuss this further? Say eight o'clock, playground in the park?'

'Eight o'clock isn't good for me mate 'cause I'm not coming. I want you to leave me alone.'

'That of course is your choice but then I have already foreseen that you will be present. Do try not to be late Joseph, not for this,' he concludes, putting the phone down at the other end.

'Please don't do this to me,' I whisper but it's too late, there is no one left to hear.

My body hangs lifelessly, my mind running riot with endless questions, the circle relentlessly turning. It spins forever, maybe half an hour, maybe an eternity. It finally comes to a stop when the front door opens with its customary force and Danny returns, storming up the stairs, his steps resounding through the floor as he crosses the landing and the door flies open. As it does so it occurs to me that I've simply assumed it to be Danny. Maybe it's that maniac coming to scoop out my eyes with a spoon? Whilst I still have them, they search desperately for a weapon in the immediate area.

'Wahay!' Danny screams as he runs into the room. Of course it's fucking Danny; intruders tend not to be blatantly carrying a nine bar of opiumated hash in their hands.

'For fuck's sake man, don't you ever knock? You could have been a maniac come to scoop out my eyes with a spoon!'

'Don't be stupid Joe, it's only me. Although talking of body parts if you ever want to get rid of one your livers I've got a mate that can get you a good deal.'

'I've only got one liver you twat.'

'Eh, you sly old dog, how much did you get for the other one?' he asks.

Despite everything, a smile creeps across my face, even if he is a cretin.

'No, we've all only got one liver,' I try and explain patiently. 'Are you thinking of kidneys?' I ask, waiting for a remnant of intelligence to make a dramatic and welcome return.

'Anyway bollocks to that, I've got some of this opiumated hash, how much do you want?'

'I told you buddy I don't want any. I'm not smoking anymore.'

'You're fucking kidding me right? This stuff is rarer than rocking horse shit.'

'Danny,' I interrupt.

'Dude.' he replies as he takes his place on the end of the bed and starts to roll a joint.

'I need to tell you something, something that's happening to me. Something you might be able to help me with,' I announce. Christ, I have to tell someone. It's either Danny or the wardrobe and that wooden bastard already heard it earlier and wasn't much help then.

'Holy crap. Should I be scared? Is this a declaration of some sort?' Danny enquires.

'Piss off. Just listen.'

'Oh Christ. This isn't going to be another Beth story is it?'

'Just listen.'

And so I tell him. For every major point there is a tangent, and so the story never seems to end. And the story wouldn't be complete if I didn't mention Beth. Danny listens carefully as I get to the present day with the letter and the phone call

161

and everything in between. He moves from boredom to interest and then finally concern. I know I made the right choice now in telling him, at last someone understands. When I finally draw to a close Danny makes his one defining comment, delivered with up most sincerity and directness.

'You're a fucking fruitcake, pal.'

'What?'

'Yeah right, messages from some geezer called The Prophet and all that.'

'Honestly mate I know it sounds bizarre but I swear its true!'

'Alright then, so you're meeting this prophet guy at what, at eight o'clock?'

'Yeah, but I'm not going.'

'Why, 'cause you've made this all up, you nutter?'

'Danny just listen to me, I had my doubts. I thought I was losing it, maybe because I smoked too much and maybe because of those other things, but I'm sure of this.'

'You have to go. If you are imagining it, which I seriously suspect you are, then you can be proven right when no one turns up, no problemo. And in the unlikely scenario that your fucked imagination does muster someone up, then I'll tell you otherwise.'

'And what if it's real?' I ask.

'Then we fucking sort out Bible boy and tell him to fuck off, no worries.'

'I'm not going!' I protest.

'Look, you're not the first person to have a breakdown.'

'I'm not having a breakdown!' I counter.

'Well there's only one way to find out isn't there? What time, eight? Fuck, its half seven now. You must have been talking for bloody ages.'

'Even if I did go, which I'm not, I think he wants me to go alone.'

'What is this? A fucking kidnapping now? No way dude, I want to check this out, get your arse in gear Joe my boy, we're going biblical.'

Before I can answer, let alone reason with him, he is out of the room and crossing the landing. In reply I raise myself out of bed and search around for my shoes and then I'm ready. Maybe Danny's right, this needs to end here and now. I remember now the Prophet's own words.

Fate is in the choices we make and the choices that others make for us.

I'm going to make all the choices you will ever need Prophet.

'How long you going to take talking to your imaginary friend Joe?' Danny asks from across the landing.

'I dunno,' I answer. 'Why?

'Just wanted to know how much doobish I should take. Maybe a Henry?' he answers. I raise my eyebrows whilst shaking my head slowly, starting to have doubts whether this is a good idea after all.

As I sit on the side of the bed, Danny eventually returns. My first sight is one of total amazement as he stands before me dressed in full combat gear. In one hand is a recently lit joint, in the other a cricket bat. Across his face are two stripes of boot polish on either cheek. He has been waiting all his life for this moment, all those wasted years watching Vietnam films finally paying off.

'What the fuck?' I ask, as any sensible person would.

'What?'

'Why the fuck are you dressed like De Niro in The Deer Hunter?'

'Do you want this to be a professional operation or what?'

'Not with you dressed like a twat.'

'Hey he'll never see me coming dude,' he answers, his index fingers pointing towards me. The pose could easily be construed as the trademark of an ageing game show host. A

163

game show that you'd never want to go on, with a host on the lookout for gooks.

'Oh for fuck's sake come on then,' I concede, leading him out the door and conscious of the time remaining.

As I walk down the stairs with Danny following eagerly behind, he provides additional commentary.

'Anyway it was supposed to be Christopher Walken in The Deer Hunter.'

'With a cricket bat?' I ask.

'Oh fuck, I nearly left it here!'

Before I have even completed my cringing facial movements he has rushed back to my room and returned with three feet of English willow.

'Can't be too careful with these fucking imaginary Christians,' he adds as he pushes me out of the door, continuing to ask questions as we get in the car.

'Dude, you know my man down Loop Road?'

'Yeah,' I reply, already suspecting that I won't like the answer.

'He can get us some shooters if you want?'

After breathing in deeply I choose not to argue with him, let alone take him up on his offer. He quickly forgets this disturbing idea as he rifles through my CDs and proceeds to put on Paint it Black by The Rolling Stones.

'Maybe then I'll fade away and not have to face the facts,' Mick sings.

If only it were that easy Mick. We drive towards the truth.

Chapter 19

Available For Weddings, Bar Mitzvahs And Missions From God

I pull up in the car park not far from the playground, Danny temporarily lost in Empire State by Mercury Rev. The stereo suddenly stops, forcing my dear friend to return to reality, the most hated of environments. Leaving the car, Danny continues to half jog/half dance as the trumpet solo continues in his head. We make our way down the hill, past the sleeping ducks that fail to notice the drug addled moron walking beside me as if he were approaching the crease in 'Nam; cue Ride of the Valkyries. Finally we arrive at the playground which is bathed in a silvery grey hue delivered by an unenthusiastic moonlight. Five minutes till eight, five minutes until I can confirm whether I'm crazy or not.

'Get your arse on the see saw dude!' Danny shouts, his voice echoing across the playground as he runs across it.

'Danny for fuck's sake!' I shout after him before breaking into a reluctant jog to catch him up. 'Aren't you going to hide in some bushes or something?'

'Alright I'm going, happy you miserable git?' Danny replies. With some reluctance he gets off the see saw, the limb rising rapidly as he removes his weight. He trundles off in the direction of the bushes and clumsily falls into them. 'Just like watching Mia again,' Danny mutters loud enough for me to hear.

As Danny settles into a commando like position I move over to the swings and sit down. Despite the urge, I manage to refrain from kicking off. Some things are best left behind in childhood like so many other memories. In compromise I scrape my feet along the dry dusty ground as I lean back. Any attempts by Danny to remain inconspicuous are somewhat reduced as I hear the click of a lighter and notice the glowing tip of another joint on the go. It takes a few moments for the smell of dope to drift its way across the moonlit playground. I study the various entrances to the playground and through to the five-a-side pitches, briefly remembering my short lived career of one game in goal and twenty four goals conceded. He isn't here, and that can only mean one thing … play it cool Joseph, he's probably got delayed polishing up his spoon, it doesn't mean you're mad. I'm glad to see Danny taking his job a little more professionally now, the orange tip of the joint extinguished. He's ready, I'm ready, come on Prophet show yourself.

One minute past and no sign. Yet as I look up from my watch, I shudder as I see a dark figure walk into the playground, some distance away, near enough to make my left knee involuntarily shake. As he skirts around the perimeter, a very large dog leaps behind him in an excited state. He's probably delighted he's going to taste blood. The initial fear is that it's that bloke with the nose. But he had that shitty little dog didn't he? Maybe he has two dogs? Maybe it's a pincer movement? He continues to move alongside the bushes, putting distance between us. He is however moving towards Danny, stopping at his precise location. Should I use Danny taking the first attack as an opportunity to leg it? Just as I place my right leg on the ground to run the dog raises his in response, and begins to urinate. The stream of piss is perfectly illuminated by the lights from the five a side pitch and falls with a splashing sound exactly where I know my friend to be hiding. Despite this, he remains perfectly still, what a professional. The wind picks up out of nowhere and the chains of the unoccupied swing beside me rattle. Suddenly, the guy looks over, staring right bloody at me. As the moonlight catches his face, I can see he is 100% good old fashioned pikey. There is awkwardness as we exchange stares

166

but he looks away as the dog lowers his leg and runs towards the other exit. The geezer promptly follows, looking briefly again to make a note of my face so he can ring up CrimeWatch next week. Within seconds his form is enveloped in the darkness of the nearby trees as he follows his dog up the path. I'm expecting the Prophet and all I get is Mr Inconsiderate Bastard. Checking my watch again I see it is now five minutes past.

Come on Joe, get with the plot, it's a wind up and I'm stuck in a playground waiting for no one. A cloud passes over the moon and the darkness stretches out before me. I give one last look around the playground before deciding to head off, having being set up good and proper. Turning my head to the right…oh fuck! OH FUCK!

I shear rapidly to the left as I realise there is someone sitting on the swing next to me. There is someone sitting on the fucking swing next to me! Instead of running I feel my body tighten in anticipation of an attack, my heart feeling as if it's stopped. All I can seem to manage is an expulsion of profanity and blasphemy.

'Good evening Joseph. Apologies for my lateness. I had to determine whether the gentleman with the dog was a threat or just an unfortunate coincidence,' the stranger declares.

My only reply is to look upon his silhouette whilst breathing heavily to supplement the now rapid beating of my restarted heart. Where the hell did he come from?

'Please don't be concerned Joseph. I have no intention of hurting you.'

I force my breathing to become more controlled as I get a grip on the situation. I don't want to die like an idiot.

'Jesus, you scared the life out of me!' I exclaim in a voice full of fear, concerned that my vital organs will soon no longer be part of me.

'Well I apologise, but things are as they have to be,' the stranger replies.

The clouds part for a few brief moments so that the moonlight shines through. For the first time since his sudden and terrifying appearance I get a brief chance to study the man beside me. I was expecting a fat balding man, smoking roll-ups, a copy of the Racing Post under his arm and a nervous twitch. He is however at first impressions a touch older than me but immaculately presented in a smart casual suit, with a well groomed appearance. Perfectly sculpted hair adds to a handsome face, oddly familiar but new, as if I were looking at an old friend whilst drunk. It is this face that he now draws into his right hand, his finger and thumb gently pressing into the corners of his eyes whilst he breathes softly into his palm. This is my chance to escape.

Run Joseph. Run for your life!

Why aren't you running? Why are you still sitting here?

'The gentleman and his dog that have just passed through and left a present on your friend could have been one of them, we can't be too careful,' the stranger reveals, releasing his fingers as if emerging from a vision.

Shit! He knows about Danny. The maniac's sudden appearance must also have caught Danny unawares, who surely now is just waiting for the prime moment to make his move. 'I wouldn't worry about your friend Daniel, he fell asleep about ten minutes ago.'

I look at the Prophet who in turn looks back at me and I can see the truth in his eyes. It hardly comes as any great surprise that that useless fool has passed out due to excessive consumption of opiumated hash. I just hope Danny is happy when he has to identify the body.

'Just to make sure that we are on the same wavelength here pal, you are the, you know, the...' I ask, stuttering as I scan his darkened silhouette to see if a can catch a glint of a spoon about his person.

168

'Yes Joseph, I am the Prophet,' he whispers as if someone were listening.

Another cloud makes way and I take the opportunity to look at him again. God I know this guy from somewhere, he's so familiar.

'I recognise you from somewhere don't I?' I ask, trying to prolong my life for a few more seconds.

'The face of a friend?'

'No,' I reply, shaking my head, 'but I definitely know you from somewhere.'

'Well I do get around in my business,' the Prophet replies with a smile that could floor a thousand housewives. There's a brief suggestion at the back of my mind. I reason the facts, I do know this guy. The clue was in the statement; his business isn't just freaking people out, it's bloody television. The man sitting on the swing to my right is none other than the actor Jack Connolly. Fuck, Jack Connolly is sitting beside me and I didn't even notice.

'I do know you,' I exclaim rapidly, any vestige of decorum lost in the animation of my voice, 'You're Jack Connolly aren't you?'

'That's not really important at the moment, what is …..'

'The failed actor!' I interrupt in my excitement.

'My career isn't really important right now, what is important is …'

'The cocaine and brothels guy right? You're an absolute legend dude, you were always in the Sunday papers.'

'That was an unfortunate chapter,' Jack Connolly replies. Bloody hell, Jack Connolly sitting right beside me. Danny would love this, if he wasn't such a useless cretin.

'Sorry man, shouldn't really go into that,' I add, apologetically. Can't imagine he's too proud of that. Best to move on. 'I saw you do that Macbeth the Return on TV ages ago, not bad.'

169

'Well I do like to think that I brought a new dimension to the character,' Jack replies, full of pride.

'What you been doing with yourself? Haven't seen you on TV for ages.'

Suddenly Jack becomes all serious, his face that of stone.

'You do remember why you are here don't you?' he asks.

Of course! I can't believe I was so stupid. It all makes sense now. I must be on one of those hidden camera shows. I must admit I would never have thought that they would go as far as actually fucking someone up. Has television become so desperate nowadays that they are really going into so much background, so much detail?

'Dude it's alright, I've twigged what's going on,' I reply. 'This is one of those video shows. You know where you wind me up and then the bloke with the beard jumps out and I look all shocked and swear a lot.'

'No Joseph,' Jack replies, closing his eyes. 'This is a situation considerably more important than that.'

'Come on, where are the cameras?' I ask, detecting an involuntary twinge of desperation in my voice.

'Maybe I should explain,' Jack announces.

'Okay, fire away!' I reply. Hey, whatever works for these guys.

'Do you believe in God?' Jack asks.

'Say again?' I request because quite frankly I wasn't expecting that.

'Do you believe in God?' he asks again, slower this time.

'I would have to say I have no real opinion on the matter,' I answer, playing the game.

'So you're agnostic then?'

'No, I'm not afraid of going outside,' I reply, giving a little smile for the cameras to pick up on. 'Isn't this a bit high-brow for a camera show?'

'Let me ask you another question. Do you believe in science?'

170

'Yeah, of course.'

'And would you agree that science and religion are mutually exclusive?' Jack asks, suggestively raising his eyebrows.

'Eh?'

'What if science could prove the existence of a Creator?'

'Oh nuts, I've read about you lot. Are you going to start banging on about Martians in volcanoes and stuff?'

'Science Joseph, not Scientology. The study of material things, from the smallest sub-atomic particle to the universe as a whole.'

'Do you have a pamphlet on the subject?' I answer, smiling towards the bushes and the cameras within.

'Joseph, will you please stop smiling at bushes. I'm finding it a little unnerving.'

'Okay,' I answer with a smile, giving a sly wink toward the trees, they could be anywhere in this darkness.

'Science has traditionally viewed the laws of nature as coincident with existence. As such life is a result of certain properties of the universe. We exist because the conditions are right for us to do so.'

'You mean life has developed from slime, then monkeys and then us,' I reply. I'm coming across well I think, funny and clever.

'An abridged version of Darwinian Theory but for the moment all I want to do is demonstrate how science and a creator are not mutually exclusive.'

'Fill your boots Jack. I'm all ears.'

'Yes indeed,' Jack answers as if he knows something I don't. Judging by the way he is speaking, he probably knows a hell of a lot more than me. 'Are you familiar with gravity Joseph?'

'Umm, yes of course,' I reply in a dumbed down voice, giving a *what's up with this guy* shrug towards the path. Of course I've heard about it, the guy with the apple discovered it.

171

'And electromagnetism?'

'Electricity and magnets right?'

'Of sorts. Now do you know what deviation is allowed between the ratios of the two in the universe before life ceases to exist?'

'I must admit I didn't bring that information with me.'

'1 in 10 with 39 zeros after it.'

'Wow, that's huge!' I reply, not really understanding what he's talking about.

'It is far from huge Joseph. It's very small. Anything outside that deviation means the universe cannot exist. You play with the ratio even the slightest bit then you wouldn't be here, I wouldn't be here, and we definitely would not be having this conversation,' Jack states.

I can't quite believe we are having this conversation anyway. I don't talk about science very often and to my knowledge never before with a failed soap actor on a TV camera show. It's probably best to be honest here.

'I think you might be losing me a little,' I admit. 'Are you saying that this ratio thing between gravity and electrothingamajig ... '

'Electromagnetism.'

'That's the puppy. That the deviation allowed is so small that it's unlikely that the universe should exist at all?'

'Yes, but let's move on. Familiar with electrons and protons?'

'Yeah, I remember them from school,' I answer although truth be told, I've blocked out a lot of things that happened at school.

'Do you want to know the maximum deviation in their masses?' Jack offers, continuing without waiting for an answer. '1 in 10 to the power of 37.'

'Yeah, but ...'

'Expansion rate of the universe since the big bang? 1 in 10 to the power of 55.'

'That's very interesting but…'

'Mass of the universe as a whole? 1 in 10 to the power of 59.'

'But what about ...'

'Finally, the cosmological constant. One part in a trillion.'

'That sounds, um…'

'One part in a trillion followed by eight other trillions. That's 1 in 10 to the power of 120. Say by some bizarre chance the universe manages to have this precise value for its cosmological constant, what about all those other ratios? They have to be spot on as well.'

'Care to explain what this all means?' I ask, both in terms of what the hell he is talking about but more precisely what the hell this has to do with a TV show. I'm trying to conceal the nagging doubt that this is a bit more than a television thing. But it has to be.

'It means Joseph that if the creation of the universe was repeated trillions and trillions of times, you might just get lucky one time and get the right values for us to exist. Otherwise it's just a bunch of elements wandering around with nothing to do, if those elements are even allowed to form in the first place.'

'So we're lucky then?' I suggest, knowing the answer is going to be anything but easy.

'Luck is simply probability, or rather the lack of it, and improbability of these things suggests that we shouldn't be here at all. And even without knowing these things mankind has always sought an answer to his own mortality.'

'Religion right,' I answer confidently. It may take me a while Jack but I'm getting there.

'Yes, religion. Now consider what I have told you so far. The chances that those variables are spot on despite probability suggesting otherwise means that the universe can only be one thing, a designed universe with the sole purpose of allowing

173

life to exist. Therefore by default, someone or something must have designed it. Call that entity God, if you like. We are here because evolution has brought a certain species of animal to the point of understanding. Evolution could be considered an extension of God's hand.'

'It sounds reasonable I suppose,' I answer. 'If I'm getting all of this right, you're saying that those ratios and stuff proves the existence of God. But you mentioned evolution. I thought your gang weren't too hot on that idea.'

'Certainly there are some factions of the Church that believe that. But religion at its most basic level is faith in a creator.'

'So what's the problem? You're happy, they're happy, the big guy upstairs is happy,' I comment looking up towards the clouds, hoping the main man wasn't listening.

'That would be true if it weren't for one factor in the wonder of creation. Religion has stumbled on some truths, you might say. They consider the concepts of good and evil as having an ultimately divine source. Good and evil, just like matter and anti-matter, are two opposing forces brought into being at the start of creation.'

'A bit like the Force then?'

'Joseph, please...'

'Do I get a lightsaber?' I ask.

'Please be serious Joseph. It's an incredibly complicated issue.'

I'm willing to let my little joke go. I thought it was funny but I suppose there are more important issues to clear up, including proof.

'So why haven't I heard about these ratios and things before?' I ask, wondering what facts he will dazzle and confuse me with next.

Jack shifts his weight on the swing so that he can lean nearer to me.

'You haven't heard about them because you haven't been paying attention,' Jack whispers as if he's just disclosed some great secret.

'Okay, so you're into the science-vicar thing. What's this got to do with me?'

'Now that's the important part,' Jack comments, taking a deep breath before launching into another monologue.

'We're gonna be here a while aren't we?' I interrupt as the temptation gets too much and I let the swing gently move with its designed momentum.

'If you accept the concept of a designed universe then probability suggests that God is watching after rolling the die.'

'Okay,' I reply as the soles of my shoes scrape the dusty ground as I swing past Jack. I could really get some height with a push but I guess Jack won't be forthcoming. All I know is that the great Jack Connolly is sitting in a playground talking to me about science and religion and stuff. If this isn't a television show, and God knows what it is if it isn't, then why am I still sitting here? Perhaps I'm interested?

'Sooner or later the basic elements of the universe move towards complexity. You are simply the universe, expressing itself as a human for a little while.' Jack comments in an oscillating tone as I swing by on another pass.

'So what's your involvement in all this?' I ask, wanting him to get back to the crux of the story.

'Well' he begins, taking a moment to consider his story. 'Everything I have explained so far is simply conjecture. What is needed is evidence. Take me. Who am I Joseph?'

'Um, Jack Connolly.'

'To be precise I am Jack Connolly, the failed actor, victim of the tabloids, a washed up celebrity perhaps.'

'I read the odd thing,' I murmur, 'but what's this got to do with me?'

175

'Patience Joseph, we'll get to that. Now where was I?'

'How you ruined your career.'

'Oh yes, well as you know my sins are well documented and this is somewhat crucial to my position as the Prophet. You see it was important for me to fall before I got back up again, stronger and with purpose. I had to see both ends of the spectrum.'

'Impressive bit of falling though,' I interject whilst being unable to reconcile Jack Connolly and the Prophet being the same person.

'And then I found my true path,' Jack continues with a knowing nod of the head.

'Let me guess, you became a born again Christian, you aren't the first person to have done that you know.'

'Oh, I'm much more than that,' Jack replies with a smile that contains a hundred secrets.

'And what would that be? Is this where you tell me that as the Prophet you have a connection with God and ask me to give you all my money? Anything above a tenner might be a struggle.'

'I don't want your money Joseph.'

'Then I don't understand. What's this all about?'

'Simply put, God doesn't want to see his creation extinguished. He wants us to flourish, to understand further. Through me God has allowed sight beyond sight, the ability to see the future.'

'That must be a handy gift to have,' I reply with a degree of sarcasm that only the English can deliver out of disbelief. He was doing so well, now he's not.

'It is not for my benefit but for all of mankind. He has recognised my sins and allowed me to grow.'

'So shouldn't you be doing some gospel thing instead of talking to me in a playground?' I ask, knowing that if he thinks that I'm a prime subject for conversion then he is very sadly misinformed.

176

'My job is not to teach but protect.'

'Protect from whom?' I ask, scanning the perimeters to check for an army of zombies, just in case.

'Do you remember I was talking about electrons and protons?'

'Yeah.'

'Well, one cannot exist without the other. They achieve a positive and negative balance within the atom to achieve stability. That is the true nature of the universe, to achieve equilibrium.'

'Sounds fair.'

'On a grander scale, God has created these universal rules and so they must be obeyed. Therefore the ability to see the future is available to both sides. Not only good but also what you could consider evil.'

'I'd keep that under your hat if I were you,' I advise.

'Unfortunately, the power to see the future has also been discovered by one intent on evil. A man like me who walks with second sight.'

'And would this guy have big horns and a tail perhaps?' I speculate, shaking my hands in a mock trembling fashion.

'The Devil? Sorry to ruin one of your precious film genres for you but evil only really exists in the hearts of mankind.'

'So if it's not the devil, then who is it?'

'That I cannot tell you until you are ready, I'm afraid. All I can say is good versus evil is played out through the actions of man, life itself defining the struggle.'

'Oh come on!' I protest.

'Joseph,' Jack states in a raised voice to end my questions, 'when you are ready you will learn his name but we must first travel the long road ahead.'

'Man, you can't just build something like that up and not finish it.'

177

A silence descends between us, enough to convince me that he won't be disclosing his identity any time tonight.

'The question you should be asking is whether you believe?' Jack asks, eventually breaking the silence.

'I believe that your whole science and the universe thing could be true, but you've hardly convinced me that you can see the future. Let alone all this good versus evil stuff,' I answer, only now aware that I have let the swing stop and am sitting motionless.

'How would you like me to prove it?'

'Is Norwich City going to win the FA Cup this year?'

'No.'

'Well I could have told you that.'

'Third round again.'

'What else you got?'

'Well I could tell you that you are currently in a relationship with a girl who thinks you're called Bruce.'

'Come on, anyone could know that.'

'She doesn't.'

'Well apart from her, then.'

'I believe the love of your life Beth is getting married soon?'

'Yeah but that's not the future. Well it is, but anyone could have told you that.'

'Only I know that it won't work out between them.'

'Really?' I reply with genuine curiosity. Perhaps she never got over me? Perhaps there might be another chance?

'And no, she won't get back with you.'

'Well of course,' I reply, slightly disappointed.

'You will have proof Joseph. All I will say is that just as you need proof, I need to know that you will travel the path with me. Look for the opportunity, look for the choice.'

'Eh?'

'Proof of your conviction and the chance to redeem yourself against your sins.'

'Could you be more specific?'

178

'All I will say is that people just don't disappear down the side of kebab shops.'

'What the hell does that mean?'

'May I ask you a further question Joseph? Do you believe that this conversation is now purely for the benefit of a television show?'

'I guess not.' I answer truthfully. I'm not stupid. I know what's real and what's not.

'So you believe what I've told you?'

'It's possible but I don't see what it has to do with me.'

'It has everything to do with you, it is your destiny.'

'It is my destiny,' I laugh falsely, 'wasn't that a line in Return of the Jedi?'

'Why isn't it your destiny? Besides, He likes to work with people who have crossed the spectrum. I can vouch for that personally,' Jack replies and I suddenly feel very angry that he has questioned how I've lived my life. He may be right but it does nothing to stop the anger rising in me. Questions, answers, a lack of clarity. Sins, yes. But why now?

Calm down Joe.

No, don't calm down Joe. You've sat listening to this drivel long enough. I don't want to remember. This ends now.

'First I thought you were just a nutter pal, and then I find out you are Jack Connolly. Now I'm thinking you're Jack Connolly, well know television celebrity and newly discovered nutter.' I answer back forcefully. How dare he comment on my past! It's buried so deep, it's not hurting anyone but me.

'The world you are about to discover contains more than you and I,' Jack replies.

'Do you want my answer now?' I ask in a tone to illustrate I will tell him anyway.

'Answer to what?'

179

'Come on Jack. I thought you were all seeing. Don't you want to know if I'm in for the ride?'

'That wasn't my question Joseph but seeing as you brought it up, no.'

'You don't want to know?'

'I already know. I knew your answer even before I sat here beside you. You're scared. You're confused. You want to say yes but fear keeps getting in the way.'

'I'm not scared Jack. I just don't believe you,' I reply, smiling for his benefit only now.

'I know you don't believe me. Well not properly anyway. That is why we take steps together towards the chasm.'

'Actually, it's because you're a nutter.'

'I wouldn't dare over rule the gift of choice Joseph.'

'You are crazy aren't you?'

'Wait for the awakening Joseph. Learn, understand, then we shall speak again.'

'Why not speak now? I'm not going to change my mind.'

'Because our time for tonight is up Joseph.'

In the distance I hear a bark and I look in the direction of the trees. From out of the shadows I see the bloke and his huge dog, jogging towards us, along the long path. They are still some distance away but getting nearer.

'It's just that bloke again,' I comment to Jack.

Oh fuck! Oh fuck! Oh fuck! He isn't there. Jack Connolly was sitting right beside me and now … I could have only been looking away for a second. How did he do that?

The dog barks again in the distance. Jack did say that bloke was okay didn't he? Oh Christ, is it one of those guys he was talking about? It would explain Jack's sudden exit. But I don't believe do I? Oh Christ, I don't know what to believe anymore.

Move Joseph, move!

The barking seems to be getting louder now as I break into a sprint towards the exit. I have to get back to the car! I have to

180

get home and tell Danny … oh shit! That cretin is still in the bloody bushes.

As the barking increases exponentially I run to the spot where I last saw my friend and start to call his name hoarsely. After a few seconds of scrabbling around in the bushes I finally locate him, lying there fast asleep. It takes a few rough shakes of his shoulders before he starts to stir and as his eyes open you can see that he has forgotten how he got here.

'Danny we've got to go!'

'Where am I dude?'

'You're in the park mate, come on let's go, we haven't got much time!' I shout as the sound of the barking dog gets ever nearer.

'What the hell am I doing in the park?'

'Look…' I start before being interrupted.

'… at night?'

'I'll explain….'

'… in the bloody bushes!'

'Mate, we've got to get out of here!'

'And what the hell is that bloody smell?' he asks and for the first time I notice the smell of dogs piss.

'Danny come on let's go, we're in danger. You remember? You were in the bushes, lit a joint then fell asleep.'

'Oh shit dude I remember, did I fall asleep? Sorry matey must have been that joint. Fuck me, I've got to cut down.'

'Dude, listen to me. We have to go!' I say for what seems like the umpteenth time. I pull Danny out by his sleeve, stumbling out of the bushes and risking a look towards the path. The figure is less than a hundred metres behind, his dog some distance nearer in its eagerness to savage us. Danny takes this opportunity to attempt to light another pre-rolled joint. We don't have time for this for God's sake. Once clear of the bushes I pick up the pace and drag Danny behind me, coughing as he tries to keep up and smoke at the same time.

'Joe man, you really need a bath', Danny incorrectly surmises as I drag him away from likely death. I decline to answer as he joins me in a full blown sprint towards the exit. Through the gate ... Don't look back, pass the duck pond ... The sound of the dog barking further away now, up the hill ... Just the sound of our feet running now.

Once back at the car and at our respective sides we look at each other over the roof. As I fumble the key in the lock Danny speaks to me from across the car, in between frantic attempts to breathe.

'So did you meet your freaky figment of your imagination?' he asks between deep breaths.

'I'll tell you all about it on the way home,' I answer, my voice changing in its projection as I move from the open air to inside the car.

We drive quickly out of the park and I do indeed tell Danny all about it, about meeting the Prophet, about the bloke and his dog, everything. For most of it he just sits there and doesn't say a thing. He doesn't even ask why we are driving home with all the windows open on a bitterly cold night so that the inrushing air hurts my face. I imagine he thinks, and he's correct in part, that this is to try and flush out the smell of dog piss, although it is fair to say he has incorrectly determined the source. It is only when we pull up outside the house and I have finally finished my story that Danny makes his one contribution to the events of the evening.

'Fuck off, Jack bloody Connolly, you're off your bleeding head!'

Chapter 20

Seeking Illusion And Revenge On Planet Gong

I don't want to remember but I know I have to. It's the only way of understanding the images of life, flickering in front of my eyes. Images of the past, projected into the present.

Saturday, 2nd February, 1980

So Mum thinks it's more important to pick Sean up from Scout camp than to come and see me. Nice parents. Nice touch. That may leave me unloved this Saturday but I've got more than enough going on to fill the time.

There's no one in the common room, good. I'm sure they are all out with some proper parents. Collapsing into a chair and flicking on the television, the first channel is showing Porridge the movie. It's the scene where Fletcher, having accidentally escaped, is now trying to break back into prison. Good old Fletch, he's got an answer for everything and always comes out on top.

'Alright son, it's nearly time for Stage Two innit.'

Who said that? Of course! He's not the main guy, not even close but he's welcome to pop by.

'Hi Fletch,' I reply.

One minute Fletch is on screen, seconds later he is forming beside me, complete with massive stomach and prison uniform. Almost instantly he's complete and more than willing to talk.

'You know I remember when Mackay was due to be replaced by Napper Wainwright so I had to come up with a plan to get Mackay back,' Fletch recalls. Series two, episode three.

'I remember, you organised a riot to humiliate Wainwright and get Barraclough back at the same time,' I reply.

'That's right. Were you there?'

'Of course not, I'm only a kid Fletch.'

'Oh yes, seems just like yesterday.'

'Fletch,' I interrupt, trying to get his attention.

'Oh and then there was the time when I got Warren to steal the exam papers for Godber. He was dyslexic you know.' Series three, episode five.

'Fletch,' I say a little louder.

'Yes son?' he replies, his concentration now more directed.

'Tell me about Stage Two.'

'Not yet son, not yet. You've not finished Stage One yet. Anyway, you know that's for our friend to explain.'

'He won't tell me, not yet anyway. Come on, you can tell me. Stage One is all planned out, what's after?' I ask, impatiently.

'Stage One my boy, Stage One,' he repeats, adding a waggle of his index finger.

'Okay, but after that I'll need to know.'

'I know son, I don't doubt it,' Fletch replies. Why does Fletch talk like my dad sometimes?

'Oh okay,' I sigh, getting up from the chair. The sigh of resignation is for external effect. Inside, I'm a bag of nerves mixed with excitement and revenge.

I catch Fletch's image fading quickly as I make my way to the door. Perhaps he'll pop along later to see how it went. Perhaps he won't be the only one.

The Foundations

I walk the gardens looking for the one person that I know will still be around, the frozen grass underfoot crunching as it becomes the first victim of the day. Wrapping my parker jacket around me tightly, this is not entirely unlike a scene from a prison film. You know what, that Fletch is cleverer

184

than he looks. Rounding the bushes and on towards the lake, I go to the one place where he'll be. Like so many other two dimensional characters in this world, his actions are ridiculously predictable: same location, same toys. I allow myself some time to watch. It's a poor storyline he's got going involving numerous Star Wars figures and it doesn't take me long to tire of it. I step out from behind the bushes and make my presence known.

'Christmas!' I call softly.

Without even looking up, perhaps paralysed by fear, the storm troopers cease entering the AT-AT walker and the pursuing band of rebels, already heavily outnumbered, fail to take the advantage.

'Hello?' Jimmy Christmas replies, his voice full of fear.

'What are you up to?' I ask even though I don't care.

'Just waiting for some friends from the year above to join me,' he lies in return.

'Jimmy, I'm your only friend,' I announce with a sinister tone in my voice.

'No, no, they'll be here in a minute,' he replies, the desperation rising in his voice. You'll have to do better than that.

'Jimmy, I have a job for you.'

'I don't think I want to,' he replies, dismissing my request without reason, silly of him. 'I heard about what you did to that boy in your dorm. I don't think I want to be your friend.' You have to be impressed that he can sum up the courage as the Eric incident is now the stuff of school legend, despite Eric's ongoing recovery. Maybe Jimmy thinks he's safe hiding behind Carter's threat. If I'm involved in just one more incident then a fate worse than death awaits, apparently. A fate worse than this? Carter's wrong and so is Jimmy here.

'I don't think you understand,' I continue.

'Please, I don't want to do it!'

185

'Jimmy, it's not a request.'
'Please….'
Jimmy doesn't get to complete his sentence.

DO IT, DO IT NOW!

By the time my mind comprehends and observation has caught up with reality, I've pulled Jimmy to the side of the lake edge by the collar on his blazer. It's not a nice experience for him.

'I have a job for you Jimmy,' I say, pushing him onto his knees.

'Please, I can't swim!' he pleads. Swimming is the last thing he needs to do.

Grabbing hold of his hair I force his head forward with a satisfying degree of force, my own knees landing in the mud as I push his head under the water. The coldness of the lake chills my hand. After a few shocked seconds on his part he starts to show some spirit and fights back. In response I pull him out; obviously I don't want to kill him. His hair flops onto his forehead in thick sodden strands, unable to hold the water within. The brown filth from the lake drips down his forehead and into his eyes, accompanied by a frantic gasping for air. I don't bother to ask him if he has changed his mind just yet, best to get the point across. I push his head into the water again, deeper this time. The force is greater in magnitude than required, but the rage has me now. But it's changed. My guide has taught me to separate the rage from reality. It allows my mind to drift towards tonight's episode of Blake's Seven as the rage acts elsewhere. Sometime later I remember Jimmy. I pull his head back out, unsure of just how long it's been. I don't remember struggling but then again I wasn't really paying attention.

Nothing. Not a thing. Then ...

Jimmy shocks himself back to life and takes a deep breath. Good lad, last thing I want is you dying on me. As he attempts to refill his lungs I bend down and whisper in his ear.

'Are you going to do as you are told now?'

'Please no,' he answers, forcing out a hoarse whimper.

My response is instinctive. I begin to push his head down towards the water again.

'Anything, I'll do anything you want!' he cries in submission, trying to turn his head to the side, away from the water.

It's best to be sure. Forcing his head into the water once more, my movement is now purely functional. I only keep him under for a short while, just long enough to prove the point. I address him as I pull his head back out.

'I'm glad we understand each other, now this is what I want you to do.'

A musty smell of dust fills the air. As I walk past the deserted classrooms, pathetic artwork hangs from the walls, filling in time and space. There is something un-nerving about the rooms, as if recent history has passed them by. Given time I intend to change that. The school is deathly quiet, the sounds present only those belonging to my friends. They are here to help. The flight of stairs now in front of me leads down to the basement, an open invitation for anyone to just go down there. The darkness of the stairwell envelops me as I make my way down, into the dark heart of the school. It feels like I've gone further than I should have. I must press on, I've come too far. He expects. He knows the path ahead. Waiting at the bottom is a maze of doors. What horrors lie within?

The third door I try is locked. Locked is good, locked means something of value within. Yet it's certainly no problem for someone like me, especially when in possession of a set of keys stolen earlier from our half demented, fully stupid caretaker. The key turns with ease and the door swings open with a gentle push. The rush of air into the room is met by an expulsion of chemical aromas, combining to form an overpowering plastic smell. I step inside, the palm of my hand running against the wall until I find the metal casing of the light switch. The overhead light flickers before stuttering into life, the light falling onto the room, reluctant to disturb the threatening shadows that hide behind the many boxes and cabinets. Against the left hand wall are two bookcases, each shelf filled with various pots, each with congealed drips down the side. It takes less than a minute to find what I'm looking for. Good old zinc phosphide: solid, reliable, perfect for Stage One.

The End Game

Look at them, filing through the gates, coming back from afternoons with their parents. Treasure it; it's all you've got. We are nothing, get used to it. Your families are fleeing back in shame. What, didn't you realise? Shame. Well, come on in. Back to the real world, the real world with God's wrath within. In comes Dean. Come on in, Dean. There's Bobby. Don't be shy, welcome back. Look, there's Michael. No parental visit for you, I expect. I know what you've been up to. Off seeing that slapper, sorry, I meant your new girlfriend Julie from the nearby town? You have your fun. Please, I insist. Come one, come all to the end game, the spectacle is about to begin.

The outside world is replaced by routine. All prisoners must make their way to the canteen for dinner. Enjoy the slop we serve. Grow big and strong for your future criminal lives. And here I am, walking amongst you, through the double doors, joining the queue. There's Michael near the front, here's I am at the back. Just as you would expect, just as I planned. The dinners are served, the queue moves forward. Most evenings I

188

retreat to the back, hiding amongst the meek. Not tonight though, tonight sees the completion of Stage One in all its glory. As Michael, Dean and Bobby sit two tables ahead, I find the nearest available seat. The other members of my table are older boys, obviously displeased with my presence. There is danger here, but then there are also rewards. To my left, I see Jimmy, dinner in hand heading towards the central aisle. He passes Michael with his head down, just as he's been told. My attention returns to the table in front. I see Michael talking, the words incomprehensible but the response from his audience obvious and predicable. They are no doubt lapping up the stories about his sexual adventures with Julie the local slapper. Poor Julie, what have you become in the words of idiots? The moronic find it hilarious, actually making Dean drop his knife onto the table with a clatter. Not to be outdone, Bobby manages to stop eating for once in his miserable life to laugh alongside. Look at him, eating with his hands like a fucking animal. Now he's grasping the sausage in his chubby unwieldy claws, waving it about. Just eat the fucking thing Bobby. Oh, there it goes, shovelled into his mouth. Next come the chips, dropping them into his mouth from above, his head craned upwards. Here comes the other sausage, there it goes.

'Wait my lad, just wait,' Fletch whispers from across the table.

'Fletch, not now, I can't speak now,' I whisper in return. I look around the table to see the other boys staring at the weirdo. It's time to withdraw from the moment and await the conclusion.

'Oh God, I don't feel well,' mutters Bobby from below, his voice piercing the silence of the dorm. It's about bloody time, I've had to stay awake until one in the morning for this.

'Oh God, I feel well rough,' Bobby groans feebly again. I'm listening Bobby, but I think everyone else is asleep. They are

189

the only ones who are going to help you now. Even Eric is asleep and I know he does so reluctantly nowadays, almost as if he's scared of being in the same room as me.

Booby starts to make the most terrible sickening sounds, accompanied by the constant movement of limbs in an effort to fight the illness. It's enough to make the other members of the dorm stir. Wake up. You don't want to miss this.

'I don't feel right,' Bobby complains between heavy breaths.

'Shut up!' Michael shouts, the first to respond.

'You alright?' Dean asks with a touch more compassion.

Neither of them gets a response, aside from a repulsive gurgling sound. Yet it's enough to force a reluctant Dean out of his bunk to cross the room. I'm almost touched by his concern. Almost. Well at least until it's replaced by pure unbridled joy. I'm lying on my bed in silence, watching the scene develop below. Bobby turns towards Dean and sends a stream of vomit flying across the space between them. It hits Dean squarely on the chest, splattering his face as a Stage One bonus.

'What the fuck? Shit!' Dean shouts in a mixture of disgust and disbelief. It's not shit Dean, I thought you of all people would know that.

Bobby in turn collapses from his vomit projecting pose, his bulky frame making the bunk shudder as he crumples to the floor. A steady flow of puke drains from his mouth onto the wooden floor. Caught in the moonlight it would be beautiful if it weren't so disgusting.

'You fucking wanker!' Dean shouts, still struggling to comprehend events.

'Oh for fuck's sake!' Michael mutters reluctantly. With an obvious effort he gets out of his own bed to investigate. Go on Michael, see what I've done.

I look at both their faces and revel in the expressions of shock as they try to take it all in. It would seem that Bobby has also managed to shit himself in his bed. Stage One,

190

double bonus! Now look at those two idiots panic, I can hardly stop myself from laughing.

'What are you looking at you fucker?' Michael shouts at me, trying to solve the situation the only way he knows. What am I looking at? Why Michael, I'm looking at my creation.

Eric is despatched to get help. Bobby is far beyond help now but I decline to mention it. Minutes later, Eric returns with Carter, dressed in an old bastard's dressing gown. Like a true professional he assesses the situation before deciding what to do. With little fear of the vomit or for that matter the shit, he picks Bobby up in his arms, no mean feat in itself, and carries him out the door. I know he suspects, but he doesn't know a thing.

The Missing Bits

Jimmy's head had only just left the water when I began to tell him what exactly it was that I needed him to do. It wasn't quite how he was hoping to spend his life but every good visionary has his disciples and I have high hopes for Jimmy. You can't be the extension of God's hand without a little help now and again.

Whilst I was exploring in the darkness of the school's basement, searching for rat poison or zinc phosphide if you want to get technical, Jimmy was busy making a difficult decision. Does he tell those three fuckers my plan? Result: Punishment by my hand of the most significant type. He's already seen this part of me. Does he tell Carter of my plan? Result: See previous. Does he go through with what I have asked of him? Ah Jimmy, poor impressionable Jimmy, waiting at the gates for the target. Next comes the clever bit.

Eric understandably left the minute I arrived in the dorm. I'm surprised he's still here after our previous encounter but never underestimate the power of school budget cuts or couldn't-give-a-shit parenting. Besides, fights between pupils happen all the time, even if it was a touch one-sided. Once alone I retrieved a convincing portion of my Christmas money from the secret hiding place. Here I am, the money in one hand, rat poison in the other. Rat poison meet bank notes, bank notes meet rat poison, if you please. Satisfied with the result, I place them back in my not so secret hiding place this time. All I have to do is bide my time.

Jimmy meanwhile waits at the gate. Bobby is the first to arrive back, obviously his parents love him that little bit less than anyone else. Not that I include myself in that equation. He should count himself lucky. Well, not exactly lucky because Stage One is about to hit him with the full vengeance of God's wrath. Why Jimmy you may ask? Perhaps because he's good at drama? Maybe that makes him a good liar? No, it's simply because he's weak, susceptible to the script.

'Bobby. Morgan tried to drown me in the lake.'

'So? What the fuck do you expect me to do about it?' Bobby no doubt replied.

'I want someone to sort him out. It will be worth it. I know where he keeps the money he gets from his parents.'

'What? What the fuck did you say about money?' Bobby replies, bound by greed.

Bobby enters the dorm at the precise moment I'm hiding the money under the mattress. Of course I had held the same pose for over five minutes whilst waiting for him but he wasn't to know that. As he punches me to the floor I'm willing to take the pain in exchange for what he will receive in return. As I act the victim, he reaches under the mattress and takes the money, counting it a couple of times to allow the poison to pass onto his hands.

'Pleasure doing business with you Morgan,' Bobby sneers, stepping over me on the way to the door.

It certainly was Bobby, it certainly was.

192

Fast forward and I watch with interest as Bobby eats like a pig, just as expected. The poison moves from hands to food and in turn to the body.

Fast forward and Bobby is writhing in agony below me. A victim of a trap that even the Emperor, the dark lord of the Sith would have been proud of. Not that it's his doing, I have The Guide to thank for showing me the way.

Chapter 21

1970s Brazil vs Accrington Stanley

Two weeks ago you would have found me sitting in a playground talking to Jack Connolly. Jack bleeding Connolly, ha. But two weeks is a long time. I never came round to Danny's thinking on the matter. That night wasn't a figment of my imagination, I could have reached out and touched him if I had wanted to. He was real, no doubt about that. When I awoke the next morning, I gave it some thought over a cheeky joint. Who knows if Jack Connolly was telling the truth or not? The only person who could answer why Jack Connolly was in a playground talking a load of religious nonsense was the man himself and I suspect shortly after our meeting was being chased by men with big nets. Maybe scaring the crap out of people like me is the sort of thing he does after managing to scale the fence of the institution? And besides, did I or did I not tell him that I wasn't interested? Without a word he shot off, enough evidence in itself to suggest he got the point, either that or he was late for his medication. With the dilemma solved I felt a whole new life unfolding in front of me. It didn't involve washed up celebrity idiots, it didn't have anything to do with the past. I descended the stairs with a feeling of triumph and congratulation. Danny was already in the kitchen, ready to deliver tea and toast into my welcoming hand as if it were a trophy to my success. And then to work.

 For the first time since I had started my overly familiar office job I actually got in early. Granted, 8:50 am is not tremendously early but considering the events of the night before you had to admire dedication like that. As I sat down at my desk an unfamiliar energy surged through me. It felt like purpose, time to move onwards and upwards. First job was a large pile of paperwork which had built from the reasonable pile I had left the week before, when I was sort of sick. Oops, that's been there a while; off you go to the ~~paper shredder~~ *ahem* automatic filing machine. Not even the shockingly unprofessional entrance of the office twats could have diminished the progress being achieved by the hand of purpose.

'Alright Joe!' it began from Marshall, as if he hadn't seen me for weeks. In a way he hadn't, not this Joe anyway.

'Morning chaps,' I replied, emphasising the period of the day.

'How are things?' Marshall added, the friendliness in his voice indicating that he was building up to something.

'Not bad, not bad. Did you enjoy the Manor and Toad?' I asked. I wanted them to know that I was cleverer than them, although I don't know whether I'm happy or sad that they made it out okay.

'Shit man, where were you? We thought you were going down there with your lass,' Magilton piped in.

'Something came up. We just went for a couple of drinks and then back to hers,' I replied. There was no real need, especially not any gentlemanly one, to divulge our eventual destination but I couldn't help myself. I can't be held to account if they reached an incorrect conclusion. Just because nothing happened didn't make it a lie.

'Yeah man, we went down the murder pub. You know the landlord? He was well funny with us. It wouldn't surprise me if we were going to be his next victims. You could see it in his eyes.' Magilton continued, retelling a story which had no doubt grown in magnitude and danger each and every time he told it. I was grateful for the abridged version.

'Joe, wondered if you could help us out?' Marshall interjected. They *were* building up to something.

'Go ahead.'

'We were wondering if you and some mates wanted a game of footy?'

196

Why I gave the answer that I did remains a mystery.

'Yeah okay,' I heard my mouth saying, my brain being distracted by the euphoria of my new life. As we arranged the time and place, the magnitude of our likely loss grew in my head. Only now had my brain returned, a visitor to a chaotic scene.

'Why don't you ask your lass to come and watch, maybe we could all go for a drink afterwards,' Magilton added.

Suddenly their plan was all too transparent, to make me look a fool on the pitch in front of her. There was but one flaw in their plan however: I just wouldn't ask her to come. Think it through lads, think it through.

And that is what led me to make my second mistake of the day.

I met Danny outside the front doors at noon, grateful he wasn't smoking. In fact, he seemed much straighter than the norm, but conditioning conceals consumption. Heading for the town centre and into the crowds of suburbia we decided to go to lunch at BurgerWorld. As we entered I realised that I hadn't been in there for years, and for good reason.

'So what's the problem dude?' Danny asked as I took my seat opposite him by the window. As I delicately removed my MegaBurger from its wrapper, Danny was already devouring his MegaKids' meal.

'How good are you at football?' I enquired.

'Why do you ask?' he asked suspiciously.

'Just wondered if you fancied a game?'

'They'll chuck us out dude.'

'Not in here you Muppet. Next Wednesday down the leisure centre.'

'Okay, who we playing?'

'Those two twats from where I work, Marshall and Magilton?'

197

'Fuck man, two a side, that'll be hard, better have a rush goalie.'

'Any chance you could round up a few of your mates?' I requested, choosing to ignore his stupidity for the time being.

Danny proceeded to make a few calls on his phone and within a couple of minutes had rounded up three others, Pikey Chris, Squirrel and some bloke called Hamster. With our team assembled I wondered who the worst player would be. A self-confessed donkey or Danny and three of his mates whose marijuana consumption probably put them on the Mexican side of the border of asthma land.

'Dude, all sorted. So, had any calls from Jack Connolly this morning?' he asked in a drastic change of conversation.

'Nope, move on,' I answered. Jack Connolly was the past as I kept telling myself.

'No worries, just wondered if he fancied being a substitute,' Danny concluded.

Two week later, time having become fluid, we are sitting in a pub near the leisure centre with my third drink in hand, the pre-match warm up fully underway. This new pub is every bit as crappy as the Manor and Toad but it's just not the same. Say what you like about Ken, but he knew how to maintain an authentic degree of crappiness, even if it was between bouts of homicidal madness.

'You having another red wine you poof?' Pikey Chris shouts across the bar at me whilst ordering the round. I'd get up and give him a slap if he wasn't bigger than me.

'Get us a pint mate,' I shout back with volume. I'm having a pint; I'm one of the lads.

Pikey Chris returns to the table with the round and rejoins the ongoing debate that has been raging for the last half hour. The only thing agreed upon so far is that the Littlest Hobo would beat Lassie in a fight, probably using a knife he had hidden in

198

his unkempt coat. Being a scholar of the genre I would have to agree.

'No way was Doctor Who better than Blake's Seven,' I add to the ongoing topic.

'Shut up Joe, your mickey mouse Blake's Seven didn't even have a robotic dog. All the best sci-fi has robotic dogs: Doctor Who, Battlestar Galactica, ummm...' Danny comments, struggling to think of further examples.

The conversation continues with renewed vigour but my interest wanes as Marshall and Magilton walk into the pub. Through no great act of deduction I conclude the three guys trailing behind must be the remaining members of their team. The group heads straight for our table, spearheaded by the twats.

'Thought you might be getting some practice in,' Magilton says by way of introduction.

'Who are these twats?' Hamster asks.

'This is our opposition mate,' I clarify.

'Fucking hell, I thought we had a game on, I didn't realise we were playing in the fuckwit league,' Squirrel adds in support.

'Yeah, well we'll see later won't we,' one of Magilton's team retorts poorly.

'Why wait? How about a game of pool to warm up?' Danny asks to all present, rubbing his hands gleefully together. My housemate is many things but he doesn't take insults lying down, good man.

'Would love to, might as well get off to a winning start,' Magilton replies. Marshall on the other hand is strangely quiet on the matter, preferring to look around the pub for what would be the absent Mia. What a moron, she ain't coming pal.

'Well, come on, who's the best player you got?' Danny asks.

'Doesn't matter, any of us could beat you. Who fancies it? Marshy? Hols? Stewey? Ambro?' Magilton asks each of his compatriots in turn whilst presenting them to us as if in challenge.

'Don't matter what monkey you put up, my boy Joe here could beat any of you,' Danny replies. Selecting me seems a little foolish considering my rather dubious pool skills. Danny's four second memory strikes again.

'Why don't we make it more interesting?' Magilton bounces back, their dispute now more personal.

'Why not indeed? Let's call it a round for the winners.'

'You're on,' Magilton replies, accepting the bet.

As I search for a legitimate sounding reason that will allow someone else take my place, I'm pulled to my feet by Squirrel.

'Go on Joe, do this twat,' he whispers in my ear.

'So where's Mia then?' Marshall asks as we approach the table.

'She can't make it,' I reply, foiling his ill thought out plan.

'Yeah she can,' Danny states from behind.

'What do you mean?' I ask, craning my neck behind as momentum carries me forward.

'I saw her in town and asked if she wanted to come, said she would meet us down there,' he replies. Bastard!

Mere minutes later the game is over and Stewey is victorious. I have no sympathy for Danny as he solemnly makes his way to the bar to buy the round. Not only did he did put me in a position where losing was a strong possibility but he also inadvertently foiled my plan to foil Marshall's plan in turn. I don't want Mia to see me playing football; I want her to love me without any reservations.

The twats sit on the next table along and laugh with excessive force, drinking their drinks with the joy of winners. In the meantime Hamster goes to the bar and orders some tequila liveners for the game. Somehow I don't think they will help. And all in front of Mia, thanks Danny, thanks a lot.

As we approach the five a side pitch, I cast a look across to the playground and remember two weeks ago. I remember that I was scared. I remember that I got angry. But as I look across to the empty playground now, the swings remain motionless, the roundabout idle. Evidently Jack must be elsewhere tonight, scaring the shit out of some other poor sod. All of this passes from my mind as I step onto the pitch and a wealth of memories comes flooding back. I had almost forgotten that immortal day long ago when my defence failed me so badly and I sent my one-time team into relegation. I know the odds are against us, but with any luck the boots I brought today, the ones on special offer, might just be magical boots. What? They could be. Both teams take to their respective sides and as if on cue we remove our tops to reveal the strips beneath. The twats unveil their shallow allegiances as Juventus, Real Madrid, Liverpool, Chelsea and Manchester United. I catch a glimpse of malice pass in front of Danny's eyes as he notices the Manchester United kit in particular. My team unveil their own kit as if in response. The first is Squirrel, peeling his sweater off as he runs back to his territory in goal to reveal an Oldham top. Pikey Chris comes next, declaring his Crystal Palace affiliations. Hamster displays the red and white strip of our local team whereas Danny has opted for a more retro 1970s Holland top and judging by the state of it, it looks original. Either that or he's never washed it, possibly both. I take off my coat to reveal my own lurid yellow top and see a couple of guys, home and away alike, smile. Bastards, if yellow is good enough for Brazil it's good enough for me. We may not have won the World Cup but you'll never take our Milk Cup victory of 1986 away from us. And then coming round the corner I see her. She looks nice tonight, all wrapped up in her jumper, coat and scarf. Bollocks to this warming up business, I'm off to speak to my bird.

201

'Hiya honey,' I say, exiting the courts through the gate and jogging up to her. I'm slightly worried that I seem to already be out of breath but I do my best to conceal it as I come to a halt.

'Hello you!' she replies, her hands remaining firmly jammed into her warm pockets. It's not exactly a welcoming stance but I kiss her anyway. In return she kisses me back with passion and dare I say it, love. The kiss lingers until the jeering from my own team shatters the moment. I cast a quick look back at them, all four of them no longer warming up, now merely watching. Dirty perverts!

'Why didn't you invite me?' she asks.

'I didn't think this would be your thing.'

'You know I wouldn't pass up an opportunity to see you running around in your shorts,' she replies with a cheeky smile.

'Oi! You playing or not?' Hamster shouts.

'Got to go honey,' I say, giving her a quick kiss on the cheek before moving off. Mia slides into one of the seats at the side.

Before it all kicks off, my team and I take a few moments to consider our game plan, meticulously constructed by Danny.

'Right boys, this isn't just a game, this is about pride,' Danny exclaims as we loosely form a circle, moving excessively in an attempt to fight the cold.

'I reckon that if I play at the back then that will free you guys up front,' I suggest. My decision is both tactical and born from self-preservation. If I play in defence my poor fitness levels won't be as obvious.

'No way dude, I've got it all planned out,' Danny orders. 'You're going up front, Squirrel you're in goal naturally, I'll play defensive midfield, Hamster you're playing a floating role just behind Joe here, and Pikey you play at the back.'

'I dunno if I should be playing up front?' I ask, desperate not to be shown up.

202

'You the man Joseph, they won't see you coming,' Danny replies. He may actually be correct, they may not see me coming but only because I'll be on the side having a heart attack. Regardless I accept my role, knowing full well that if I get knackered or look bad I'll just fake an injury so I can go in goal.

'Okay let's go!' Danny shouts fiercely, met by an array of unenthusiastic sighs. The rest of the team have already accepted their fate and now I'm starting to have doubts myself.

I turn away from the group as Danny is swinging his elbows roughly to the sides of his chest whilst exhaling rapidly. Squirrel lurches in the direction of the goal, slouching with his hands in his pockets. Pikey Chris seems intent on staring at the ground whilst Hamster is nowhere to be seen, perhaps taking the definition of a free role literally and has now gone back to the pub. At the other end of the pitch the twats are undertaking a staggered choreography of jumping up and down in preparation. My God this is going to be embarrassing, and with that I would like to pass you over to our commentary team.

'Good evening and welcome to the local five-a-side pitches for a fascinating contest. It's safe to say there's no love lost between these two sides. Wouldn't you agree Ally?'

'Absolutely John.'

'Of course we are familiar with many of the players here tonight.'

'Who could forget the season that the twats won the Outer London amateur league by an astonishing twelve points. Looking at the other side one would say that they are somewhat untested as a team having never played together before tonight.'

'It will be a tough introduction to the game for these boys, although we are all of course familiar with the career of the forward for the underdogs.'

'Who could forget that momentous day John, young Joseph playing his one and only game in goal.'

'Somewhere in the order of twenty goals conceded if I remember correctly, Ally.'

'Looking at the crowd it is obvious they are supporting the underdogs here tonight.'

'A small but enthusiastic crowd indeed.'

'Aye, what a pretty lassie she is.'

'Looks like things are about to start here, Ally.'

'Very pretty indeed, lovely eyes.'

'Any final words Ally?'

'Very pretty indeed.'

'Ally?'

'Oh yes, sorry John, well I can't see any other outcome than a resounding victory for the twats.'

'I'm afraid to say that I would have to agree but you never know, after all anything can happen in a game of two halves.'

'Well John, it looks like things have started down there. And it's the twats that have kicked off. Straight away it looks like young Joseph is going to try and intercept Hols on the line.'

'All to no avail Ally, Hols has evaded Joseph's clumsy tackle and delivers a sweet ball back to Magilton, a real opportunity to break for the twats so early in the game.'

'Oooooh, a crunching tackle from Danny sending Magilton to the floor. That was harsh John.'

'Not a legal move surely but when you don't play with a referee then you expect such shenanigans. But wait, the ball has broken to Stewey who has a clear run on goal, he has to score! Stewey unleashes a fierce drive which is bound for the bottom corner.'

'My God, Squirrel pulls off a wonder save, smothering the ball!'

'What do you make of that Ally?'

'Ho ho ho, well he was certainly living up to his name there, he smothered the ball like a secret supply of nuts.'

'Yes Ally. Squirrel is in action again and kicks the ball far up-field hoping to find Joseph who is standing in a blatant offside position. Joseph takes the ball on his right foot and passes across the field to no one in particular, poor vision there, he didn't even look up. Ambro collects the ball comfortably but hang on ... '

'Oh no, John, the boy Danny has come in with a sliding tackle taking the ball and the player. Somehow it's made its way to Joseph who controls it this time and is clean through on goal!'

'Joseph.......'

'Yeeeeeessss, the underdogs take the lead, a good old fashioned toe punt which clips the inside of the post and goes in, magnificent!'

'A surprise lead here and it looks like Joseph is revelling in the moment as his team swamp him over by the corner flag.'

'Looks like the twats aren't impressed, there are some words being said about Danny's unorthodox play. Magilton has kicked the ball in dissent and it's sailed over the fence. Looks like he will have to go and get that back from the playground, John.'

'You would expect the twats to come back from this, wouldn't you Ally?'

'Absolutely John, I canny see them taking this lying down.'

'Magilton has returned with the ball and the twats have kicked off.'

'The underdogs are certainly protecting their lead well John, the twats have continued to probe but the fierce tackling of Danny and the numerous kicks by the underdogs over the fence have left the opposition infuriated.'

'Do you think that's deliberate time wasting Ally?'

205

Unfortunately not John. Most are shots.'

'Looks like another hoof from Hamster here.'

'Ock no, a complete slice of his boot and its gone like an Exocet missile.'

'Wait a minute Ally. The ball has hit Joseph on the back of the head whilst he wasn't watching and straight into the goal. I don't believe it!'

'The underdogs go 2-0 up. Well, I wouldn't have expected this, John.'

'Certainly not. Is this a case of underestimation by the twats, Ally?'

'It could be John, it could be.'

'Looks like the young lady in the crowd is particularly pleased that Joseph has scored again.'

'And she certainly is lovely, John.'

'Without a doubt Ally, and now she's signalling that half an hour has passed. Half time!'

'Joseph my boy, genius man, genius!' Danny exclaims, running up to me and launching into an uncharacteristic hug.

'Cheers buddy,' I reply. Be the Fonz even if in truth I want to run round the pitch screaming.

'Hamster, Pikey, Squirrel, nice work fellas!' Danny congratulates the others as they approach.

'Dude, that was a monster tackle on that twat!' Pikey comments as he accurately defines Danny's playing style.

'Which one?' Danny asks. Judging by the last half hour it isn't modesty, he's fouled everyone on the pitch so many times he can't remember.

'The one limping,' Hamster points out. We look over to confirm the fact but my attention is drawn elsewhere. There she is, Mia, looking angelic and beautiful in the passing glimpses allowed as the other team file past us, cursing us as they go. In between the passing of Magilton and Stewey I receive a shock when I see who is sitting beside her.

206

No! No bloody way! Jack Connolly, here, smiling.

Hols blocks my view for a second as he passes, get out the bloody way! When my line of sight is restored I see Jack again, faking a yawn and stretching his arm around Mia in the classic teenage cinema manoeuvre. That dirty bastard, I'm gonna bloody … shit get out the way Marshall you lanky git. I duck to the right to look around the twat but in the intervening seconds he's disappeared, leaving Mia sitting there alone. Where the bloody hell did he go? How does he do that? Come on Joe, calm down. You've been running around for half an hour. That and the tequila must have given you a rush of blood to the head or something. I've got to be sure though.

'Back in a bit lads,' I say, jogging over to her.

As I reach her, she smiles, her hair flowing magnificently in folds out from under her beanie hat. God, I love this girl. Calm down Joe or you'll have to play the second half with a woody.

'Hi,' I say, leaning across the railing to kiss her.

'Are you winning?' she asks nonchalantly in reply. Crap bags, I'm playing the game of my life and she wasn't watching.

'We're two nil up and I scored both,' I reply. Be the Fonz.

'Yeah I know silly, I was only joking. That second goal was somewhat creative.'

'Cheers honey!' I reply, my pride restored.

'First goal was good as well, apart from the fact that you were offside,' she comments. Beautiful, funny and knows the offside rule. Can't argue with that.

'Ah, only just,' I retort, waving my hands like a young Tommy Cooper. Of course my definition of *only just* covers about two metres.

'I think your friends are calling for you honey.'

To my disappointment I turn around to see this is true. Looks like the second half is about to kick off. But before I get a chance to go she pulls me across the railings, my arms trapped behind. She kisses me fiercely and taking my head in her hands she moves her mouth to my ear and whispers softly.

'Play like that again and you might get to celebrate tonight.'

Am I reading too much into this or are we going to have sex tonight? As she releases me I really don't know what to do next. I'm lost in a world that seems extremely unfamiliar.

'Football,' she comments as I remain in my vegetative state.

'Sorry?'

'You're playing football, remember?'

'Oh yeah of course.' I reply. With reluctance I turn and head back to the pitch, hoping dear God that my semi subsides before I get there. I turn and ask her one last question as I jog backwards.

'Mia? Was anyone sitting with you whilst you were watching the game?'

'Only some bloke with a hook nose,' she replies.

Calm down Joe, there could be thousands of people in this town with a nose like that. Remember, there is no Prophet, there are no agents of evil.

'Okay boys, no mercy alright. These guys are going down!' Danny shouts as I rejoin the team.

'Hurghhhhhhh!' Squirrel screams, fists clenched, in time with the beginning of the second half.

I put thoughts of Jack Connolly to the back of my mind for the time being, there's a game to be played.

'Welcome back for the second half of what promises to be a fascinating contest.'

'It certainly will John, can the twats make their way back into this game? Or with Joseph in such scintillating form can we expect more goals?'

'A fascinating half hour awaits.'

208

I think I lost count after I scored my fifth. I'm sure this won't be the greatest day of my life but for the time being I can't imagine anything feeling better.

'Ho ho ho, who'd have thought it eh John? The lovely lady has signalled for full time and we have seen a tremendous game here.'
'Completely against our predictions, Ally.'
'What will a result like this mean for the local teams John?'
'Well, a result like this will send reverberations around the Outer London Amateur league for sure.'
'It certainly will John.'
'Who stood out for you Ally?'
'Well you couldn't ignore the tremendous display of football from Joseph. We thought he would struggle against the well-disciplined and practised defence of the twats. In the end I don't think anyone would have expected him to get nine goals in his lone role up front.'
'Any final comments Ally?'
'I think the result speaks for itself, John.'
'And so with that we bid you farewell from the local five a side pitches.'

'What a game, what a game,' Pikey exclaims as I jog towards my team.
'You the man, Joseph you the man,' Squirrel contributes.
'Cheers lads!' I reply, struggling to contain my modesty.
'Well played lads, well played,' Danny comments casually as he arrives.
'You know what lads, I thought we might struggle in the second half but I think the turning point was …' I say before suspending my analysis when I see that the rest of them aren't that interested. Their new mission is for each of them to take a pre-rolled joint which Danny is handing out like cigars at the

birth of a baby. I decline the one offered to me, let's not forget Mia is waiting for me. Squirrel is the first to tilt his head back and blow the smoke dramatically into the cold air, mixing with the condensation of his own breath.

'Nice,' Hamster remarks as he repeats the action prior to bursting into a fit of coughing.

'Anyone fancy a pint?' Danny asks as he cups his hand round the lighter and lights his own.

'Yeah I'm in,' Pikey says.

'Me too,' Squirrel agrees.

'Hell yeah,' Hamster grunts.

'What about you, golden boy?' Danny asks. I like being called that.

'Can't do lads. Got an appointment with a young lady,' I reply. I'd love a pint but Mia, Joe, need I say more?

'You're bailing on us for a lass?' Squirrel asks.

'No fair play lads. Look at her, what would you choose?' Danny comments in support.

'Fair enough,' Hamster replies, nodding his head.

'Okay lads, have to catch up for a beer soon,' I suggest.

'Yeah,' one of them mutters. Beer is important, but joints come first.

The walk across to where Mia is sitting allows me a few moments to consider the game. I can't believe how good I was. I was doing tricks that I didn't even know I could do. I wasn't even knackered, maybe I'm not as unfit as I thought. To emphasise this, I sprint the remaining distance towards Mia. If she wanted to sleep with me after my first half performance then she couldn't fail to be impressed by the second. This could turn out to be a very good evening indeed and not a sign of Jack nutcase Connolly or anyone else for that matter in sight.

Chapter 22

Never Write Off The Voice Of Reason

'Come on, answer the phone,' Katie muttered under her breath for the fourth time. The previous three attempts had been met with a distinct lack of response, but Katie wasn't one to give up.

'What's the problem honey?' Harriet asked as she entered the front room, a cup of tea in one hand and a half closed book in the other, a finger marking her place.

'Joe. He won't answer his phone because he's in a strop.'

'You guys had an argument or something?'

'We had a fight over his girlfriend and now he won't speak to me.'

'Joe's got a girlfriend?' Harriet asked, over dramatically.

'Yeah, but he's an idiot. That's the forth bloody time I've tried.' Katie replied as a shudder ran through Harriet's body as she contemplated why he wouldn't answer.

'You don't think it's because he can't get to the phone?'

'Nah, he's just being a moron.'

'What if he's injured?' Harriet asked, panic in her voice. Katie registered the emotion but merely put it down to how Harriet viewed the world. She was the ultimate actress, living the life but over-compensating the role.

'He's not injured, he just won't accept when he's wrong.'

'I could go round and check to see if he's alright?'

'Asshole!' Katie declared with anger, slamming the phone down in defeat.

'I don't mind.'

'Don't worry about it,' Katie replied, regaining her softer side. 'I'll go round and sort it out.'

211

Ten minutes later and as Katie's car pulled away from the house, Harriet relaxed into the chair, a soft rounded smile forming on her lips.

The drive to Joe's house only took five minutes but it did allow Katie enough time to think. She couldn't deny the fact that Mia seemed nice enough, and she undoubtedly made Joe happy. Yet she didn't appear stupid, and so she must realise that Joe wasn't Bruce or Bruce wasn't Joe, whatever the insane arrangement was. If that's the case then what was her motivation? Money? Katie gave out a little chuckle to herself for even thinking this. Sex? Somehow she doubted that. Nutter? Now that made sense and given Joe's history, it wouldn't come as any great surprise. Katie knew that they had to be friends again, and once back in the fold she intended to watch Mia very closely indeed.

After pulling up outside Joe's house, Katie stared out of the car window and marvelled at its decrepit state. Finally and with a feeling of resignation, she got out of her car and walked towards the house, taking a careful route around the shopping trolley whilst avoiding the stinging nettles to the side.

'Why can't he live somewhere nice for a change?' Katie muttered under her breath as she manoeuvred her way around the obstacle course.

'Alright treacle?' Danny announced, opening the door in his dressing gown despite it being early evening. A number of thoughts entered Katie's mind, the majority of them unsavoury.

'Hi Danny, Is Joe in?'

'Sorry sweetheart, he's out with Mia. Want to come in?' Danny asked, easily one of the least appealing questions Katie had ever heard.

'No thanks, do you know where he went?'

212

'I think they probably went for a drink. They could be in The Manor and Toad. I hear it reopened today, new landlord and all.'

Even with a new landlord Katie doubted that that it would be any less crappy. Luckily there weren't many places left that could be used to impress in this town.

'What about that trendy bar we all went to?' Katie asked, thinking of Joe's attempt to project the image of a modern, stylish guy. Everything Bruce probably was and everything Joe definitely wasn't.

'Yeah, I suppose,' Danny replied.

'Well cheers anyway,' Katie replied, attempting to round off the conversation.

'Sure you don't want tea?' Danny enquired and unsurprisingly Katie wasn't the least bit tempted. For two main reasons: firstly she had heard about Danny's tea, secondly, she had heard about Danny.

'No thanks.'

'What about a drink?'

'I've got to get going I'm afraid,' Katie replied, casting a glance over her shoulder to convey a sense of urgency.

'What I meant was, would you like to … you know … go for a drink someday?' Danny stuttered. Katie in response looked at him and saw the vulnerability in his face.

'No thanks Danny, but thanks for asking,' she replied, smiling as she did so to project an image of sincerity.

'Okay, no problems. Of course I meant like, you know, the four of us, like last time,' Danny answered, trying desperately to dissipate the awkwardness.

'Of course,' Katie replied, assisting the escape plan as she backed down the path before getting into her car.

'So no chance of a shag then?' Danny whispered softly, hardly moving his lips.

It was just the sort of thing Danny would say, at least the Danny that he tried to portray. No one heard him. Certainly not Katie as she pulled away. Certainly not the shopping trolley as it dreamt of its long desired return to the supermarket. And certainly not the man who sat in the black car with tinted windows on the other side of the street. He had been listening intently to the exchange, confident that the Joe they were talking about was the one he had been told to find. The only thing left to do was coincidentally the part he enjoyed the most.

Chapter 23

Out Of The Frying Pan, Into The Wok

I'm in the same wine bar where four of us sat not so long ago, now only two remain. Soon it will be one. Where has my deception got me? Bloody nowhere, that's where. We've sat here for an eternity and we've completely failed to string a decent conversation together. I know what a strained conversation means, I've had enough practice.

'So ...' I ask with no particular topic in mind.

'So …' Mia replies, friendly but waiting for the moment.

'You look very nice tonight,' I whisper. When struggling I reach for unbridled flattery, compliments of the house. I may not be Bruce but I'll make damn sure I'm hard to dump. And to think less than an hour ago at the football I thought it was perfect between us.

'Thank you,' she replies, staring intently at the grain of the wooden table. She's not going for it. The compliment, the best one I had, bounces off her cold heart and flies off to find the others. Come on Joe, think! Say something.

My hands are in loose fists and I drum the joints of my little fingers against the table. If ever a sound was needed to heighten the silence then this was the one. But it's not over yet, I can save this. Bruce wouldn't give in so easily would he?

'So what do you fancy doing after?' I ask. Witty? No. Clever? No. First thing you thought of? Yes.

'What do you fancy?' Mia sighs in resignation.

Come on, give me something to work with here. I close my eyes and contemplate the situation in the darkness of my soul. I can't think of anything I've done wrong. I hate not knowing what she knows and what, probably, I should know too.

'Is there something you want to talk about?' I ask bravely.

The resulting silence is so noticeable it probably registered in Japan.

'This isn't really the place honey,' Mia replies after giving her response some thought. Of course I don't actually want to know. Who would? However, if we can't talk about anything else, we may as well talk about the inevitable. Once it's out in the open, I can start to fix it.

'Please,' I ask.

'It's us, Bruce,' she replies.

Here we go. I know the next bit. Oh Bruce, it's just not working. Oh Bruce, things have changed. Oh Bruce, I'm going to dance around the subject and pad out the reasons before delivering the terminal blow.

'Okay...' I reply timidly as if it were a great shock.

'It's us Bruce, I've been thinking.'

'Thinking about what?' I ask with the stupidest question of the night. Why do we ask such things? Is stupidity going to soften the blow any the less? Or do we have to be one hundred per cent certain that the maximum amount of pain equals maximum amount of understanding.

'You have to admit that things between us aren't quite the same as before,' Mia murmurs.

'Elaborate?' I ask, knowing full well why.

'Well, you've changed so drastically,' Mia comments.

'For example?' I question. It's a question that we both have the answer for but again it's a one sided knowledge as to why.

'Well, your friends for example. You never used to have friends like that,' Mia declares.

That's because, and I'm guessing here, Bruce never had friends like that. A drug dealer and a paranoid woman who keeps ringing me as I'm sat here (one thing at a time please Katie). Not exactly the ideal companions for the ideal man.

'And your job, why the sudden change?' she continues.

It hasn't changed, it never changes.

216

'And you, you seem so different.'

Okay I think I get the point now.

'Well, it has been a while,' I reply. I don't know how long a while has been? I can't live this lie anymore. I can't pretend to be Bruce because Bruce is seemingly nothing like me. Well what if Bruce wasn't me? Joe as Bruce seems to have failed, what about Joe as Joe? Can't get any worse can it?

'Mia,' I address her, my head bowed as I close my eyes and breathe in deeply. I'm unable to look her in the eye as I tell her the truth.

'What is it?' she asks, providing me with the one moment to deliver the ultimate line, the one thing that can save our relationship.

'I think it's about time I told you something,' I begin and a silence settles over the table before the horsemen come charging.

'Bruuuuuuce!' shouts a voice behind me. 'Bruce is that you? I don't believe it!'

Our attention is immediately shifted from the declaration never made. Before I even have time to consider whether this is a good or bad thing, two firm hands grab me from behind by the shoulders.

'Bloody hell Bruce what are you doing here?' the voice behind the hands asks.

'Hi' I reply nervously, looking first at what I can see of matey and then at Mia to see her reaction. If Bruce knows this guy then by default so must I.

'My God, Bruce! What are you doing in this shit hole of a town?'

'Oh well you know how these things work,' I reply, slipping back into my disguise as easily as ever. Suddenly my shoulders are released and Mr Mystery makes his way around the table. He looks at me as he moves and then at Mia. I recognise that look in his eyes.

217

'Hi,' he says to Mia as he takes in the vision before him.

'This is Mia' I begin, fighting the urge to kill him.

'Hi, I'm Rob,' he slimes towards my beautiful angel.

I'm more than grateful to know his name but I'm far from happy as they shake hands, the touch lingering a little too long for my liking.

'Hi,' she replies, letting her hand slip from his grasp. Good girl.

'Not *the* Mia?' Rob asks, turning his attention back to me. Don't look at me pal, how would I know?

'Bloody hell. This guy here never stopped talking about you when we used to hang out together,' Rob continues.

'Really?' Mia replies, acting all shy. Of course she knows. If I was Bruce, who I suppose I am, I wouldn't have shut up about her either.

'Yeah,' Rob states as if it was obvious, which of course it is.

'How long is it since you two have seen each other?' Mia asks.

'Dunno? Got to be …' I muse, taking the risk that Rob will finish the sentence.

'Got to be two years,' Rob interrupts upon my hesitation. Good lad, like a dream.

'That's great,' Mia says with a warming smile.

'You know I didn't think this boy would ever get over that incident, good to see you alright again,' Rob pipes up. Eh, what's this incident Rob? I don't know this bit.

'The incident?' Mia asks, looking at me inquisitively.

'Yeah, he must have told you about the incident?' Rob enquires. Rob, dear boy, I would have told her about the incident if I knew what the fuck you were talking about.

'I don't think so...' Mia replies, lost for the time being.

'The South America thing,' Rob expands.

'The South America thing?' asks Mia in return. What the hell is the South America thing?

218

'Yeah the South America thing,' Rob confirms. For God's sake Rob she doesn't know, just tell her.

'New one on me,' Mia affirms. Don't worry Mia, new one for me as well.

'Surely you must have told her about the whole South America hostage situation?' Rob asks. The … South ... American ... hostage ... situation? A voice in my head is chuckling mildly to itself, somewhere unknown.

'What's the South America …' Mia says, pausing before continuing with a sense of disbelief '...hostage situation?'

'Nothing,' I interrupt, a little too suddenly to seem natural. Every conversation has its truths, it really was nothing, at least to me.

'Nothing my arse!' Rob retorts, taking a seat without invitation on the sofa opposite to go into more detail. As he relaxes into his seat a feeling of panic floods my body. Suddenly the idea of being Bruce isn't very appealing.

'Tell me more,' Mia asks. Come on Mia, let the guy go.

'This man is a legend, saved all our arses,' Rob says as if a great weight had been lifted from him.

'How?' Mia asks as the worms in the can begin to warm up.

'Well,' Rob begins, and the floor is his. I have to let it roll as I have no other option.

'Bruce and I were trekking through the jungle right, South America and all that. There was huge group of us right, dunno fifteen, sixteen, something like that. One night we were all sitting round the camp fire in the jungle. With me?'

'Absolutely,' Mia confirms. I'm nodding my head in a calm collected fashion even though I'm anything but.

'We're all sitting there, right,' Rob continues, leaning forward with his open hands near his face, trying to recreate the scene. I have to stifle myself from saying 'go on.'

'All sitting there, complete darkness, beautiful stars,' Rob continues, looking up at the ceiling as if it were the night sky.

219

'Wow!' Mia adds in one of the rare pauses that Rob permits as he rattles through the story. My old friend is pressing his fingers to his temples now, suddenly he releases them, suspense instantly added to the story.

'Then from out of nowhere comes seven guys. All kitted up with machine guns and the like,' Rob adds and moves his hands in a flash to holding an imaginary machine gun.

'Anyway, these guys take us all hostage,' Rob continues, relaxing back into the chair, the master story-teller giving us a brief moment to catch our breath.

'Bruce, I didn't know,' Mia exclaims.

'So we're all held hostage, right,' Rob says, leaning forward in his chair to add an air of suspense and danger. Mia in response leans forward, great stuff this, great stuff.

'We're all marched off to this camp somewhere. You know, guns poking in our backs and all that, just to prove some political point or some bollocks like that.'

'So what happened?' Mia asks with genuine interest, luckily saying this as I open my mouth to say the same.

'Well. We're kept hostage for about two weeks and things aren't going so well. You know Bruce knows a bit of Spanish?'

'Yeah of course,' Mia replies. Judging by my own knowledge I'm not sure *where is the bar?* is appropriate here.

'Well Bruce starts picking up on little bits of information that the gang are talking about. Something to do with the government not listening to their demands.'

'Oh my God!' Mia blurts out in concern for her beloved Bruce.

'Even when he hears that they are going to kill one of the hostages to make people listen he doesn't say a word so as to not cause panic.'

As Rob continues with his monologue, Mia's response is to turn and smile at me sympathetically. I shrug as if it were nothing.

220

'At night when we sleep, these guerrilla guys take turns in watching us. But this one night...' Rob leans forward again to emphasise the climax of the story as Mia gives out a gasp. 'One of them falls asleep. Anyway I get woken up suddenly by Bruce here, pointing across to the sleeping guard and signalling that we should do something. Now I'll be honest here, I thought he was mental. But before I can signal to him not to do anything, Bruce is already moving across the clearing. He manoeuvres himself quietly around the back of this guy and does this thing on his neck, sort of like that Star Trek geezer. The guy goes down like a sack of shit and the machine gun drops from his grasp. Bruce here just calmly picks the gun up.'

You can feel the climax of this story building. I can feel it, Mia can feel it, and Rob knows it.

'So there are three guards left, all still asleep. Bruce here moves quietly towards one of the others. Suddenly he brings the butt of the gun down onto the back of his neck, you know like in the films and this guy just goes down,' Rob continues, repeating the action with his imaginary gun. 'The only thing is, it makes this dull sound and the two remaining guards start to wake. Before you know it, Bruce is on this other guy. Bang!' Rob brings the imaginary gun down again, 'one to go!'

What happens next Rob, what happens?

'What happens next Rob?' Mia asks.

'So the one guy remaining jumps up and starts shouting mad stuff in Spanish. He's waving his machine gun at all of us in turn, threatening us. Bruce is talking back to him in Spanish and I ain't got a bleeding clue what's going on. Suddenly the guard grabs a girl from the ground and he's holding her in front of him, pressing the gun against her temple or waving it at us or some other crazy shit. Suddenly the terrorist guy just falls to the ground as the sound of a shot, the loudest thing I

221

have ever heard, echoes round the clearing. Bruce here has shot this guy right between the eyes!' Rob announces, illustrating the point by pressing his two fingers into the centre of his forehead.

'Oh my God!' Mia says, looking at me once again.

What do I do? Do I smile? Do I frown? Being undecided I do nothing. My motionless face hopefully portrays a sense of a dark yet tortured history.

'So anyway,' Rob says wrapping up the story casually. 'We're all free, right, all thanks to this guy. Then Bruce leads us through the jungle for two days before we find our way out.'

'I never knew!' Mia gasps.

'Well you know I didn't want to make a big thing out of it,' I reply, the guilt almost too much to bear.

'You saved all those people and at such a sacrifice,' Mia replies and I can see that my worth is bang on top again. This is the Bruce she used to know.

'Damn right, he saved us all. I owe my life to this man,' Rob concludes. It was my pleasure Rob.

'Oh, Bruce!' Mia says and leans across the sofa and kisses me delicately with passion and understanding.

'So anyway, what are you doing back here, mate?' Rob asks.

'Well you know, it sort of freaked me out a bit,' I mutter, sharing my tormented soul. An ideal opportunity to justify why Bruce is now Joe even though I'm pretty sure this is a touch on the dodgy side. 'Just sort of wanted a normal life after that,' I lie. This is why I am different from Bruce, Mia. It's not because I'm not him, it's because I killed a man and that sort of thing can mess you up.

'It must have been horrible to have to hear that again,' Mia surmises and looks down to see my empty glass before declaring 'you need a drink.'

As she gets up for the bar she kisses me and I can tell that she loves Bruce again. Once she is gone I turn back to Rob on the

222

other side of the table and feel awkwardness by not knowing what to say to him.

'So what brings you here yourself?' I finally muster.

'What?'

'What are you doing here?' I repeat.

'What do you think I am doing here?' Rob states in a scornful voice.

'Did you come in with some mates?'

'No.'

'Just a quiet drink then?' I enquire. His response is one of contemptuous body language. Why are you being aggressive all of a sudden Rob? I saved your life, remember?

'Let's just cut the bollocks, Joseph,' Rob replies.

I must have misheard, I thought he called me Joseph.

'Sorry, not with you,' I reply out of defensive instinct. I'm beginning to feel like I am waking from a dream.

'What's wrong with you? Why are you pretending to be this Bruce guy?'

A feeling of panic floods through my body. Can I get out of this? Can I convince him? How did he know?

'Rob I am … '

'You can be yourself Joseph when she isn't here,' he interrupts.

I don't know how he knows the truth but I do know that he doesn't seem too happy about it. It's almost too much to think about.

'How did you know?' I reply timidly, admitting defeat under the weight of overwhelming evidence.

'Where do you want me to start?' he asks, not expecting a reply.

I may not be able to convince him I'm Bruce but it may be possible he won't tell Mia.

'Who are you then?' I ask, trying to get him on the defensive.

'Who am I? Who do you think I am?'

223

'Bruce's mate from the jungle?'

'No of course I'm not. I was making all that jungle shit up. I was sent to tell you something.'

'So you don't know Bruce?'

'Ain't got a clue. It's your deception pal, not mine. I was just helping you out before she dumped you.'

'She wasn't going to dump me!'

'Yeah right.'

'She wasn't,' I reiterate.

'And you could really save loads of people in a hostage situation,' Rob replies sarcastically.

'Are you going to tell her?' I ask with my best pleading voice.

'Of course not. Look, I may not like what you are doing here but we are on the same side remember,' Rob announces.

The same side? The only side I knew I was on was the one I didn't want to be on in the first place. How the hell has Jack Connolly got some other stupid bastard believing his crazy ramblings? Just in case I'm wrong I shrug my shoulders like an idiot.

'You do know the Prophet isn't exactly impressed by this whole Mia thing. But he knows he must tolerate certain things if you are indeed the one.'

'I don't know what he told you but …' I counter, oh shit, it is another Jack nutcase. 'I told him and I'll tell you, I'm not interested in your whole good versus evil thing,' I reply as confidently as possible. Rob however continues as if he hadn't even heard me.

'What's wrong with you Joseph, can't you get a girlfriend through conventional means?'

'Not really, no,' is my matter of fact reply.

I look across to the bar and can see Mia handing over the money to the barman. Rob sees it too, yet he doesn't seem to notice the pure white snow beginning to fall outside. As I sit here, either being beset by religious ideology or living the lie of a lifetime, the sight of snow reminds me of the past. I want to be outside and away from this, to feel the snow falling on me, cleansing my soul.

'Look, we don't have much time,' Rob cuts in. 'The Prophet says that something is going to happen, to do with proof of conviction. I'm just here to remind you about it as The Prophet knows that remembering things isn't one of your strong points.'

'What?'

'The Prophet says that when the moment arrives to prove which destiny you believe, do not hesitate.'

'What do you mean?'

'Dunno, I'm just the messenger, ain't I. Well, not The Messenger obviously, he couldn't come because he's looking after his mum tonight.'

'What am I supposed to do?' I ask.

'Look pal, do what you have to do and everyone will be happy,' Rob delights in telling me as if it were the easiest thing in the world. How can it be, Rob? I don't know what I have to do, when I have to do it and which world I'm even occupying in the first place.

As Mia comes back to the table, Rob changes from religious nutter back into his original character.

'Sorry treacle, got to go,' he speaks, rising from the chair.

'Oh okay Rob. I was hoping you could tell me more about Bruce.'

'Maybe another time, eh.'

And with that he is gone. All that is left is Mia, Bruce, a well delivered but ultimately complicated lie and yet another unresolved situation for Bruce's alter-ego.

'So was all that true?' Mia asks.

'Yeah, but I don't really like talking about it.'

'I understand honey,' she says and leans across to kiss me passionately. Everything she needs to say and understand is in

225

that kiss, from sympathy to a burning desire to help me through this terrible mental conflict. Never underestimate the power of wanting to believe, both for Mia and myself. Situation restored. All units stand down.

Conversation from this point onward flows. God I love this girl. So does Bruce, so does everyone she seems to meet, but I got here first and I refuse to give her up. A few drinks later we can both tell what we're both thinking. All in one night the situation had turned from hope to hopeless and then back again. It's obvious what is needed, the ultimate understanding, the final connection. Bruce is about to get his reward for saving all those people.

Chapter 24

An Age Of Reason Suspended For The Chemical Generation

Stepping out onto the street with a sense of anticipation, I wonder what sex will finally be like for us? Mia wraps her thick scarf around her tender beautiful neck as I look up at the sky and watch the snow fall towards me, as if the stars were embracing us. Mia slips her arm alongside mine and we take our first steps into the layer that has settled. For this time of night there are still a few people about, hardly even noticing the wonder around them. Mia and I know how special this is, the defining moment in every relationship when you both realise that you are now one.

'Shall we build a snowman?' I ask. There isn't enough snow but this is what young couples in love do.

'Don't be silly honey, there's not enough snow.'

'How about a snowball fight then?'

'How old are you eh?' Mia asks with a cheeky smile. Come on Mia, that's the sort of thing you do with your bird in the snow, feel the connection, feel the love.

'Hang on,' Mia responds as she releases my arm and crouches down to do up her laces. It's not quite the dream, maybe there won't be a snowman, maybe there won't be a snowball fight but pretty soon there will be sex and that's alright with me.

'Baby, why don't we go back to yours?' I ask hopefully as my gaze takes in the beauty of the winter world ahead of me.

With no warning a snowball hits me between the neck and hair, the coldness making me draw my shoulders up in reflex. I turn around defensively to see Mia standing up again with a look so innocent her guilt is obvious.

'You!' I reply with a smile on my face.

'Wasn't me!' she replies, looking so innocent, looking so in love.

'Right,' I reply with friendly determination. I crouch down and take a pile of snow, shaping it into a rough ball, the coldness just enough for my hands to bear. As I do so Mia backs away a couple of steps, vainly protesting her innocence. I toss the snowball a few inches into the air and then back into my hand. I seem too close to throw it at her, not that that stopped her, so I opt for selective placement somewhere about her person. Mia guesses my plan instantly, benefiting from our connection just in time. She backs away to mid-range, far enough away to avoid a Joe lunge, not nearly far enough away for a launch. I laugh out loud, unable to contain the joy that floods my heart.

And then it stops.

A hoarse voice echoes across the street. Turning in its direction we both see a tramp, the same nutter tramp that accosted me outside the wine bar when we first met. He stumbles across the road towards us, rambling.

'Pal, spare some change for a cup of tea?' the mad tramp asks. His definition of tea may actually be extra strength lager but it is snowing and we are in love. I can spare him that and so fumble in my pocket for some change.

'No problem,' I reply, getting my response in early and taking a step towards him so he doesn't bother us for long.

'You're a star,' the tramp says as he gets closer. Will you just hurry up and leave us alone.

What happens next doesn't happen in slow motion. Time, I realise, is uniform, it's just your perception of its passing. It's the sound of the car engine I hear first, then the sliding of the wheels on the snowy road and finally the horn as the car slides out of control. Unfortunately, it is the same bit of road that the tramp is currently occupying. As I hear Mia gasp to the side of me, the tramp doesn't move, he just stops dead,

228

looking at the forthcoming horror. Move you stupid fucker, move!

Don't hesitate Joe, do it.

But …….

Joe!

I can't.

Bruce!

Bruce isn't here right now.

I don't want to watch but I can't help it. My eyes remain open, my mind long since gone into observation mode only. And then just as quickly, my comatose state is broken as I feel the air move against my face, my body being jolted forward. Am I moving? Am I going to save him? No! The feeling of adrenalin without thought shoots off into a cloud of incompetence as I see the reason for my movement. From my right comes a blurred figure dressed in what seems like a beige raincoat, moving with speed into the road. As my body tenses in anticipation of the result, the mystery figure with the dramatic entrance grabs the tramp around the chest. They turn. They fly. To the sceptic you would only see a tremendous jump, but I know what I see. They fly! The tramp's saviour takes them to the side of the road as a combined bundle. After the car has careered past, the scene is revealed. They made it. The tramp's saviour is already getting to his feet, brushing down his raincoat and moving into the shadows so that his face becomes hidden. Move into the light my friend, be the hero. If it wasn't for him then the tramp would be dead. I look up the road to see the car turning the corner at speed, bastard didn't even stop. Mia joins me at my side and I can sense the overwhelming relief that she feels also. As the tramp starts to throw up in the gutter the hero directs his gaze towards me. Not at everyone, not even at Mia and me. He looks straight at me and all I see are eyes that pierce deep into my soul. With one look he knows everything,

229

all because I did nothing, all because nothing was the easy option. And then just as quickly the look is broken.

Like a rocket he is away, running from the scene, away from the crowds. Mia breaks my daze by dragging me across the street towards the tramp as he wipes his mouth of stray vomit on his sleeve. At the same time another onlooker arrives, another useless bastard who didn't do a thing.

'Are you okay?' Mia asks the tramp frantically, standing a good two feet clear of any potential trajectory.

'I fooking luv you pal,' the tramp replies as he rolls onto his back.

'Did you see that jump? It was like he was flying!' Newly arrived matey asks.

'Yeah, it was a pretty good jump,' I reply, knowing what I saw and what I say are two completely different things.

'Where did the guy go?' matey asks as if he wants his autograph.

'I don't know, he just ran away,' I reply.

'Bloody hell, do you think we should go and see if he's alright?'

'Yeah I think we should,' I confirm. My reasons for catching him up have a deeper purpose. Looking up the street I can see the hero's pace falling to a gentle jog some distance ahead.

'Come on then,' my acquaintance orders and starts to run at speed after him.

'Mia, help this guy, I'll be back in a bit,' I announce.

Before I even know what I'm doing, I'm running catch up, first to matey and then to the hero in the distance. We are running at an unrelenting speed, darting in and amongst the scattered crowds who remain dazed by events. As we get within twenty metres he turns and sees us bearing down on him. Suddenly and without question he breaks into a run again, accelerating to a sprint in seconds. The speed he quickly builds is staggering and is already putting distance between us. Why is he running away from us? Why won't he

230

wait for me? I have questions I need to ask. I'm struggling to keep up with matey and he in turn is struggling to keep up with the tramp's rescuer. Without warning the hero darts round a corner and into a side alleyway at what must be an instant ninety degree turn. Matey and I are soon at the entrance to the alleyway ourselves and slow down to make the turn.

The alleyway is illuminated from the light inside the adjacent shop, shining through the frosted side windows. The smell of piss and something I can't quite identify is overpowering, the light is unforgiving to every nook and cranny of the narrow alleyway. In amongst the boxes and large industrial dustbins, there is no sign of our quest, not anywhere. There's no way he could have escaped from here, I didn't see him come back out and there are no doors to which he could make an escape. The alleyway is bounded on all sides by the tall buildings which surround it. There is no escape. There is no frigging escape.

'Hello?' my companion shouts at a volume more than sufficient in such a confined space.

'Hello!' I shout at an equal volume.

'Where is he?'

'I dunno, did you see him come out?' I ask.

'No way, he came in here. I saw him,' my companion insists. I would have to agree.

'Then where is he?' I ask, desperate for some form of answer.

'I have no idea. Still if the bloke doesn't want to be found, so be it. Let's get back to the accident and see if the tramp's okay,'

It is only as I start to leave that I notice a scattering of something near one of the bins.

'What's that?' matey asks as he notices the same.

'What's what?'

'There by the bin?' he asks, pointing towards it.

We both move closer and as I do so I finally recognise the smell that I first noticed but couldn't identify: it's the smell of meat. I look back to see the rotating agglomeration of reprocessed lamb in the window of the kebab shop.

'Fucking hell!' matey exclaims and in response I take in the sight before me. There are feathers everywhere, glimmering like silver in the artificial light.

'Oh shit,' I mutter.

'You don't think... you know?' Matey asks.

'I don't know what to think any more,' I whisper under my breath.

Both my companion and I exchange a look. I can see in his eyes how he is already formulating what he's going to say. He's seen a guy fly. He's seen a guy disappear, leaving behind only an array of feathers. He's seen what he thinks is a miracle. The story has already formed and he will do his best to convince everyone of what he has seen here. I would have to agree with his rather obvious conclusion, however in my case I think I may know a bit more of the story than my friend here.

Chapter 25

He's A Complicated Sergeant But No One Understands Him But His Inspector

Any other day, the sergeant would have parked his car outside the Inspector's house with a feeling of dread and resignation. Another day in Suburbia, another day in lateral law enforcement. However, last night and today hadn't been like before. Walker was now inspired to look upon the Inspector's dilapidated house with dreams of potential. He could really do something with a house like this. No, correction; they could really do something with a house like this. They would clear away the crap, paint it, have a nice garden, fill it with stylish furniture, anything and everything to erase the history of the previous owner. It would be a house filled with little touches that only two people in love could provide. Give it a couple of years and some children would come along, hopefully with her beauty and his intelligence.

The sergeant gathered himself, unable to conceal a broad smile as he made his way from the car and up the path, forcing the snow underfoot into a grey sludge. As he rang the doorbell, Walker pondered a future where he would be painting a door like this. She would probably bring him a cup of tea, not because he was thirsty but because she loved him.

'It's about time you got here,' Polston commented as he opened the door to his subordinate in a tweed jacket and elasticated trousers straight from the back pages of the Daily Mail.

'Sorry boss,' Walker replied, stepping uninvited into the house.

'So what the hell is going on? What's so important that the chief inspector makes you come and pick me up on my day

233

off?' Polston asked gruffly as he made his way into the lounge.

'Haven't you seen the local news?' Walker asked. Callahan idly stood up on the sofa and began to growl at the intruder.

'This morning? No I was doing something else,' Polston replied, neglecting to mention that *something else* had been Trisha on the other channel while indulging in one of his other favourite past times.

'Boss, it's all over the local news!'

'What is, Walker?' Polston asked, irritated that Walker seemed to know something he didn't.

'Well boss, there was, how can I say this, a sighting of an angel in town last night.'

'A what?'

'An angel boss, you know one of those guys from heaven.'

'Yes Walker, I know what an angel is!'

'By the kebab shop.'

'And who saw this angel? Junkies, drunks?'

'Well, one of the witnesses was a tramp. He believes this angel saved his life. Asides from him there are over ten witnesses so far. Most of them were people in the street but also a few have made statements from the wine bar.'

'So let me get this right, an angel saved a tramps life? A tramp is the main witness?'

'I believe so boss.'

'This is unbelievable!' Polston clamoured. 'And where is this angel now?'

'He ran away. Some witnesses chased him but he disappeared down the side of the kebab shop.'

'He ran away?' Polston enquired mockingly.

'Get this boss, they found a pile of feathers where he flew away.'

'Where he flew away?' Polston asked, heightening his condescending tone. 'This is a joke right?'

234

'The chief inspector doesn't think so boss. He asked CID to investigate immediately. I hear the media attention down at the station has been unbelievable.'

'Oh for Christ's sake, it's probably bloody students. I'm going to get my jacket from upstairs. Don't touch anything,' Polston ordered.

The inspector left the room and made his way up the stairs, convinced that his stern tone was enough to prevent the sergeant snooping around and finding his cupboard of videos.

As Walker heard Polston walk across the landing he seized the opportunity at hand. He removed a bone from his pocket and as the aroma drifted across the room, Callahan's distrust of the big nosed man gave way to a thousand years of instinct: he scurried across the room without a second thought. As he got within a foot of the sergeant (or to give its technical term: striking distance), Walker lashed out with his foot. Callahan came to a halt near to the other end of the coffee table, sufficient distance for Walker to make his exit as revenge filled the small dog's mind. Closing the door behind him the sergeant delighted in hearing the soft thud of dog colliding with wood.

While we wait for the inspector to return we can revisit the life of Sergeant Walker as part of our ongoing documentary Super Sevens.

Year 0

Just born, we find Mr and Mrs Walker cradling the infant Lionel Agnes Walker as we begin to follow him throughout his life at seven year intervals.

'So, Mrs Walker, is motherhood everything you expected?'

'To be honest, I've found it difficult. He seems to cry an awful lot.'

'And what about you, Mr Walker?'

235

'Crikey, have you seen that nose? Are you sure he's mine Marjorie?'

Year 7

At seven years old, we find the young Lionel Walker sitting on his own in a playground.

'So, Lionel, what do you want to be when you grow up?'

'I'm going to be a detective, the greatest detective the world has ever seen!'

'Do you think you'll be well suited to a life in the police force?'

'Well I already have a list of people I'm going to put in prison.'

'And what have they done?'

'Does it matter?'

Year 14

At fourteen years old we find Lionel Walker on prefect duty at his school.

'Lionel, how are you enjoying your teenage years?'

'Well, I haven't got a girlfriend yet.'

'And how does that make you feel?'

'It's okay. I have my job as a prefect to keep me busy. I'm currently undertaking a mail order course on advanced prefect skills.'

'And when you leave school, do you still wish to join the police force?'

'Absolutely! I'm going to apply at the first opportunity. I want to be an inspector by the time I'm 25. I call it my master plan.'

Year 21

At twenty one years old we find Lionel working as a road sweeper.

'So Lionel, can we ask how life is at twenty one?'

'Actually, it's quite rewarding. I work outdoors and I can take my broom home at night.'

'And what about the career in the police force? Are you still trying to get in?'

'Yes, I'm trying again next week.'

'And are you confident this time?'

'Absolutely. I'm applying for the Goodison police force. I hear they have a severe shortage of officers.'

'And what about romance? Do you have a girlfriend yet?'

'I haven't got time for that. I'm just concentrating on my career.'

Year 28

At twenty eight years old we find Lionel fulfilling his dream at Goodison police force.

'So, Lionel, you have finally achieved your dream.'

'Yes, I've been here six years now. I'm still a constable but I'm sure promotion is just around the corner.'

'And is working in the lost property section how you imagined a career in law enforcement?'

'Well it's certainly an unorthodox route to the top but I'm convinced things will turn out okay.'

'And what of romance?'

'There's a Constable Fox, she's just arrived. I'm thinking of asking her out, I'm pretty sure she'll say yes.'

Year 35

At thirty five years old we find Lionel working in CID at Goodison police force.

'So Lionel, we see you've moved departments.'

'Yes, there was a clerical error which it turns out couldn't be rectified for procedural reasons. So, here I am.'

'And what does the future hold?'

237

'I think they are really impressed with my work. So much so, they have even offered me a promotion to sergeant if I agree to move to another police station.'

'And may we ask what happened with Constable Fox?'

'This interview is over. I have nothing more to say.'

Year 42

At forty two years old we find Lionel sitting in his car outside a wine bar, watching a suspect having a conversation with a young woman and another gentleman who is talking about the jungle a lot. Unfortunately Lionel has declined to be involved in the documentary at this stage and so we will respect his wishes for privacy.

As Walker waited, watching Joe and Mia through the window, lingering doubts questioned whether there might be a conspiracy at work here. *'But then maybe there is!'* his brain shouted back at its own rebellious parts. After all, Walker speculated, why else would she be going out with a guy like that? He chose to ignore the idea that they didn't go out with guys like him also. Snow began to fall heavily onto the street and settle on the Sergeant's car as Walker muttered to himself.

'Having a nice little chat are we Joseph? Now she's gone to the bar. What kind of man are you Joseph, not getting the round in ... You don't know who you're messing with here ... No, stop kissing. Please stop. Sweetheart, please … '

The weight of his anger grew stronger as Joe and Mia made their way out of the bar and into the snow. As they kissed again he could hardly contain himself.

'Please darling, stop kissing him. Fight his powers. I know you can do it.'

As they played in the snow Walker's hand involuntarily moved towards the ignition. For a moment it all made perfect sense. An accident, or so it would seem, as his car careered

238

onto the pavement, problem solved. Simple enough to explain if he got caught, the snow, a dreadful error, something like that. Yeah, he would probably go down, but he would be free one day. Was it worth the price? Prison in return for justice as it should be, the criminal gone forever and his love on the outside waiting for her hero. His body tightened as the demons inside churned up his sense of morality, the fire growing in his stomach and the eyes glazing over as a new Walker emerged to replace the old. His fingers gripped the key, his foot hovering over the accelerator.

Then something unexpected happened. A small voice at the back of his mind spoke with clarity through the rage. It was reason, waiting until the last possible moment to deliver its contribution with maximum effect.

You aren't a murderer, despite the situation. Prison is no place for someone like you, especially with that nose. Besides cars that career onto snowy pavements are not the most accurate of weapons, what ... what if you hit her as well?

Walker gasped as he contemplated a course of action that might take her away from him, his fingers trembling as they moved away from the key. Unbeknown to the sergeant, a defining point in the master-plan was only seconds away.

Walker looked up sharply as he heard the sound of a car racing past his window, his attention focused as it applied its brakes and skidded forward. The sergeant let out a primal scream as the car lost control, fear swamping his senses with the thought that fate could be so cruel as to take her away from him, right in front of his eyes. But within seconds he was relieved beyond belief that the car was going to miss her, instead heading towards a tramp in the road. Then came the disbelief. From out of nowhere ran a man in a beige raincoat, snatching up the tramp and making a tremendous leap to safety. How could a man jump so far? Walker didn't care. Instead every instinct told him to go to her, and comfort her

239

from the near miss. Yet all he could do was watch and fall more in love with her than ever before now that she was safe. He did such a good job of this that he failed to notice anything else. That was until Constable Rosario turned up. He watched the future Mrs Walker provide her statement, he seethed as Joseph gave his. Then came the local reporter and her film crew. She wasn't short of interviews from witnesses who seemed as keen on sharing the experience as Walker was to avoid it.

A feeling lingered in the air like hidden electricity. Walker of course failed to notice it. He did however recognise the woman he had followed before when she turned up. Katie Rose he confirmed, checking his notebook. When another police car turned up Walker considered that perhaps it was time to make an exit.

At his one bedroom flat, Walker slumped onto the sofa with a bottle of lager in one hand and the television remote in the other. He sat in silence for a while trying to work out what had happened. When no answer came to mind he flicked on the telly to see if divine inspiration was scheduled and was surprisingly rewarded by the story being beamed into his front room. Here on the local news was the very story he had just observed. Walker watched as they ran the interviews with the numerous witnesses. It was an angel all right, no doubt about that, or so the sergeant was told. Walker drained his bottle and chuckled to himself that he was there, he could tell them what really happened. Of course he couldn't because he wasn't there, officially, and even if he were, he hadn't been looking anyway.

The sergeant got up and made his way across to the fridge to get another beer. As he opened the door the internal light shone back at him. A plan burst into his mind, his eyes fixed to a distant point at the back of the fridge as he considered that this could be the best plan yet. Walker knew that within

240

days, if not hours, the angel story would be dead and with that his chance would be gone. Over the last couple of days it was becoming obvious that he would eventually have to account for his time. He was sure that Polston was going to scrap the surveillance as there was no actual evidence linking Joseph with the Post Office robberies. Even the evidence that Walker had been somewhat creative with was tenuous at best. Yet he simply couldn't let her be at the mercy of Joseph. It might not be orthodox or even legal but Walker knew that he must do anything and everything to prevent that. What he needed was a fresh round of surveillance, one without interference. He needed his own case, one that no one else wanted but one that he could string out without ever being expected to get results.

Walker returned to the sofa with a new bottle of lager, draining it quickly. Picking up the phone, he hit the fast dial number for the police station, right next to the only other entry for his mother.

'Hello, Carrow Road Police Station. How may I help?'

'Hello, put me through to the chief inspector will you my good man?' Walker asked in a ridiculous Scottish accent.

'I'm sorry sir but the chief inspector is unavailable at this time of night,' the duty sergeant replied.

'Ock no, I was hoping for a comment for our newspaper, Glasgow Star,' Walker exclaimed.

'I'm sorry sir, a comment on what?'

'Are you mad? The angel sighting of course!'

'I'm sorry sir, the angel sighting?'

'This is the police station correct?'

'Yes, sir.'

'Well you must have heard about the angel sighting there tonight?'

The line went quiet as the duty sergeant took it all in and considered his response. It would seem that Constable

Rosario hadn't yet returned to the station with her incredible story.

'Yes, sir. Of course.'

'Well do you have any comment to make?'

'Yes, I mean no. I mean that perhaps it would be best to speak to the chief inspector in the morning.'

'Okay my good man. Tell him I rang,' Walker concluded, hanging up the phone.

Another beer later Walker was back on the phone as the Newcastle Recorder.

'Eh up lad,' Walker began.

'I'm sorry sir?' the duty sergeant replied and so it continued.

For the rest of the night Walker made innumerable calls of a near identical nature, new accent every time, new newspaper every time, same old Walker. As morning broke and feeling he had done enough, Walker made his way out of the door and to his car.

By the time he was getting out of it, the sun was rising above the horizon. Walker was the first officer at the station, conveniently at hand to deal with the media circus that the duty sergeant had assumed and Walker had created. The chief inspector was just a phone call away and within minutes Walker was now instrumental in investigating a case that he himself had invented.

'Wake up Walker!' shouted Inspector Polston.

Sergeant Walker came round quickly and found himself sitting at his desk at the police station. The drive here with Polston had flown by as he thought about events of the night before. And when Polston had headed upstairs to talk to the chief inspector he must have fallen asleep. No surprise really, given his activities of the night before.

'So what's the plan boss?' Walker asked, stifling a yawn.

'These surveillance techniques that you learnt at Goodison?' Polston enquired.

242

'Yes boss?'

'I think that it's about time that we let you try them out, don't you? I want you on this case, sergeant. The chief inspector was extremely keen on getting you involved Walker, and so am I.'

'It will be a pleasure, sir. I was thinking that perhaps I could start by examining the histories of some of the witnesses. It may take some time of course.'

'Now listen Walker. You know how much press attention this case has got. It's imperative that you stick with the surveillance until you get a result.'

'I understand sir,' Walker replied, almost punching the air in triumph.

'Good stuff, sergeant. I'm counting on you.'

'I won't let you down Inspector Polston.'

Five minutes later they were pulling up outside the Inspector's house and like a flash Polston was out of the car and making his way up the pathway to his door. Callahan followed his master, looking back at Walker to give menacing growls through his muzzle, dog talk for *'I've got your number sunshine.'*

'You want answers? I have just the man,' Walker quietly whispered to himself as he began to drive away.

Inside, Polston picked up the phone and rang the chief inspector.

'It's Polston here, sir.'

'How did it go John?'

'He went for it. No questions asked.'

'Excellent, hopefully we can get rid of that idiot for as long as possible,' Chief Inspector Goss commented cheerfully. Polston smiled in return.

243

Chapter 26

The Count Of Planet Gong

People don't know the first thing about seeing things. Maybe some things you aren't allowed to forget.

Wednesday, 20th February, 1980

The air around me is warm, charged with a comforting static. I wait in the laundry room for my Guide as others are elsewhere. Michael and Dean are probably off bullying some other poor sod in my absence. Who knows where Bobby is nowadays after his parents pulled him out of school? He just wasn't the same once the hand of revenge touched him with such devastating effect. It brings a smile to my face just to think about it again. What do you think Avon?

 From around the back of the tumble drier my friend and Guide appears. Kerr Avon, the greatest enemy of the federation and the leader of Blake's Seven (series three and four). There was no point asking anyone else from the spaceship Liberator (and the later and more rubbish Scorpio) because they all die on Gauda Prime at the end of series four. Even Roj Blake managed to come back after an absence of two series to make sure he was killed. Avon, on the other hand was much cleverer. Surrounded by Federation troopers, the screen faded to black. Did he live or did he die? I think the fact that he's just walked out from behind a tumble drier answers that.

 Avon struggles to the bench carrying a heavy super computer. When you get Avon you get Orac. Despite appearance of a fish tank with flashing Christmas tree lights, Orac is in fact the cleverest creation in the Universe, as super computers go. It's unfortunate that the BBC couldn't quite manage to extend the budget for him beyond four pounds fifty though.

'Good evening,' Avon says, placing Orac between us as he takes a seat on the other side.

'Hi Avon, how's things?' I ask. We've become good friends since that first night when he began to form in the shadows.

'We aren't here for pleasantries if you'd forgotten.'

'I saw you on telly the other night. I can't believe you got tricked by Servalan,' I reply, trying to lighten the mood of the galaxy's greatest hero. It's no good, he's as serious in real life as he is on Saturday evening television.

'Servalan tricked me? I doubt it,' Avon replies confidently, despite the weight of evidence against him. Knowing Avon and the sound of the secrets in his voice it must be all part of some greater plan.

'So why did you want to meet?' I ask, knowing the answer.

'It's time.'

'Stage Two?'

'Stage Two, are you ready?'

'Yes of course I'm ready. I've been ready for weeks,' I reply with a hint of frustration, just so that he knows that I've been kept waiting.

'May I say the near drowning of young Christmas was an inspired piece of violence on your part.'

'Thanks Avon.'

'So, your thoughts on Stage Two?'

'Well I was thinking about poisoning again,' I begin to explain to my companion before the thought of Michael writhing in agony makes me break out in giggles.

'We need to be more adventurous, less repetitious,' Avon explains, his index finger pressed firmly against his lips as I let the giggles run their course. Suddenly a mass of twinkling lights and electrical hum erupts between us as Orac comes to life.

'That does not compute!' Orac contributes in his half human/half electronic voice.

'Sorry?' I question.

'Explain, Orac,' Avon asks, stirring from his thoughts.

'There is no logic in your revenge. Stage One relied on a chance factor of 3 to 1 with a standard deviation of 0.008. That is too high to be deemed acceptable.'

'Suggestions?' Avon asks.

'To reduce the level of risk to a more acceptable value I have calculated that a new element must be introduced to the equation.'

'Tell us, Orac,' Avon orders, growing frustrated with the super computer. Before he does, I have a more pressing question that comes to mind.

'Will this get me out of here Orac?'

'Not at this present time. My calculations predict release at Stage Three level but first we must complete Stage Two. I will explain all.'

And explain he does.

Stage 2, Sub-stage 1

It wasn't easy getting out of the school at night but then again, it wasn't hard either. The world at this time is peaceful with only myself on the streets with thoughts of Stage Two. When we set off, there were four of us, Morgan's Four I like to call it. After one hundred yards Fletch dropped out because frankly he's not in best of shape. Five minutes ago, Avon started to lag behind because he insisted on bringing Orac with him. Let's face it, Avon's not getting any younger and Orac isn't getting any lighter.

I followed Michael two days ago and he led me to this nice middle class street filled with nice middle class houses. In the daytime, it's probably a safe street to live in, as I walk down it

247

in the darkness, things have changed. By association young Julie, you have changed everything. The private road is lined with aged oak trees and it is behind one of these just outside Julie's house that I hide in the shadows. Over the course of the next hour the last few remaining lights in the house flick off and then I wait the specified one hour and twenty four minutes Orac insisted upon. Just to be sure they are asleep, safe and sound as it were.

Stepping out I walk slowly but purposefully across the road. My trainers with the Velcro double fastening bands make scuffing sounds on the nicely paved front path as I walk up it. I am invisible. I bring stealth and revenge to Suburbia. Negotiating the long alleyway between fence and house I soon find myself at the back of the home. The garden in the moonlight is beautiful, the grass blending effortlessly with the woodland. Nice touch, if you can afford it. Slowly, the wind picks up and the branches of the trees sway before settling back down again for the night. The sound of a train somewhere in the distance rises and falls without a soul noticing.

My first attempt to enter is via the patio doors. Locked! No surprise really but then Orac had already anticipated this. I slide the crowbar borrowed from our ever resourceful caretaker out of my jacket and line it up where the two doors meet. Very slowly but forcefully I begin to lever the doors, feeling the resistance of the lock. At this point, perhaps guided by unseen forces, I choose to look up and notice the window above the barbecue slightly ajar. I let the crowbar relax in my hands and the door settles back into position. They really should have made the effort to close all the windows, anyone could just climb in.

Once inside my Action Man torch picks out the forms of furniture in the darkness. There is a distinct silence inside, deathly you might call it. As I move towards the door my clothes move against each other, the slight sounds amplified ten-fold by the silence. Orac warned me this might happen and so I move in time with the ticking of the mantelpiece clock, becoming background noise. I'm on automatic, auto-pilot for the soul, expertly weaving my way around furniture, through doors and arriving at the bottom of the stairs. It's not anger that drives me up the stairs, I have evolved. I am new.

I let the light from my torch play across the five doors along the landing when I get to the top. Which one? Where are you Julie? As I think through the dilemma my eyes catch an image forming at the end of the landing. The shadows merge and Avon brings himself to life, nodding towards the door to my right.

This door here?

'That door there. The one with the name Julie on it.'

Now what?

'Go in.'

But what if …?

'Go in ... NOW!'

One more breathe in, one more breathe out, turning the handle, becoming the plan.

'Slowly, and turn that fucking torch off!' Avon orders in a whisper that reaches my ears but passes out of existence soon after.

As I flick the torch off I continue to turn the handle slowly, feeling the lock of the door release. Looking back I see Avon's form dissolving into the air. I guess this was for me and me alone.

I enter quietly, Julie having been an immense help by leaving her curtains open. The light from the full moon pours into the room, illuminating a bookcase just slightly jutting out. On the top shelf I look down to see a line of cassettes, ready to be knocked over. I've never really been into music, maybe I'll start to take an interest when this is all over. At the other end of the room is a double bed, the form within amply covered

249

by folds of duvet and this presumably being Julie. It may be warm but it only protects against the cold. My legs move independently of me, they want to go to the bed and my brain is in no mood to object. There is the sound of my trousers rubbing against my thighs again. Don't wake up Julie, it will only make things harder. My breathing sounds heavy, am I scared or excited?

Looking down, I notice the long hair, probably blonde in daylight, and an innocent face. She is really quiet pretty, a little chubby but pretty still. I suppose it's about time I was interested in girls, it's just I have so much else to do at the moment. Oh Julie, you may make Michael happy but not for much longer. I'm going to take you away from him and not even he will be able to turn back time. I lean over her, the weight of the crowbar in my hand seeming heavier than ever before. Please forgive me Julie, I know you didn't ask for this.

My lips connect with her soft skin just above the temple and she stirs beneath me.

'What are you doing?' Avon shouts from inside.

I … I was …

'Are you insane? You could've ruined everything!'

I couldn't help it, I just wanted …

'Forget it. Get on with what you have come for!'

I stand up straight quickly, giving a quick look to see Julie toying with her dreams below me. I can't believe that I could have ruined everything on one simple impulse. Avon's right, he's always right. No more mistakes!

Moving away from the bed I slowly make my way across to the dressing table opposite the window. Propped up against the mirror is exactly what I'm looking for, a photo. I reach across to take it and as I do so I catch my reflection in the mirror. It doesn't look like me. I don't recognise myself anymore.

'Look at the photo.'

250

Two people from different worlds. The girl from a world I once knew, the other from one I was forced into. Both worlds come crashing together in this one photo and I slip it into my jacket inside pocket and proceed to get the second item required.

The top draw scrapes slightly as I pull it slowly towards me, glancing back to ensure Julie is still asleep. Good, she doesn't want to see this. I take a pair of her panties out of the drawer and let them fall across my face, feeling the soft cotton brush delicately against my skin. I know Avon wouldn't approve but I don't give a fuck. The smell of the panties in my nostrils and the sounds of my excitable breathing accompany me as I creep from the room. A sense of reality dawns as I descend the stairs and make my way through the lounge. It all seems so real, so terrifying. Once I have climbed through the window and the cold breeze is hitting my face as I run, I can't quite describe the emotion, somewhere between the excitement and the horror of what I have become. All in all, the rush should be enough to cover the guilt. It's necessary.

Stage 2, Sub-stage 2

Back at school I sit up in my bed. I'm tired of course, having been out half the night but the anticipation of the events of the day will keep me going. It's time for the final act, time for Michael to follow the trail towards the truth, or at least my version of it. Michael begins to wake and he doesn't have a clue what the day has in store.

After breakfast we trudge back to the dorm. Unless of course you are Dean who is off somewhere on a small diversion. Eric trails behind Michael by design and I am further back still. Eric knows exactly what to do one minute and forty two seconds after I enter the room.

251

The clock begins. I slide into the room innocently to see Michael smoking a cigarette out of the window. Eric is on his top bunk and I see his brain start to count. He knows what will happen if he doesn't. I hope you haven't just lit that cigarette Michael, the clock is ticking.

20 seconds ...

I'm resting on my own bed, Michael ignoring me (for the time being) and Eric is looking for encouragement with a sideways glance. I don't offer it.

40 seconds ...

I cross my legs and relax a little. Why not? Sixty two seconds left to enjoy the silence.

55 ...

56 ...

57 ...

'Michael, can I ask a question?' Eric asks nervously, forty five seconds early. Not perfect but pretty good for someone scared shitless.

'Fuck off, mong,' Michael replies predictably. I would listen if I were you Michael, it's the most important thing you will hear today.

'I wanted to ask you about girls, Michael,' Eric asks, the fear making his acting appear unrealistic. Luckily his real life character isn't that much different.

'Why do you want to know about girls you poof?'

'Okay, sorry,' Eric stops.

Why the fuck have you stopped, Eric? A fierce look across the bunks jumps him into life again.

'Michael...' Eric continues.

'Piss off, gay boy!'

'Does it bother you about Dean?' Eric asks. Just as instructed Eric delivers the one line there is no going back from.

'What the fuck are you talking about?' he asks, not quite listening.

252

'About Dean and your ex-girlfriend,' Eric blurts out, almost crying as he does so.

'What ex-girlfriend?' Michael asks, his back still turned to the room but you can see he has started to think.

'Your ex-girlfriend Julie.'

'What did you say?' Michael shouts, turning back into the room, the cigarette dropping from his fingers as he hears the name.

'Julie?' Eric stutters. Conviction is quickly deserting him but it's nearly over.

I don't think there is a clock fast enough to measure the time it takes Michael to cross the room and pull Eric from the top bunk, connected by fistfuls of clothing as Eric crashes to the floor.

'What the fuck did you say?' Michael screams at him, phlegm flying into Eric's face.

'I didn't say, I didn't!'

'What did you say about Julie and Dean?'

'It's just what I heard!' Eric cries out as Michael grabs his hair and pulls him up.

'Who's been talking about Julie? Who's been spreading bullshit about her and Dean?'

Eric doesn't answer, I don't think he can.

'Who?'

'Jimmy …' Eric splutters. 'Jimmy Christmas.'

Michael doesn't reply, he doesn't need to, his clenched teeth and stiffened posture say enough. Releasing Eric and letting him fall back to the floor he storms out of the room, looking for Jimmy, looking for the truth. Follow the trail Michael and see where it leads you. First things first though.

'Eric, piss off,' I demand, now that there are only two of us.

'I don't understand why?' he whimpers.

'I said piss off!' I shout with venom. He drags himself off the floor, his part in Stage Two coming to an end. As he trudges out the door, my part has just begun.

I do what I have to do before making my way over to the window to see Jimmy standing with his back against the tree, just outside so I can see the brilliance of my creation first hand. All Jimmy has to do is wait with his one piece of information. He doesn't have to wait long. Enter Michael, stage right. He's on him in seconds, pushing him up against the tree, making Jimmy reveal the facts willingly. Now for the hard bit.

I decide to wait on the side of Bobby's bed, after all he's not using it anymore. I don't even have time to read the first page of my Transformer comic before Michael barges back into the room. I let the comic drop from in front of my face, my smile already extinguished seconds before.

I don't know how many punches I've taken. Up to this point I was in a much happier, tranquil place. But I'm back now, at the crucial moment.

'Answer me you stupid fuck!' Michael shouts.

'I'm sorry, were you speaking to me?' I answer smugly as blood drips from my mouth.

'Who fucking told you about Julie?'

'Who's Julie?'

'Don't be fucking clever with me Morgan, why are you spreading bullshit about Julie and Dean?'

I want him to see the coolness despite the pain, so later on when he gets a brain he knows it's me. He just needs a little push.

'I wasn't, I saw them!' I shout back, wanting him to believe that I'll tell him anything to make him stop. I will, just not the truth.

'Bollocks, you fucking knob!' he screams.

'I'm not, please don't hurt me. I saw them in town.'

254

'Don't fucking lie to me!'

'I'm not. He keeps a picture of her under his bed!' I scream in desperation. The things I will do to make the pain stop, if only you knew.

I feel the lessening of the force at the back of neck. The great moron known as Michael releases me.

From my lowly observation point I can see the vacant and betrayed look on his face. Not betrayed Michael, just exploited. He crosses over to the other bunk and on his hands and knees pulls out the box from under Dean's bunk. Sitting neatly on top is the picture I took from Julie's room, now with my own modification. He takes in the sight of the picture of his girlfriend/ex-girlfriend/whatever and realises it's only half the original. A tear straight down the middle, removing his presence, as if she had done so in preference for Dean. And then he sees his next surprise. The panties rest just underneath the photo and he recognises them. You know, don't you Michael? For once he doesn't explode. The anger and violence is waiting for direction and I know exactly how that feels.

'Fuck off,' he mutters slowly in a deep guttural voice with a slight quiver as he fights the tears. Oh well.

At the bottom of the stairs an old friend of mine passes by right on time.

'Alright, fuck face,' Dean proudly exclaims as he passes me, making his way to the dorm.

Enjoy the moment Dean, whilst you can still talk.

I reach the tree and slump against it in pain, the window to the dorm room coming into view. Just in time as it looks like it's all starting.

First, the argument ... Now the sound of someone being pushed against some furniture, and my moneys on this being Dean ... Dean's shouting now... Dean's not shouting anymore…

255

Fifteen seconds is all Michael can hold his rage for before it comes flooding out, all of it in Dean's direction. Wonderful. What follows next is the sound of Dean screaming, intermittently punctuated with the sounds of violence. It doesn't take long for Dean to stop screaming, maybe he can't anymore. It doesn't stop Michael however, burying himself ever deeper in my plan. The next set of sounds are more conventional, more expected. The shouting of Mr Carter flies around the dorm as he enters. You can tell that he's never seen anything like this before, but then he has never met me before, has he?

I let out a laugh. Victory in Stage Two! I have beaten you. I have beaten all of you.

My laugh has only just subsided when I notice Mrs Bonnell, the Geography teacher striding towards me.

'Hello,' she says as soon as within distance.

'Hello,' I reply casually, fighting the giggles.

'Mr Brown would like a word. Would you follow me please?' she asks with a slight element of nervousness in her voice.

This wasn't in the plan. This wasn't in Orac's calculations. Why the hell does Mr Brown want to see me? Michael? No, he couldn't have worked it out. Why the hell don't I know?

I trail Mrs Bonnell into Mr Brown's outer office and I'm shaking. At the future, at what lies beyond that door. As instructed I sit on the chair outside, the same chair I remember sitting in when my mum first brought me. In the corner Carter is leaning across the secretary's desk, whispering excitedly. No surprises what that's about. What could be more important than Michael trying to kill Dean? Why does Mr Brown need to see me now? Can't it wait? Obviously not. Oh God, they know. Somehow they know.

'Mr Morgan, would you care to join us?' Mr Brown asks, leaning out of his office.

256

'Yes Mr Brown,' I reply and rise to enter. I thought the game was won, I cannot lose, I will lie, I will cheat. I will survive to fight another day until the game is won.

Walking into the office behind Mr Brown I see two men of different ages sitting to one side of the desk. One is smartly dressed, the other, the younger one, more scruffy and fighting a losing battle against hair loss. I know who they are, I can tell. They're police officers and the game is slipping away.

'Hello son,' the older one speaks, the younger one taking notes, learning his trade.

'Excuse me gentlemen, I shall let you conduct your business whilst I sort out our other situation,' Mr Brown announces and leaves the room.

'Hello,' I reply nervously before finding more confidence in my voice. I cannot be nervous, not now. I don't know how they've found out but they still have to prove it and I have no intention of making a blubbing confession.

'My name's Inspector Goss and this is Sergeant Polston,' the older policeman reports. I nod to confirm that I have heard before he continues. 'I'm afraid we have some bad news for you.'

I can feel the numbers building…

1, 2, 3 …

'There's been an incident I'm afraid.'

6, 7, 8 ...

Is Michael half killing Dean just an incident?

9, 10, 11 …

'There was a fire at your parent's house last night.'

What? What did he say? I come over cold suddenly, fighting to control the feelings of disbelief.

'A fire?' I whisper as if on automatic.

'I'm afraid that your parents died in the fire, son,' Inspector Goss replies with sincerity. Each word comes crashing down

257

upon me, each making my body shudder as if from repeated blows.

'I'm sorry?' I ask, not quite understanding.

'I'm sorry son, but I'm afraid your parents died last night. I'm very sorry.'

'No you must be thinking of someone else,' I reply.

'I'm sorry son, but your parents, Peter and Katherine Morgan died last night.'

'How? Why? You're lying!' I shout. Where are the numbers? Where is the rage?

'I'm sorry son, but the fire took hold too quickly.'

'But why?' I ask, my voice hardly registering through the tears and emotions flooding back into me as reality returns with deadly vengeance.

'Luckily your brother Sean was at Scout camp, he's okay, don't worry about him.'

There is nothing. No numbers. No rage. No Avon. Nothing to go back to.

'How did it happen?' I ask, forcing my voice through the terrible choking sadness which engulfs me. With my head bowed the tears fall to the floor beneath me.

'Do you know of anyone who might want to hurt your parents?' Sergeant Polston suddenly asks, raising his head from his notepad and looking at me with questioning eyes.

'What? No! I don't know,' I force out.

'For Christ's sake Polston! The boy's just lost his parents!'

I fail to hear any of this. One word, above all else, is paramount in my mind. The universe at this precise point in time revolves around this one word. Why?

Saturday, 23rd February 1980

I know what they are all talking about. There's the kid who's lost his parents. There's the kid who hasn't said anything or moved from the tree outside his dorm for days since he found

258

out. I've seen it all happen from here. I've seen Dean being taken away in an ambulance, never to return. I've seen Michael being removed from the school and taken somewhere between a mental institution and a hospital. It's the same teachers that have forced me to eat, forced me to sleep. I've seen the sun and moon trace their paths across the sky in front of me. And what does it matter?

Why did they leave me a second time? Why? Auntie Sarah has said I could leave the school and stay with her. But it's all too apparent. The outside world isn't for the likes of me. There is only one place I truly belong. Here. I want to get better. I want to do it for them. And there is only one way to do that and it must start with this.

'Hi Avon,' I say tiredly as he rounds the tree with Orac in his arms. My voice is hoarse as it remembers how to form words.

'I'm sorry for your loss,' Avon replies with genuine emotion.

'You understand why I needed to see you both.'

'You require advice,' Orac postulates correctly.

'How can we help?' Avon offers.

'I need to know how this is going to end.'

'I'm sorry but we do not know,' Avon replies.

'What do you mean you don't know? You know everything. You said you would be my guide!'

Orac starts to blink and whirl as he recalls information from his data banks.

'The definition of a guide is one who shows the way or instructs. A person who is able to define future events is referred to as clairvoyant, oracle, prophet … '

'Yes Orac, we get the point,' Avon interrupts. 'You know why you can see us, don't you?'

'You're a figment of my imagination right?'

'To be precise,' Orac computes, 'we are a representation of you that can only exist in third person form. It was logical for

259

you to construct your plans from a viewpoint which allowed objectivity.'

'I always knew that you weren't real.'

'While we served this purpose you chose to ignore the underlying truth,' Avon contributes.

'Then why are you still here? I know you aren't real and yet here you are.'

'A remnant experience, a trace thought process that remains whilst reality catches up with the present,' Orac replies.

'I don't need you any more do I?'

'We exist for a reason, that reason is no longer valid,' Orac concludes.

'And what happens after you go?'

'Life is a journey,' Avon suggests, 'for the most part one travelled alone. You will forget us and progress from this state. You will attempt to bury these moments deeply.'

'Will I ever see you again?' I ask.

'If you need us then we will return,' Orac replies, his voice now more human. 'We may be buried so deep that in the future it may be difficult to recognise us. Just as Fletch is Avon and Avon is Orac, we are all part of you. We are a representation of what you see with your eyes made real. Logic dictates what you see in the future will define our form. Do not forget.'

'I'll be alone.'

'We are all alone,' Avon comments.

Maybe it's the knowledge that they will never truly leave me. Maybe it's the realisation that I cannot move on with them. To be the person my parents wanted me to be I make my decision, to let them go.

'Thank you,' I whisper into the passing breeze.

The shadows cast by the branches of the trees move apart as the wind picks up. As the shadows split, the forms of Avon and Orac begin to fragment. What was once an arm returns to being the shadow of a branch. What was once a body thickens and extends to meet the trunk of the tree casting it. The last thing I see are Avon's eyes fading into nothingness. They were gone.

From here to the end

The rest is history. Auntie Sarah continued to ask the question but I could see the fear in her eyes. Is he still mental? My dear old auntie, with all her Christian goodwill, offered me a home because that's what her God would have wanted. Well God took my parents and handed me a shitty deal. By the time God finally gave up messing me about, Auntie Sarah wasn't asking anymore. So yet again Sean got it all.

I seem to remember someone once telling me that you go through life alone. It's probably the most truthful thing I've ever heard.

At sixteen I left the school and the world was waiting for me. The rest, well you know all that.

Chapter 27

Squeezing The Sponges Of Expansion

'I don't believe you sometimes,' I say to Katie, half in jest, half serious. It may have been a strange night but it did have its positives. One, Katie and I made up. Two, we'll get to that in a bit.

'What?' Katie replies, pretending she doesn't know what she did. Her front room has never seen such a bare faced lie as she sits opposite me, the morning after.

'I was going to get laid last night until you turned up,' I retort, in complete belief of my statement.

'Sorry, I must have missed that,' Katie replies and a look between us determines that everything is back to normal.

It's all true of course. Everything was going well with Mia in the wine bar, post Rob of course. You can't have that good a day without it culminating in mutual love. I was most definitely going to make love to my beautiful girlfriend. And then it all went wrong. Not just normal wrong, but *you don't see that every day so let's call it a night* wrong. First the whole angel thing. Whilst everyone else was saying miracle I knew that the tramp wasn't saved because there happened to be an angel knocking about. It was because I hesitated. The universe had set up the play and ensured I was there to save the day. But just in case they had the wrong man, the angel was at hand to make sure no one got hurt. After all the big man upstairs doesn't make a habit of knocking off tramps just to make a point, does he?

You know the rest, and how it didn't go quite as planned. After such a damning realisation of my own failures what I really needed was the comfort and understanding of my beautiful Mia. Lo and behold who suddenly pops up?

Frigging Katie, that's who. Of all the times she could chose to mend fences, she picks the first moment in ages that I'm likely to have sex. So it's no surprise that with Katie hanging around, Mia and I couldn't excuse ourselves without admitting what we were both thinking. On the way back to Katie's after walking Mia home bits of my brain answered her questions, and even had a go at conversation. The rest of it however was dedicated solely to processing what I had seen. I believe now, don't ask me how, something important happened in that street and I was right in the middle of it. Was I starting to believe?

Back at Katie's she could tell that my mind was elsewhere. All those years of friendship came into play, knowing that I didn't want to leave, not tonight. As she was in the kitchen making tea I wondered if this was something else, maybe she did love me after all? Was this an implausible suggestion? We must have argued a thousand times but she's never been the first to apologise. Insanely jealous of Mia? Concerned for my welfare? The signs were all there. We chatted about the night and I tried to subtly steer the conversation around to us. I wasn't going to leap across the room and kiss her or anything, I needed to build up to it.

So here we are the following morning sitting in her lounge, after spending the night on her sofa. I can't believe my luck sometimes, I really can't. I can't believe that I was even thinking about trying it on. She's my friend and yes, I may have had feelings about her in the past but I'm with Mia now.

'I was going to get laid I tell you,' I repeat.

'Well, you are a love machine.'

'I was doing alright until you turned up.'

'Until I turned up? Didn't this angel you saw put her off at all?'

'You don't believe what I saw last night do you?'

'I think a lot of people saw what they wanted to see. You, for example, saw an angel.'

264

'You have seen the local news this morning haven't you? Everyone but you thinks it was an angel.'

'Only because you and some bloke saw a pile of feathers down an alleyway and told everyone about it,' Katie replies, always the disbeliever.

'Well, how else do you explain it?'

'I dunno, maybe someone stepped on a pigeon?' Katie speculates.

'They were white feathers, pigeons aren't exactly known for their dazzling plumage are they?'

'I dunno, maybe it was a pigeon on a mission from God.'

'Very funny,' I sneer. 'Look, I can't really go into the details right now but I know what I saw meant a lot more than a reluctant hero on a pigeon stamping session.'

'What details? Is this another Joe thing?' Katie asks with a cheeky smile. It's just enough of a smile to illustrate that she may have heard the story before but she's not being nasty about it. Perhaps she wouldn't be so bored if I expanded on the abridged, all-over-the-news version. No chance of that though: she'd only end up doing her best to convince me not to do what I'm thinking of doing anyway.

'Look, you believe what you want to believe and I'll believe what I saw,' I answer, giving a concluding statement to end the conversation on a light but definite note.

'Well sod you then, I'm gonna watch Trisha,' Katie announces, dismissing the previous conversation instantly. If only it were that easy for all of us. Shortly afterwards as Trisha is introducing another reject from the gene pool the message tone goes on my phone. It's the message I've been waiting for. Once in the fold there's no way back.

We have some things to discuss.
11:30 am, St Mary's.

'I suppose I better get to work then,' I suggest to Katie with a certain modicum of the truth.

'Okay, I'll see you later,' she replies, taking a few precious moments to acknowledge our reinvigorated friendship before re-immersing herself. It's shocking really, she should be at work and all she can do is watch television. Having said that, I have no intention of going to work either. The difference is that I'm on a mission from God and I've only just realised it. It may not look good on a sick form but I'll worry about the details later.

Location: St Mary's Church
Time: 11:25am GMT
Purpose: God's work

'His logical reasoning's off. Joseph, you've turned your logical reasoning off. What's wrong?'
'Nothing, I'm alright.'

St Mary's sits proudly, delivering optimum presence and salvation on top of the hill. I pass the primary school that remains quiet as the sleeping commotion inside awaits the bell. I wish I could go back to those days, those days at the very beginning. But there is no going back for any of us, especially me. Crossing into the church grounds I make my way up the path, past the graves which line either side. So much history, so much to be written. The oak door looms in front of me and I take a few moments to consider what I'm going to become because of this. This is the right choice, for all of us.

The heavy door opens easily as I apply a small amount of pressure, no grating against the floor, not even a horror movie squeaking. I take my first few steps inside, feeling more alive

266

than ever. I should have come back a lot sooner, I should have confessed to all those sins. But I'm here now and that's what counts in the end game. The lingering smell of incense fills the air as light streams from the overhead lamps, humming in the silence. The church is empty, all except one person sitting near the front. It would seem The Prophet is early. I really shouldn't have stopped off for that pint. I walk up the aisle towards where he is sitting with his head bowed in prayer. As I get nearer I realise that I've seen this scene a thousand times in films and my entrance is crucial. I could silently place myself beside him without a word and be rewarded with a typical spy film meeting. Alternatively, I could approach with caution and lay my hand on his shoulder to make him quietly aware of my presence. However putting your hand on someone's shoulder in such a fashion usually leads to disclosure of full zombie status and a lust for brains. My first impression has to be subtle and the surroundings deserve the utmost respect.

'Alright?' I cheerfully announce, leaning into his space a little too enthusiastically from the aisle.

'Why don't you sit down?' The Prophet asks quietly. It takes a few seconds before that face comes flooding back from a multitude of poor television programmes. Jack bleeding Connolly, who'd have thought it.

'Don't mind if I do,' I reply, sliding onto the cold pew beside him.

'We have a lot to talk about, wouldn't you say?' The Prophet asks with a knowing look.

'I guess so.'

'Let us start with the most pressing shall we? How do you think last night went?'

'Well, the evening with Mia went well. I mean Katie turning up wasn't the best thing.'

'Joseph, you've misunderstood the question,' The Prophet interrupts.

'Oh right sorry.'

'So?' The Prophet asks with the mother of all questions that needs no further explanation.

'The tramp? Honestly Jack, I didn't see him in time,' I reply. I reassure myself that although the lie might be inappropriate given the surroundings, I'm sure the end result makes it excusable.

'Your hesitation would have had the most conclusive of consequences if every eventuality hadn't had been considered. Our friend was there in case you didn't find the conviction in yourself. Probability remember?' The Prophet replies, dismissive of my excuse, knowing of the lie. 'We discussed previously how the true purpose of the universe is to understand itself as it moves toward complexity. One of the fundamental forces of this progression is time, or rather the illusion of it passing. You see time should perhaps be viewed as a stream descending from the mountains and winding its way towards the sea.'

'Eh?'

'Time began with the creation of the universe as a trickle high in the mountains. What you would perceive as the present is simply a short stretch of this stream through rolling pasture that you, Joseph, are able to stand in, to let the waters of time swirl around your feet. If we look further upstream, nearer the mountains, neither you nor I are there as we haven't been born yet. As we look towards the sea we have since faded as we were not able to walk that far. Although you managed to walk further than I.'

'And this relates to last night how?' I ask, pondering his conversation.

'I am able to observe the small eddies and vortices within the stream, to read in what direction they swirl and what happens to the elements of life when they pass through. The tramp was

268

one such passer-by and under normal circumstances would have been swept into the current. Foreknowledge allowed us to change ever so slightly the turn of the water and as such events as they would have been. The stream still continued to flow towards the sea yet in this one action I was able to show you that when I speak of my powers I am not dismissive of them lightly. And of course its main purpose was of course a test of faith and conviction Joseph, nothing more, nothing less.'

'A bit of warning would have been nice,' I suggest.

The Prophet Jack Connolly looks down towards his shiny expensive shoes for a few moments before answering me.

'Do you think that when Moses ascended Mount Sinai to receive the Ten Commandments, he said, hang on I've got to have a sandwich first?'

'No I'm sure he didn't, but then there is a slight difference between the guy with his hedge on fire and an angel disappearing into thin air down the side of a kebab shop,' I reply with more than an hint of frustration.

'Different circumstances for different times, Joseph.'

'So I suppose I failed the task then?' I enquire.

'Joseph,' The Prophet replies in a soft understanding voice, 'I knew you would come to believe just as I knew you would fail the test. Sometimes we have to fail to see the true path.'

'Eh? Are you saying I passed?'

'Yes Joseph. I was expecting you to, in an unorthodox fashion.'

'So what now?' I whisper subtly. I know that secrecy is paramount now that I am in the fold. I like it here, I should've arrived a lot sooner.

'Unfortunately I have foreseen that we will talk about your mission and then you will be unwilling to accept the true face of The Seer.'

'Sorry Jack, you've lost me.'

269

'Actually I think you will find that it is I that will lose you, for the time being at least.'

'I'm sorry Jack, could you explain? Am I not coming to your secret base or wherever?'

'Not as such,' Jack replies, seemingly caught off guard. 'First Joseph I must ask you to open your heart and soul. I have to know if you believe without reservation, for the hearts of men cannot be seen.'

'I don't ... I'm not one hundred ... well probably ninety nine per cent, what I mean is ...' I splutter.

'Do you believe?'

'Yes, yes I believe!' I blurt out. 'I know that it goes against everything I should believe. I can't help thinking that I should be telling you that I don't but I can't. I believe Jack. I believe with all my heart. I know things like this don't happen to guys like me but too much has happened to dismiss it. Not just the angel, I feel it's the right choice. It seems so obvious.'

'Then you must promise me one thing Joseph. You must remember what you have just said in the coming days. Those words will be the cornerstone of everything that follows, once your initial fear has subsided.'

'What fear Jack?'

'The fear borne of the inner turmoil between what you feel in your heart and what others want you to believe.'

'I'm sorry Jack. I'm not with you.'

'Then perhaps we should start at the beginning,' The Prophet Jack Connolly suggests and looks up towards the front of the church and the figure of Jesus hanging from the cross. Five minutes ago I was convinced there were only two people having this conversation. Now, as I look upon that gentle forgiving face I realise that there are three. The Prophet and I take it all in before he speaks again.

'We have spoken about probability and that forms the core of what I am about to reveal. If you want something or perhaps someone to remain secret, then you choose the most

270

improbable person for that task, whether Prophet or Seer. Now I know what you're thinking Joseph. You're wondering why not someone a bit more anonymous to be The Prophet?'

'The thought had crossed my mind.'

'Judgement day is approaching and God has a message to tell. As such he has chosen the most powerful medium for its delivery, one that can reach the largest audience. Church numbers are falling so why not try a different approach?'

'And what has this got to do with you?' I ask.

The Prophet in turn waits in silence for me to answer my own question.

'Television!' I blurt out, the word leaving my lips automatically.

The Prophet turns to me and smiles.

'The people's entertainer is being turned around Joseph. It shall become more than it is now. It shall guide and it shall spread the message.'

'Ummm Jack I don't mean to piss on your bonfire but have you watched that religious rubbish they put out on Sunday afternoon?'

'Joseph. When the skies rain fire and the ground opens, people will need to be guided away from the underworld. Who will you believe? The Politician? The church? Or the newsreader?'

'The newsreader of course!' I exclaim.

The more he speaks the more sense it makes. Of course it doesn't end here and now, Jack is just the focal point of a world behind that screen that nobody knows about. He's probably been recruiting for ages, I wonder who he's got on board?

'You clever bastard Connolly,' I retort with a smile.

'Not my idea Joseph,' The Prophet answers, directing my gaze forward once more towards the figure on the cross, perhaps to illustrate the point, perhaps to draw attention to the fact that I keep swearing.

The ensuing silence must last for at least a minute as the Prophet and I sit in quiet contemplation. I can't say for sure what he's thinking but I know what's on my mind. A revelation of the beauty in the world and a disgust for everything that threatens it. With beauty comes happiness and I can't let anyone take that away from me. I love Mia, I can't contemplate a life without her. And what about Katie? I love her too, in a different kind of way. At a stretch I even sort of love Danny, not in a gay way of course. He needs protecting because without me he will be one of the first arriving at the gates of Hell. No I won't let this happen. I have to do this for them. I have to save them just as I have to save myself. Eventually Jack speaks.

'Joseph, I am glad that you now see the world as it was meant to be.'

'I just can't believe it. It was like it was always there yet I couldn't see it,' I reply.

'Then it is time for you to understand your position within the new world.'

'Okay,' I reply, drawing out the word as if the truth of responsibility is bearing down on me.

'We must fight the evil. The Seer has been hidden for so long. He has convinced so many. Yet he has made a fatal error. He sees his enemies as those who wield power but has foolishly disregarded the common man. Joseph, you are equal amongst men in the eyes of God. Yet within society you are at the very bottom. You are the last man he expects to be a threat.'

'Hang on, I wouldn't say that I was …' I complain before The Prophet interrupts me. I can't help but feel a little offended.

'You said our method of bringing God's message to the people via television was clever. We are unfortunately not the

272

only ones to think so. Our enemies are also using the same means. There are reality shows to dull the waking responses, incessant violence to inflame the reactive senses, quiz shows to increase competition and greed. The amoral content of television is not the result of a collapsed society, rather the means.'

'So let me get this straight. This Seer guy is making everyone more evil by corrupting them through television?'

'Desensitisation through familiarity. And it's getting worse. The Seer must be stopped and that's where you come in.'

'How?' I reply suddenly becoming extremely nervous as to what lays in front of me.

'It is time for you to look behind that locked door Joseph,' The Prophet declares as if reading my thoughts.

'I don't think I'm going to like this am I?'

'The Seer holds within his hands the opportunity to swing the balance of power towards a world without hope. He has achieved great steps towards his ultimate purpose. Therefore it won't come as a shock to learn he is also a well-known television celebrity.'

'So who is he then?' I ask, genuinely excited that I will be one of the first to know the great secret.

'To know the Seer is to take a step that you may never retrace.'

'I want to know,' I plead. I need to know. I cannot carry on my life and not know after coming so close.

'Are you sure?' the Prophet Jack Connolly asks.

'Yes, will you please just bleeding tell me?'

'The Seer...' The Prophet starts, adding a dramatic pause, 'is Anthony Chambers!'

There is a deep heavy silence between us as I consider what I've heard. The church feels even emptier all of a sudden, the warmth and beauty of the outside a long way away. Anthony Chambers? Mr Lottery? Mr guest presenter on that word

273

game? Mr right-on Christian? Half of me is telling myself that this is the most ridiculous thing I've ever heard, the same half that's trying to cling desperately onto the life I knew before. Another half is telling me that The Prophet is speaking the truth, channelling a voice from above. The final half is suggesting I don't want to believe, because I'm scared of what's required of me. In all, three halves don't make for a very stable whole.

'Piss off!' I reply with a small fake laugh attached. 'I take it all back, you are a bleeding nutter,' I reply, a controlling influence having taken over. Perhaps I'm scared. Perhaps I would rather live in ignorance in the world I left behind.

'If you think about it, it makes perfect sense,' Jack comments.

'It makes no bloody sense at all,' I answer in confirmation of the new path I have chosen. *Double back, you took a wrong turning Joseph.*

'It doesn't make any sense because you cannot see beyond your pre-programmed response. That is exactly why he is The Seer, the least probable person is the most likely. If evidence is what you require then let me share something with you. Anthony Chambers' initials are AC, correct? Ring any bells?' Jack Connolly, the so called Prophet asks.

It takes me a few seconds to run the initials round my head, trying to think of names that match. When it finally comes to me I give out a small laugh.

'So you're saying that your evidence is the coincidence that Anthony Chambers has the same initials as the Anti-Christ?' I reply. As I say the name I feel its effect on the surroundings, an awoken power in this peaceful place. Involuntarily my eyes drift towards Jesus on his cross hanging in front of me and the sobering effect stops me laughing.

'No Joseph, not only the initials. To get the Seer's true identity one of us managed to infiltrate his organisation. That person is no longer with us, a person not unlike you, yet

274

extinguished from this world by the hand of the Seer. If he were still here, my friend would …' Jack pauses as a tear rolls down his cheek before stumbling on. 'If he were still with us then he would be more than happy to provide the evidence you seem to require. But he can't and I refuse to let his suffering and the suffering of countless others from this day onwards be in vain.'

Someone just like me? Am I here because my predecessor is no more? I'm simply a replacement and that does little to reassure me. I want to pretend none of this has ever happened. I want my old life back. It may not have been much, but it was a hell of a lot less scary than this one.

'Jack?' I mutter softly.

'Yes Joseph?' Jack replies, wiping his cheek with the back of his hand.

'Anthony Cambers is known as AC who,' I pause, 'is also the Anti-Christ, right. And you are not only the Prophet but also the actor Jack Connolly,' I say, rolling the words around my mouth.

'Correct.'

'Jack Connolly also known as JC, ring any bells?'

'Well observed, I have often pondered the irony myself.'

'So Anthony Chambers has the initials AC, and your initials are JC but you aren't....' I question but refrain from mentioning his name, resorting to merely nodding subtly to the figure in front of me.

'Think of it as a twist in the rules of probability.'

'What about Judith Chalmers?'

'Sorry?' The Prophet enquires, genuinely confused.

'Judith Chalmers, JC. Is she in on this? Is she with this organisation? Is she on a mission from God?'

'I don't understand why you feel the need to make jokes about this.'

'What about John Craven?'

275

'No.'

'And what exactly is my role in all this? Tell me, or I walk right now,' I command.

'As I've already mentioned, when I tell you, you will walk anyway.'

'Tell me!'

'All I can say is The Seer and his people are moving against us and it's a war he's winning. There are so few of us left now. The Seer must be removed to reset the balance of the Universe.'

'Are you saying you want me to whack him?' I ask, raising my eyebrows.

'Joseph. What you will witness soon will be the point of understanding. The Seer must be stopped or our suffering will have been in vain. Your actions are yours alone and they will become clearer in time.'

We sit in silence for a few minutes as I run the thoughts around my mind, to a point where I hardly notice the Prophet sitting next to me. Every time I decide yes, the part of my mind conditioned by society sneers at the craziness of the whole thing. Then I look up at Jesus on his cross and feel that I still owe him. The absurdness of it all, Jack Connolly the Prophet, Anthony Chambers the Seer, this doesn't happen to other people. I don't know how long I have been thinking when the Prophet finally asks for my decision.

'And so your answer?' The Prophet asks.

My mind is running at a hundred miles an hour, swinging wildly between the two choices. Then from the swirling mists of uncertainty the old Joe returns and delivers his one-time stop card.

'No,' I find myself saying.

'As expected my friend,' Jack replies.

'Let me explain,' I reply hurriedly.

276

'No need. Remember certain futures are written, ones that can be foreseen. Our suffering will provide the emphasis for the cause.'

The Prophet rises from the pew and begins to make his way along the bench towards the side of the church.

'Wait, I want to tell you why?' I shout after him, desperate for him to know, not to have him judge me on a misunderstanding.

'Goodbye Joseph, until the next life,' The Prophet states, not once looking back as he slips behind a column.

'Please, I need to explain!' I cry out at him, manoeuvring myself on the pew, swinging from side to side to gain a better view.

Nothing, again he has slipped out unseen. How does he do that? Suddenly a suggestion of not being alone brings my gaze forward once more so that it falls onto Jesus in front of me. Was it disbelief that made me say no? No, it was fear, of what was involved, of what I would become. The question I should have asked myself was did I have the courage? No. Not then and not now.

'Forgive me, Lord,' I ask softly and rise from my seat quickly, making my way swiftly from the church because I am a traitor here, a coward in the face of the future, a coward from my memories of the past.

Chapter 28

Bjorn And Benny Save The Day

I'm running, not just from destiny but also from the past. Who knows what would have happened if I just tried that little bit harder with Beth? Who knows what would have happened if I tried that little bit harder with what Jack Connolly has just told me? I'm running scared, have been since that fateful day so long ago.

Get in the car, drive.

I slide into the driver's side and pull away, killing the radio so I can be alone. Where am I driving to? I have no idea. I'm so caught up in my thoughts that it takes me ages to notice the car in the rear view mirror. It's just paranoia, I tell myself.

No Joseph, not this time.

A silver saloon car is following me, I've seen enough spy films to tell. It's trailing far enough behind as to not arouse suspicion, a professional without a doubt. The fatal error they have made however is that I'm always expecting someone to be after me. My initial attempts to remain cool with only occasional glances in the rear view mirror soon go the way of the chocolate teapot and fear prevails. I can't take my eyes from the image of the car behind. This is about to change. Any panic I was already experiencing has just paled into insignificance compared to the horrific, stomach churning, heart rendering, shit yourself fact that the traffic ahead has stopped suddenly. I rapidly come to the reluctant conclusion that I am about to test the law of physics that concern the force of a speeding object meeting the resistance of a stationary one. However this is no time for physics, get a grip. My instinct takes over and I slam the brakes on so that I lurch forward violently with the momentum. Thankfully I am

279

restrained by my seat belt whilst everything else in the car flies forward. Physics, it seems, is not without a sense of humour as a polystyrene hamburger carton clips the back of my head on its journey forward. The tyres screech on the road and with a distinct smell of burning rubber, the car comes to an abrupt halt. How close to the car in front? Let's just say, very fucking close. Gravity suddenly remembers that it was invited to the party and every single particle of my car rocks in protest as my heartbeat races beyond the speed of a drunk at last orders.

The car in front eventually moves forward and sensibly puts more distance between us than a joint paper. In reply I move forward, slowly, very slowly. And then I remember the reason I nearly crashed in the first place. As I glance backwards, any hope that a near death experience would cancel out all previous events in time and space are instantly dismissed. The sunlight is glancing off the front windscreen of the car behind so that it is almost impossible to see the occupant inside. Yet from behind the glare is the all too visible hook nose of the driver. All too visible and all too recognisable. The memories come flooding back. Everywhere I go, the nose follows. It started at the beginning, the beginning of all of this. I remember all too clearly now what The Prophet said. They are everywhere, The Seer is tracking us down and we are the only thing he fears. My face screws up and tears form in my eyes as I realise that there is no way back. They are after me, simple as that. What the fuck do I do?

Joseph, there is only one person that can help you at this precise moment.

I close my eyes, realising what this means.

That's right. Now get your act together and do what has to be done. You haven't watched all those car chase films for no reason have you?

Now?

Now!

I slam my foot down on the accelerator. The car tries it best to comply with a grinding of metal on metal, surely not good. *Easy Joseph. Be the Fonz.*

I relax the accelerator so that the car returns to a more sensible *really? I didn't realise anyone was following me* speed. The last thing I want to do is alert that big nosed bastard until I've got an opportunity to escape. The only way I stand a chance is by using a combination of speed, local knowledge and trickery. My car continues to whine in protest at going above thirty miles an hour and so I conclude that local knowledge and trickery/lunacy are the only things left available. I have to break away from this heavy traffic and make my way out of this two dimensional town and into the pretend countryside that surrounds it. I take the main road out of town, watching the silver car following fifty yards behind.

Don't worry, be the Fonz. It's all in the plan.

One left turn, one right and then I'm now on the dual carriageway, leading out of town, all the way to the next one. My driving is casual even if my foot is shaking uncontrollably on the accelerator pedal. I recognise a bend coming up ahead and know that this is my chance. Suddenly I hit the accelerator and wait for my dear car to remember its past glories. A few seconds later the car flies forward at a speed which surprises even me. It knows, just as I do, that this is its last chance for glory and you can't beat the Austin Maestro for the element of surprise. Every light is flashing on the dashboard and an acrid smell is encroaching from the engine yet my speed continues to increase and I swing into the outside lane. At this speed I soon come up behind a slower car and dart into the inside lane, undertaking to a symphony of angry horns. Looking back I see the silver car attempting the same manoeuvre. Returning my gaze ahead and with the corner rapidly approaching I begin to pass a Swedish furniture lorry to my left. The lorry as if on cue cuts into my lane on the

281

turn and so I attempt the ridiculous. I attempt to squeeze through. I can't really explain the feeling except as one between excitement and absolute terror as the distance between me, the lorry and the crash barriers reduces at every moment. The car and I both scream in a duet of horror as the corner reaches the apex with nothing to spare on either side. And then just as I'm on the brink of death I find myself racing through and away. I glance back to see evil attempting the same foolish manoeuvre through the ever decreasing gap before sensibly dropping back under heavy braking. Thank God for the Swedish, birthplace of Abba and now saviours of mankind.

The freedom from pursuit for the time being gives me the opportunity I was looking for, swinging into the left hand lane and preparing to exit the dual carriageway in the most absurd manner known to mankind. Less than twenty metres on the left is a small slip road leading to a local village. I wrench the steering wheel and swing the car into the narrow lane. On doing so I'm instantly confronted by another sharp corner, tricky for tractors, bloody insane for speeding cars and I slam the brakes on hard, giving a dangerous glance backwards to see the silver car and the enemy within scream foolishly past the turning. That leaves me, an Austin Maestro and a corner that I'm about to die at.

Stttttoooooooooooopppppp!!!!

The car grinds to a halt on the apex of the corner, rocking from side to side as steam starts to bellow from the bonnet. A smile creeps across my lips, buoyed by feelings of achievement. The countryside stretches out before me and there isn't a sign of the Devil or any of his shitty little minions.

Now I just have to get the hell out of here and that requires fixing the Maestro. I'm guessing the unrelenting steam cascading from under the bonnet is indicative that any water that my car once possessed has long since evaporated during the insanity. After searching it would seem that for all the crap littered under the seats, water is inconveniently absent. No worries though, I do find a warm can of beer rolling around, fair's fair, half for me, half for the radiator. With that, service is restored and the car rises from the grave with its usual background noise of defects, nothing that turning up the radio doesn't fix.

That was too close. Yet I feel more awake than ever. Up until this point I have lived a variety of lives, trying to find a purpose like everyone else. It's time to consolidate this splintered, complex life, a dawning of a new age, one of Joseph the truthful, Joseph the decent. I just hope that I have enough time to escape with the one thing that I love before The Seer calls again. There is only one way to do that. You can't live the dream and not expect to wake up.

Chapter 29

The Three Monkeys Philosophy

I feel like it's a first date as I pull up outside Mia's house. Part of me doesn't want to do this, the same part that wants to be happy at any cost. But I have to tell her, it's the only way.

'How's the coffee?' Mia asks, settling down beside me on the sofa.

'Yeah, good thanks.'

'It's good to see you. I kind of wanted a chat.'

'Okay,' I reply, my mind elsewhere. The only thing I can concentrate on is how I'm going to break the whole Bruce thing to her.

'I've been thinking that we've been seeing each other for a while now haven't we?'

'I suppose we have, yeah,' I reply, glancing uncomfortably around the room.

'Well don't you think there is something missing for the both of us?' Mia asks.

All of a sudden it dawns on me what this conversation is actually about. I may not have been listening before but I'm all ears now. What we are missing is the definitive act of love. If you think about it, it has to be. In response my brain starts throwing a party in celebration.

Weren't you going to tell her something Joseph?

No, I don't think so.

The truth, remember?

Just once, I think I am well within my rights to lock my consciousness in the airing cupboard of my mind until the moment finishes. I promise I will tell her but let me have this one moment of beauty and joy, please. I will set her straight afterwards, well maybe not immediately afterwards, I'm not completely unromantic.

'Yeah I suppose there has been one thing missing,' I reply, fighting to conceal a smug grin erupting onto my face.

'It's not so much one thing, it's more a number of things wouldn't you say?' she replies and I wonder what these other things could be, hoping for some examples of moderate deviancy.

'Umm maybe,' I reply, shyness prevalent now that the time has come.

'I guess what I'm trying to say is...' Mia says, timid with her words as if also embarrassed. 'That you want to make love!' I blurt out, finishing her sentence off for her. The words come out as if someone else had spoken them.

'No, I want to split up.'

'Sorry?' I say as if I haven't heard correctly.

'I want to split up. I'm so sorry.'

My ears hear but my brain doesn't quite register. When it does finally catch up, my whole life drains in an instant. The party is over and all I can hear is a gentle chuckling coming from the airing cupboard.

'But why?' I ask, genuinely confused.

'It's not your fault,' Mia replies.

'Is it because you know we haven't made love?' I enquire, opening my soul with the truth.

'Don't be silly,' she retorts as if she wasn't expecting such a frank exclamation, 'I know you have been through a lot but you've changed and things aren't the same.'

'I know they aren't because...' I start but then hesitate, scared of telling her the truth whilst still clinging to the lie. But I have no choice, it's the one thing that can save us.

'Because why?'

'Because...' I stutter, thinking of what to say. Should I lead with the truth or expand on my adventures in the jungle.

'Why?' Mia asks again.

286

The truth Joseph, tell her the truth.

'Because, how can I say this? The thing is...'

'What is it, Bruce?' she asks, the question rattling something deep inside.

'Because I'm not Bruce - I'm Joe.'

A silence fills the room as she stares at me, not a glimmer of emotion on that beautiful face. It's a silence that invites the truth.

'Look I know I should have told you earlier but I think we have got our wires crossed a bit.' I begin to explain.

'I don't understand, Bruce.'

'The thing is, I'm not really Bruce.'

'Why are you saying this?'

Finally she knows the truth: we stand at the edge of a cliff, facing a whole new chapter in which we either walk away hand in hand, or fall to the rocks below. All my life I have taken tiny steps towards the abyss, looking over to stare at the crashing waves below. Every step fills me with fear but the curiosity is too strong. What will it be like to fall? Isn't just seeing the churning sea enough? Joe as Bruce has no right to walk anywhere with her. If she is going to take my hand and lead me to safety then she has to know the truth.

'What I'm saying is that you've got me confused with someone else. This Bruce chap, I realise that he was important to you in the past but I'm afraid that was never me.'

'Why are you saying this Bruce, didn't I mean anything to you?'

'I'm not Bruce!' I reply, getting frustrated that she can't make this difficult task just that little bit easier by realising the obvious truth.

'Please Bruce, don't let it finish like this. I don't understand why you are saying this.' Mia cries.

287

I hear the words, I see the light but I can't stop even when ahead of the game. The truth is flowing out of me, suppressed for far too long.

'Listen to me, I may look like him, I may even sound like him but you have to realise that Bruce and I aren't the same person. I'm sorry that I've led you to believe otherwise.'

'I don't believe you!' she screams, on the edge of tears. 'Why?'

'Why? Because you're beautiful and clever and funny and, and... and I love you.'

'Noooo!' she cries, her face buried in cupped hands.

'Now that you know, do you think you could love me as much as you loved Bruce? Do you think you can love plain old Joe?'

'Who's Joe?'

'Oh Christ. I'm Joe!'

'You're not Bruce?' she asks timidly.

'My name's Joe. I want you to love me as Joe, not Bruce. Can you love me for who I really am?' I ask, getting up from the sofa to beg for her love standing.

As I await her answer I look down at my feet so as to not intimidate her. Unfortunately by doing so I fail to notice her fumbling around near the table. A sound alerts me to lift my head just in time to notice a vase leaving her hand and flying through the air towards me. I take it all in in a split second, time I really should have been using to evade the incoming object. With a resounding thump it connects with the side of my forehead and I fall to my hands and knees, my vision going out of focus. I can sense her rushing towards me. I may be heavily concussed but she is obviously horrified that her anger has led to this. Pretty soon she'll be covering me with kisses and apologies. A few seconds later I realise that I may have been a little presumptive. The sharp point of her shoe connects with my ribcage and flips me onto my back.

288

'You bastard!' Mia shouts, kicking me again, even though I'm only midway through my scream from the last.

'Please Mia!' I plead as another kick comes in, not a hundred miles away from my groin.

'Get out!' she screams through her tears.

'Please!' I splutter from the floor.

'Get out!' she repeats and I can tell she most definitely means it. It's not like I'm in a situation where I can present a convincing argument. I don't need to ask if she still loves me, the blood beginning to trickle down my cheek is evidence enough.

'I'm sorry,' I say, concealed in a cough.

Her reply is to tighten her face muscles, whether from anger or sorrow I can't tell. My automatic pilot rules in favour of self-preservation over any slim chance that might remain, and I find myself stumbling down the stairs. As I reach the front door the level of crying elevates from the living room above and my hand hesitates on the catch. Perhaps I should go back? As I place my foot on the first step she appears at the top with a cricket bat in hand. Given my existing pain and the likely outcome of her rush towards me, enough is probably enough. I open the door and throw myself out. As I do so I touch the tender area of my forehead which recently met with ceramic, ignoring (for the time being) the excruciating pain racking every other part of my body. The sight of blood on my fingertips is enough to convince me of reality and I half collapse out of the building and into my car. It takes a few moments of restraint before the inevitable happens. I should be expecting it by now.

How could you be so stupid? What did you think was going to happen?

I didn't want this to happen. I thought I loved her.

Start the car Joseph. Move on.

Where to?

289

Where else is there?

The journey takes five minutes, nowhere near enough time to reflect on recent events. Jack gave me the opportunity to make something of this life and I turned him down. Now, irrespective of whose side I'm on, The Seer is after me. Where's the fairness in that? I'm scared. Correction: I'm absolutely petrified. I have to escape this town, I have to make a fresh start. I so wanted Mia to be a part of this but it's clear now. I never really loved Mia, I was merely infatuated with her. It's fairly bleeding obvious that she didn't love me. She loved Bruce and try as I might, I'm not Bruce. Never was, never will be. That leaves one option left, and the more I think about it the more I realise that I should have made this choice long ago. It took a vase to the head and a rain of kicks to the ribs to show me the true path.

'Hi Harriet.' I say solemnly as she opens the door.
'What happened to your head?' she asks, sounding genuinely concerned. Maybe there's hope for her acting career after all.
'Just an accident.'
'Can I ...' Harriet asks before I interrupt.
'It's nothing, is Katie in?'
'Yeah, she's in the front room, are you sure I can't help?' Harriet asks as she moves aside gracefully.
In the front room Katie acknowledges my presence without drawing her eyes away from the local news.
'Hello, Pickle,' I announce as I enter. The very action of speaking makes me grimace in pain, although I wonder if the pain in my voice is exaggerated for the sympathy.
'Bloody hell, look at your head!' she cries, finally looking up and taking in the sight before her. Before I know it I'm swept up in her concern and she whisks me upstairs to the bathroom.
'Who did this?' Katie asks as she slams me over the side of the bath, taking handfuls of cold water from the tap and

splashing it onto my wounds. The stinging sensation is only slightly lesser than the pain I feel inside.

'Would you think any less of me if I told you it was a girl?' I reply.

'Was it who I think it was?'

'Probably, yeah.'

'I told you to stay away from that old woman with no teeth at The Manor and Toad.'

'For fuck's sake, Katie, it wasn't Crazy Yvette! Do you think I'm stupid or something? It was...it was someone else.'

'Who then?'

'It was Mia, alright! Happy?!'

'Mia? Mia did this? Why?'

'Because I told her the truth. I told her who I actually was.'

'I assume she didn't take it too well,' Katie comments, taking a brief moment to brush back my hair with her hand.

'I think a vase to the head sort of confirms that,' I reply.

'Oh Joe,' Katie sympathises, leaning softly onto my back and holding me so I can feel her soft breasts gently pressing against me. It is in this moment that everything makes sense.

'Katie,' I speak, heralding the importance of what I'm about to say.

'What is it?' she asks as she holds me a little tighter.

'Can I ask you a question?'

'Of course you can,' she replies as if it were a ridiculous thing to say. It's a question that we've both been waiting a long time to hear.

'Katie, I don't know how to say this.'

'Don't be afraid,' she states, waiting for the truth to come out so we can acknowledge our love finally.

'Katie, I love you.'

Suddenly everything goes quiet except for what seems like the deafening roar of water from the tap. Loud, but not loud enough to mask the cry from outside the door. Without saying

291

anything further Katie rises and crosses to the door, opening it quickly. There is nothing there bar the muffled sounds of Harriet moving along the landing quickly. Katie closes the door and leans her back against it in a casual manner.

'Sorry,' Katie finally replies as I turn my head towards her.

'I know what Harriet is like.'

'No Joseph, I don't mean Harriet. I mean I'm really sorry.'

'What for?' I ask, before the stupidity of the question and the accompanying realisation strikes home.

'I know, I've always known. But you know that we have always been friends.'

'But I thought...'

'This is just a rebound thing Joe, you've broken up with Mia and you said something that you shouldn't have said. Again.'

'What do you mean, again?'

'Christmas, a few years back.'

'I don't remember that.'

'You wouldn't. You were drunk.'

'Okay but at least now we know the truth, we've both admitted it.'

'I'm sorry Joe, I love you too but only as friends.'

'But what about just then when you were holding me?'

'I didn't mean it like that.'

'I love you,' I say in a retiring timid tone, trying to convince her in case she doesn't believe, doesn't want to let go.

'Please Joe, don't let this ruin our friendship.'

'Ruin our friendship? Ruin our bloody friendship?!' I answer, raising my voice.

'Can we forget it?' Katie asks stupidly, as if something of this magnitude can ever be dismissed so easily.

'I can't forget it, I can't forget you,' I reply, my voice quivering as I stand on the edge of unwelcome tears.

'I'll always be here for you Joseph, but you don't want me, you want Mia.'

'I think I should go,' I declare apprehensively, accepting the losing battle. I can't believe I was wrong. Not this time, please not this time.

'Don't leave like this, please.'

'I have to. It's the only thing I know how to do properly.'

Raising myself from my position over the bath I stand and approach the door, and I approach Katie. Without saying anything I halt a good foot from her, followed by a few moments of silence before she finally moves aside and I leave, having ruined our friendship. My mind is in turmoil as I walk across the landing and down the stairs. The physical pain from my encounter with Mia has been replaced, possibly usurped, by the more dreadful emotional pain of realising what I've done. I wanted it to turn out like I've always dreamt it but now it's worse than ever. It's over, no way back and I've lost them both. As I leave Katie's house, leaving a dreadful silence behind me, the cold hits me and the darkness of the evening envelops me.

The door to this shit hole fails to yield at first but submits under the excessive force of my second attempt, swinging open and colliding with the wall. Without hesitation I am moving up the stairs as Danny calls me from the front room.

'Where you been dude?'

'Nowhere, just going to bed, had a bad day,' I reply through the grimaces of pain.

'Dude, what about that game last night? Fooking wicked man.'

By the top of the stairs I've remembered the game, when I was so good, when Mia was in love with me, when Katie and I were friends, when neither of them knew the truth. It seems such a long time ago now.

'Yeah mate, good one,' I reply softly, just enough sadness to indicate the fact that I want to be left alone. No distractions, nothing to stop me shutting myself away from this world.

I lie on my bed for a good five minutes before Danny knocks on the door.

'Dude, thought you might like a cup of tea. I'll leave it outside,' he says, his muffled voice finding its way easily around the ill-fitting door frame.

'Cheers mate,' I reply timidly as I hear him retire to his own bedroom. He's a good lad Danny, just the sort of mate you want in situations like these. Blokes realise that when a mate is in the pits of despair he needs this time to himself. Women, all they do is fuss over you. Women, who needs them? I'm going to drink my tea, watch television and try to block out the frightful pain spreading from my forehead to behind my eyes. If the TV doesn't work then I'll skin up some skunk joints and take the emergency bottle of Crème De Menthe out from under the bed.

By the time the late night news comes on and with a strong alcoholic haze on my breath I can hardly focus, unconsciousness creeping up on me. My vision begins to fade and not even the main story on the news about how Jack Connolly has gone missing can halt my welcome descent into peacefulness.

Chapter 30

The Book Of Revelations In Aisle Number Three

My head! Oh my God, why does my head hurt so much? No, hang on, it's a hangover I think. Why? Ssssssh Why? Something to do with some gear and that ropey bottle of green shit under the bed. My head is throbbing, particularly around the forehead. Why the hell does my body feel like it's been kicked all over? What could possibly have made me drink so much?

In your own time.

Oh fuck! It all comes flooding back to me, not minuscule snippets but in one big sodding revelation. Mia, Katie, that booze my Auntie brought back from holiday, oh my God the booze, the news on the telly, falling unconscious. Why would the thought of last night's news be hanging around?

Again, in your own time.

The news! Jack Connolly going missing! How the hell could I have fallen unconscious at that point? The Prophet has gone missing! What does this mean?

Come on Joe, you know what it means.

It's about what he said in the church, about not being around and all that stuff about the stream and how I was nearer the sea or something. Jesus, any doubts I had about his powers just instantly evaporated. My God, he foresaw his own capture by The Seer and he knew that I would be the only one left after he was gone.

I sit up in bed despite the pain from my ribs, with my hung over brain screaming for us to go back. In the ashtray is a half smoked joint and after lighting it, I lie back and stare at the ceiling for an eternity. He knew our meeting at the church was never going to be my final decision. That choice occurs here and now. A decision between saving mankind or running away. I suppose it boils down to this:

Option No. 1
Forget. Go back to being the Joe of old. It's easy, convenient and the one option that I have the most experience of. But now there is no Katie to share it with. More importantly, if The Seer found me yesterday then he can find me again. I wish I could, but I've turned a corner. If I stay then I will be going the way of Jack Connolly and no one wants that, especially me.

Option No. 2
Run away like a big girl. I'm pretty good at running away. I've been doing it all my life. But I don't want to go on my own. No more Mia. No more Katie. No money to do it. I could take Danny but I'm not that desperate.   Well that's that buggered then.

Option No. 3
Do what Jack wanted, join the fold and fight the fight for nothing less than saving the future of mankind no less. That's all well and good but I'm scared, terrified, frightened, hey just name the adjective. Well with options 1 and 2 dismissed that only leaves this one. Oh, bloody hell.

As I desperately try to think of another option, a wave of conviction surges through my body. I don't know where it comes from but I know where it's heading. It's as if, quite unexpectedly, my whole life has been leading up to this point. Arghhhh! Come on! Why not? Why bloody not?! What have I got to lose? It may be over for Katie and me, and Mia for that matter, but I can't bear the thought of The Seer hurting them. You wanted me Jack, well you've bloody got me. It's time for

Joseph to take the chance. Straight after I've had another cup of tea and some toast.

Returning to my room with a mug of tea in one hand and a slice of toast in my mouth I begin. I'm just not quite sure where?

Fifteen calls later I've had fifteen people tell me that their first name isn't Jack and they have never heard of this Prophet guy I'm asking about. Ex-directory eh? Clever. As a matter of interest I check to see if a listing for Prophet exists but this also unsurprisingly fails to yield results. Perhaps I can catch some more details from the news? Unfortunately all that is on is Trisha. I could watch the parasites of society but I need to get moving on this.

Two minutes later no ideas have presented themselves, so I switch on the games console. The final level of Inferno starts, the main character falling into a vast underground cavern. The walls are covered in ice, with shadows of harrowing figures within. It would seem it's impossible to climb back out again and with no save function there's no going back. One chance, no extra lives, no way back. When I finally get to the end I'm confronted by the end of game baddie, and they haven't held back on this one. Every time you think you gain a slight advantage he just swipes you with his terrible claw, or not fancying the elaborate, simply eats you. Just as I'm about to be beaten for the umpteenth time a thought, a beautiful glistening thought fights its way through my stupidity and a thousand horns of hope erupt in triumph. How could I have missed it? There is a link, a way to find the path. The Prophet told me so himself, I just had to work it out.

When did it all start to make sense, I ask myself? When did they first let me know of my destiny? When did they first try to save me from my sins, the betrayal of Mia or the lusting after Katie? Remember. The fair, where I first took Mia when I was still living the wrong life. It began with the letter. The letter as delivered by The Messenger. Remember what he was wearing, a Salisbury's supermarket uniform if I'm not mistaken, that's the link. The Prophet said that there would only be a few left in the end game. Let's just hope The Messenger is still with us. There is hope for us all. I promise you Jack, your sacrifice won't be vain.

To Salisbury's and quickly, Joseph!

They say the strange ones come out at night, but the slowest on the roads come out at midday on a Friday to converge on the local supermarket. Eventually I fight my way through the traffic and swing into the car park, managing to cut up a teenage boy pushing a line of trolleys as haphazardly as I'm driving.

'Wanker!' the kid calls after me as I fall out of the car and start to run towards the entrance. I can't help but think that he'll be thanking me later.

I enter the store and take in the multitude of shoppers teetering on the brink of politeness. But I'm not here for them. I'm here for The Messenger. As I scan the line of cashiers, the penultimate one catches my eye. Sitting there in her unflattering uniform is Harriet, scanning a huge trolley-load with equally huge contempt. I don't know if she feels the intensity of my glare or intended to look longingly at the exit, but as she looks up she recognises me. Her first instinct is to quickly duck below the till, hoping I haven't seen her. Shortly afterwards a customer queries what exactly she is doing and under duress she pops her head back up and produces a nervous wave. In return I wave back accompanied by a warm smile. It's not pity or amusement on my part, I'm just happy to see her. It may well be the last time I do see her. I hope my smile will tell her I no longer feel bitterness, I just hope that everything will come together once she has ridden the storm. But the answer I'm looking for isn't here. Casting my mind back I recall The Messenger had off-white stains on his coat, and working on the assumption that they weren't put there by unsavoury means he must have got them from the section where he worked.

To the yoghurts, and quickly Joseph!

'Excuse me?' I ask a small dumpy woman with a ridiculous perm. She reaches for the top shelf whilst balancing on her knees on the fridge edge, the back of her plump calves presented to me.

'Yes dear?' she answers as she loads the raspberry fools into a mechanically unstable structure. Somewhere a health and safety expert is feeling a sense of dread.

'I'm looking for someone who works here.'

'Not me is it?' she answers, giving me a wink as she fights the pains of ageing and steps back to the floor.

'No, it's a bloke, moustache, greasy hair.'

'There's a few like that here darling.'

'Looks a bit like a pervert,' I add, quietening towards the end.

'You mean that one?' the shop assistant asks, pointing behind me.

As I turn and follow the path of her multi-ringed finger I see The Messenger wheeling a trolley unsteadily around the corner. He struggles to bring it to a halt as he sees me rushing towards him, the stack of yoghurt trays swaying as he does so.

'What do you want?' he asks nervously as I approach.

'I need your help.'

'Not here, okay?'

'Where?' I ask impatiently.

'Toilet rolls, five minutes.'

I stroll around the shop nervously for five minutes before eventually making my way towards the toilet rolls, finding

299

The Messenger already there. He has obviously called upon his knowledge of the store to choose the quietest location. Any customers seem to grab their bog roll of choice before moving on quickly. It's almost as if they can't even see us.

'What do you want?' The Messenger asks as I approach.

'I want to know what's going on, has there been any news?'

'News? I just do what he asks. What happens after that I have no idea.'

'I need your help,' I plead.

There is a look on his face that I can't quite figure as he reaches into his pocket and pulls out an envelope, thrusting it into my hand.

'All I know is that he told me that if you ever came looking for help then I should give you this letter.'

'What does it say?'

'Dunno, like I said, I just do as I'm told,' The Messenger replies, beginning to move away.

'I could do with your help on this one!' I shout after him.

'You're on your own pal,' he answers, disappearing around the corner as if he had never even been there.

Like it or not, it looks like I am on my own. Jack knew this and left a message to that end, to show me the path ahead. With the aisle now empty and free from spying eyes I open the envelope and pull out a small cream letter folded down the middle.

Dear Joseph,
I once saw this day, and therefore knew that you would pass through the shadows and see the path which lies ahead. The rest is up to you, it's time to save the future of mankind. May God's light shine down on you this day.

Badger's Rest
St Bernard's Hill
Weybridge
Surrey

Your friend
Jack Connolly (The Prophet)

A tear runs down my cheek as I finish the letter. I know in my heart that this letter would have been his last, and the determination comes rushing back to me. I must put aside any fear about what has to be done. The Prophet has made the ultimate sacrifice, I must make my own. Before I do I need to do a little shopping: one writing pad, one pen, one pack of Rizla and one sandwich for the long road ahead.

I wait in the queue for the prettiest girl on the checkouts, who passes a number of nervous glances in my direction.

'Hi Harriet,' I announce when it's finally my turn.

'Hi Joe,' she replies, relaxing in full resignation that her secret is now out. I'm proud of her more than anything and what follows is a friendly conversation as if we've just revealed our true selves. I could chat for longer but more oppressing matters are at hand; that and a disgruntled queue behind me.

Back in the car, I write my own letter, detailing everything that is about to occur, hoping history will be kind to me. There is only one person I can trust with this. One short drive later and I'm posting it through the letterbox, knowing that by the time it's read, the job will be done. I still have a few hours before the darkness I require descends, so I take the opportunity to drive to my house for a few essentials, not forgetting something to go with the Rizla packet.

Abort, abort, abort. You have to stay hidden. You have to stay smart.

Of course. I change direction and realise going home would simply be stupid. It's the first place The Seer will be looking for me. Instead I decide to take one last look around this town, just in case I never make it back.

My car cruises pass The Manor and Toad, the pub of a previous life. I need a name. Jack is The Prophet, Weird Guy is The Messenger, who will I be?

The playground now to my left. Where I first met Jack, poor noble soon to be avenged Jack. The Avenger? No, sounds like a Charles Bronson film and Michael Winner has ruined that one for me.

St Mary's church passes on my right. That was where it was revealed to me that I was the extension of God's hand. The Extension? No, sounds like building work on the back of someone's house.

The Angel kebab shop passes by the window. The Angel? No, not yet.

The Retaliator? Sounds like a sex toy.

My thoughts come to an abrupt halt as I inadvertently, or perhaps sub-consciously begin to drive down Mia's road. As I toy with the idea of stopping I notice the silver estate car parked opposite her flat. Waves of panic crash onto me as I recognise the car as the same as the one that chased me yesterday.

Be the Fonz.

I drive casually past, no sudden screeching of tyres, no hot pursuit. My goodbye will remain unsaid as I drive away, away from evil, out of her life.

302

'Take care Mia, I hope that your Bruce turns up one day,' I whisper.

This town is too dangerous for me now. It's time to move on and take the next step in life, to save the future of mankind, no less.

Chapter 31

The Fracture Of Time To Counteract A Linear Nature

You would think that the rich would have better security than this. Any old nutter that wanted to get in to Anthony Chamber's private estate could simply scale the same wall in the same secluded spot that I did. If it wasn't too hard for me, imagine how easy it would be for a deranged madman.

I eventually find the house in question, the high walls and security cameras confirming the fact. One problem Chambers, it's not safe enough. To prove the point I enter the garden by sneaking around the back of one of his neighbours, and in a shaded spot and with the aid of a barbecue that holds my weight with only minimal warping, I clamber over the wall. Twilight is flooding the world, a world where the righteous will strike. Now for a place to hide, these bushes look good. I settle in and wait, the descending darkness embracing me.

Two hours later my patience is rewarded as the electronic gates swing open, followed by a black BMW rolling up the gravel driveway. Its headlights swing across the lawn as the car comes to a halt, illuminating the bushes in which I hide. He can't see me though, he's not looking. I on the other hand see everything. I see you Anthony Chambers. I see you Seer.

He walks in through the front door but I remain hidden. There are no sudden movements, no rash decisions, the fate of the world depends upon it. First I have to know if he's alone. No great big sodding Dobermans chasing me please. Just in case, I've come prepared for the possibility, carrying in my right hand a string of sausages. I just hope those comics didn't lie to me. In my left I continue to run my fingers over the crowbar.

You have come so far. Just one more step.
Yes, you're right, just one more step.

For the Prophet.

FOR THE PROPHET! I shout in every corner of my mind.

I'm up. I'm standing. The body obeys the mind and the mind of yesterday's Joe is nowhere to be found. Whoever is in charge now is damn sure they know what they're doing. With purpose I'm up and out of the bushes, hugging the boundary of the lawn as I run, slipping easily in and out of the shadows. Before I know it, I have rounded the house and can see the back door, just as The Seer comes out. Impeccable timing, perhaps timing that only God could arrange. And then I'm on him, pushing him to the ground. As he recovers from the initial shock he looks up at the sight of God's vengeance standing over him.

'Stay down or you'll get some of this!' I shout in my best cockney gangster impression, lifting the crowbar into the air. He initially looks more confused than scared. It dawns on me that I am holding not the crowbar in my raised hand but the sausages, and try as you might there is nothing remotely menacing about constrained meat swinging over one's knuckles.

'Please, don't hurt me,' The Seer calls out as I make the presence of the crowbar known, belatedly.

'Get inside!' I order, dragging him up by the collar. He stumbles towards the back door, initially falling onto his knees before the fear makes him struggle through.

'Please take what you want!' The Seer cries as I close the door behind us.

'First things first pal. Is there anybody else here?'

'No, there's no one else here,' Chambers pleads as he lies slumped on the floor, cowering from divine justice.

'There better not be or I might have to use this,' I threaten, realising yet again that I've held up the sausages, for fuck's sake. Frustrated with myself, but also as a reminder I fling the sausages at him. They wrap around the top of his head before carrying on with their momentum and hitting the wall behind.

306

This has not been the most successful of starts, I have to improve.

'Take a seat, while your legs still work,' I growl. I'm good, I'm very bloody good.

Gingerly the Seer lifts himself from the floor and takes a seat on a nearby chair. As he does so it gives me a chance to take in the grandeur of his magnificent kitchen. Obviously evil pays well but it does nothing for one's courage. Behind that hand knitted jumper and receding hairline is the heart of a coward.

'What do you want?' The Seer cries as tears start to roll down his cheeks. 'Please take whatever you want!'

'I don't want anything of yours,' I reply forcefully.

'Money?'

'No.' Tempting, but no.

'Drugs? I don't have any of that here.' Again, tempting, but I must decline.

'Let's start with information shall we?'

'I don't know anything.'

'I think you know a lot,' I assert confidently.

'Please what do you want to know?' the Seer whimpers.

'Well let's start with Jack Connolly, what have you done to The Prophet?'

'Jack Connolly, the actor?'

'Better known as The Prophet to you and me, wouldn't you say? I know you've taken him hostage, probably killed him, you bastard!' I shout, the anger rising in me.

'I don't even know Jack Connolly.'

'How do you explain his disappearance then?' I ask.

'I didn't know he had gone missing,' the Seer stutters.

'You're going to have to do better than that. I might have believed you if I was your normal type of nutter but you've forgotten one thing,' I declare.

'What have I forgotten? I don't understand.'

307

'Just the small fact that I know who you really are Mr Chambers, or should I say The Seer!'

'What?'

'I know behind your so-called righteous image lies the heart of evil. That's why you killed Jack Connolly, that's why you tried to have me whacked.'

'What? Why do you keep calling me this Seer?' Chambers asks, trying to persuade me of his innocence. There can be no doubt because if I let even a tiny glimmer exist then he will strike when I'm least expecting it.

'Stop pretending and we can finish this!' I shout.

'I'm Anthony Chambers, you know, television celebrity.'

'Exactly! The perfect disguise for evil.'

'You can walk away now, I promise I won't file charges, I can get you help. '

'Shut up,' I implore, trying desperately to shut out the seed of doubt he is attempting to plant.

'You don't have to do this,' The Seer chances, seeing that slight hint of uncertainty in my eyes.

'Then how do you explain your initials. AC, sound familiar?' I counter with facts. 'You have the same initials as your master, The Anti-Christ. Did you think no one would notice?'

'AC... no, you misunderstand. Anthony Chambers is my stage name.'

'Can we finish this?' I query although I don't know why I'm asking.

'Anthony Chambers is my stage name, please believe me,' he stutters 'my real name is Sean, Sean Morgan. It's like Jack Connolly, his is a stage name too. His real name is something like Christmas, James Christmas. That why we change our names, to make us sound better.'

'Are you finished?' I ask, ready to finish this once and for all. I'm not even sure I'm even hearing what he's saying anymore.

308

'Please for God's sake, please don't hurt me!' Chambers pleads.

'You should have thought about that before you killed Jack Connolly,' I counter.

'I haven't killed anyone. You've made a terrible mistake.'

'Shut up!' I shout in return taking that first step towards him. Suddenly that lingering sense returns and hesitation stops me.

'Tell me you're the Seer!' I shout, the anger now replacing the calm and collected nature I came in with. 'Admit it!'

'I'm not, I promise. Please don't hurt me.'

As the pleading continues I come to realise something. Simply put, I would already be bashing his head in if I had complete faith. But is it a lack of faith or a lack of courage? I just need that edge. I have to know for sure that he's The Seer, and that's the only thing keeping him alive for the time being. With faith I would strike even if I had doubts. With faith I would save mankind. It's time to make up for my failure to believe in its entirety. I shut my mind, the sound of the world fading away, the scene in front of me just images projected onto a compliant desire. I raise the crowbar in a swinging action above my head. Every thought, every memory, every suggestion directed towards this one action.

DING DONG.

What?

DING DONG.

Ding fucking dong? Is that the fucking doorbell? There's a slight flinch in my arm as my urge runs ahead of my self-control. No, not now, I'm thrown, I've been distracted. In contrast a look of hope spreads across the Seer's face.

'Who's that?' I mutter menacingly through gritted teeth.

'I don't know,' he whimpers.

What do I do? Do I go ahead with the whole beating The Seer to death with a crowbar scenario? Or do I play it cool? What would The Fonz do? I don't think he ever found himself in this situation. I'm the one in charge here, I'm not the bleeding Fonz. I make the rules.

'Right, you're going to go to the door and see who it is. Nice and cool, you know how it works. No mention of me, just make them go away as quickly as possible.' I order.

'Yes, of course,' Chambers obeys, the element of fear returning as he remembers who's in control here. I follow as he leads the way out of the kitchen and into his expensive hallway, stopping a few steps behind the dark oak door.

'Ask who it is then,' I whisper. Fucking idiot.

'Hello, who is it?' Chambers asks nervously through the door.

'Hello, sir, it's the police.'

The police! What the hell are they doing here? Working on the assumption that it's not Sting and his pals, the situation has just got very dangerous indeed. Perhaps it's just routine stuff but I still have to make them go away, regardless. Chambers looks nervously at me, wanting to know what to do next. A nod of the head towards the door indicates that he should convince the police that this is just another harmless night in. As he reaches for the handle I take up position behind the door. The door opens as a name enters my head and the presence of the police now seems all too obvious.

Joseph, you're a plum. What did you think she was going to do when she got the letter?

'Hello, Mr Chambers is it?' asks a voice from the porch.

'Yes it is,' comes the nervous reply. Chambers is all too aware what will happen if he lets on.

'Hello, sir. My name is Inspector Polston and this is Sergeant Walker,' the police confirm. Where have I heard those names before?

'What can I do for you, inspector?' Chambers asks.

'I don't mean to alarm you, sir, but we have reason to believe that you may be being targeted by a mentally disturbed member of society,' the inspector announces.

310

If he means me then I'm hardly mentally disturbed, am I? But it's enough of a distraction for Chambers to seize the opportunity.

'He's here! Help me, he's right here!' Chambers shouts, nodding in my direction as he leaps out of the house.

I hardly have time to respond before the two coppers come barging in, pushing the door into my nose with a sickening crunch. As I collapse to the floor with a warm feeling of blood spreading across my face I catch a brief glimpse of the two of them rushing into the house. The blur conceals their features except for a large nose on the one to the left. Pain rages through my chest as I feel a heavy kick to the ribs seconds later.

'Walker, not in public you idiot,' one of them says.

The words drift through the air and gently fade away as I slip into unconsciousness alongside them.

You're safe now Mr Chambers.
Who is he? He tried to kill me.
Mr Chambers has had a lucky escape, sir.
Walker, for once you've actually got it right.
He's coming around, sir. Shall I kick him again?

Just keep him pinned down Walker, if you can manage that.

A glimmer of light in the darkness. A tunnel? Am I ... Is this ... But why the pain? Why the horrible agonising pain? Oh shit I'm not ... I think I'm coming round.

When I finally emerge on the other side, an onslaught of yellow light accompanies the pain of something pressed into my back. The source is quickly identified as a knee being forced down, holding me to the floor. Truth be told, it isn't necessary considering the rest of the pain. Just as I'm getting to grips with the discomfort everything is eclipsed by a sharp pain that awakens and spreads across my whole face. It's as if someone has just shoved a wasp sandwich up my nose.

Perhaps clearing it will lessen the pain? I attempt to blow and a combined mixture of snot and blood shoots across the carpet. If the unparalleled view of this horror isn't enough, the pain returns and brings me to the brink of losing consciousness again.

Stay focused!

How did this happen?

How do you think?

Katie! She must have got the letter early and grassed me. Why couldn't she have trusted me just this once? Katie's lack of faith may well have killed us all.

'Thease, ou've mathe han orful ssistake,' I splutter before a new wave of nausea terminates my attempt at speech. I don't know if they fail to understand, regardless the two coppers carry on talking as if I weren't there.

'You know boss, when I was at Goodison it was procedure to put all arrests in handcuffs at the first opportunity,' the one with the hook nose says as he continues to pin me to the floor. The nose. I know that nose. He's one of The Seer's men. Has evil infiltrated the police as well?

'Shut up Walker. Just put him in the car.'

'All I'm saying boss is that at Goodison...'

'Shut up, sergeant!' the older one replies again, his voice getting more and more aggravated.

The sergeant with the hook nose pulls me to my unsteady feet. Fuck you, nose!

Fight, don't give up.

I can't. I can hardly stand. The nose has a tight grip on my left arm and forces my limp, non-resistant frame out of the door and into the cold night air.

Fight, just one last time.

Nothing. My body has nothing left. Through blurred vision I make out the overweight form of the older copper overtaking us. A few feet ahead a yellow light illuminates in the darkness as I feel my head being pushed down. I'm being put in the back of a car aren't I? Was this how Jack met his end? No! I won't go out like this. All I need is one last surge of strength and a healthy dose of luck.

'You know boss, when I was at Goodison...'

'Walker, I'm warning you.'

'But boss, you never listen to what I learnt there.'

'Walker!'

'Goodison,' the nose blurts out in a childish fashion.

'What?' the fat man questions.

'Goodison, Goodison, Goodison.'

'What the hell are you talking about?'

'Goodison, Good....i....son,' the nose replies, almost as if speaking in tongues.

'Walker, I'm warning you.'

'When I was at......'

What happens next is somewhat of a surprise. To the casual observer with slowly regaining vision and raging pain (namely me) the overweight guy, the inspector I think, has lost it. With it comes the sound of fist on jaw, followed by the sensation of release as the nose goes into defensive mode.

Run you fool, run!

I take the opportunity without hesitation. The sergeant falls to the gravel as I'm leaping from the open car door. God in his infinite wisdom has allowed me one last roll of the dice. My legs could go from under me at any moment but they must hold out, they will hold out.

'Get him Callahan!' the fat one shouts from behind.

I sweep my head back at full pace to see who the hell Callahan is, and as I do so I see a small dog leap from the open front car window and look in my direction. God gave me strength. God gave me luck and he's not finished yet. Instead of chasing me as instructed the dog makes the short journey to where sergeant big nose is lying. As I begin to clamber over the electronic gates I glance back and wince as I see the dog

313

biting him in the you-know-where. That's got to hurt. I drop to the other side as the fat one waddles down the driveway in pursuit. Too slow fat man, I'm gone. I don't think the one with the nose will be running anywhere any time soon either.

Drawing on an extensive knowledge gleaned from Hollywood films and late night police chase documentaries I'm running through the back gardens and along the dark lanes of the estate. Countless security lights automatically activate; no good, need to stay undetected. A siren starts up in the background as I fling myself over one final fence and crash into the nearby woods. I run as far I can through the threatening shadows before my strength finally deserts and I fall to my knees, breathing frantically.

How far did I come?

It wasn't far enough.

I can't go any further. I can't.

Then regain your strength, stay hidden.

A ditch lies a few feet away and I crawl into it, covering myself with leaves and dirt from the immediate area. It's the best I can do. I just hope it's enough. For the next couple of hours I hear the far off cries of police search teams. They come close, but they don't come close enough. I am the truly blessed.

Chapter 32

Hmmm, I rather Like You, Said The Vacuum Cleaner

'He was a cop living on the edge. His target, a loose cannon on the wrong side of the law. One of them was going to lose. In this year's must see film, the showdown is set and the end game begins.'

Katie turns the key in the door and enters the house, her thoughts troubled. On the table of the front room lies a letter, opened the night before.

Sergeant Walker follows behind. He has a bruise to the face and walks with a pronounced limp. He carries a look of smugness, derived from the knowledge that the punch and the dog bite to his upper thigh (dangerously close to his groin) will end the career of his superior.

> **Walker:** Don't you worry Miss, we'll find your friend and we'll be able to give him the help he needs.
> **Katie:** Do you want a coffee, sergeant?

Walker raises an eyebrow, believing the question to be an overture to a sexual encounter.

> **Walker:** Yes miss, coffee would be (pause) very acceptable.
> **Katie:** Will he be alright, sergeant? What if you never find him?
> **Walker:** Don't worry miss, I've locked up loonies like him before, they always turn up.

Katie lets her jaw drop slightly in disbelief as they both enter the kitchen.

> **Katie:** Loonies?
> **Walker:** My apologies. Your friend will receive the best treatment possible, I can assure you that.

Walker tries to stifle a look that betrays his thoughts.

> **Katie:** May I ask you a question, sergeant? Have I met you before? You seem awfully familiar.

Camera pans out whilst zooming in on Walker's nose, reminiscent of Roy Schneider in Jaws.

> **Walker:** I don't think so Miss but a lot of people do think that I look a bit like a certain Mr Williams.

Katie looks into the middle distance, wondering if he means Robbie or the more apt Kenneth.

> **Katie:** Can I ask, sergeant? What punishment is Joe likely to receive if you catch him?
> **Walker:** That would be up to the judge, miss.

Walker raises his eyes from Katie's breasts and takes the coffee from her. Both enter the front room.

Cut to five minutes later as Katie pushes Walker out the front door. Tracking shot of Walker getting in his car, silently mouthing the word lesbian.

'Starring that bloke from EastEnders from five years ago as Joe and some geezer who was once in a talent show as

316

Sergeant Walker. It's the straight to DVD classic that nobody's talking about. And it's coming soon, from a cupboard near you.'

How long are they going to be speaking in there? I couldn't have chosen a worst place to hide. Of course when I got here I was hoping that she would be home but at least I knew where she kept the spare key. The very last thing I was expecting her to do however was to bring some copper back with her. I had to dart into the nearest hiding place, namely the fricking cupboard under the stairs. I can't even move for fear that the smallest movement will reveal my presence. I wish someone would tell that to the nozzle of the vacuum cleaner that's making homosexual advances upon my person. The copper's voice sounds familiar as he attempts to chat her up, and it doesn't take a genius to work out he's failing dismally. Don't worry mate, you wouldn't be the first to be turned down. He finally gets the message and leaves, and about bloody time too.

Certain that she is finally alone I straighten up and attempt to make my way out from under the stairs. Unfortunately as I start to move, any item not able to withstand an earthquake topples over, creating a symphony of clattering noises. I crawl from the cupboard into the hallway, instantly overcome by a tremendous onset of pain between my shoulder blades. The clang of metal on bone suggests my friend has just slammed a heavy cooking pot down onto my back.

'Jesus, for fuck's sake Katie!' I blurt out as the dull but immense pain spreads down my back and into my stomach, making me want to throw up.

'Joe?'

'Yep,' I whisper through the pain.

'What the hell were you doing in the cupboard, you stupid bastard?'

317

'What do you think? I was hardly going to have tea with your new boyfriend was I?' I splutter, my strength returning incrementally, allowing me to raise myself gingerly from the floor. The pain between my shoulder blades accompanies me into a cautious standing position.

'How did you get in?'

'Key under the flowerpot. Look, can we discuss this somewhere a little less obvious?' I reply, nodding towards the glass in the door to indicate we could be being watched.

'Get your arse in there you cretin,' Katie orders, pointing toward the lounge and as always I obey.

As I enter the front room I go across to the curtains and draw them. Katie flicks on the light and I slump into the nearest chair.

'Why did you bloody hit me?' I complain.

'Because you came crawling out of my cupboard. You could have been anyone. First things first, why is your nose at that strange angle?'

'Well,' I reply, adopting a sarcastic tone, 'people keep attacking me.'

'I can't think why,' Katie replies. Nice touch.

'My bloody nose hurts like buggery but I don't think it's broken.'

'Well if you don't start telling me what the hell is going on then I assure you I will be correcting that,' Katie demands, dismissing my fragile state as inconsequential. Shame no one has told my back, ribs, nose, and generally, my whole body that.

There is a time for holding information back and a time for divulging all. Considering how much trouble I'm in, it's probably wise to choose the latter. And so I tell her the whole sorry story. Katie finally breaks her silence when I bring events up to the present.

'Are you off your bleeding head?'

'Eh?'

318

'Are you telling me that you have been chosen for the fight against evil by what was his name, Jack Connolly?'

'More or less.'

'And do you still think that?'

'I don't honestly know. I was so sure before but when I went round to see Chambers he almost had me believing that he was just an ordinary celebrity.'

'Of course he did you stupid bastard!'

'You mean you believe me?'

'No you idiot, he's a television celebrity who's had the misfortune of being attacked in his own home.'

'Then how do explain the fact that I met Jack Connolly who told me all these things and then I saw on the news that he'd disappeared, probably dead?'

'I don't know what you saw, but it wasn't on the news.'

'And how would you know? You never watch the news,' I reply, confident that this hasn't all been a dream.

'Because, Joseph, the police rang him up last night when I was at the station to check you hadn't tried to abduct him as well.'

'And they spoke to him?' I ask, astonished.

'Yes,' Katie replies slowly as if explaining it to a child.

'Are they sure it was him?'

'Well the recently deceased aren't known for answering the phone.'

'Then what did he say?' I ask, continuing to test her.

'What do you think he said? He's never heard of you.'

I take a few moments to consider it all. Every thought I have had recently has been directed towards a single purpose. Now I have my oldest friend telling me otherwise. Who to believe? What to believe?

'He must have pretended not to know me!' I cry out when the only option that satisfies all criteria finally comes to mind.

'Joe, I don't know what is going on but you have to accept that last night you attacked a well-known television celebrity. Not only are you now wanted by the police, but pretty soon your face will be all over the media.'

'I have to finish this,' I declare.

'You don't have to finish anything. It's not real. Get it in your head for God's sake!' Katie shouts, getting angry with me.

Who to believe? What to believe? Believe in what you know. Believe in what you goddam know. Something is not right here and I'm stuck in the middle. Katie or Jack? Jack or Katie?

'What am I going to do?' I ask tearfully. Whether it is fact or imagination, I'm pretty much stiffed here and Katie is the only person left I can trust.

'You hand yourself in,' Katie orders as if it were the only logical choice.

'What?'

'The police. They can help you.'

'No way!' I reply in defiance.

'Then what else are you going to do?'

'I don't know, run away or something.'

'Where to? You don't have any money,' Katie answers, somewhat accurately.

'Anywhere. Spain. Amsterdam. I don't know if it's the police or The Seer chasing me but I'm pretty sure I'm in a lot of trouble.'

'Running away isn't the answer, not again. You do it every time you fall in love with some bird and then ...' Katie hesitates.

'When I fell in love with you?' I ask.

'I don't know, Joe, but you've been running away all your life.'

'Well are you going to help me or what?' I ask, determined.

320

The way I see it, this is the only way out. I have to get away, at least for as long it takes for all this to die down. It's a scary thought but I feel a sense of excitement, a life unplanned. All I need is Katie's help. I'd like her to come with me but I better not push my luck.

'Well?' I ask as she takes all things into consideration.

'Of course,' she answers, 'I would do anything to help you even if I thought you were making the wrong decision. If you're not going to get help then I suppose it makes sense to get yourself away until all this blows over or at least until you aren't mental anymore.'

'Thank you,' I reply in all sincerity. I don't think I have ever meant it so much.

'So how are you going to do this?' Katie asks.

I take few moments to consider my plan. Nothing immediate comes to mind even if I'm doing every deep-in-thought pose I know. As my finger rests on my lips for the fifth time and Katie begins to get impatient my mind finally kicks in with something useful.

'The way I see it is that everyone is looking for me, right?'

'Yeah, one or two people.'

'So do you think they will be watching the airport?'

'It's possible.'

'I can't leave that way, then.'

'Not unless you have a false passport,' Katie comically suggests, not realising that she has ignited a spark of inspiration.

'Not yet Katie, not yet,' I reply, a smug grin spreading across my face as I see the exit in the distance.

'How the hell are you going to get a fake passport?'

'Ah, now that is the clever bit.'

I'm making my way across the playing fields at the back of the house whereas Katie has opted for the more traditional

321

method, by her front door to get her car. The rendezvous is set, the plan begins. Within minutes I have exited the playing fields and find myself sitting on a small wall waiting, my head bowed and my hood pulled up. Again I try to phone my critical hope. Yet again it merely rings into eternity. When Katie pulls up I get into the car silently.

'Were you followed?' I ask.

'Nope,' Katie replies with a sense of achievement.

'Excellent. So let's just play it nice and cool, okay,' I instruct, nervously.

'So tell me again, why the hell are we going back to your house? That's the last place you want to be isn't it?' Katie asks, pulling out into the road.

'Because I need something and it's an unavoidable risk I have to take.'

'What do you need? If I'm going to help then you have to tell me everything.'

'Okay. The way I see it is I have to leave the country. Therefore I need a passport.'

'I don't mean to call you stupid, even though you are, but if the police are watching the airports then surely your passport will be the first thing that gives you away?'

'I didn't say my passport, I said a passport.'

'I don't understand,' Katie replies and it's perfectly understandable why. I don't want to be harsh but she doesn't quite have the imagination for this sort of thing. She's good at her thing, I'm good at mine, even if it is for the first time.

'My passport will be no good, but a fake one might just work.'

'Where in hell are you going to get a fake passport?' Katie exclaims as she swings the car gently down some side roads.

'Danny,' I reply.

'I didn't know Danny did that sort of thing. Anyway why do we have to go back to your house, can't you ring him up and get him to meet you somewhere?'

322

'In theory yes, but the stupid bastard's not answering his phone and we don't have the time to wait until he does. He knows this dodgy bloke down Loop Road who deals in these sorts of things.'

'Then why are we going round if he's not in?'

'I didn't say he wasn't in, I just said he wasn't answering his phone. This is Danny remember, and it also happens to still be morning. I guarantee the lazy git is still in bed.'

'So what happens when we get there?'

'I sneak in, wake up Danny, find out where this dodgy bloke lives, pick up some clothes and stuff and then we're on our way, simple as that.'

'Sometimes Joseph I don't think you know the meaning of the word simple,' Katie replies and to my dawning horror I realise she has turned the car into my road.

'What the fuck are you doing, you're driving down my road!' I shout in terror.

'So?'

'You do remember the police don't you, not to mention the agents of evil?' I cry, ducking dramatically. As my head hits the glove compartment I catch a glimpse of the silver estate car parked opposite my house.

'Don't worry, I'll just drive past casually,' Katie comments, finally understanding the reality of the situation.

'Shit, that silver estate car, you see it? That was the car that chased me. That's the Seer's men. They must be waiting for me.'

'The Seer's men?' she asks disbelievingly. 'If you mean that silver car parked opposite your house, it definitely isn't evil incarnate or whatever.'

'Eh?'

'The bloke in the car is Sergeant Walker. I should know, having just spent an entire night with him. He even tried

323

chatting me up while you were hiding in my cupboard like an idiot.'

'Are you sure it's him?' I ask, realising that there's something to work out here. I feel my centre of gravity moving as Katie makes the turn into the next road.

It's all in the nose. I remember the name now from last night. His boss mentioned it after the bastard smacked a door into my face. However, the fact that he is waiting outside my house doesn't change anything. I already worked out he's the one who has been following me around. He's the one working for The Seer. As Katie brings the car to a halt I slowly raise my eyes above the base of the window and look around to see the road that runs behind my house.

'What did you expect Joe? If the police want to arrest you then the first place they are going to look is your house. Where did you think he'd be?'

'No, you don't understand, that copper.....'

'That copper wants you locked up. I thought that was fairly evident when you were hiding in my cupboard.'

'No, just listen. That copper, I think he works for The Seer!'

'What!' Katie exclaims a little louder than I would have wished.

'Look I don't have time to go into the details right now.'

'Oh no, please do, you crazy bastard.'

'Okay, okay. He's been following me everywhere and Jack told me that I wasn't to trust anyone.'

'And that's your evidence?'

'Jack told me.'

'Did Jack tell you that Sergeant Walker specifically worked for The Seer?' Katie asks, the disbelief and anger evident in her voice. I take a few moments to consider the facts of the matter before reluctantly coming to a conclusion. Yes, he's everywhere. Yes, he tried to break my nose. No, no one actually said that he worked for The Seer. Why was he

324

watching me then? Why did he chase me in his car? That's a lot of questions that I need answers to.

'Then how do you explain the fact that he's been watching me? Not just today, but for weeks now,' I ask, hoping she can work it out for me.

'Maybe because you live with a drug dealer? Maybe because he knew you were planning to kidnap a famous television celebrity? I don't bloody know.'

Am I right? Is Katie right? The only thing for certain is that I am in a lot of trouble and that running away is the only way out of this. Once I have escaped from the police, The Seer, or whoever else fancies chasing me next it will be a whole new life, a new beginning. All it needs is one fake passport from Dodgy Fuck and then I will have the life that I've always dreamed of. It will be the chance to be someone new. A fresh start, living the dream, as it were. If Jack is right then it will be fairly evident when I see four horsemen ride past my kitchen window. I've done my bit for the cause and now it's time to move on.

'Okay, let's do this,' I utter with a sense of calmness in my voice.

'Well, it's about bloody time,' Katie replies.

Chapter 33

Confessions Of A Nutcase

After taking in the view of the deserted street around us, I turn to Katie and give her a smile.

'So what now?' she asks.

'You stay here. I'll be five minutes.'

'How do you know that there won't be police inside?'

'This is Danny we're talking about here, he's hardly going to be letting the Old Bill inside is he? Plus our friend Mr Policeman is sitting outside trying to be discreet, just waiting to nick me on the sly. It hardly adds up to walking into a copper frenzy.'

'It's an awful risk you're taking.'

'Just one small step and we can get out of here. Trust me,' I comment, opening the car door and stepping out into the bright winter sunshine.

'I'm coming with you,' declares Katie as she also gets out.

'What are you doing?' I whisper across the roof.

'I don't want anyone breaking your nose again.'

It's fairly evident that she has no intention of listening to me as she starts to make her way up the passageway towards the back of the house. All I can do is catch up and plead for her to change her mind.

'This fence?' Katie asks as we reach the half rotting collection of planks at the bottom of my garden.

'Yeah, but Katie please,' I request.

My protestations are simply ignored as she begins to clamber over. I feel ashamed to be looking at her arse as she goes but I can't really help myself, after all it may be the last time that I get to see it.

Once Katie is over she calls softly from the other side and I begin my own ascent. My entrance isn't quite as graceful, the fence swinging and creaking wildly as I straddle it at the top. As I begin my descent I slip and fall the rest of the way and into stinging nettles.

'Don't swear,' Katie whispers as she stands over me.

'What do you fucking mean, don't fucking swear! I've just fucking hurt myself, for fuck's sake!' I whisper back, a little over-enthusiastically.

With my right hand and one side of my face stinging like a bastard I get to my feet. A lifetime of non-gardening has created the perfect camouflage from which to watch the house. A few minutes later nothing remotely interesting has happened, so it's probably safe to conclude that the only danger lying inside is from a disgruntled Danny when I wake him up.

'Looks fine,' I whisper.

'Are you really going to do this?' Katie asks as if it were the last chance to turn back.

'Yeah of course,' I reply, suppressing the urge to do a runner. Breaking into three houses in less than twenty four hours is more than enough for me, even if one of them is my own.

'Then let's do it!' Katie exclaims and before I can stop her she is making her way silently towards the back door. I quickly follow, catching my clothes on the brambles as I make my way out of the bushes. When I finally catch up with her at the back door I slip past her and gently turn the handle to find it locked.

'It's locked. I could break a window?' I suggest.

'Or you could try your keys.'

'Oh ... yes,' I reply, embarrassed that I'm acting the amateur.

After fumbling in my pocket I finally find my keys, slipping the largest one into the lock and turning slowly. The door unlocks easily and as I gently push it, a slice of Joe's kitchen life is revealed. A hazy orange light penetrates the seventies curtains. The cartons of half-eaten curries and pizza boxes are

328

the first obstacles to be overcome. If we make it through the genetically mutated bacteria then the rest will be child's play.

'Doesn't it ever occur to you to clean up once in a while?' Katie whispers from behind as we stealthily make our way through the danger.

I decline to reply as there really is no reasonable explanation. I do however resist eating the cold slice of pizza lying on the table. We make our way into the hallway and the light from outside streams through the frosted glass door, making sharp parallelograms of light on the hallway wall. With some trepidation I slowly open the door to the front room, half expecting the local constabulary to be waiting, drinking tea with Danny handcuffed in the corner. Luckily they have chosen to look elsewhere. I smile as I think of the copper in his car outside. Hey big nose, I'm in here, missed me. The house remains silent with only the distant echo of a dog barking somewhere nearby.

'He must still be in his bedroom,' I whisper to Katie as she silently falls in beside me.

'You think?'

'Let's go wake him up,' I mutter with a feeling of mischief and take my first steps onto the creaking staircase.

As I reach the top of the stairs with Katie a few steps behind, I am greeted by a dimly lit landing. It may look miserable but I'm happy to work in the reduced light, if not for the security then at least for the atmosphere.

'Danny!' I whisper urgently through his door, my voice breaking into a hoarse rumbling halfway through.

'Wake up you lazy bastard!' Katie shouts, rapping on the door.

In order to stop her kicking the door down I give her a calming hand gesture and try the handle with the other. As usual it's locked and yet again I'm appalled that my friend doesn't trust me not to enter his room. Okay, if he had caught the news recently then perhaps I could understand his concern. The second I release the handle I see a flash of boot connecting with door, breaking the fragile lock and sending the door swinging into the room wildly. The boot retreats, taking a flash of smooth, provocative leg with it.

'Well you did say it was urgent,' Katie justifies and we both stare into the darkened room. Before I can complain, let alone comment that she seems to be enjoying herself perhaps a little too much, she is already crossing the room.

'Danny, time to wake up,' she announces, pulling the curtains back violently to allow the outside world to flood the room. The scene revealed is of a remarkable tidy room and a bed not slept in: not slept in because Danny isn't here.

'Will you close the bloody curtains!' I bark. Amateurs, the lot of them.

'Oh, sorry,' she replies, drawing the curtains but leaving a small gap remaining. The light that filters through is enough to provide the room with a sinister illumination.

'Where is he?' I ask.

'I don't know. Maybe he didn't come home last night? Maybe he got lucky?' Katie speculates.

'Danny?'

'Okay maybe not.'

'Maybe he's lying low in case the police come round?' I contemplate.

'Maybe he thinks you're going to come home and kidnap him for the forces of good,' Katie heartlessly replies, pouring the cold water of cynicism onto my already delicate personality.

'What are we going to do now?' I ask.

'Well, you need the address of this Dodgy. Danny must have it written down somewhere.'

'Yeah, you're right,' I concede.

I start to check the bedside cabinets as Katie starts to look through the chest of drawers. I'm ashamed to admit that I

330

once lived like this, the hollows of dust left by recently removed coffee cups all too apparent. I continue to search until Katie asks a definitive question.

'Does Danny have many clothes?'

'Not really no,' I reply as I open another empty drawer.

'What I mean by that is, does he have any clothes at all?'

'Yeah of course he does.'

'Then why is this chest of drawers completely empty?' Katie asks.

I'm slightly annoyed that Katie had brought this up when she knows we don't exactly have a lot of time here. I grudgingly cross the room to the chest of drawers before standing beside her and looking down. She's not wrong, the drawers are indeed completely empty, save for a base lined with old faded wallpaper.

'Maybe he doesn't keep his clothes in there?' I suggest, making my way across to the wardrobe.

'Joe, he's done a runner,' Katie states as if it were obvious.

'Nah, Danny wouldn't do that,' I reply as I pull open the wardrobe door. I am ill prepared for the heavy plastic object which had previously enjoyed the support of the closed door, which falls from the top shelf and connects with my head.

'Shit!' I mutter, rubbing the impact point.

'You moron,' Katie adds.

As the object clatters to the floor, I look down to see the identity of my attacker. Resting at my feet is a symbol of another age, one I recognise instantly because of the memories it brings back. As a child the Star Wars X-Wing fighter with battle damage stickers was all I ever wanted. It was something I never got. This X-Wing has evidently suffered more battle damage than perhaps the manufacturers intended, one of the wings having been broken off. Still I would've been happy with even a damaged one when I was a kid, and despite various heartfelt pleas it never arrived. I think

331

my parents felt that the stick-on battle damage stickers, symbolic of a history of intergalactic violence, were not quite in keeping with their modest religious leanings. Still, thinking about it, maybe I should ring them when I'm finally safe and away from all this. After all, pretty soon they will probably be wondering why their son has tried to kidnap Anthony Chambers. Then again, maybe I won't, that will teach them for never getting me the X-Wing. I should be beyond all that now but everyone else had one, even Danny. One question remains though as I continue to stare at the floor. Why has Danny kept it for so long as it's obviously broken? Perhaps it has some deep meaning for him also, after all we are not that much different. We both love football, computer games and a bit of a smoke. We both have an older brother, his is called Sean or something. Alright, his parents died in a fire and mine are alive and well in a village in Kent but it's much the same.

I take in the rest of the room and come to the conclusion that the assorted crap left behind is just the sort of thing that someone running away would leave.

'He's bloody run away,' I concede to Katie.

'Any sign of Dodgy Fuck's address, an address book, anything?' Katie asks, emphasising the urgency of our breaking and entering. I quick rummage through the dust and collective crap of the wardrobe, revealing nothing of interest.

'Not a bloody thing,' I reply in anger, much too loudly.

'What now?' Katie asks.

'I don't know, let me get my stuff and get out of here and we'll worry about it later,' I reply, trying to forget that my one and only plan is in total ruin.

We make our way across the landing and into my room, chucking anything at hand into a rucksack. I toy with the idea of taking my games console with me, hoping that at some point I will get to finish Inferno. However, some situations are more important than others. I must be strong and realise what's important here.

332

'Joe,' Katie whispers as I start to unplug the leads to the console.

'What?'

'I heard something.'

'Don't be stupid.'

'I heard something. Downstairs.' Katie repeats.

Trusting my friend a lot more than my own hearing I stop and listen. Cutting through the silence is the slightest of sounds emanating from downstairs. Shit, someone else is here.

'There's someone downstairs,' I whisper very quietly to Katie.

'Is there any other way out of the house?' Katie asks, worried.

'It could be Danny. Maybe he forgot something?' I suggest.

'Does it look like he's bloody forgotten something?' Katie answers as she gestures towards the emptiness of the room across the landing.

'Who else could it be?'

It takes a few seconds of Katie looking at me in contempt before I realise.

'Fuck, the coppers!' I whisper, as we hear the sound of the door to the front room being opened. From what I can gather it sounds like just one copper, but one is more than enough.

'Quick, we can make it out the back door while they are still in the front room,' I blurt out, realising that this is our one and only chance.

Without further contemplation I sling the rucksack on my back and take Katie by the hand. I must admit her hand does feel good in mine as we step softly onto the landing.

Not the right time Joseph. Not the bloody time!

We descend one step at a time, the stairs creaking under my weight. Luckily, no immediate frantic, arrest-the-nutter sounds emanate from behind the door, which lies ajar. As we

333

reach the bottom and turn towards the kitchen, escape is almost within grasping distance. Slowly, softly, very quietly. Suddenly from behind, a voice erupts as the unwelcome visitor makes his way out of the living room. We could run. We could fight. For some reason however, we both stop as a voice booms around the narrow hall. It's not Danny, it's not the coppers, it's not even the agents of evil. It's much worse than that.

'Alright boys,' comes the unnecessarily loud voice of my landlord Mr Smith, trying to stretch the words to infinity.

'Hello Mr Smith,' I reply tentatively, turning around slowly to face him, half expecting pain to swiftly follow.

Smith takes a few moments before replying, preferring to take a huge swig from his compulsory can of Guinness which he raises to his lips. In his other hand is a white carrier bag which I presume holds more beer.

'So this your bird?' Smith asks in an informal manner, as if he's known me for years.

'No Mr Smith, just a friend.'

'Always hold your friend's hand, do yer!' Smith retorts, laughing loudly. As I shudder with the volume of his voice I feel Katie's hand slip from mine.

'Um Mr Smith, did you see anyone outside the front?' I ask.

'Nah, I came in the back door. You wanna lock that, anyone could just come walking in.'

'But there's no way of getting into the back garden from the outside,' I question.

'Your fence has been kicked down, mate. I want that fixed,' Smith orders. I strongly suspect that Mr Smith's entrance to the back garden was not quite as graceful as my own.

'Why did you come in that way Mr Smith?' I ask quietly.

'Can't be too careful, not in my line of work. I'm a player, you remember that.'

Katie remains silent beside me, her desire to leave all too apparent. Katie, you're not the only one.

'Of course Mr Smith,' I reply in submission. Smith drops his now empty can of Guinness onto the hallway floor and proceeds to pull another one from his deep jacket pocket and opens it.

'So where's that little shit you live with then?' Smith asks.

'It's not rent day is it?'

'Nah, came to drop of this little delivery for him,' Smith answers, throwing the crumpled white carrier bag in my direction. It falls awkwardly into my hands, the objects inside rattling against each other. As I look inside I see a multitude of vials and small bottles.

'What are these?' I ask, confused.

'I dunno. Danny pays me for them. The missus works down the hospital, well the morgue to be honest, she gets them.'

'Are you Danny's supplier?'

'Supplier? Fuck off kid, I'm a face, I don't get mucked up in that filth.'

'But these are drugs, right?'

'Drugs, medicine, it's all the bloody same.'

'What do they do?' I ask.

'Dunno, the missus told me once, she read all about it on that Internet thing. Something about using it on patients to make them more suggestive or something.'

'Suggestive?'

'Look kid, do you want them or not?'

'Well, no,' I reply, the details beginning to work themselves out at the back of my mind.

'Two hundred quid you owe me,' Smith replies, choosing to ignore my previous statement.

'But ...' I start to say before Katie interrupts me.

'Here you go,' Katie says, passing over the money from her purse. I don't ask why she has that sort of money at hand but it would seem to Katie that two hundred is a small price to pay for freedom from this maniac.

'Nice one,' Smith replies, finishing his second can and letting it drop to the floor. I, on the other hand, am transfixed by the contents of the bag and what it all means.

'Mr Smith, do you know where Danny is?' I ask, now knowing that this question is perhaps more important than I first assumed.

'Dunno mate. Look, I'd love to chat but I've got to go see some other muppets. Stay lucky,' Smith comments as he barges past us, pulling another can of Guinness from his other pocket.

'What was that all about?' Katie asks softly.

'I think I understand at last.'

'Understand what?'

'I'll tell you, but not here.'

'Where then?'

'I know just the place, where no one goes.'

Chapter 34

We Don't Need No Education, We Don't Need No Thought Control

The trappings of a crime scene have, if anything, added to the appeal.

It's been a long time since Katie and I came to the Manor and Toad and I know for a fact that since it reopened people have been staying away in droves. No change there then. It's apparent now that most of the brave souls who entered before never left, present company excluded. I would like to think those poor locals that Ken dispatched weren't murdered but rather caught up in an eternal lock-in. I can imagine the scene from the netherworld now, one draped over the bar, one piling coins into the fruity and that annoying ghostly bastard on the jukebox who keeps playing The Jam. All in all, it's probably the busiest the Manor and Toad has ever been.

'I can't believe you've brought me here,' Katie murmurs as we slide in through the door.

Bar the ghosts, the pub is completely empty. It's a shame as the brewery has obviously spent some money doing the place up in order to bury (no pun intended) the past.

'What do you want?' I ask as we approach the bar.

'Well, how about you start telling me what the hell you've worked out?'

'I meant drink-wise.'

'Is this place actually open?' Katie asks, looking around at the empty tables. Even Ken had the decency, albeit between killing sprees, to man his own bar.

'Hello!' I shout in a friendly fashion to anyone present. After a few moments, I hear someone running down the stairs and am pleasantly surprised when a bloke stumbles out to greet us.

'Hello there folks, what can I get you?' the new landlord asks, in an excessively friendly manner that conflicts with memories of the previous tenant.

'Just a couple of pints of lager, please.'

'No problem at all,' the new landlord confirms and moves over to the pump. As he flicks it on, a spurt of foam erupts into the glass and his face signals dejection as lager fails to heed the call.

'Ah, looks like the barrel needs changing.'

'We can have something else if it's a problem?' Katie suggests.

'No, no. It's no problem. Olive, can you change the barrel love?' he shouts up the stairs to his wife.

'Piss off. I'm not bloody going down into that cellar,' his wife replies. With an embarrassed smile the landlord moves to the small door which leads into the cellar and opens it, taking a few moments to summon up the courage before disappearing into the depths of the infamous room.

'So are you going to tell me what's going on?' Katie asks.

'In a minute, why don't you take a seat and I'll bring the beers over.'

'Where?'

'Where else?' I reply.

With a shake of her head she moves over to our table. At the same time and with a speed that would have terrified his predecessor, the landlord returns, slamming the door dramatically behind him.

'Two beers was it?' he asks between heavy breaths, returning to the bar.

'Yes please.'

As I join Katie at the table, I'm reminded how beautiful she actually is. But it was never meant to be. Some things should have remained unsaid. Some things should have definitely remained undone.

'Now are you going to tell me?' Katie demands as I slide in beside her.

'Let's pretend that I've made a dreadful mistake. Let's pretend that this Joseph you know has been set up,' I begin.

'What do you mean?'

'Visualise this: I'm not actually an extension of God's hand, Anthony Chambers isn't in league with the devil and Jack Connolly hasn't been visiting me on behalf of the big man upstairs.'

'I had sort of assumed that already,' Katie replies.

'Okay. So there are two options left. One, I've gone crazy or two, this has been a set up.'

'I know which one I'd go for.'

'I'm not bloody crazy, alright?'

'Okay, I believe you.'

'So that leaves the set-up, right? The question is who has set me up and how? Mr Smith kindly provided that information,' I reply, pulling the carrier bag from my pocket and rattling its contents.

'Danny? Why the hell would he set you up?'

'You heard what Smith said. The drugs make people more suggestive. I just don't know why he would do it to me.'

'But Danny... he can't even arrange his own personal hygiene!'

'I don't know why, but at least I know how. It must be down to the drugs.'

'But what about Jack Connolly?' Katie asks.

'Drugs.'

'What about The Messenger?'

'Drugs again.'

'What about Mia? I know you didn't imagine her. Has she anything to do with this or was that the drugs as well?'

'I prefer to think that was my charm,' I suggest.

'We'll chalk that one down to the drugs as well then,' Katie retorts.

'It has to be Danny, There's no other explanation,' I conclude as Katie buries her face in her hands for a few moments before emerging.

'If I could just ask one thing? How come this morning you were all *let's kill Anthony Chambers* and now it's a sinister conspiracy perpetrated by your housemate?'

'I guess I've been working it out since last night. There was something at the back of my mind when I confronted Chambers, like I was making a mistake. Only after running into Smith has it become clear. Why else would Danny be buying drugs to make people suggestible? Why else has he done a runner? Danny knows that I'm not in police custody and it's only a matter of time before I work out it was him.'

'Joe, I don't mean to sound patronising but wouldn't it make more sense if we just said you had gone a bit loopy?'

'I admit that I did go crazy for a while but that was to do with the drugs. You know me, I may be a miserable sod at times, but I don't make a habit of trying to kill television celebrities.'

'Okay,' Katie sighs in resignation, 'let's say it was Danny. Why would he go to all that hassle?'

'I don't know.'

'And how are we going to find him?' Katie asks.

'For the time being let's stick to the original plan. We need to find this dodgy fuck and get a fake passport. I'll work out the rest later.'

'But we don't know where he lives.'

'I never said I had it worked out completely, but I'm due a bit of luck. Come on, drink up, we're leaving,' I declare, not entirely sure I know what the hell I'm doing.

It's not exactly far, this Dodgy's house, but as we pull up in Loop Road I can feel something. I'm not sure what it is but it's getting nearer.

'So how are we going to work out which house this dodgy bloke lives at then?' Katie asks as she switches off the engine.

'I'm not sure,' I reply.

I've heard Danny talking about his mate Dodgy Fuck enough times to know he lives down here somewhere. I could knock on everyone's door and ask whether a dodgy fuck lives there, but I imagine most people won't take kindly to that approach. Instead I wind down the car window to get some fresh air, hoping a flash of inspiration will follow. As if by design I catch a small but familiar smell.

'Can you smell that?' I whisper.

'Have you let one go?'

'Um no. That, my girl, is the smell of skunk weed,' I correct her.

'So?'

'Katie my dear, that is what brings us here,' I conclude and before I know what I'm doing I've removed myself from the car. Katie follows behind as the sweet aroma brings me to number eleven.

'This is it,' I announce as we stare at the 1970s wallpaper through the kitchen window.

'Are you sure?' Katie asks.

'Without a shadow of a doubt,' I reply. Houses like this, people like these, this is my area of expertise.

Ringing the bell we wait until the door begins to open slowly. First comes the overpowering smell of skunk, next the creature within.

'Yeah?' matey asks, looking over his visitors, yawning as he does so. He's probably average height, average build, and not overtly good if judging by the haziness of his eyes and inability to focus. I can spot a dodgy fuck when I see one.

341

'Hello there. My name's Joseph,' I begin, somewhere between country gent and undercover cop although I'm not sure what approach I'm going for here.

'Is this about the milk bill?' Dodgy asks.

'I'm a friend of Danny Morgan. Can I come in for a chat?'

'Why?' Dodgy asks, passing his eyes over us in judgement.

'A bit of business.'

'Ah, business, you should have said,' Dodgy replies, lazily stepping to one side to allow us in.

We follow Dodgy over an obstacle course of assorted crap which covers the hallway floor and then up the stairs, passing a slumped mattress at the top.

'So what can I do for you?' Dodgy asks as we enter his bedroom.

'I hear you are in the business of selling certain items,' I enquire. If there's one thing I've learnt from Danny, asides from not to trust the fucker, it's that Dodgy here does a nice line in counterfeit items.

'Yeah, don't be shy. Tell us what you want?'

'I need a fake passport.'

Dodgy breathes in as if this was the rarest thing in the world.

'A passport, that will cost yer.'

'How much?' I ask.

'Seeing as you're a friend of Danny, and I wouldn't want to get on the wrong side of him, let's say £150?' Dodgy demands, raising an eyebrow Roger Moore style.

'Will you take a cheque?' I ask. I'll be long gone by the time that puppy bounces.

'No son, don't do cheques,' Dodgy replies, fighting back laughter as he begins to drag on a Camberwell Carrot joint.

From behind, I hear Katie open her bag, no need, this is my world now. I pull out the bag of Smith's drugs and place them on the bed beside Dodgy.

'What about a swap?'

Dodgy looks carefully in the bag, taking a few moments to summon his pharmaceutical knowledge.

'Nice, you've got some good stuff here,' Dodgy states.

'Well?'

'Okay sunshine, call it fifty for these, and the passport another hundred.'

I admit that I don't actually know how much the bag is worth, somewhere between the under-valuation of Dodgy and the over-valuation of Smith. Done on all fronts, but once I get my passport it simply won't matter anymore. Katie must be thinking the same thing as she pushes past me and hands over the remaining hundred. She is just fantastic. With the necessities completed Dodgy walks across to the wardrobe, pulling a dusty crumpled cardboard box from the top. He grabs the first passport on top and throws it across the room to me.

'That will do yer,' Dodgy comments, accompanied by a wink.

'Cheers,' I reply, flicking through it.

'You see that bit at the back, where the photo goes? Just get yourself one of those machine jobbies, peel back the acetate and whack it in there,' Dodgy suggests.

As I turn to the back page I notice the name on the passport: Hamish Hussein. I can't believe this will be my name now, I mean I hardly look like a bloody Hamish.

'Hamish?' I enquire.

'Take it or leave it.'

'I'll take it,' I reply. Anything to get away from Dodgy, away from this house and away from this stupid bloody town.

'Excellent!' Dodgy exclaims with a grin that hints at something else. I suspect he's been trying to get rid of Hamish Hussein for quite some time, either that or every name in there is the same.

'One last thing,' Katie interjects.

'Can I get you something else? How about a shooter?' Dodgy asks, trying to flirt with Katie in pretend gangster style.

'We wanted some information. Do you know where Danny might be?' she asks with the limited amount of feminine charm she can bear to use on this bastard.

'Ain't got a clue. Try not to get involved with that Danny if I can help it, too dangerous. Why do you ask?'

'He's done a runner,' I reply.

'Bloody hell. Been busted at last has he? Well I tell you what, if I had a bird like his I wouldn't be getting myself banged up if I could help it.'

'His bird?' Katie asks, surprised.

'Yeah, he brought her round here yesterday. I'll tell yer, she was well fit.'

'What did she look like?' Katie asks as a horrible thought begins to fight its way to the front of my mind.

'Dunno, long hair, square glasses, you know, well fit.'

Don't be stupid. Danny? Mia? There's no way she would get involved with that fuckwit. But remember the sly looks between them, that deep unwelcome feeling that she wasn't ever telling the whole truth. I have to know for sure, don't I? It's the very last thing to do before I get on that plane.

'So anything else I can sort you out with?' Dodgy asks.

'No thanks,' I conclude before turning and ushering Katie out of the room.

'Where are we going?' Katie asks, descending the stairs.

'Unfinished business.'

344

Chapter 35

Invasion Of Planet Gong

'So you're now saying that Danny set you up because he was secretly in love with Mia?' Katie asks as she pulls the car to the side of the road, fifty metres from that traitorous witch's flat.

'That's the only reason I can think of for why Danny would go to so much hassle. I've always had this feeling that there was something between them and you heard what Dodgy said about Danny turning up at his with some fit bird. The more times I run it round my head, the more I'm convinced. I can just feel it, instinct or something.'

'Yeah but Danny?'

'If he was knocking her off then it makes perfect sense. He set me up because he wanted me out the way. I was never going to get away with kidnapping Anthony Chambers. It's the oldest trick in the book.'

'Jesus, what book you been reading? I'm sorry Joe but I just can't see Danny with Mia. I was struggling with you, no offence, but Danny? He hardly strikes me as her type.'

'Alright Katie, I get the point. You never liked her.'

'Joseph,' Katie says dryly.

'I just thought something was going right for me,' I declare, looking down at my feet.

'Joseph,' Katie continues.

'Look I know what I did wasn't right, the whole Bruce thing but ...'

'Joseph for Christ's sake, will you shut up and look who's just come out of her block of flats?' Katie shouts and I look up as instructed.

There, coming down the steps, the black clothes, that stupid fucking haircut. Danny boy, I've got you. Up until this moment, I was never quite sure. Now that I see him, all the answers to this whole sorry mess is standing fifty metres from me. I'm going to make him explain every single detail, whatever the cost. I'm out of the car, my adrenaline pumping, slamming the door behind me. Unfortunately the sound of an oncoming maniac set upon revenge seems to alert him.

Under forty metres. He's still looking, not moving, trying to work it out.

Twenty five metres. Our eyes meet and it's only then that he finally recognises me. All of a sudden he's off, running scared.

Ten metres, Christ my lungs are burning. He's running at full speed now but by small increments I'm clawing in the distance.

'Stop, you bastard!' I shout after him between heavy gasps for air.

Danny starts to slow. Then suddenly his decrease in speed makes sense as he darts right, squeezing through a hole in the wire fence that runs alongside the road. On the other side lies a deserted playground and within seconds I'm also at the opening, squeezing through. I emerge into the playground to find him trapped. Wrong turn Danny boy, no way out except through me. To the left and right are high brick walls, at the back and beyond the swings, a collapsed fence covered with empty beer cans and syringes. Beyond the fence lies a canal and no one in this world could make that jump. Danny comes to the same conclusion and comes to a skidding halt, frantically looking for another way out. I take the opportunity to catch my breath, breathing deeper and slower now, feeling the strength return. When Fuckface finally works out there are no options left he turns to face me.

'Look Joe, I don't want any trouble,' he declares, attempting to appear innocent.

346

'You don't want any trouble?' I question disbelievingly, taking a step towards him. 'You should have thought of that before.'

He matches my movement and moves backward, maintaining the distance and keeping the roundabout between us.

'I heard what you did Joe. Look, I don't know what's going on in your head but I can help you through it.'

'What are you talking about?'

'I saw it on the news. When you were going on about that whole Jack Connolly thing, I should have realised things weren't right. I didn't realise you were having a proper breakdown, like. How was I to know that you were going to go off and try to kill Anthony Chambers?'

'Danny, I think you knew that was going to happen all along,' I retort, suppressing the urge to jump forward and make him pay.

'Joe, mate. Listen to me. I don't know what's been going on in your head but there are people that can help you.'

As he's talking, I'm taking small steps around the roundabout, hoping to gain an advantage while he's busy trying to talk his way out of this. I can see what he's doing, trying to act innocent, trying to be my mate again.

'It was always you Danny.' I reply. 'I know about the drugs. I know you set me up.'

I feel the anger rising. It's a dull ache at first in the pit of my stomach, becoming a tingling sensation that travels up my back to the base of my skull. Yet there is something else, a small thought, camouflaged for the most part by the fury. It's doubt, just enough to activate a deeply buried sense of morality. Please, not now, don't let me lose the moment.

'I had nothing to do with this,' Danny states.

'Then why did you run away?' I ask, confident he can't answer.

347

'Because the last I heard, you were wanted by the police for trying to kill Anthony bloody Chambers,' Danny replies.

'Then why have you taken all your stuff from the house?' I ask. Another question. Another damming piece of evidence.

'Why do you think? One moment my housemate is on the news, the next thing the filth are all over the house. I had to get out of there before they busted me. I had a bloody nine bar of opiumated hash stashed there.'

I suppose that would explain the sudden runner. But it's not enough. The anger wants results, not the musings of a reasonable mind.

'Bollocks Danny, too many things are unexplained. Don't forget I've just seen you leave Mia's house. I know.'

'You know what? Me and Mia? Jesus I just went round to ask her if she knew where you were. I was trying to help you dude. I'm your mate. I wouldn't do that,' Danny proclaims.

'Why should I believe you?' I shout, a hint of desperation in my voice.

'Because listen to yourself mate. The whole thing is ludicrous.'

'Then what's been happening to me? How could I have thought that you were with Mia?' I mutter, shaking my head.

'What do you mean?' Danny asks.

'Well, no offence, Danny, but you're hardly her type,' I say, lowering my head in shame. How could I have been so wrong?

'I'm not with you.'

'Well if you think about it,' I begin, 'she's hardly going to be seeing you whilst going out with me. Even if she wasn't with me, I can't quite see it happening between you two,' I reply with a slight chuckle.

'Joe, let's be realistic. I could if I wanted,' Danny replies. I've obviously offended him.

'Come on Danny. She's out of your league,' I announce. He has to be told, for his own sake.

348

'Fuck off, Joe!' Danny shouts, the anger quickly rising in him as he reaches down and swings the roundabout wildly.

'I'm only telling the truth,' I answer, opening my palms towards him. 'You must have tried it on with her. After all you try it on with every other girl you meet. There's nothing to be ashamed of, being blown out. It just happens to you a lot.'

Danny's response is to clench his teeth as his head moves from side to side involuntarily. Next his eyes begin to stare wildly, his hands becoming fists. Every nerve, every blood vessel, everything capable of explosion does so.

'You want to know the truth? I've been shagging her for years!' Danny shouts with venom, his Welsh accent now firmly replaced by a dry, outer London alternative.

Why the change? I don't give it a second thought. I'm too busy giving Danny a knowing look to indicate that he's not the only one who can trick people by design. The doubt stopped me with Chambers, to a point it stopped me with Danny, all I needed was confirmation and suddenly the barriers are down. That's how you conquer doubt.

'You bastard,' I spit, 'I knew it was you.'

There's a look on his face that signals that the game is up, no way back.

'Oh so fucking what! You don't even know what happened to you!' Danny shouts, moving, now on the offensive. In response I move around the roundabout, clockwise and maintaining the distance. Time.

'Why Danny? Was it Mia?'

'You fucking knob. You don't have a clue. You think her name is Mia?' Danny asks with a snort. 'She was just the start, something to raise you up so you could come crashing down again at the right moment.'

'You're right, I don't know, but I'm going to make you tell me,' I reply, moving against the spin of the roundabout.

349

Danny maintains the balance and begins to move in the opposite direction. Time.

'Oh I'll tell you. I'll tell you because you should see genius for what it really is. The more I pushed, the more you submitted to suggestion.'

'It was the drugs you got from Smith wasn't it? How did you get me to take them?'

'Why do you think I was always making tea? It wasn't out of the kindness of my heart.'

'I knew it. They made me see Jack Connolly, they made me paranoid.'

'You think you can achieve something like that with a few drugs? You don't know how long I had to wait in that shitty house, sharing with pathetic knobs until you came along. The right person for Stage Four.'

'Stage Four?' I ask.

'Stage fucking Four, wanker. You wouldn't even begin to understand.'

'Then are you going to tell me or are you going to continue dicking about?' I demand.

'Stage Four is when everyone pays.'

'Is this where you tell me how hard a life you've had? Boo fucking hoo, my mum never got me a bike and so it's all her fault I'm a homicidal maniac?'

'Don't you dare talk about my mum!'

'Why not? I hear everyone else does.'

'Shut up! You don't know the first thing about me. You don't know what I'm capable of!'

'Well, I'm pretty sure ...'

'You want to know? You want to fucking know?' Danny interrupts, 'that bitch, she never believed in me. So if you want to know what I'm capable of, maybe you remember that fire I told you about? The one that bitch and my useless bastard of a father died in? They never listened, they never understood. I burned them. I fucking burned them. And then

350

when the police came snooping I played the heartbroken little boy act. It was so good I almost convinced myself.'

'You're sick in the head,' I declare, worried he's actually telling the truth here.

'I watched it, the heat on my face, the flames in the night sky. That's what I'm capable of. They were Stage Three. My brother, Stage Four. There wouldn't even be a need if I hadn't miscalculated. My brother wasn't even in the house, the lucky one as always.'

He begins to laugh and a strange glaze passes over his eyes. I'm making sure that there's definitely a full roundabout between us. He's in a dangerous place. Time.

'Out of all of all them, he was the one who deserved it the most yet he was the one who got away. I couldn't exactly go after him straight away, a double murder had already raised a few eyebrows. I had to take my time, construct the ultimate plan, Stage Four in all its majesty. He grew up to be a lovely Christian boy, you know. Of course you've met haven't you? Although you probably know him by his stage name, Anthony Chambers.'

It's coming together. Time.

'The drugs,' Danny continues, 'they were the trigger for what was hiding inside you. The rest is Stage Four in all its genius. You think I could make you hallucinate Jack Connolly? The great B-list celebrity in the flesh.'

'You're talking shit. How would you get Jack Connolly to do that eh?' I ask.

'Let's just say Jack owed me one last favour. Although I must admit I prefer to call him Jimmy Christmas, call it nostalgia.'

'And The Messenger? I suppose he was real too?' I question, trying to take it all in.

'The Messenger?' Danny chuckles, 'that weak fool Eric, sometimes you have to work with what you've got.'

351

'And Rob from the pub?'

'Rob? I don't know, just some jobbing actor who knows Jimmy. Same as the angel. Mia spiked your drink and your mind went into overdrive. Fucking actors everywhere, they'll do anything for a few quid. Plus give a tramp a few cans and he'll walk wherever you tell him.'

'Mia had nothing to do with this. She couldn't have done,' I plead. Please let that, of all things, be a lie.

'Joe don't be naïve. I told you, she's been doing exactly what I've wanted for years now. Not bad is she? Used to belong to an associate of mine before he went a little crazy.'

'You're lying!' I shout. 'I saw it all on the telly. I saw Jack at the beginning, and then it was on the news when he went missing.'

'Video.'

'Nice try, but it couldn't have been because I haven't even got a video.'

'No you haven't, but I have. A few hidden wires here and there and the next thing you know you're watching exactly what I want you to. I told you, I've been setting this up for years.'

'You're making this up!' I shout, the whole array of facts now totally bewildering me.

'No Joe, for the first time in a long time you're actually near the truth,' Danny confidently replies.

'But why me? I thought we were mates. What about the football match? We were a team, me and you.'

'Just a little fun you could call it. It's amazing what you can achieve with a combination of drugs and idiots. Do you really think I would be so stupid as to put you up in a pool competition? I wanted you to lose so I could buy the round for the other team and spike it with sedatives. That and some speed in our drinks.'

'Why me?' I ask timidly in the face of such ferocity. I can't believe everything was a lie.

'Why not? At first, you seemed okay. Then you started to bore me. Do you know how many times I had to listen to you going on about Katie or Beth? How much you loved them or some bollocks like that. And if you're not talking about them you're talking about your supposed drug past. Christ, it's not like you're Howard Marks, you've only got a police caution for cultivating weed in someone else's garden.'

'That was years ago, it was nothing,' I reply.

'Well the people at Blue Peter didn't think so. And if it's not the police you constantly expect to come crashing in at any moment it's being visited by the ghost of that gardener they used to have on the show. Christ, it's pathetic. The more you talked, the more perfect you became for the plan. You've been constantly looking over your shoulder, waiting for something to happen, simply to convince yourself that you deserve the life you lead. Or maybe just smoking pot makes you feel part of something bigger, an alternative view of society perhaps. Who cares? It all leads to the same thing. You needed something bigger than what you were and then you happened to meet me. You wanted a new life? You should be thanking me, I gave you that new life.'

'So you wanted your brother dead because you're a psycho. Why go to so much effort? Why involve me?' I ask.

'What better alibi could I have than my own housemate doing it? Think about it. My brother recently dead, parents dead in mysterious circumstances. It's not going to take that fat fucking cop too long before he's knocking on my door. He never believed me, even back then. You however, that's different. You've got the connection to Sean through me, plus the motive of a madman. Whilst you're trying to explain to the cops your whole Jack Connolly story I'm trying to come to terms with the loss of my brother, on the surface at least.'

'You really had it all worked out didn't you?' I ask scornfully.

353

'All except the bit where you fucked it up. All that planning, down the fucking drain because you can't do one small thing.'

'You mean murder?' I exclaim disbelievingly.

'Call it what you like, it doesn't matter anymore. It's over.'

'I'll tell the police everything,' I warn.

'Tell them what? No copper is going to believe your story about me as much as they would have believed the one about Jack. You're still in the shit.'

He's right. I hate to admit it but nothing's changed. The cops are still chasing me and with good reason. There's no denying the fact I tried to kill Anthony Chambers/Sean Morgan, whatever the fuck he's called. It looks like I've gone crazy and the only people that know otherwise are Danny and me. Maybe Katie could speak up for me, maybe that bitch Mia could tell the truth for once? But what would be the point? I did the crime, regardless of the motivation, guilty as charged. Well fuck you Daniel Morgan, if I'm going to prison then I'm going to make it worth my while. Time stops.

'I'm going to kill you!' I shout, moving with purpose around the roundabout.

'Oh please,' Danny replies with contempt, his confidence delaying his reaction.

I push the roundabout with force and jump on, the world flashing past. Within seconds I've swung round to the other side and leap off, my knee connecting with his chest. Danny falls to the floor and I tumble over the top of him. The plan, if there ever really was one, was to follow this up with a forward roll and then back to my feet before executing a number of debilitating karate moves. In reality I land awkwardly, the pain from the numerous attacks over the past few days returning instantly. When I do finally manage to scramble to my feet, Danny is already up and advancing on me. Before I get a chance to get into a defensive stance his fist connects with my nose and a cracking sound reverberates around my head. As I go down, I just manage to catch a

354

glimpse of the silver estate car screeching to a halt on the other side of fence. Through the pain I see Danny standing above me, pulling his leg back, preparing to strike.

FIGHT!

With a distinct lack of nobility I swing my fist up and catch him squarely in the nuts, feeling my fist connect with the lower angles of his pelvis. That's got to hurt and Fuckface would seem to agree. As I force my way up to an unstable standing position, Danny goes down and he goes down hard. I stand above him, swaying, blood dripping from my nose on to the dirt. Danny lies, crying a primal, almost inaudible scream. But like always, I've run out of time.

Through the hole in the fence I see the copper with the big nose squeezing his way in, emerging into the playground with his eyes fixed on me and me alone. I can tell what he's thinking. The moaning Danny below me is just another victim of the religious nutter. Who needs the truth when there's glory to be had?

Run!

But Danny?

Run, goddam it, RUN!

I burst into life. No way back to the road, except in the back of a police car, only one way out remains. I sprint past the swings and over the fallen fence, the wooden panels spongy underfoot. And then in a moment of madness I try and achieve the impossible, leaping from the canal bank, trying to reach the other side. About half way across I concede that I've made a dreadful mistake. There's no way in Heaven or Hell that I'm going to make it and I begin to descend towards the murky waters below, my legs flailing as I fall. I feel myself tipping backwards, the clouded sky above me coming into view. From behind a cloud the sun breaks through, the light blinding as it traces past me, enveloping my person. I close my eyes and hold my breath, ready to feel the water rush over

355

me. Then something happens, I'm not sure what but it feels as if I'm being held from below by unseen hands. As I'm carried to the other side of the bank it's not a wrenching change of direction, more an alteration of how I'm expecting it to turn out. At this precise moment physics doesn't quite behave as I would expect it to. Instead I just make it, my feet slipping in the mud as I land, my left leg sliding into the water. My eyes hover over the edge of the bank and beyond the grassed wasteland the main road lies less than a hundred metres away. Salvation lies that way. I pull my leg clear and scramble onto the grass, so close now. Yet something tells me to look back. I see big nose attempting the same jump, only this time it results in a more predictable outcome. He falls way short and plunges into the dark water feet first, quickly followed by the rest of him. He quickly surfaces, gasping, his hands desperately trying to grab at anything.

'Help, I can't swim!' the copper shouts, the water spilling into his mouth as the struggle seems to be reaching a terminal climax.

I hesitated before, but not this time. I look across the canal and see Danny limping the other way towards the fence. Within seconds he will be gone but I can only think of what the right thing to do is. Revenge? Escape? It doesn't matter. Saving a life means everything. I find a long branch lying nearby and take up position on the bank, extending it towards the copper's grateful hands. Big nose grabs it willingly and embraces it like a child, making no effort as I pull him in. When he finally reaches the bank, his feet find purchase and he stands up straight, knee deep in water, covered in shit and mud.

'Joseph Gbhllurghh,' he forces out, my surname garbled as he temporarily vomits water onto his shoes, 'I am arresting you ...'

'What?'

'... for attempted murder, resisting arrest,' he continues, trying to make his way up the bank towards me, 'breaking and entering, criminal damage with intent, suspicion of ...'

And there it is, a good deed repaid by ingratitude. Still what did I expect? What he doesn't know is I'm not going out like this. With a swift lunge I connect my flat palms with his chest and push him backwards, his feet finding little grip on the slippery mud and he falls backwards with a splash into the canal. I didn't go as far as saving him first time around to have to do it all over again. Luckily there's little chance of drowning in less than a foot of water, so I take my leave by legging it across the field toward the road. Running across the grass, my feet find a rhythm beneath me. I risk a glance behind and in true B-movie fashion, big nose emerges and begins to chase, fired by humiliation.

The next time I hazard a look is when I reach the pavement, my mind filled with thoughts of escape. So much so that I fail to notice the car screaming to a halt in front of me. The passenger door swings opens but having neither the time nor the athleticism to avoid it, I slam into the car.

'Get in!' a familiar female voice screams.

Slumping onto the car and peering through the window I see Katie frantically gesturing for me to get in. It's always rude to refuse a lady, especially one trying to save you from prison. I hardly have time to get in and close the door before she is driving off at an alarming speed. I give one last glance back and see the copper finally reach the pavement but I'm gone, no more looking back.

'Joseph, you're a moron,' Katie insults as way of introduction.

'Katie Rose, I love you,' I reply, grateful as always that she's saved me. The wider use of that statement always was and always will be true.

'Yeah, well let's save the pleasantries for later. I think it's a bit more important that we get you away from here.'

'Where to?' I ask.

'Out of this bloody town before you cause any more damage.'

Chapter 36

Watch Me Urinate On Goodison As I Pass, That Will Teach 'Yer

As Walker pulled into the police station car park, he remarked to himself that perhaps the master-plan hadn't quite gone how he had intended. On the face of it, there was no denying that he hadn't exactly planned on being punched in the face, being bitten perilously close to the groin or nearly drowning in a canal, yet it had had its positives. A wry smile slid across the Sergeant's face as he thought of the situation within the station. Yes, the suspect had been allowed to escape but was any of that his fault?

Failure to handcuff the suspect: *Polston.*

Assault on a sergeant of HM Criminal Investigation Department: *Polston.*

Further assault by dog under direction of a superior officer: *Polston.*

Further failure of arrest whilst conducting unofficial surveillance of future wife: *Let's move on shall we.*

Failure to provide adequate support to Sergeant Walker in his courageous solo attempts in the apprehension of the suspect: *Polston.*

Continual undermining by a superior officer in the career of one the police's brightest talents: *Polston, Polston, Polston.*

'Oh dear, oh dear, oh dear,' Walker chuckled to himself. The shit was about to hit the fan and Polston was going to get a substantial dollop of turd to the face.

Chief Inspector Goss hung his coat on the stand in his office as a knock came on the door.

'Come in,' the chief inspector sighed.

'Good morning, sir,' announced Constable Rosario, stepping into the room. 'You wanted to see me, sir?'

'Yes, thank you, constable. Take a seat.' The chief inspector replied, gesturing to the chair opposite as he sat down behind the desk.

'Thank you, sir.'

'It would seem that a delicate situation arose last night. I believe you were the first officer on the scene after this rather unfortunate display?' he asked.

Constable Rosario pulled a small book from her pocket and began to recount the events of the night before.

'Well, sir, it would seem that our suspect, a …' Rosario hesitated as she flicked forward a few pages '… a Joseph Carpenter, was arrested last night while attempting to kidnap Anthony Chambers.'

'Anthony Chambers, the television celebrity?'

'Yes, sir. By all accounts, the two officers who made the arrest failed to handcuff the suspect. Following some sort of disagreement between the two, the suspect was allowed to escape.'

'And tell me about this …' Chief Inspector Goss sighed as his eyes flicked to the window '… disagreement.'

'Well, sir, we are unsure of the precise details but it would seem that following a comment from Sergeant Walker, Inspector Polston punched the sergeant in the face,' Rosario commented with a wry smile on her face.

'This punch, do you think it hurt the sergeant?' Chief Inspector Goss asked.

'I believe so, sir,' Constable Rosario replied as the two of them exchanged a look.

'Now constable, isn't there something about Inspector Polston's dog being involved?'

'It would seem that the Inspector's dog assaulted the sergeant by delivering a bite close to the groin. I have the pictures from the duty nurse if you want to see them, sir?'

360

'No thank you, constable. And it's at this point that the suspect escaped?'

'Yes, sir. Search teams were dispatched to the area but no trace of him could be found. Until this morning. It would seem that the sergeant drove the informant, a Miss Katie Rose, back to her residence. On his …' Constable Rosario stalled, '... somewhat long drive back to the station he encountered the suspect in a fight with his housemate, one Daniel Morgan. He is on our records as a suspected …'

'I know the file, constable,' the chief inspector interrupted. 'How does the sergeant explain his coming across the suspect? A coincidence?'

'No, sir, the sergeant has indicated that it was his instinct that led him to the location the suspect.'

The chief inspector lowered his eyes before adding in an incredulous tone, 'and the suspect escaped again?'

'Yes, sir. The details are somewhat sketchy from the report radioed in, sir. However I believe that the sergeant has just arrived back at the station.'

'And Daniel Morgan. What happened to him?'

'No sign yet, sir. We have issued descriptions to all available units.'

'Good work constable. On your way downstairs, please inform either Inspector Polston or Sergeant Walker that I want to see them.'

'Who would you like to see first, sir?'

The chief inspector relaxed back into his chair and took a moment to consider his response.

Limping into the chief inspector's office with dramatic effect, Sergeant Walker gratefully sat in the chair opposite.

'Good morning, sir,' Walker announced with added grimace.

'A terrible situation this,' the chief inspector mused as studied the notes in front of him.

361

'I only wish it wasn't me that had to bring this complaint against the inspector, sir. He's been like a father to me,' Walker replied.

'Yes, well, why don't you tell me your version of events and perhaps we can remedy the situation.'

Upon this request, Walker divulged his own particular recollection of events. Any detail that could be exaggerated, fabricated or distorted was embellished, expertly so. History, it is said, is written by the victor; Walker in his retelling was a God of his own creation.

'And so you see, sir, I have only made the complaint for fear of Inspector Polston's health,' Walker drew to a close.

Chief Inspector Goss sat back in his chair and stared out of the window as he made his decision. For Walker it seemed like an eternity before he turned back again.

'Firstly, I would like to thank you for your recent work,' the chief inspector announced, returning his gaze to his sergeant.

Here it comes, thought Walker; goodbye Inspector Polston, hello Mr Promotion.

'I'm afraid that despite your complaint, I feel it would not be in your best interests to take further action against Inspector Polston regarding the events of last night.'

'I'm sorry, sir?' Walker asked, thinking he had misheard.

'If you would bear with me, sergeant. We both know that Inspector Polston will be retiring soon. It would be a tremendous shame if this were to affect his final moments with us.'

'He attacked me, sir,' Walker argued, not quite believing. Still, Walker thought, if the chief inspector wanted to drag himself down with Polston then so be it. There were other people he could go to, higher people.

'I would like to take this further, if only for Inspector Polston's health.'

'I understand, sergeant,' the chief inspector replied before letting the facade of procedure slip. 'But then of course we have *this* to consider.'

The chief inspector raised two beige files from his desk and placed them in front of Walker. The sergeant looked inside as Chief Inspector Goss continued.

'Of course, sergeant, you will be aware that before speaking to you I had a conversation with Inspector Polston.'

'Uh huh,' Walker muttered, confused.

'It would seem that Inspector Polston has uncovered some unfortunate facts about your behaviour during working hours. In that first folder you will find a comprehensive review over a number of years where it's believed that you acted inappropriately.'

'But sir, I can explain,' Walker mumbled.

'The second file you have there is a complaint from a member of the public that you've been stalking her. A certain Miss Julie Evans has accused you of following her around, watching her. Is this correct?'

'No sir, of course not,' Walker blurted.

'At first both Inspector Polston and I thought that you'd been caught out again during surveillance. However when we checked the database there was no record of any interest in her activity at all.'

'Sir, let me explain,' Walker cried. In all the time he had been watching her, he never checked up on the details. He thought he had heard her being called Mia but he must have been wrong. She was his angel, his love, but never Julie.

'Of course, this will have to go to an official review. Inspector Polston has agreed to speak up on your behalf but then there is this ...' the chief inspector declared, pressing his index finger firmly down on top of Walker's complaint.

The chief inspector gave Walker a few moments to consider his thoughts.

'Well sergeant, have you made a decision?' Chief Inspector Goss asked momentarily.

'I'd like to drop my complaint against Inspector Polston, sir,' Walker replied timidly.

'Excellent.'

'What happens next?' Walker asked.

'Well how about getting on with some work?' The chief inspector ordered, nodding towards the door.

'Yes, sir,' Walker replied and made his way from the room, carrying less of a limp than when he came in.

Back in the CID room, Walker found Inspector Polston awaiting his return with a smile.

'Sir,' Walker announced, coming to a halt a few feet from his nemesis as a thought entered his head: murder, sweet beautiful murder. Around them the room was abuzz with activity.

'Sir,' Sergeant Fleck interrupted from across the room 'Culverhouse and Bowen are outside Carpenter's house and Sutton and Gordon are en-route to his workplace. Plus airports and ports have been notified of his name.'

'And has anyone been able to find Daniel Morgan?' Polston shouted back, 'I've been after that little shit ever since he got away with murdering his parents.'

'We're on it, sir,' Fleck replied.

Walker wasn't really listening to any of this, his mind was on other things. What did he have left? His angel? No, she had betrayed him and he couldn't forgive her, not this time. All he had left was his work and that was in tatters. He may have suffered a major setback but he was convinced that he could make it back. All he needed was one big arrest and as far as he could tell, there was still one going.

'Sir. How can I help?' Walker asked, fired with enthusiasm.

'I'm glad you asked that sergeant,' Polston replied, 'I do have an important task for you as it happens.'

364

'Yes, sir?'

'Take Callahan for a walk will you?' the inspector ordered, the smile returning to his face.

As Walker traversed the streets, thoughts of revenge flooded his mind. Callahan jogged on ahead, eager to exploit the full length of the extendable lead. The reasons were two-fold: one, it was Walker; two, a rather attractive pug was being walked along the other side of the street. Before he knew it, instinct took over and the canine super cop was already half way across the street before Walker noticed the whirling of the extendable lead in his hand, quickly followed by the sound of squealing brakes filling the air.

'No, no, no!' Walker cried as he ran into the street towards the victim.

'I'm sorry mate. He just ran straight out in front of me,' the driver called as he emerged from his car.

'Oh just fuck off!' Walker shouted back, looking down at Callahan.

How could life be so cruel, Walker thought. Yes, they hadn't always got along but it shouldn't have happened like this, especially today of all days.

'You little bastard! You did that on purpose,' Walker commented, detaching the lead from the lifeless body.

Half an hour later Walker re-entered the CID room, making his way over to Inspector Polston.

'For God's sake, Walker. Didn't I tell you take Callahan for a walk?' Polston fumed.

'Yes boss, it's just that I have some good and bad news.'

'What are you talking about? What bad news?'

'I'm sorry, sir, there was nothing I could do. Callahan just ran out into the road,' Walker replied.

'What?' Polston shouted, jumping to his feet 'What did you say?'

'Callahan, sir, I'm afraid he got run over.'

'You stupid bastard, please tell me he's alright! Is that the good news, is Callahan alright?' Polston pleaded, tears beginning to stream down his cheeks.

'The good news? No, sir; I managed to get your lead back.'

Seven years on we revisit Lionel Walker as part of the ongoing documentary, Super Sevens.

<u>Year 49</u>

We find an ageing Lionel Walker working as a road sweeper having left the police force some years previously.

'So, Lionel, we understand you had a few problems in your police career.'

'Yes, unfortunately I was a victim of budget cuts.'

'Really? We heard you were sacked.'

'Well, my superiors at the time were somewhat judgemental on my performance if you wanted to call it that.'

'And how does that make you feel? Does it keep you up at night?'

'It's not that that keeps me up. It's him.'

'I'm sorry, who are you talking about?'

'Every night, when I turn out the lights I can hear him, growling in the shadows.'

'And where do you think your career path lies in the future?'

'Well I keep applying for a post back at Goodison but for some reason they don't seem to reply. I'm thinking there must be something wrong with the postal service.'

'What about applying for another London Suburb, say Barking?'

'Did you say barking? Can you hear a dog? Oh God, he's back, he's watching me!'

366

At this point we decided to terminate the interview with Lionel Walker out of concern for his mental health.

'No, it's not over. He's real. Why doesn't anyone believe me?'

'For goodness sake man, pull yourself together.'

'He's real I tell you, real!'

CUT!

Chapter 37

She Just Smiled And Gave Me A Vegemite Sandwich

I can almost touch it, freedom from the past, stepping into an unknown future.

'Where now?' I ask, stepping into the chaos of the crowds of Heathrow Airport.

'You need to get a photo don't you?' Katie asks.

'Yeah, I'd almost forgotten about that,' I reply. No almost about it, I had forgotten about it.

'Okay, I'll meet you in the coffee shop in twenty minutes, we'll sort out the rest then,' Katie confirms, disappearing into the crowd.

That leaves the small matter of the ticket to deal with. A quick visit to the cashpoint yields a disappointing one hundred and ten pounds, including the theft from a stretched overdraft that I have no intention of repaying. I might have got away with it ten years ago had the bank not got wise about nine years and eleven months previous. If there were a reason to leave, besides the warrant out for my arrest, it would probably be the hit-man the bank will hire when they learn of my flight from the law. Hey, you never know, Katie might just chip in with the cost of a ticket. God bless her, she's already shelled out quite a bit to help. I did ask her why she had that sort of money at hand around Dodgy's house. She couldn't quite answer that, something about a dream and some geezer with a halo suggesting she visit the bank. Frankly I had no idea what she was talking about but it was probably just another Roger Moore dream, I have those all the time.

Second stop, photo booth. I sit there like a fool, having the flash dazzle me into numerous criminal looking poses. Of course manufacturers of such machines are inherently evil and make you wait an eternity for the photos to drop out. Despite a readiness to snatch them up, the machine cunningly waits until I have a slight lapse of attention just as the most beautiful yet nosey girl walks past.

The final stop is the second cubicle on the right of the men's toilets. You know the one I mean, the cubicle without the coat-hook and next to the bloke having the mother of all shits. Pulling the fake passport out of my pocket, I flick to the back page. Using the scissors on my Swiss Army knife I cut the least embarrassing photo out, no easy task in itself. Peeling back the acetate I place my photo inside, a pretty top notch job if I say so myself. Getting up to leave I leave the penknife resting on the toilet roll, it cannot accompany me on this journey. No more slips up, not anymore.

Goodbye Joseph Carpenter, hello Hamish Hussein.

'Everything done?' Katie asks as I find her in the coffee shop, sipping a latte.

'I think so,' I reply, sliding onto the seat opposite her.

'This is it then,' she announces.

'I guess so.'

'I wish you weren't leaving. I wish there were some other way.'

'I'm sorry Katie, it's the only option. The one thing I have to work out now is where to go,' I say, conscious that a hundred and ten quid isn't exactly going to get me very far. I'm thinking Europe if I'm lucky, Bognor Regis if I'm not.

'How about Australia?' Katie asks, ludicrously.

'Um, I don't think that's going to happen,' I reply, trying hard not to laugh.

'Then maybe this will help,' Katie replies, opening up her bag and sliding a ticket across the table for me to look at.

'Are you serious?' I ask. Australia, Jesus, Australia of all places.

'Yeah, I guess I am.'

'But Katie, you can't afford this!'

'Yes I can, anyway I have my reasons.'

'I don't understand.'

'Joseph, you've always talked about a new life, this is your chance. Besides I want you to give Danny a kicking from me.'

'Are you saying Danny is in Australia?' I ask, excited by the thought. 'But how do you know?'

'Well, while you were having your chat with Danny, I had a little talk with Mia.'

'You talked to Mia?'

'Not so much talked, more sort of slapped her around a bit.'

'What did she say?' I ask, trying to suppress an illogical urge to protect Mia.

'Well, she more sort of gurgled through the toilet water that Danny was going to Australia.'

'Katie, you are without doubt the most beautiful girl I know,' I declare, grasping the ticket in my grateful hand. I lean across the table and give her a brief kiss. As I move away from those soft lips I have to fight the urge to kiss her again. I may be mistaken but there's a look between us, as if she wants the same. But what if I'm wrong? I've been wrong about so many things recently. It's best that I savour the thought for what it is: a *maybe* is better than a no and I fully intend to enjoy the speculation on the long flight ahead.

'Will you just get on the bloody plane,' Katie orders.

Ten minutes later I approach the line through to the departure lounge. I can see it, twenty feet away and past security, a new world just waiting for me. It's the one thing left to do.

Chapter 38

Welcome To Australia, You Might Accidentally Get Killed

When I finally touch down after a long arduous flight, Sydney is everything I hoped it would be. Not even a stopover in Los Angeles and a sudden desire to carve out an acting career could stop me getting here.

Stepping out into the bright sunshine I take the train to the city in the blistering heat and book into the first hostel I find. Days pass and new friends emerge, plans evolve. In England I was nobody, now I'm Hamish Hussein and I can be whatever I want to be.

There's even a bloke in my dorm that looks like Avon from Blake's Seven. He carries around what I suspect is a fish tank, concealed in a black nylon bag. We haven't spoken yet, but I'm sure we will.

Kirk St Moritz lives on a small island in the English Channel where he divides his time between writing and working for a top secret department of Her Majesties government (only one of these facts is true). Born in 1974 in the suburbs of London he has lived in Australia and Norway before settling in Guernsey and deciding to write his first novel The Day Jesus Rose Into Croydon. He is currently working on his second novel Kayfabe Sunset but keeps getting interrupted by the various henchmen of dastardly new world orders.

The Day Jesus Rode Into Croydon has been a long time in its writing. As an author I cannot thank enough those who helped along the way, you have made the experience undoubtedly shorter and less arduous than perhaps it might otherwise have been. A special thank you must go to my editor Ant Skelton who despite an almost fanatical hatred of the character Callahan persevered with my insufferable grasp of the English language. I must also thank my dad who encouraged me to begin writing in the first place and is remembered dearly.

Printed in Great Britain
by Amazon